MW01128845

BLOOD CHARGED

BOOK THREE

LINDSAY BUROKER

Blood Charged

by Lindsay Buroker

Copyright Lindsay Buroker 2014

Cover and Formatting: Deranged Doctor Design

FOREWORD

Welcome back, good reader, for the third adventure in the series. This novel brings back Ridge, Sardelle, Tolemek, and Cas (oh, and let's not forget Jaxi, who always has something to say). I hope you'll enjoy taking a new journey with everyone.

Once again, I would like to thank the behind-the-scenes people who helped me get Blood Charged ready to publish: my beta readers, Cindy Wilkinson and Sarah Engelke, my editor, Shelley Holloway, and the cover art designers at Deranged Doctor Design.

CHAPTER 1

S ARDELLE WAS BEING FOLLOWED.
She hadn't seen her pursuer yet, but her sorceress's senses told her a woman was back there, skulking through the slushy alleys of Pinoth. Her senses also told her the woman was armed. The large hunting knife hanging from her belt shouldn't prove too much of a threat, but the six-shooter nestled in her palm? If prepared, Sardelle could shield herself from bullets, but doing so in the middle of the magic-fearing Iskandian capital with dozens of witnesses around… even if she wasn't physically harmed, she would be in trouble.

Sardelle quickened her step.

You should have brought me with you, Jaxi, her sentient soulblade, spoke into her mind.

As I've pointed out several times, women wandering around with swords are an oddity in this age. For the first couple of weeks she had been in the city, Sardelle had worn Jaxi beneath her cloak, in part because she hadn't wanted to risk losing her after working so hard to retrieve her from that mine, and in part because she hadn't realized how much fashions had changed during the three hundred years she had slept in that mage stasis chamber. Soldiers still carried swords as part of their uniform, but firearms were the norm, and women who worried about defending themselves on the streets preferred pistols they could slip into their handbags. Thanks to her relationship with the most famous pilot in the city, if not in all of Iskandia, there were already enough rumors floating around about her. She didn't need to draw extra attention by not fitting in with the locals. Fortunately, without the soulblade, she looked no different than any other Iskandian woman, dark hair, pale skin, a few freckles across the nose...

And the ability to flambé hordes of enemy soldiers with a wave of your hand.

Sardelle snorted. *Pyrotechnics are* your *specialty.*

Yes, and I'm quite fabulous at them. After a pause, Jaxi added, *Your shadow has taken to the rooftops to keep up with you without being noticed. Her finger is tight on that trigger too.*

I know.

You could hop onto the roof, pin her down, cut off her air for a while so she knows you're serious, then demand to know why she's following you.

Unless you're suggesting I impose upon her physically to do all those things, I would be confirming something she can only suspect at this point.

Physical imposition is perfectly acceptable, but from the way she's hopping from rooftop to rooftop, she may be more than your match in that area.

Sardelle thought about pointing out that she had hopped a few rooftops in her day, but Jaxi was fully aware of her abilities... and weaknesses.

You tripped and skinned your knee the last time you hopped a log.

Thanks for the reminder. Sardelle turned down a side street, hoping her spy would be slowed down by having to cross the wide boulevard before skimming up to another rooftop. A sudden hope kindled. *She's not Cofah, is she?*

Pale skin. She looks like a native.

Sardelle sighed. She would have worried less if a spy from the empire verified her secrets. Nobody here would listen to a Cofah woman's accusations against her.

A steam wagon mounted with large guns trundled down the street, clattering and clanking across timeworn cobblestones. The cargo area in the back was covered. On impulse, Sardelle jumped onto the back and clung to a bar at the corner.

Very nice. You didn't even skin a knee.

Ignoring Jaxi, Sardelle watched over her shoulder, hoping she would spot her follower stuck up on a rooftop and quickly falling behind. The woman didn't show herself.

The steam wagon belched stinky black smoke into the air, and the bumps and shudders from driving on the cobblestones made Sardelle's teeth clatter together, but it moved along at a faster speed than she could walk. They cruised past shoppers, workers, and bicycle messengers braving the slushy streets and fearlessly weaving past steam vehicles, horses, and donkeys pulling carts. The miles-long harbor came into view, a mixture of fishing vessels, freighters, and warships on maneuvers out in the water. Sardelle's gaze drifted to the butte towering at the south end. From the ground, she couldn't see much of the airbase, but she had been up there enough times to imagine the runways and its hangars full of mechanical dragon fliers. The sky over the sea was clear, the wind stiller than usual. Maybe the pilots would have practice maneuvers scheduled for the day.

Isn't your doting lover going to a meeting this morning?

Ah, that was right. Ridge wouldn't be out there, even if the fliers did take to the sky. Not unless an alarm sounded, and his whole squadron was called to duty.

Your spy is falling behind, but still following. She may know where you're going.

Unfortunately, that was a possibility. This was Sardelle's third day heading to the public archives building for research. Maybe another visitor had noticed her there yesterday and thought her suspicious, or maybe the woman who worked at the assistance desk had reported to someone about Sardelle's unflagging interest in the place—judging by the dust smothering the shelves, very few had even passing interest in the archives building.

I'm not going to turn around and go back to Ridge's cottage to weep quietly over my lost friends, family, and life while waiting for him to come home for the night. Sardelle had done enough of that during her first weeks in town. True, she had been working on those communications devices for Ridge's squadron more often than she had been mourning—sulking, Jaxi had called it—so it hadn't been wasted time, but she was eager to make headway on the mission she had given herself: to track down her kin, however many generations removed, and search for other Iskandians with dragon blood. Then she would teach those who were willing how to use their powers. It would be the mission of a lifetime, and finding those people wouldn't be easy, not when anyone with inexplicable talents learned to hide them early on. The archives building was the only place in town that might tell her if her brother or any of her cousins had survived the purging of the Referatu and had children who had kept the line alive through the centuries. She particularly wanted to find her brother's descendants, to make sure they were well. He had teased and tormented her relentlessly all through childhood, and she had rarely visited him in adulthood, but now that it was too late... a lump of regret formed in her throat whenever she thought about it.

I wasn't suggesting you abandon your quest or fill your days with knitting scarves like the old woman next door, but you could come home to get me, so you'd be better able to defend yourself.

I can defend myself fine on my own.

I never would have chosen to bond with you if I'd known you would leave me under the bed for days on end with nothing for company but dust balls.

I'm quite positive there are no dust balls under Ridge's bed. The wagon turned off the main street. When a bicycle wobbled into its path, forcing it to slow down, Sardelle hopped off. *Besides, a couple of days of inaction should be nothing after three hundred years of being cooped up inside a mountain. It's scarcely been three weeks since you had that big adventure with Tolemek.*

You mean the big adventure where he used me as a lamp, because I can glow nicely?

You also incinerated a deadly weapon that was seconds away from killing thousands of people. Something Sardelle wished Jaxi had figured out she could do *before* Sardelle had promised to help rescue Tolemek's sister from some sanitarium an ocean and thousands of miles away and to teach her how to use magic.

Fussy, fussy. I thought you wanted *new students.*

I do, but it would be more feasible to look for them here. Maybe it was selfish, but Sardelle was more interested in teaching her own people than someone who came from the continent that had been trying to conquer Iskandia for centuries. Nor was she positive Tolemek's sister, reputedly disturbed in the mind, would be teachable.

She hiked up her skirt and walked up a side street full of melting snow and steaming horse piles, glad her fur-lined boots kept *most* of the road decor away from her legs. Her destination, a drab gray three-story building looming at the next intersection, had the architectural allure of a doorstop. The usual woman was sitting behind the desk, reading a book and scowling at people who left puddles of water on the threshold floor. She also had the allure of a doorstop.

"You again?" the archivist asked when Sardelle walked in, then glanced toward the door, as if she expected someone else to come in behind her. Interesting.

"Yes, I believe this will be my last day of research." Sardelle signed her name in the register at the desk, using the same made-up surname she had been using since waking up in this new era, Sordenta. Only two people had signed in after her yesterday, and she was the first visitor today.

"You going to be looking in the red books again?"

Sardelle paused, the pen still on the page. "Pardon?"

"I have to report that, you know."

Sardelle thought back to the previous two days. She had looked into archive books with red bindings, but she hadn't thought anything of the colors. Others were black, blue, and green, seemingly arranged on the shelves at random.

"I didn't know. What does the red signify?" she asked, though a feeling of unease settled about her shoulders like a cold, wet cloak.

The clerk's eyes narrowed to slits. "Ancestral lines with witch blood."

It took her a moment to do so, but Sardelle hooked two fingers before her chest in a warding-off gesture, having learned this was the appropriate sign one should make when magic or witches were discussed. "I had no idea."

She had been aware of the clerk ambling around the building from time to time, pretending to dust and to arrange books, but she hadn't realized the woman had been spying on Sardelle's research material. Or that a genealogy book could be so condemning, to the one reading it *and* the ones listed in it. Were the descendants of known sorcerers from centuries past monitored to this day? Or were they simply listed in these archives in case the names came to the attention of the law? The archivist would have known, but Sardelle dared not ask her further questions on the matter.

The woman was still squinting suspiciously. "No? Most people who come here are looking for information on their ancestors. But some are also hoping to contact descendants of witches for nefarious reasons."

"I was simply researching lines I found mentioned in historical texts that are related to the Referatu," Sardelle said, "because there's been a renewed military interest in the artifacts from that culture."

"You don't look military." The woman frowned at her dress.

Maybe you should have brought a sword.

Hush.

"I don't believe the military is interested in witches, either," the archivist added.

"Not the magic users specifically, but some of the artifacts that civilization once left behind." Technically true. The Referatu light fixtures were now powering Iskandian fliers, not that anyone had seemed to know that's what the power sources had originally been.

"People's names are listed here, not artifacts."

"I understand that, but I may gather a few leads here." Why was she explaining herself to this woman when she had such a poor history of lying convincingly? "Unless you intend to stop me from doing so, I shall continue to do my research." Sardelle raised an eyebrow, almost hoping the woman would pester her further and give her a reason to deliver an unseemly rash.

Don't start with that again. That's almost as suspicious as deflecting bullets in public spaces.

I hardly think that's true.

It got you in trouble last time.

That was, alas, true, but it had been more the discovery of her picture in that book that had sealed the condemnation.

"It's not my job to stop you from researching," the woman said and waved for Sardelle to continue into the building.

No, she'll just report what you're researching to someone dastardly.

That's the impression I'm getting. Sardelle headed into the library-like room, turning down an aisle to escape the woman's view. *Let me know if my rooftop pursuer comes in the door, will you?*

I'll consider it if you agree to take me out next time you go. I like to feel the warmth of the sun on my pommel.

Agreed.

Sardelle headed for a narrow hallway in the back of the building. She hadn't discovered it, and the stairs at the end that led to a basement, until the archives had been on the verge of closing the day before. There were a lot of red-bound books down there. She took the stairs three at a time, having the sense that she should finish her research today; someone more intimidating than the archivist might be waiting for her if she showed up again tomorrow.

She grabbed the knob and almost smashed her face on the door when it didn't open. It hadn't been locked yesterday...

It didn't need to be locked until you showed up with an interest in the contents.

What is this? Some way to trap innocent people who are simply intrigued by genealogy? Sardelle could bypass the lock without much effort, but she felt affronted anew at this small betrayal. Maybe because there had been so many betrayals already. Learning about the demise of everyone she had ever known and loved had been difficult enough to grasp, but knowing her own people—Iskandian soldiers—had been responsible for the purge, as they called it... The Referatu had worked side-by-side with the military for generations, helping defend the continent from invaders. The only thing that made it possible for her to look at those around her as normal human beings and not mortal enemies was that this genocide had been three hundred years in the past for everyone alive on the continent today. Or so she had thought.

Sorcerous genealogy, yes. For once, Jaxi sounded more grim than sarcastic. The Referatu had been her people too. Even if she had lived and died centuries before bonding with Sardelle, she'd had friends from that era, too, sorcerers and other soulblades. *I could peruse the contents if you don't want to go in.*

There were several thousand books in there.

I read the entire prison library at the Magroth Mines.

That was fifty books. And you had three hundred years.

There were at least sixty books. Jaxi sniffed. *And they were only there for the last fifty years, thank you very much.*

It'll be faster for me to look in person, but thank you for the offer. Having Jaxi do the research from the safety of Ridge's house *would* keep Sardelle from going out in public, but it was a lot more efficient to be here, looking at titles—and red covers—in person. And this was her quest, not Jaxi's. The names of Sardelle's relatives wouldn't mean anything to someone who had been born centuries before.

She used air pressure like a key to push the lock pins above the sheer line, then opened the door. She stepped into a dark, musty room and made sure she didn't sense anyone else in there before she shut herself in. Pitch blackness surrounded her. She thought about simply making a mage light, but there were lanterns with oil hanging by the door. She produced a spark of flame, lit one, and carried it with her into the room. Her footprints from the day before were visible in the dust on the stone floor, along with another set that hadn't been there when she had left. They weren't much bigger than hers, and she guessed they belonged to the archivist.

Sardelle took her notepad out of her pack and selected a few registers with names and addresses from families in towns in the Ice Blades. Of course, there was nothing anywhere about Galmok Mountain, the subterranean fortress where she had trained and where so many Referatu had lived and worked when the stronghold was destroyed. But people didn't move to the mountain until they were identified as gifted. She had grown up in—

Problem, Jaxi chimed in her mind.

Someone coming? Sardelle looked toward the door and listened for footsteps.

Someone is peeking through the windows here.

At Ridge's house?

Unless you left me under a bed in someone else's house, yes.

Is it Lieutenant Colonel Ostraker's grandmother again? Sardelle referred to their usual snoop, a woman who liked to do favors for Ridge and who wasn't above peeping into his windows while trimming the hedges.

No. Two women in green cloaks with the hoods pulled low. They're skulking around in the backyard. With more alacrity than the ninety-year-old woman next door.

Maybe leaving Jaxi at the house had been a mistake after all. She could keep herself from being stolen, in a deadly manner if she wished, but it would be condemning if a magical sword were found at Ridge's house. Not just to Sardelle, but to Ridge, as well. She didn't have a lot left to lose, but he could lose his career, his reputation, and all of his comrades if it came out that he was sleeping with a sorceress. *Knowingly* sleeping with a sorceress. Not for the first time, she wondered if it was selfish of her to stay here, to risk everything he had worked for over the years because she cared for him—maybe even loved him—and enjoyed being around him.

One just took out lock picks and is heading for the back door. I'll see if I can keep them from noticing me. In case the dust ball camouflage fails.

There are *no dust balls*, Sardelle thought reflexively, but she was more worried about the intruders. Should she run home to deal with them? When this might be her last chance to access these archives? What would she do even if she arrived and the intruders were still there? Confront them?

Fine, but I do find this collection of beer steins from around the continent somewhat alarming in its thoroughness.

At least Jaxi didn't sound that worried about the intruders. Meanwhile, Sardelle was once again reconsidering her decision to come to the city with Ridge instead of staying in his cabin by that nice little lake. Just because she couldn't do any research there or get on with her life in any way...

I thought it was your unwillingness to give up the long nights of bed bouncing with your soul snozzle that prompted the move.

Not... entirely.

They've opened the back door.

Sardelle tried to remember if she had engaged her booby traps that morning after Ridge had left. She thought she had, but after several days without trouble, she might have grown lax.

Are they—

A creak on the steps outside her door interrupted her thoughts. Sardelle swept out with her senses. Yes, someone was walking down the stairs. The archivist. Sardelle lowered the lantern to the tiniest of flames. She didn't think the light was bright enough to been seen beneath the door crack, but no need to take chances.

The doorknob rattled. She hoped the woman would assume nobody was inside since Sardelle had relocked it, but she doubtlessly had the key. If she decided to come in and check...

The steps creaked again. Sardelle let out a slow breath. The woman was going away.

What's your status, Jaxi? She grabbed the most promising registers and stuffed them into her satchel. She was going to have to borrow them, whether that was permissible or not. She would find a way to return them later.

You know that large copper soup pot?

Yes...

It fell on the head of one of the intruders.

That's impressive considering the pot rack is over the stove and not the walkway through the kitchen.

Yes, isn't it?

Sardelle started for the door but paused next to a bin of large rolled scrolls, each one at least three feet wide. She hadn't investigated those yesterday and wondered if they might be graphical representations of lines. Three of them had edges that had been dipped in red dye. She grabbed them for a quick look. The scrolls wouldn't fit in her satchel, but on the off chance they held something important, she didn't want to abandon them without a glance. As she unrolled the first, it occurred to her that if she had known about the red-for-evil-witchiness categorizing system, she could have limited her search to those records to start with.

"Lesson learned..."

She sucked in an excited breath when she spotted a familiar surname at the top of the first scroll. Maricoshin. That family had founded Referatu and had claimed numerous powerful sorcerers even by the standards of Sardelle's day. She was taking these scrolls with her whether they fit in her satchel or not. She would simply sneak past the archivist on the way out...

A click sounded in the corner of the room near the door.

Before Sardelle could do more than wonder what it might be, orange light flashed, and a cacophony of noise roared in her ears. A wave of power slammed into her, hurling her from her feet. She crashed into a wall of books, and pain pummeled her body from all sides. Her lantern disappeared beneath falling furnishings—or maybe breaking beams and a falling ceiling.

Blackness swallowed the room.

* * *

Colonel Ridgewalker Zirkander ambled through the courtyard of Harborgard Castle, giving cheerful nods and smiles to the dour-faced soldiers stationed next to the doors to the various towers, halls, and dormitories that opened up off the main driveway. Most stared stonily forward, refusing to acknowledge him—there was some rule on the books about castle guards not interacting with anyone, except to skewer intruders with swords—though a few offered quick grins and abbreviated waves when they thought none of their stolid brethren were looking.

The dourest of the dour stood in front of the grand marble doors leading to the king's audience chamber. They were open, letting in the sunlight—a welcome change from the rain and snow of the past three weeks—but one had to pass the guard's scrutiny before entering, or so the rifle crooked in the man's arms implied. The weapon was one of the few modern inventions on open display within the castle walls. A steam-powered crane sitting next to scaffolding erected against one of the towers marked another exception. The castle had survived nearly a millennium and was considered a Super Important Historical Landmark, meaning about seven hundred people on a dysfunctional committee had to approve architectural additions and changes. It had taken twenty years for them to decide to fix the holes in that tower after the last castle bombing. Fortunately for the castle—and the committee—attacks on the capital had been rare since the dragon flier base had been built above the harbor.

The dour door guard knew who Ridge was and knew the king was expecting him, but he lowered his rifle and opened his mouth to start the familiar state-your-name-and-your-business-and-whether-you-swear-undying-fealty-to-the-king-and-Iskandia preamble that all guests had to endure.

"You forgot to button yourself in," Ridge said, pointing to the man's crotch.

The guard blinked and looked down. It only took him a second to see that it had been a joke, but by then, Ridge had slipped inside, avoiding the spiel. He caught Mister Dour's sigh at the same time as a familiar gray-haired man stepped out of the alcove by the entryway and held up a hand. His dress uniform was immaculate, the creases in his trousers pressed to rigid crispness, and his boots polished so brightly one could shave in the reflection. Neat rows of medals and ribbons lined the breast of his jacket.

"General Ort, you were invited to this meeting too?" Ridge asked, though he was used to higher-ranking officers being present whenever he was invited to the castle. He was just the trigger for the gun that was his squadron, not someone who had enough clout to be a part of the decision-making process.

"Someone has to hold your hand and make sure you don't put your feet up on the king's furniture. Or make inappropriate jokes about his wardrobe." Ort frowned at Ridge's leather jacket, olive green flight uniform, and mud-spattered boots—they had been clean when Ridge left the base, but it was sludgy and wet out there. Ort must carry a boot-polishing kit in his pocket.

"I would never do such a thing," Ridge said. "The king's furniture is all five-hundred-year-old wood and scratchy upholstery. It's not nearly as comfortable as the leather chairs in your office."

"They didn't keep you in that frozen hole in the Ice Blades nearly long enough. Your sense of military courtesy and propriety hasn't improved one iota." Ort jerked his head toward one of the high-ceilinged hallways that opened up on either side of the entryway. The king wasn't sitting on the ceremonial dais at the end of the runway of a throne room, but the general apparently knew where he could be found.

"I don't think one goes to Magroth to improve *anything*," Ridge said.

He followed Ort down the hallway, through a side door, and onto a balcony with glass ceilings and walls warming the space. Snow might still blanket the garden outside, but inside, the vines of tropical plants twined up support posts and along beams, and birds from all over the continent chirped contentedly from the branches of broad-leafed shrubbery and dwarf orange and lemon trees. A few windows were open along walls lined with flowering plants and bushes, but the birds didn't appear tempted to escape.

King Angulus Masonwood the Third sat with two uniformed men at the head of a wrought-iron table covered with a floral cloth and doilies that Ridge chose to believe were the queen's influence rather than a suggestion of his taste. He was a stocky man with a broad face, a creased brow, and curly brown hair shorn close to his head, probably because his hairline was receding like troops fleeing an overrun front line. Despite that concession to age, he still had the muscular stature of a soldier, even if it had been twenty years since he had served. He'd been a cavalry officer in one of the few remaining units and was usually depicted on horseback in portraits. On paper, the king was only a few years older than Ridge, but he seemed far closer to sixty than forty. A stressful job, doubtlessly. He watched Ridge and

Ort's arrival, though he kept glancing down at a rolled up scrap of paper in his blunt hands.

The general stopped at the foot of the table, clicked his heels together, and saluted. "General Ort and Colonel Zirkander reporting, Your Majesty." He glanced at Ridge, probably to make sure he was saluting.

Ridge was. The king had always treated him with respect, and thus he reciprocated, even if he often got the feeling Angulus wasn't a fan of pomp and circumstance and would have preferred slaps on the back.

"Good." The king waved to seats near the head of the table. "Sit."

He wasn't a fan of long-windedness, either.

The men sitting to either side of the king didn't budge from their positions. Both wore the uniforms and jackets of infantry officers, and both had the addition of silver badges highlighting crossed swords on their chests. The badges signaled placement in one of the army's elite troops units. The stone-faced colonel sitting to the king's right, his meaty arms folded across his chest, gave Ridge a hard, challenging stare. Ridge resisted the urge to make the same comment he had made to the door guard. Barely. The captain to the king's left had a bland, forgettable face, brown eyes, dark brown hair, and tanned skin that, given the winter season, hinted of mixed blood.

General Ort gestured for Ridge to sit first. Ridge sat beside the other colonel, bumping elbows as he pulled his chair into the table, and giving the man an insouciant smile as he apologized. The colonel's fingers flexed, as if he was considering how much trouble he might get into for throttling someone at the king's table. Ridge didn't recognize the man, but he'd met any number of ground troops who were unimpressed with pilots and spouted nonsense about how real men fought hand-to-hand and face-to-face. As if most modern ground fighting didn't involve hiding behind something and shooting at people from as far away as possible.

"Gentlemen," Angulus said briskly. "You're here to be briefed on a secret mission you'll be taking into the Cofah homeland."

Ridge sat up, all thoughts of annoying his table neighbor rushing out of his head. He hadn't been sure what this meeting would be about—for the last few weeks, he had been living in a low-grade state of paranoia, worrying that someone would realize Sardelle wasn't an archaeologist from Charkolt University on the east coast, as he'd been telling everyone—but he hadn't expected a mission. Even if the snow outside was melting today, it was still the middle of winter.

"My best spy was fatally wounded acquiring this information." Angulus glanced at the captain—the man clenched his jaw but said nothing—and spread out the roll of paper, revealing a hastily sketched map with two lines of writing at the top.

Ridge twisted his head to try to read the words, but they were encoded. The king gestured to the captain. "Nowon."

"Cofah intelligence has obtained viable samples of dragon blood," the bland-faced officer recited, his fingers tented before him. "Experiments are ongoing in a secret facility. Viable prototypes have already been created."

"*Dragon* blood?" Ort asked. "And viable prototypes of *what?*"

Ridge was glad his commander had been the one to ask the questions. Of late, he had been hearing too much about magic and sorcerers and how dragon blood in their veins explained their powers. He didn't want to pretend he had any knowledge of the matter, though, because the average Iskandian subject—pilots included—shouldn't. He certainly hadn't before meeting Sardelle.

"Dragons have been extinct for over a thousand years," Ort said. "How could anyone have blood, viable or otherwise?"

The king looked at the captain, but Nowon shook his head. "That's all the note says. We've been aware that the Cofah have been working on weapons and military-funded science projects for some time, but this is the first time we've gotten... someone inside one of their secret facilities." Nowon's jaw had ticked during that pause before the word someone. He must have known the spy who had died, maybe been close.

Ridge leaned back, framing his chin with his fingers. He knew the government had spies, of course, but he had never been invited into their world.

"Is it possible your man was mistaken?" Ort asked. "That the Cofah are simply trying to synthesize dragon blood somehow? Maybe they've found some fossils or something." The general's forehead wrinkled. "Can blood be fossilized?" He looked at Ridge as he asked this last question.

Ridge swallowed, hoping he wasn't about to mention Sardelle. Was he supposed to be some archaeology expert now because he was supposedly living with one? Sardelle probably knew the answer to the question, but Ridge sure wasn't going to volunteer to have her brought into this meeting. The last thing he wanted was for her to come to the king's attention.

"This man was very good," the captain said. "It is unlikely he would have been mistaken. I not only suspect they've acquired blood, but from a few messages we've intercepted, I believe the Cofah might be very close to weaponizing it somehow."

"I want a more complete report," the king said, holding the flimsy sheet of paper in the air with an irritated quirk of his lips. "And if they have dragon blood, I either want it destroyed or I want it brought back to Iskandia for our own new scientist to analyze." His unsubtle gaze landed on Ridge.

Ridge slumped back in his chair. Was that why he had been called in? Because of his dubious relationship with Lieutenant Caslin Ahn's new... pirate? Ridge didn't doubt that Tolemek "Deathmaker" Targoson could contribute on a scientific level, but Ridge had been somewhat bullied by Sardelle—and her telepathic sword—into vouching for the man. Even knowing what the man had done to help the city, Ridge worried that his loyalty wouldn't last much longer than his infatuation with Lieutenant Ahn. There was a reason the man's lab had guards on it at all times.

"You know Deathmaker," the king said. "How far can he be trusted?"

Insofar as what? He seemed contented enough in his lab, but... Ridge shrugged. "I don't know him well, Sire. He is—*was*— Lieutenant Ahn's prisoner. I do trust Lieutenant Ahn."

The colonel's eyes closed to slits. Ridge doubted the man

knew anything about the situation, but he sensed a judgment there. He hoped this mission wouldn't require working with the other officer. Judging by the gray in his hair, he probably had seniority.

"I want you to talk to him, Zirkander," the king said. "If you don't think he's a flight risk, he might be worth taking on this mission."

The colonel's nostrils flared. "Sire, I protest. Deathmaker? The pirate? I don't care who he's mounting now; he's killed thousands of our people."

Ridge's fist balled. He could only imagine the expression that must have been on his face, but it made General Ort kick him under the table and tilt his head toward the king with great significance. Ridge kept his temper. Barely. But he loathed the way the other colonel—what was this bastard's name anyway?— gave him that challenging look again.

"Colonel Therrik," the king said, the censure in his tone present but far too mild for Ridge's tastes. "Lieutenant Ahn is a national hero—all of those in Zirkander's squadron are—and an unparalleled asset to our armed forces. Respect, if you will."

Therrik, bah. Zirkander had heard that name from young officers recently out of the military academy. He'd taught combat classes there for the last few years and had a reputation for humiliating and pulverizing young men and women, particularly those going into non-combat branches of the army. Ridge wouldn't have guessed he was still going out in the field. Maybe he was here to advise.

"Of course, Sire," Therrik said, though his face didn't soften, nor was there anything apologetic in his expression.

"If anyone can identify dragon blood and what strange things are being done with it," the king said, "Deathmaker probably can."

Actually, *Sardelle* probably could. Ridge tapped his fingers against his thigh, wondering if there was any way he could take her without revealing... anything. Even though they had only been in combat together once—and technically it hadn't been all that together since he had been flying and she had been fighting a shaman on the ground—he would much rather have *her* at his side than Deathmaker or Thugly the Tormentor of Young Pilots.

"He has no loyalty to our people," Therrik said. "He'll go right back to them if he's given the chance."

"He has no loyalty to the Cofah, either," Ridge said. "Nor would they be happy to have him. My understanding is that he... plugged up both outhouses on the property, as one of my country-bred pilots would say."

"Classy," Ort murmured with another head tilt that was probably supposed to remind Ridge that they were in the presence of royalty. Eh, if the king had been a soldier, he had surely seen an outhouse once or twice in his life.

"I gather that he can't return to the pirates, either," Ridge said, "at least not to the Roaming Curse. His... lady friend is here. He has more reason to stay loyal to Iskandia than to leave us."

"Oh, sure," Therrik grumbled. "I'm sure that's the sort of romance that books are written about."

Ridge hadn't been enthused at the idea of a mass-murdering pirate for his young lieutenant, but he would defend her right to pick whomever she wanted, with fists if necessary. Even if that would get *him* pummeled.

"Get him on the team if you can," the king said.

"The team for what, exactly, Sire?" Ort asked.

"Zirkander and the necessary pilots will fly Therrik and two of his best men—" the king nodded toward Captain Nowon, "—into Cofah territory to infiltrate this research facility. I want the dragon blood destroyed or brought back, and I want any progress they've made likewise destroyed. I also want to know where that blood came from in the first place."

"Who's in charge of the mission?" Therrik asked, his face cool as he regarded Ridge again.

"You are, Colonel." The king pulled a folded piece of paper out of a pocket and pushed it toward Ridge. "These are the coordinates for the secret facility." Turning back toward Therrik, he continued, "Zirkander and his people will get you and your men where you need to go and wait for you to return."

Ridge scowled—he was being assigned rickshaw service?—at

the same time as Therrik issued his first smile. It was an alarming thing, like a wolf curling its lips.

"That's acceptable, Sire," Therrik.

Ridge opened his mouth, and Ort kicked him under the table again. Ridge scowled at him. It was worse than having dinner at a girlfriend's parents' house with her stomping on a man's foot to ensure he delivered the proper responses. General Ort utterly lacked any of the girlfriend qualities that would have made such interference bearable.

"I must respectfully object to Deathmaker's inclusion on the mission, Sire," Therrik added. "He can't be trusted. Why can't he just study the dragon blood when we bring it back? And I assure you, we *are* good enough to bring it back."

The captain's eyebrows twitched ever so slightly at the word we. Ridge wasn't sure whether it indicated doubt as to the colonel's abilities—probably not—or doubt as to whether the colonel was needed at all. Maybe this had originally been Nowon's mission. He was the one who knew about the spy and had decrypted the message, after all.

"If there's anything more troublesome than samples of blood in vials, you may need his help," the king said, giving Ridge a nod.

Ridge had been the one to explain how Tolemek had destroyed a device full of a deadly toxin to save the city. He hadn't been able to mention Sardelle's role in the event—or rather her *sword's* role—so Tolemek had received full credit. Ridge didn't resent that exactly, but it rankled him that he couldn't speak openly about what Sardelle had done to help defend their homeland. It rankled him even more now that Ridge had learned that the pirate's infamous potion-making abilities weren't entirely mundane.

"Speak to him and come to an understanding ahead of time if necessary, but plan on taking him," the king said, staring steadily into the colonel's eyes.

"An understanding." Therrik flexed his fingers, then curled them into a fist. "Yes, Sire."

Therrik planned to beat Tolemek into loyalty? Oh, yes, that

would work well.

"Zirkander, choose three good pilots to take with you. You'll fly the two-seaters and each take one of Therrik's three-man team, along with Deathmaker, if he'll come. Therrik, you can decide whether he's going into the compound with you or not, but I urge you to take him so he can help identify what's worth taking and what's not."

"What can kill you in the blink of an eye and what can't," Nowon murmured. He obviously knew a little more about what was going on in those Cofah facilities than what was on the note.

"While you men complete your mission," the king went on, "The pilots will wait in a safe area with the fliers camouflaged. It probably goes without saying, but my preference is to have you all in and out without ever being seen. The repercussions might be less harsh if the Cofah can't prove we had anything to do with their missing samples."

"We understand, Sire," Therrik said.

Ridge nodded, though he still hated the idea of having Therrik in charge of this. He supposed the colonel couldn't be too much of an ass on the mission, not when Ridge's team would be his only way home.

"Dismissed," the king said.

Ridge pushed back his chair, as did Ort and Nowon.

"May I have one more word with you in private, Sire?" Therrik asked, glancing at Ridge.

The king nodded. Ridge didn't like that quick glance, but he walked away with the others. He *did*, however, dawdle, pausing on the other side of a large shrub to prop his boot on the pot and tie the laces.

"What is it?" Angulus asked.

"Captain Nowon's people handle external intelligence gathering," Therrik said, "but my old unit handled internal, and I've been made aware of some interesting developments of late."

That might explain how the colonel knew about Ahn and Tolemek's relationship, something Ridge hadn't thought would be common gossip outside of his squadron. He lifted his other boot to retie the laces.

"Your point?" the king had moved away from the table, and Ridge barely heard the words. He parted the branches of the shrub. The men were walking toward one of the windows overlooking the garden.

"Zirkander's witch," Therrik said, and Ridge's heart nearly stopped. "Are you sure we shouldn't—"

"Colonel," Ort hissed from the doorway. "What are you doing?"

Ridge wanted to wave him away, to shush him so he could hear the rest, but the king and Therrik had moved out of earshot, anyway. Damn, he needed to know what they were talking about.

Ridge raced toward the doorway, almost knocking Ort aside as he blurted, "I'll meet up with you at the hangar, General. I need to piss."

He glanced back, catching Ort giving that potted plant a long, concerned look. Ridge ran through the hallway, but instead of racing toward the front door, he ran in the opposite direction, then swung into a narrow staircase that led down to a door to the gardens. He vaguely remembered indoor latrines somewhere in that direction and thought his excuse might be plausible. Even if it wasn't, he would risk demerits from Ort. He had to know what they were saying about Sardelle. It wasn't surprising that the intelligence department had put the pieces together—just because he hadn't mentioned her role in the battle back at the mines didn't mean there hadn't been witnesses and that the truth would come out—but if someone like Therrik knew about her, how many other people might know? And what did the king think?

The side door was thankfully unguarded. Ridge charged out and hopped the fence into the gardens. Despite the day's sun, three inches of snow blanketed everything. He ran through the melting stuff, following the side of the building, forcing himself to slow as he neared the first open window on the greenhouse balcony above. He hugged the wall so nobody looking out from above should see him. The sounds of birds chirping floated out, but he couldn't hear voices. He crept to the next open window. A shadow moved behind the glass. The king? The faint murmur of a conversation reached his ears, but he couldn't make out the words.

The skeleton of a vining plant, its leaves shed months ago and snow blanketing its brown limbs, snaked up the brick side of the building, passing the window and reaching all the way to the roof of the greenhouse. Ridge had no idea if it would support his weight—the center trunk was about three inches thick, but didn't look very hale beneath the snow—but desperation drove him to try.

He gripped the plant and pulled himself off the ground. The trunk shivered, and snow splatted down his shoulders, but it didn't crack or pull away from the wall. He hoped the two men inside were too engrossed in the conversation—about Sardelle, damn!—to notice branches shivering in the utter lack of wind.

Ridge stopped before his head drew level with the bottom of the window. Besides, the trunk had dwindled in thickness from three inches to two, and it was starting to slump. His boots were pressed into the plant below him, but they kept slipping. Dry wood and cold snow pricked at his fingers. He should have put on his gloves before jumping onto the vine. His efforts were rewarded, though, for he could hear more than chirping birds this time.

"—told me," Therrik was saying. "The officers in my old unit don't miss much."

"I suppose it'll be all over the city before long." The king sighed.

"I can't understand why you let her into the city in the first place, Sire. Why wasn't she shot as soon as someone figured it out?"

Ridge gritted his teeth, in part because a piece of the vine had snapped away from its anchor on a post above his head, and in part because he wanted to lunge through the window and strangle Therrik.

"I believe she was shot any number of times during the battle with the Cofah," the king said dryly. "A sorceress isn't easy to kill."

Sorceress. He hadn't called her a witch. Could the king know everything? Intel must have interviewed that research-happy Captain Heriton from Magroth.

"Not when she's awake, likely not," Therrik said. "We have snipers. One of our men could take her out in her sleep."

If Ridge had disliked the colonel before, he was ready to hurl the man into a volcano now. His shoulders flexed, and he caught himself climbing another foot on the vine with an image in his mind of leaping through the window, repercussions be damned. But another limb snapped away from the wall overhead, and he found his perch sagging a couple of inches away from the window. He gritted his teeth and eyed the ledge. He might be able to make the lunge...

"That would be a poor reward for Zirkander's years of loyalty," the king said, his tone still dry.

Therrik snorted. "If you want to reward the man, give him a medal, not a witch. Sire, do we even know he's voluntarily housing her? She could be using him—*controlling* him—without him even knowing it."

Not that idiotic argument again. Everyone seemed sure Ridge had a mind feebler than that of an eighty-year-old amnesiac.

"I've read her record," the king said. "If she had been one of the rogues from her century, she would already be dead. She was a healer who worked with the army."

Huh, the king's research had been even more thorough than Heriton's, it seemed.

"Her... century, Sire?" Therrik asked.

"Never mind."

"Please, hear me, Sire. I don't think Zirkander's a suitable guard dog for a witch, especially not if he's sleeping with her. Besides, he's not even here half the time, and she's free to roam at will."

"I have people watching her. If it becomes a problem... I'll reassess the situation."

People watching her? Ridge swallowed. And here he had joked at Sardelle's assertion that she didn't feel safe doing her work on base. Maybe the grandmother next door *was* keeping an eye on her.

"This is a bomb waiting to detonate, Sire. If you don't do anything about her, you can trust that someone will. A lot of people are very afraid of magic."

"I'm aware of that, Colonel," the king said, his tone cooler now.

Sardelle is in trouble! The words and an image of the old archives building in town blasted into Ridge's mind like a foghorn, startling him so that he lost his grip.

He tried to catch himself, his fingers wrapping around a branch, and he thought he might have saved himself, but the brittle limb snapped. He plummeted to the ground. He bent his knees, trying to soften the landing and keep himself from making a lot of noise, but one of his heels struck something slippery. His leg flew out from beneath him, and he landed on his back. He rolled and came up in a crouch, ready to flee away before anyone could look out the window and spot him. With his first step, he almost crashed into General Ort.

"Are you *insane?*" the general whispered, glancing up at the open window and keeping his voice low. He grabbed Ridge by the arm before he could answer, dragging him toward the garden gate. "Are you *trying* to throw away a twenty-year career?"

"No, sir," Ridge responded, but his focus was inward. That had to have been Sardelle's sword that had yelled into his thoughts. It had never spoken to him before, but he knew it communicated with Sardelle, and apparently it had done so with Tolemek, as well. Another time, the telepathic intrusion would have made him as uncomfortable as ants crawling on his skin, but the content of the message was more important than the fact of it.

What do you mean? he asked in his mind, having no way of knowing if the sword could hear him. *What kind of trouble?*

"Don't tell me you were looking for a place to piss in the garden," Ort growled. "I'm sure there's a rule on the books somewhere about leaving yellow snow on the castle grounds."

Ridge shook his head, hoping for clarification from the sword. But nothing came.

"I wasn't thinking, sir. That's all. If this mission starts tomorrow, I have to run to the hangar, select my team, and make sure everyone and everything gets packed and ready today." By now, they had reached the main courtyard, with its guards stationed all around. Ridge couldn't have gone back for more spying, even if he dared. It didn't matter. Sardelle was in trouble. He quickened his steps. "I'll report back to you at the end of the day, sir." Not waiting to be dismissed, he broke into a run.

"You better," Ort called after him.

Ridge raced through the castle gate with little more than an acknowledging wave. He sprinted down the icy street, ignoring the startled looks he inspired from passersby, and headed for the archives building.

CHAPTER 2

S ARDELLE HUNKERED ON HER HANDS and knees in a corner as books and pieces of the ceiling continued to fall onto the shield she had gathered around herself. Her lantern was buried, and she couldn't see a thing, but she sensed two people at the top of the stairs leading to the basement. They were armed. Somehow, she doubted they were patrons of the archives, simply curious about the noise. Rubble blocked the doorway on her side, so they wouldn't be coming to investigate soon. She muffled a cough—some of the dust flooding the basement had gotten to her before she had formed her shield— not wanting to make noise, regardless. Let them think her dead.

When the final book fell, she risked lowering her shield, so she could create a light. A soft orange glow filled the space, its influence dimmed by the haze in the air. It didn't matter. Her other senses had already told her the story. She was blocked in until she cleared that doorway—or someone else did. Going out that way might not be wise, anyway. She touched the wall behind her, stretching her mind out in that direction, wondering if there might be more than dirt and earth out there. In a city this old, one expected layers upon layers of civilization.

Hm, yes, there *was* a passage out there. Or, more likely, a sewer tunnel. Either could offer her an alternative exit. The mortar holding the old, chipped bricks together was already crumbling. It shouldn't take much effort to tear away at it. She let go of the light—maintaining two ongoing forms of energy was always a challenge—to reestablish her shield, in case her architectural deconstruction resulted in a cave-in. Another one.

She could have pulled down the wall in one quick move, but she didn't want to make noise. The people on the steps were still there, waiting like snipers. They might decide to close in if they thought she was escaping. Sardelle didn't know who they were, but she didn't want to deal with them.

The bricks slipped free with soft clunks and thunks. Of course, there was another layer of bricks behind them. Time ticked past as she removed the puzzle pieces one by one.

A soft rattle came from the other side of the rubble pile, someone trying the doorknob. Her snipers had grown tired of waiting. The door opened inward, so she ought to have more time before they could clear a route.

"No," came a distant, shrill command from the stairwell. "No more explosives. Not in my building."

Sardelle recognized the archivist's voice—and the fact that she might have run out of time. She pulled down the bricks more vigorously, wincing when they banged and clanked as they landed. A musty scent wafted in along with a cool draft. It didn't smell like a sewer. That was promising.

"—hear her," someone said on the other side of the door.

They heard *her*. Not *someone*. There was no question for them as to who their trapped prey was. Well, Sardelle wouldn't be trapped for long.

Judging the hole large enough, she started to squirm through. She halted in the middle, her stomach draped across bricks, remembering the scrolls with the genealogical trees. She created her light again and stumbled across the rubble to the spot where she'd last seen them. A broken table lay across the bin of scrolls. She flung debris aside, no longer worrying about making noise, and yanked out the red-banded ones.

"Hurry," someone urged on the other side of the door.

Sardelle didn't hear or sense the archivist. She must have been ushered away somehow. Who were these people, anyway? Government spies with orders to get rid of her? She had sensed people watching Ridge's house—watching *her* in the past weeks—but they had never approached her.

A question to answer later. With the scrolls unceremoniously stuffed into her satchel, along with the books she had grabbed earlier, she climbed across the bricks. She was about to crawl into the space on the other side, which turned out to be tighter than she had estimated, when a boom sounded behind her. Whoever wanted her didn't care a whit about destroying public property.

Sardelle used the noise to bring down more bricks and hide the hole she had made. They would find it eventually, but not right away. She hoped.

She pulled herself upright in the passage outside of the basement and found she couldn't walk through it, not without scraping her hips and shoulders into a pulp. The floor was uneven and littered with rocks and sticks or some other type of debris she didn't bother to identify. She didn't bother with a light, either—she wasn't certain how effectively she had covered that hole and didn't want any rays seeping back into the basement for those two people to see.

Turning sideways, Sardelle shuffled along, her heavy satchel bumping against the walls, impeding her progress. When she checked to see if there might be a room on the other side of the crawlspace, she found nothing but filled-in earth for several meters. At least she was heading in the direction of the street.

Her satchel snagged on some obstacle in the way. She tried to push it aside, but it stuck out of the wall. She leaned forward and patted around, trying to figure out if it went all the way across or if she could climb over or duck under. Something else snagged her hair. Grumbling, she tried to draw back. Her knuckles brushed against the wall. It had turned from brick into dirt at some point. The thing in her path seemed to be a branch, or maybe a tree root. Had she gone the wrong way? Maybe she wasn't heading toward the street at all.

Sardelle risked a small light and gasped, stumbling backward. The human leg bone sticking out of the wall wasn't what she had expected at all. Her heel caught on one of the rocks, and she almost pitched to the ground. The narrowness of the passage saved her, for she flung her arms out, catching herself. What she'd thought was a rock was part of a skull. There were a number of them behind her—she had been stepping all over them, kicking them to the side. Nubs of bones were sticking out all along the dirt wall.

It took a moment for her heart to quiet its rapid beating... and for her to realize this must be the edge of some old cemetery or catacomb. The bones were yellow and brittle with age; they had been residents of this place for a long time.

"What a strange research trip this is," she whispered.

Back in the basement, rock or brick shifted, reminding her that those people would be expecting to find her in that room. She hustled forward, crawling awkwardly under the bone obstacles. Noises came from ahead, clack-clunks that echoed oddly in the small passage. Horse hooves? On cobblestones? She thought she might find a way up to the street, but ultimately her passage simply continued under it. It turned and she stumbled across more debris, this time broken ceramic jugs. She touched the wall in spots, trying to sense an opening ahead or another basement nearby. Finally, she found the latter. There was nobody in it, and the wall was in poor condition here as well. She carefully tore away bricks, feeling bad about her vandalism, but she had no intention of wandering this maze beneath the city all day.

She squeezed through her hole and into a basement full of old distilling equipment. She climbed creaking wood stairs that led to a ground-level building. Clanks and the smells of food wafted down the hall, but she turned in the opposite direction, finding a door leading to an alley. Outside, she slumped against the wall, relieved to be in daylight again. Horses and wagons passed in the nearby street.

Disoriented, Sardelle crept to the end of the alley to see where she was. She snorted. The front door of the archives was across the street and only one building away. It had seemed like she had been underground far longer than that. She poked her head out and peered in both directions, then yanked her head right back into the alley. There were two slender figures in cloaks watching the archives building. The same two that had been blowing their way into the basement? No, this felt like another two. Both women. Interesting.

Sardelle backed up and nearly cried out when she ran into someone.

"Most people have to go inside the archives building to do research," a familiar voice drawled, "but I suppose you have those special powers."

"Ridge," she whispered with heartfelt relief, facing him for a sound kiss, though she wasn't ready to turn her back on the street—and those spies—for long. Those women hadn't moved. They were like statues watching the front door.

"What are we spying on?" Ridge slipped his arms around her waist and hugged her from behind. It wasn't always easy to tell when he was worried, since he made flippant remarks no matter what, but she sensed his concern wrapping around her along with his arms. For a moment, she basked in it, admiring the handsome line of his jaw over her shoulder. A month of living together had yet to dull the almost giddy pleasure she experienced in his company. Then it occurred to her to wonder what had brought him here in the middle of the day. And why he was breathing so heavily. With sweat trickling down the side of his face. Had he run all the way here?

She squeezed his arm to let him know she appreciated the embrace and answered his question before asking her own. "Those two women in the cloaks. There are more inside who tried to trap me in the basement. How'd you know I was in trouble?"

"Your sword chose an inopportune moment to jump into my head." Ridge dropped one arm to rub his backside.

"Jaxi? I told her not to do that to you. I—Jaxi! I forgot about her."

"She's in danger too?"

"In danger of being discovered, anyway. Someone was sneaking into your house." *Jaxi? Did you and the beer steins drive away the intruders?*

"More women in cloaks?"

"I don't know. She's not answering. Do you have time to stop at home before going back to work?"

He hesitated, and she flinched inwardly. He probably hadn't had time to come to her rescue in the first place, but he had clearly made it.

"Yes." Ridge stepped back and dusted a cobweb from her hair. "But I have to tell you about my latest mission on the way. You're not injured, are you?"

"No." She swatted at dust clinging to her dress.

Ridge frowned at her, as if he wasn't sure if she was telling the truth. He didn't question her, though. He pointed toward the archives building. "Not that you need my assertive and manly help in matters, but do you want me to question those women and get some information before we go?"

"I don't know... Would you be getting information with force or with charm?"

"If I follow in my already established pattern for the day, I'd dangle from a vine outside their window."

"There's a story I'd like to hear about."

"And yet, oddly, I'm not inclined to share it." Ridge grinned, then tilted his chin toward the street, silently asking his question again.

It was probably a vain hope, but Sardelle didn't want to drag Ridge into her trouble. He stood to lose so much if people found out he was protecting a sorceress. A witch, they would call her.

"No," Sardelle said. "Leave them be. Better to just disappear."

For a moment, he looked like he would argue, but he sighed and said, "As you wish."

He released her from his hug but held her hand as he started toward the opposite end of the alley. He paused before he had gone more than a step. "Ah, by *disappear*, did you mean walk briskly back to the house to check on your sword, or did you mean something more..." He waved his hand in the air and raised his eyebrows.

Sardelle smiled and started walking at his side. Someday, she would give him the full list of what she could and could not do, but the notion that she could do anything magical at all hadn't stopped making him twitch. It would take more time for him to grow accustomed to her abilities. Assuming she remained in the city and they had that time. She gave a long look over her shoulder before letting him lead her into the next street.

* * *

"How long will you be gone?" Sardelle asked as the gate guard passed them onto the installation. She was worried about Jaxi and setting a fast pace, but Ridge's proclamation that he was heading to Cofahre, for what could only be a dangerous mission, had her doubly concerned. "And would it be terribly inappropriate if I arranged to be on the continent at the same time? I promised Tolemek I would find a way to get his sister, and…" She groped for a way to suggest that she could be useful if she were there with Ridge without implying that he needed her help.

He gave her a sidelong look. "Tolemek should be coming with us, if Colonel Ice Butt doesn't offend him so deeply that he flees the country ahead of time. Albeit, this isn't a quest to get his sister."

"Will Lieutenant Ahn be going too?"

Ridge nodded. "I'm not sure I could get anyone else to willingly fly with the Deathmaker sitting in the back seat. That would even make *my* shoulder blades itchy."

"Ah." It was silly—Sardelle wasn't a part of his world and certainly not trusted by his military, so she couldn't expect to be invited along—but she already felt lonely at the thought of the few friends she had made all leaving her. As the weeks had passed, she had grown more distressed about the comrades and kin she would never see again, rather than less. In the beginning, it had been as if she had been off on some adventure in a strange new land, with her family waiting back at home. But she'd had more quiet time of late, and it had finally sunken in that there was no one back at home. There wasn't even a home anymore.

"I'd rather have you with us than roaming the continent on your own." Ridge chewed on his lip as they rounded the corner onto his street. "And I'm not enthused about the idea of leaving you here, either, especially when there's so much interest in you right now."

"I don't suppose there's a luggage compartment on those fliers that you could stick me in."

"Uh, they're not really made for long-distance voyages. Just ask Ahn about the tube."

"The tube?"

"Never mind. You'll find out when you ride in one." Ridge

squinted down the street toward his house. It had come into view and was still standing. There wasn't any smoke billowing from broken windows. "If you'd agree to do the work of my machine guns, we might be able to mount you in front of the cockpit."

Sardelle was trying to imagine the feasibility of this—thus far, she had only seen the fliers from the ground—when she caught his quick smirk. "Ah, that was a joke."

"Let me mull on things. I might come up with something."

"Don't get in trouble on my behalf, please." She already worried they would find trouble at his house when they arrived.

Yes, about that... You might not want to bring the homeowner in just yet.

Jaxi! Why haven't you been talking to me? And what do you expect me to do with Ridge? We're only a half a block away.

I've been using a lot of effort to remain hidden. Those women had some sort of device with them that could detect magic. I had to figure out how to thwart it. I don't care for all these new technological advancements. This century is complicated. As for your pretty pilot, take him for a few laps around the block.

He's not a dog, Jaxi.

Fine, but I can't be blamed. I was only defending myself. I'm pretty sure those women were looking for me specifically. They kept muttering about swords.

"Jaxi says the house may not be as we left it," Sardelle said, following Ridge up the walkway. "The intruders weren't tidy. She's trying to clean up now."

Ridge stopped with his hand on the door. "Do you know how strange that sounds?"

"The idea that Jaxi would do something so helpful as cleaning? Or the fact that she can?"

"All of that, yes."

Sardelle put a supporting hand on his arm, in case he needed it when they walked inside. He opened the door, and a picture frame zipped past, inches from his face. He blinked slowly as he turned to watch it float across the room and affix itself to the wall above his stove. Then his eyes lowered and stayed closed. He took a deep breath.

Sardelle winced and walked inside for a closer look. *You made this mess? Or the intruders did?*

It was them. But possibly they didn't start throwing things around in disgust until I started dropping pots on their heads.

The awful green-and-yellow couch didn't look any more appealing when it was lying on its back, its cushions thrown across the room. Chairs and tables were likewise overturned, and Ridge's picture collection was all over the floor and dusted with something white. Oh, a flour canister had been knocked over, the powder strewn everywhere. Pots and pans littered the floor in the kitchen. Something that looked like a smear of blood decorated one of the counters.

A cold draft rustled Sardelle's dress. Ridge had opened his eyes, but he was still standing in the doorway, staring.

She grimaced. "Are you dumbfounded because of the mess? Or because your pictures are rehanging themselves?"

Ridge shut the door, removed his cap, and scraped his fingers through his hair. "All of that, yes," he repeated.

He managed one of his quirky grins for her. It didn't seem forced—he had looked more stunned than truly upset—but that didn't keep her from feeling bad. This was her fault.

"Let me check on Jaxi. And make sure she's still snuggled in with your mug collection."

"My what?"

"You have a number of glass steins under the bed. We've, ah, discussed them."

"Oh, I was wondering where those went. People always give them to me whenever the squadron helps out in different parts of the country and lands long enough for a drink. I started to get concerned about my reputation after I received the tenth or twelfth. I do like a drink now and then, but does the average Iskandian subject think I'm perpetually drunk?" A heavy thud sounded as Ridge pushed the couch into the upright position. He was the first to admit it was loathsome, but he sprawled on it to read every night. Sardelle wondered if it was telling that it was the first thing he straightened.

"Probably not if they've seen you fly." Sardelle fished Jaxi out from beneath the bed and tucked her purloined scrolls behind the box of steins at the same time. "Those loopy loops and twisty screw moves you do would be difficult in an inebriated state."

It's about time. None of this would have happened if you'd taken me with you in the first place.

Keep nagging like that. It'll ensure I want to take you places.

Please, you know I'm perfectly capable of nagging, no matter where in the world you are.

"Loopy... loops? I'm going to make sure nobody ever puts you on a committee for naming things."

"Is there such a committee?" Sardelle had met a number of his pilots and had to wonder who had thought Pimples, Duck, and Weasel would be good names for brave young men who risked their lives daily.

A knock sounded at the front door, and Ridge didn't answer her.

Same people, Jaxi?

No. A man I haven't encountered before. He has two pistols and a number of knives hidden under his jacket.

Sardelle hurried out of the bedroom and entered the living room as Ridge opened the door. His hand twitched toward the pistol under his own jacket, and she tensed, ready to defend him.

The man standing outside wasn't tall, broad, or beefy, but he wore black trousers, a black turtleneck shirt, and a black jacket. He had fine features, a cleft chin, short sandy hair combed to one side, and frosty green eyes. Though he stood several inches shorter than Ridge, he had a presence that made him seem larger. Intimidating. Ridge didn't take a step back, but something in the way he held his shoulders made Sardelle believe he wanted to. The man's gaze swept past Ridge, taking in the disheveled living room—and her—with a faint sneer.

"Ahnsung," Ridge said. "I'd feign surprise that the guards let you on the post, but I suppose you go where you want."

"They don't know I'm here."

"Seems they don't know a lot of people are here these days. I'm going to talk to someone about additional training."

The man—Ahnsung—didn't smile or give any indication

that he appreciated the humor. It was the opposite, rather, with his brows lowering, as if he was considering a punch to Ridge's nose. Or something worse. Sardelle might assume this was some superior officer, since Ridge so often butted heads with them, but if this man were in the military, wouldn't he be wearing a uniform? It was the middle of the workday.

"You here to threaten me again, Ahnsung?" Ridge asked.

"No." The green eyes closed to slits. "Though you're fortunate you weren't here last month. I would have shot you if you had been."

Sardelle gaped. Ridge merely grunted and said, "Not surprising."

Last month? What had been happening then? She and Ridge had still been up at that fort.

"You're about to take her into trouble again," Ahnsung said.

All at once, the puzzle pieces snapped into place. Her. Ahnsung. Last month, Lieutenant Ahn had been reported dead. This must be a relative. A father? Nobody had spoken of such a person to her, but other than the weekends at Ridge's cabin, when she had been more intent on teaching Tolemek, Sardelle hadn't spent much time with Ahn. The man was old enough to be her father. Late forties.

"Amazing how quickly news from secret meetings with the king gets around," Ridge said.

How could this man know what members of his team Ridge was choosing to take on this new mission? He hadn't told anyone except Sardelle yet, had he? Unless Ahnsung had been spying on them while they'd been walking. If so, he was good. She hadn't sensed a thing. Jaxi hadn't warned her, either.

I was busy picking up pots and picture frames. And might I point out how lowly a task that is for someone with my talent? You'd think I was someone's apprentice.

Those years of demeaning tasks shouldn't be so far back in your memory. You were barely past your apprenticeship when you stored yourself in the soulblade.

Please, I'd been a full-fledged sorcerer for years.

I did look up your history before we bonded, Sardelle pointed out.

You hadn't even finished your final papers.

Because I knew I was dying by then. As if I was going to waste my last months writing papers when there were enemies to turn to ash.

Ah, my apologies.

Jaxi seemed to have come to terms with the shortness of her life long before Sardelle had met her, but every now and then, a sense of wistfulness or regret slipped past the sarcastic irreverence.

"If you take her to Cofahre," Ahnsung said, "I'll hold you responsible for her."

"I consider myself responsible for all of my pilots," Ridge said.

"I also consider you responsible for the fact that she's running around with that—" the man's lips twisted into a much more open sneer than the earlier one, "—*pirate*." Sardelle didn't need a sorcerer's talent for telepathy to know that wasn't the first word that had come to his mind.

"I don't see how I can be responsible for who she's involved with—"

"If you hadn't let her get shot down, she never would have been a prisoner of war." Ahnsung leaned forward, pointing at Ridge's nose. "She never would have met that beast."

"I wasn't there when she was shot down. I was following my orders to be elsewhere. Even if I had been there, this is a dangerous job, and it's possible that something will happen someday, something I can't stop. You'd better reconcile yourself to that. Or, here's a thought: why don't you talk to *her* about her work and who she's sleeping with?"

Ridge was tense. Ahnsung was tenser.

Sardelle loosened the barriers she usually kept around her mind, both for her sanity and to give other people their privacy, trying to get a feel for what Ahnsung intended to do, besides scowl. Was he truly a danger?

His mind was more schooled than Sardelle would have expected from the glacial expression fixed on Ridge, and he didn't give away much, at least on a surface reading. She did catch Tolemek's face floating around in his thoughts. This confrontation had more to do with Cas's new friend than the danger she might be in from Ridge's new mission. Sardelle didn't dare dig deeper. Aside from the morality issue, some people could sense sorcerers poking around in their thoughts.

He's a sniper, and he wouldn't mind putting a hole into your lover's chest—they seem to have a history of arguments. Even if she had been young—and hadn't bothered with those final papers—Jaxi had been a more skilled telepath than Sardelle ever would be, and she could slip into and out of another's thoughts without alerting them, usually even when dealing with sorcerers. Not that they encountered many of those these days. *It seems he doesn't randomly kill people, though. Only if he's paid. He has contemplated finding someone to pay him to shoot Colonel Zirkander.*

Sardelle clenched her hand into a fist. Ridge wouldn't appreciate having a woman protect him in a fight, but that wouldn't stop her from doing it if he was in danger. *Why?*

Because Ridge was the one to encourage his daughter to join the military, and he backed her up when she wanted to attend flight school. Ahnsung wanted her to follow in his footsteps. Join the family business.

The family business? Shooting people?

Apparently he's quite well known for it.

Lovely.

"I gather you haven't spoken to her in years," Ridge said, after they had glared at each other for a while. "She might appreciate it if you stopped by to check on her." As if the man's icy stare mattered nothing to him, Ridge offered a wry smirk. "Let her introduce you to her pirate. Maybe they'll take you out to dinner. Wait, that might not be a good idea. I hear he has a number of strange potions he can slip into a man's food."

Ahnsung stood there seething for a long moment, but he finally lowered his finger. "You like to walk the cliff's edge, don't you?"

"Just living up to the name Dad stuck me with."

Ahnsung snorted softly.

"We're leaving in the morning," Ridge said. "She'll be packing tonight. Plenty of time for you to stop by, say a few words. Give her some fatherly advice on staying alive in enemy territory."

Ahnsung clasped his hands behind his back. He'd recovered

his equanimity and didn't react to Ridge's words, other than to look past him again, considering Sardelle and the mess around her.

"Your home is in disarray," he said.

"It must be those keen observational skills that make you such a fine sniper."

Ahnsung reached under the flap of his jacket. Ridge tensed again, and Sardelle felt the surge of concern go through him as he wondered if he had pushed the man too far. But Ahnsung merely withdrew a business card and extended it.

"Er?" Ridge frowned at it without taking it.

"In case you are in need of my services." Ahnsung laid the card on the side of an upended bookcase near the door, then walked away without another word.

Sardelle waited for Ridge to close the door before saying, "Did that man just offer to kill your home intruders for you?"

"I believe so." Ridge pushed a hand through his hair, leaving it in a state of disarray that matched the room's, albeit the hair was attractive like that, the room less so. "For the right price. I don't know what he thinks officers make these days, but I doubt I could afford him."

Sardelle stepped past a potted plant, the dirt spilled onto the carpet, and slipped her arms around Ridge's waist to give him a hug.

He returned it without hesitation, resting his cheek against her hair. "What's this for?"

"All the craziness I've brought into your life."

Ridge chuckled softly into her hair. "I'm not above accepting affections given out of guilt, but I should inform you that my life was hectic before I met you too. In fact, certain colleagues have suggested that my unique personality and unconventional approach to life attracts interesting people and unorthodox situations. So if you're some kind of repository of craziness, it was probably inevitable that you found me."

"Were these colleagues who respected you or were they trying to point out a character flaw?" Sardelle appreciated his attempts to make her feel better—and let him know with a touch to the cheek and a fond smile—even if she couldn't shirk her guilt that easily.

"I believe so, yes." Ridge sighed and released her with reluctance. "I need to get up to the hangar. General Ort's already going to be wondering about my diversion. I need to pick the rest of the team, not to mention visiting Lieutenant Ahn's pirate."

It amused Sardelle that Tolemek was still Ahn's pirate to him, even when the four of them had spent several days together out at his cabin and she had started teaching Tolemek to recognize his talent and apply it to more than the creation of potions. Of course, Ridge had done his best to pretend nothing of a magical nature was going on by wandering out to fish, never mind that he had to break a hole in the ice and sit on a snowy stump in freezing weather to pursue the hobby.

"I have to convince him to come along," Ridge added.

"Tell him you'll fly past his sister's sanitarium."

"That did occur to me. But it's a big continent, and I don't know if our destination and his are within a thousand miles of each other."

"Your fliers cover ground quickly. If you flew at night and weren't noticed…" Sardelle shrugged. She shouldn't push too hard. It would be convenient for her, certainly, if Ridge could pick up the sister while he was there anyway, but she would find a way if he didn't. It would be interesting to see the world and how much it had changed during her sleep. Granted, her Iskandian complexion would be troublesome for navigating Cofahre, but she could manage.

"Two problems," Ridge said. "First, we still wouldn't have a spot for an extra passenger. Second, I'm not in command of the mission. I'm just… the flying rickshaw service."

"No chance the mission commander can be enticed to deviate?"

"It would take someone a lot prettier than me to entice that man to do anything." Ridge gave her a farewell kiss and opened the door. "My apologies for leaving you with a mess. I'll come back and help clean it up tonight." He waved and jogged down the path to the street, his pace quick enough that Sardelle regretted having delayed him by bringing him back here.

She didn't want to spend their last night together cleaning, either. Of course, if she could figure out a way to go with him, it wouldn't *have* to be their last night together.

We're going on a trip? Jaxi sounded excited.

I'm not sure. Are you willing to ride strapped to a flier like a machine gun?

The view would be better than from under the bed. And you can escape these people trying to blow you up and steal me.

Yes, but I'd rather solve that problem than run from it. Can you describe the people who were here, throwing things around?

Women in cloaks. Not a uniform, but they were wearing trousers rather than dresses.

Like the woman who was following me earlier?

Yes.

Sardelle wondered if she had time to do a little research before Ridge returned from work.

It depends. Are we going to clean the house or leave that for him?

I thought you could clean the house while I went to a library. Sardelle smiled. She didn't truly intend to leave Jaxi again, not with people hunting for her, but it was fun to tease her from time to time.

You know, I don't have *to stay out of your thoughts when you and old Ridgewalker are enjoying your athletic embraces. I could comment on your technique.*

Sardelle grimaced. *Given that you've admitted you passed away before garnering any personal experience in that area, I don't think it would be fair of you to judge.*

Oh, but I've read a lot of books. And had some handlers who were much more libidinous than you. I've seen much.

Why don't we just clean up this mess as a team, then go to the library together?

What a marvelous idea.

CHAPTER 3

RIDGE KNEW HE HAD DAWDLED too long when he found General Ort—scowling as usual—and the bland-faced Captain Nowon waiting inside the hangar door, along with a third officer, who wore the elite troops silver badge on her uniform. Yes, her. Ridge blinked and looked twice. Women weren't allowed into the infantry units, and while the elite troops were a somewhat different creature, since some of the operatives were trained for spy missions as well as for fighting prowess, he wouldn't have thought many—if any—could pass the rigorous physical tests. She was taller than Captain Nowon, though—only an inch shy of Ridge's own six-foot-one—and had the lean rangy look of an endurance runner. Her nametag read Kaika, and she wore captain's tabs on the collar of her uniform. Ridge expected a rigid attention stance and a snappy salute when she turned toward him, figuring a woman would have to be the model of military professionalism to be considered for the elite troops, but she gave him a perfunctory salute, followed by a handshake and a sultry smile that seemed out of place on a rawboned face without a speck of makeup softening the features.

"Colonel Zirkander, it's a real honor to have been chosen to work with you and your team."

Despite the sensual smile, she didn't hold the handshake longer than appropriate, nor did she do anything so brazen as giving him a head-to-toe look of consideration, such as he occasionally received from women. Still, something about the cant of her lips and the twinkle in her gray eyes said she knew how to have fun on the weekends. Her hair was short enough to be regulation without pins, but she managed to give it a flirty sway as she turned her head toward her comrade. Captain Nowon was in the middle of something that almost looked like an eye roll, but the movement was so slight, it might have been part of his perpetual scanning of the area around him—and above him.

"Well," Ridge said to Ort, whose scowl was definitely directed at him and not anyone else in the hangar, "I like her better than Therrik."

"I'll bet," Ort said.

"That's not much of an accolade," Kaika whispered to Nowon, and clasped her hands behind her back in a loose parade rest.

"Where have you been, Ridge?" Ort snapped. "Your elites are packed and here—" he waved toward a couple of duffel bags near the wall that, judging by the bulges, were loaded with weapons rather than clothing, "—and you haven't even picked your team yet."

"Sorry, General. Had a break-in at the house I had to check on, then I needed to make a quick stop for a necessary purchase." Ridge rattled a brown paper bag in his hand.

"Break-in? What do you mean, break-in?"

Ridge shrugged. For all that he would love to hurl all of the army's forces after the intruders, he wasn't about to explain that someone was after Sardelle and her sword. That would raise far too many questions as to why. "I don't know who was responsible, but I'll be having a word with General Domhower about installation security. My house was demolished, and I'm not certain yet if anything was stolen."

Ort's scowl faded and was replaced with a faintly hopeful expression. "Was your couch irreparably damaged, by chance?"

"Nope, just tipped over."

"A shame."

Ridge arched his brows.

"About the break-in, I mean."

"Careful, General. Make fun of my couch, and I won't invite you to my next beer, blood, and brisk-ball summer gathering. You won't get to take your shirt off and flex your muscles for Lieutenant Colonel Ostraker's grandmother."

"I still have a scar from your last gathering," Ort grumbled.

"That'll teach you to play drunk. The ground crew officers are feisty."

"I think they just like an opportunity to throw an elbow into a general's ribs."

"That's what feisty means, isn't it?" Ridge asked.

Ort grimaced and rubbed his side.

"What's in the bag?" Captain Kaika nodded toward the crinkled paper with curious eyes.

"Just something to watch over the house while I'm gone." Ridge kept it shut. As captains, these two probably wouldn't mock him to his face, but he didn't need any rumors about his quirkiness floating around the intelligence units.

"Break-ins regardless, I need you to pick your team and get ready," Ort said. "You'll need to leave two hours before dawn if you want to time your arrival to cruise into Cofahre after dark but with most of the night still ahead of you. That's why I told Therrik to send his gear and team early, so you can get everything sorted out today."

"Yeah, yeah, got it." Ridge ignored Ort's customary bristling at the lack of honorifics and military courtesy, and waved to the captains. "Before I do anything else, I've got to tell you two that half of *that*—" he pointed to the lumpy duffels, "—will have to stay here."

"That is mission-essential gear, sir," Nowon said. His facial expression didn't change much, but his words came out rapidly. That probably passed for urgency from him.

"If it's half as heavy as it looks, it'll be too much weight. Even the two-seaters—*especially* the two-seaters—have very strict maximum loads, and if we don't pay attention to them, we'll be sailing over to Cofahre instead of flying. I'm already going to have to lose half of my ammunition to make room for all of Therrik's muscles." Ridge gave Ort a sour look before heading into the hangar.

"Find a lighter pilot to take him," Ort called after him.

Ridge waved his hand in acknowledgment but wasn't sure he could justify tormenting any of his people with that personality. He had Lieutenant Ahn in mind for the mission—she was the lightest of anyone on the squadron—but planned to assign Tolemek to her plane. He hadn't been joking when he had told

Sardelle he couldn't see any of his other pilots flying across the Targenian Sea with Deathmaker in the seat behind, not without sixteen hours of tense shoulders and quiet suffocating terror.

It was a maintenance day, without any drills scheduled, so all of the Wolf and Tiger squadron fliers were in. Tiger squadron had their physical efficiency tests today, so Ridge's pilots had the building to themselves. The men and women had their checklists and technical manuals out as they ran through inspections of engines, wiring, and cabling, though they had all been glancing toward the door while he and the colonel talked. They had to be wondering why the elite troops were here and if the squadron was heading off on a mission. Ridge wasn't sure whether to feel bad for those who had to stay behind or not. He would be enthused about this adventure if *he* were in charge, but he had misgivings about Therrik.

No, he admitted to himself, he just didn't like Therrik and didn't want to work with him—much less *under* him. Most likely, he was a perfectly competent commander and very good at skulking around behind enemy lines and setting bombs or whatever these people did. Ridge glanced back, catching Nowon and Kaika with those duffels open, arguing over the contents. Several pistols and boxes of ammunition lay on the floor around the bags, while wires and bulging apparatuses poked out of the top. Bombs, yes, that appeared likely.

"Morning, sir," Lieutenant Ahn said as he approached. She glanced at the paper bag in his hand but didn't comment on it.

He should have left it by the door, but then one of those other officers might have peeked inside.

"Is it still morning?" Ridge asked. It seemed like he had been awake for hours and hours.

"I think so, sir."

"Up for a special mission to Cofahre?"

She hesitated, but then nodded firmly. "Always, sir."

He mulled over that hesitation for a moment. She hadn't said a word about what she had endured during her weeks of being a prisoner, but it couldn't have been anything pleasant. He had spent time in a Cofah prison himself a few years back. He doubted the guards had grown any more accommodating. Still, she had proven herself capable in battle three times since returning, and he didn't doubt that she could handle any lingering nightmares.

"If everything goes well, we'll slip in at night, drop off our cargo—" Ridge waved to the two captains, "—and then slip out again the next night, without ever getting into a battle. In fact, I think the king is hoping we won't get into battles. It's something of a spy mission, and there'll just be a handful of us going."

"Oh?" Ahn perked up, clearly intrigued. Or pleased to be picked for an elite task force.

"Yes, and I've been asked to talk Tolemek into coming. I thought you might be willing to help."

Her expression grew a little wry. "I assumed you were picking me for my unique skills, rather than who I'm sleeping with, but I suppose I want to go along if he's going, to keep him out of trouble."

Ridge stifled a grimace at the words "sleeping with." It was true that Tolemek had acted like a perfectly decent human being so far, but Ridge still felt protective toward Ahn, probably because he'd first met her when she was barely more than a kid, and some notorious pirate was *not* who he would have picked for her to fall in love with. The decision wasn't his, of course, and the fact that her dad loathed the idea almost made Ridge want to champion it. None of that was important at the moment, though.

"Oh, I have your unique skills in mind, trust me," he said. "Take your Mark 500 and plenty of ammunition for it. Just because we're *supposed* to get in and out without a fight doesn't mean we will. You know plans are worth spit until they've been put into action. And if our friends over there get into trouble, it's possible we'll have to get them out." Oh, and wouldn't he appreciate the expression on Therrik's face when Ridge's pilots were the ones to rescue him from some Cofah prison? "We're leaving two hours before dawn, so start packing. But I do want you to meet me at Tolemek's lab after lunch."

"You don't think he'll want to come along?" Ahn lowered her voice. "Or are you afraid he'll want to come along too badly?

So he can get his sister? He *is* happy here, sir. He just wants to make sure she doesn't have to stay in that place any longer than necessary."

"I know. I understand. Unfortunately, I'm not going to be in command of the mission, but we'll find out where she is exactly, and if it's anywhere near and it's at all possible…" Ridge finished with a shrug, not wanting to promise too much.

"Thank you, sir. He'll appreciate you thinking of him. *I* appreciate it."

Ridge gave her a parting nod and headed down the line toward the next pilot he had in mind for the mission. Ahn's gratitude made him feel a little guilty, since he wouldn't be thinking of going out of his way to help Tolemek if not for Sardelle and the promise she had made to the pirate.

As he passed Pimples, Beeline, and Crash, Ridge gave them quick nods and greetings, noting their hopeful expressions, but he didn't stop. He could only take two more men, and he hadn't been buttering Ahn's toast—he truly wanted people with talents beyond flying for this. Talents that might be useful if he needed them. Besides, he needed to leave some good men for Major Pennith, who would command the squadron in his absence.

"Duck and Apex." Ridge gestured to the two men at the end of the line of fliers. "Come see me."

A wide grin split Duck's face, and he thumped his fist on Apex's shoulder as he ran past. He was twenty-five and would make a good captain once he settled down, but Lieutenant Wasley "Duck" Antilon still seemed more a kid than an officer. He and Pimples might have a few years on Ahn, but she always seemed the oldest of the group of young lieutenants.

Duck almost skidded in his hurry to meet Ridge and snap to attention. "Yes, sir?" Almost too tall to be a pilot, he had big ears, big feet, and a big grin that he always had to struggle to rein in. He wasn't doing a good job of that at the moment.

Apex walked over, his stride more measured, his expression one of curiosity but not avid hope, like Duck's. Though he was also a lieutenant, he was in his early thirties since he had come later than usual to the military, finishing eight years of university classes and two years studying fossils in the field before having his hometown of Tanglewood destroyed by pirates. More specifically, by Deathmaker's biological agent. Ridge had been watching him since Tolemek had come to the city, but Apex was good at hiding his thoughts. He had seemed stiffer than usual around Ahn these last weeks, but to Ridge's knowledge, he hadn't confronted her or made a problem. Under any other circumstances, Ridge wouldn't do something as foolish as putting him on a team with Tolemek, but the man knew everything there was to know about dragon history. Sardelle knew a lot about dragons and history, too—Ridge still hadn't figured out if she had always been academically inclined, or if Referatu children had simply received more thorough educations than anyone else—but he still didn't know how he could bring her on the mission, especially if he wasn't in charge.

"Sir?" Apex asked, falling in beside Duck.

Ridge opened his brown bag and held it toward him. "The vendor promised this is an authentic Peruvashian Prosperity Dragon carved from the finest redwood burl. It's guaranteed to bring luck to my home. What's your professional opinion?"

Apex peered into the bag. "That the vendor saw you coming and knew colonels make good money."

Ridge snorted. "I only paid ten nucros for it."

Apex lifted his gaze to the flier at the front of the queue, where Ridge's little wooden dragon carving hung in the cockpit. "It looks heavy. You're not going to replace your current charm, are you?"

"Nah, this is for the house. It's been under assault of late."

"I see." Apex clasped his hands behind his back and refrained from saying his commander was a superstitious dolt. Good man.

"Any idea what dragon blood might be used for?" Ridge asked.

Apex's eyebrows rose. "Dragon blood was exceedingly difficult to acquire. There were cases of swords stained with dragon blood during the Rider Wars, and of minute quantities being scraped away for study, but that was fifteen hundred years ago, and science was primitive back then. Speculation ranged from the blood itself having healing properties to the possibility of it being an energy source. It was proven any number of times that the offspring of those who mated with dragons gained access to otherworldly or perhaps mental powers that normal humans couldn't tap into. Is this what you're referring to? Human blood mixed with dragon blood? If so, it's been nearly fifty generations since the last dragons were seen in the world, and the dilution factor means there's little difference now between a human who had a dragon ancestor and one who didn't."

"Yes, I've always wondered how those matings went," Ridge said, though in truth, he hadn't thought much about it until he had met Sardelle and she had explained that all sorcerers had a dragon ancestor somewhere in the family tree. "But what I'm actually asking about is what pure dragon blood might be used for now, because it sounds like the Cofah might have some."

"I don't see how that's possible, sir. It sounds like propaganda." Apex eyed the elite troops captains. "Unless we have some kind of proof? In which case I would be most intrigued to examine it. It can't possibly be live, viable blood, but perhaps they've found some trace blood molecules in a fossilized mosquito or some such. If a mosquito could even pierce a dragon's scaled hide. I'd be skeptical, but I know there were some bigger blood-harvesting insects in past eras."

"The impression I got from my meeting was that this was live blood," Ridge said.

"Impossible. Unless they've got a live dragon too."

"That's... an interesting notion. Or a disturbing one. If anyone is going to have dragons on their side, I'd much prefer it be us rather than the Cofah. Still, you'd think that if there were dragons left in the world, one would have shown up now and then in the last millennium."

"Science hypothesizes that they went extinct due to changes in the atmosphere that came with the increased human presence in the world," Apex said. "The bonk-a-doos say the dragons got tired of this world and migrated to another one, though there's no evidence that dragons could fly through space or create portals to other planets."

Bonk-a-doos, indeed. "Is it possible the Cofah could have

figured out a way to *create* dragon blood through some scientific or mechanical means? Like if they did find some fossilized remains?"

"*We* can't make blood, and we're at least as far along, scientifically and technologically speaking, as the Cofah."

Duck scratched his head. By now, Apex probably knew why he was being invited along, but Duck looked a little mystified.

"Wondering what your role is going to be on this mission, Duck?" Ridge asked.

"No, sir. Well, yes, sir." Duck lowered his hand. "But I got stuck on the idea of dragons and people making like jacks and mares in heat."

Apex tilted his head. "An inaccurate simile, since the offspring between a horse and a donkey is sterile. The human children born to those matings were perfectly viable, as evinced by the fact that people with dragon blood were born for centuries after."

Duck's face screwed up. "But how... I mean dragons are—" he stretched out his arms to their fullest spread, "—and people are..." He pulled his hands into encompass something much smaller.

Ridge smirked, but he eyed Apex as well. He was just as curious about the answer. He supposed Sardelle would know, but he had never thought to ask. Talk of magic and the origins of magic made him twitchy. He ought to put this whole conversation to bed and send these men off to pack.

"According to the histories, dragons could take human form," Apex said. "Like many other species, there were always far more male dragons born than female dragons, and only the strongest and most desirable males were taken as mates. Those who wanted offspring, or were simply feeling randy, shape-changed and mated with other species. Not only humans. This all happened so long ago that it's difficult to prove any of it, mind you, but some of the rarer and quirkier species out there with inexplicable traits that border on the magical—such as unicorns, winged tigers, and flash apes—are believed to have come about due to dragon blood. Most of these creatures are nothing more than stuffed reproductions in museums now, having either been hunted to extinction or having had their blood diluted through the generations until the peculiar traits disappeared, but you still hear stories of them now and again, especially in the wilder and less explored areas of the world."

"My father brought a unicorn horn back from his travels," Ridge said.

"Now I'm imagining dragons and horses..." Duck shook his head. "Never mind."

"Apex, your knowledge could be important on this mission," Ridge said. "You up for an adventure into Cofahre?"

"Yes, sir."

"And, Duck? Can you forage and survive in some random Cofahre wilderness as well as you can here?"

"Ahh." Duck nodded, understanding his role finally. The kid had practically grown up with wolves, at least according to the stories he told, before his family had joined a farming community so their children could be properly educated. During an exercise the year before, he and three other soldiers had crashed in the swamps off the Temeron Keys, and Duck had kept everyone sheltered and fed until the team had been located. "Yes, sir. Reckon I can forage and survive just about everywhere. There's ways to test what's edible and what's not, even if you're in a new area."

"I hope we won't need your skills..." Ridge had no intention of having his team shot down deep into enemy territory, but he'd make a poor commander if he didn't plan for every contingency. "But I'd like to be able to call upon them just in case."

"Yes, sir. I'm happy to go along."

"Good. We're leaving in the morning. I'll have the ground crew prep the two-seaters. We'll all be flying an extra passenger." Ridge nodded toward the two captains.

"You've selected four pilots, sir," Apex observed. "Who else is coming?"

"There's an elite troops colonel that will be leading his men. And the fourth person... I'm going to go check to see if he's available." Ridge waved and hurried away before Apex could ask who that fourth person might be. Best to see if Tolemek wanted to come before worrying too much about personality—and history—conflicts.

Still, Ridge could feel Apex's eyes following him across the hangar as he walked away.

* * *

The receptionist in the research building pursed his lips in clear disapproval of the mud Ridge left on the white marble floor when he entered, or maybe at Ridge in general. His flight suit and leather jacket weren't uncommon wear in the city, but everyone walking in and out of doors up and down the hall wore white lab coats and tidy civilian suits. Mud-free footwear.

Lieutenant Ahn was leaning against the end of the receptionist's desk. Her boots looked as muddy as Ridge's, but there wasn't a line of prints leading from the door to her spot. The receptionist sighed and pushed something under his desk, eliciting a thunk. A door opened down the hallway, and something that looked vaguely like an upturned mop bucket with gears rolled out. Damp sponges between its wheels deployed, wiping the floor clean. Ridge stepped aside for it as soon as he realized it was on some kind of circuit that wouldn't be stopped for innocent bystanders.

"Tolemek's lab is this way, sir," Ahn said, pointing down the hall.

Ridge watched the cleaning contraption for a moment before joining her. "Should I be jealous that a notorious pirate and enemy of the nation works in a much fancier building than we do?"

"From what I've seen, the fancy toys are just distractions. The other day, I walked in on Tolemek using his mechanical spinner and some liquid gas to turn milk into ice cream."

"No wonder the king was excited to turn him into an ally." Ridge gave the sponge machine another wistful look before they turned into a stairwell and started climbing.

"You could get Wrench or Dantalos from Tiger Squadron to build you a self-propelling mop bucket if you were really motivated, sir."

"I'm not sure the minds that thought up an ambulatory beer dispenser for the break room could be trusted to create something as useful as a cleaning device."

"Maybe not." Ahn led him onto the second floor to a door with a frowning guard standing next to it. His shoulders were slouched, almost in a cringe. Odd. Was he that alarmed by Tolemek's reputation?

The guard straightened as soon as Ridge and Ahn approached. "Colonel Zirkander, sir." He glanced at the closed door. "Is... Deathmaker in trouble, sir?"

"I don't know. Is he not sharing his ice cream?"

A puzzled furrow creased the guard's brow. "I don't know, sir. I just mean... another officer. It *sounds* like he's in trouble." He frowned at the door again. "He's been decent to me. I know about his past, but I didn't think he'd done anything to—"

Ahn pushed past the guard, a worried frown forming on her own face. She opened the door, and a wisp of smoke wafted out. Ridge hesitated, imagining some experiment gone awry and spilling poison into the air, but the guard had been worried *for* Tolemek, not because of him. Ahn rushed in without pausing, and Ridge's heart jumped when a slam almost as loud as a gunshot came from the other side of the room.

Ridge strode in, slipping his pistol out of his holster. Towering equipment and cabinets loomed on either side of him, but he focused on the far side of the room, trying to figure out what had caused that noise. But smoke thickened the air, dulling the sunlight filtering in from the single window and dimming the influence of the gas lamps mounted on the walls.

"Tolemek?" Ahn asked.

"Get back, woman," a man said. It wasn't Tolemek, but Ridge recognized the voice. "Quit hiding, you pirate coward. Face me like a man, not a child full of tricks."

"Colonel... Therrik?" Ridge asked. He lowered his pistol. Ahn had her own firearm out and hadn't bothered lowering it yet.

Ridge stepped forward and pressed down on her forearm. "That's our commander for our mission. Shooting him would be frowned upon by our superiors."

"Tolemek, are you all right?" Ahn asked, her arm tense. She lowered the pistol but didn't put it away.

"That depends on whether this... person is done assaulting me," came the pirate's voice from a corner of the room. It sounded like he was hunkered behind a lab station.

"Colonel Therrik," Ridge said, hardening his voice—he knew Therrik wouldn't be intimidated by him, but he wanted a serious response, not to be ignored. The colonel was visible in the smoke, his broad shoulders heaving, as if he'd run a sprint. Or been in a fight. His face was covered in soot, lined with sweat streaks. Or maybe those were tear streaks. "What are you doing here?"

"Getting information from this homicidal ass," Therrik snarled.

"He barged in here, wanting to interrogate me," Tolemek said.

"We don't *need* information from him," Ridge said slowly, not sure he understood Therrik's intent. "We're taking him with us so he can be a mobile resource for us. If he agrees to come, that is. Your method of enticing him to join our quest is lacking."

Ahn pulled away from Ridge and walked toward the sound of Tolemek's voice. She kept an eye on the colonel—she'd yet to holster that pistol.

Ridge wanted to warn her not to do anything to jeopardize her career, but Therrik was talking again.

"I'm not taking this hairy gorilla anywhere. He'll tell us what he knows about dragon blood, if I have to carve it out of him."

"Come close to me again, and the next grenade I throw will do a lot more than tear up your eyes," Tolemek said.

Therrik shifted, and Ridge spotted a big knife in his hand.

Seven gods, what was the man *doing*? "If you're looking for an expert on dragon blood," Ridge said, "I suggest you talk to Apex, one of my pilots. He studied archaeology and dragons specifically before joining the military. Tolemek is supposed to come along to analyze the Cofah lab and figure out what they're making. I sincerely doubt he can do that until he actually sees the lab." Of course, if Therrik and his team objected to Tolemek's presence, that might be the perfect time for Tolemek to slip away and find his sister. *Ridge* wouldn't want to go into an enemy scientist's lab without a scientist of his own to point out the booby traps, but Therrik didn't seem to share that feeling.

"We're *not* taking him with us," Therrik repeated. "Not on my team, and not on my mission. There's no way I'd trust that animal at my back, and you're a fool if you would, Zirkander. Get him back in his homeland, and he'll turn on us quicker than a cobra escaped from its cage."

"Anyone want to tell me about this mission I may or may not be going on?" Tolemek rose from behind the lab station, a ceramic oval device in his hand. He gestured for Ahn to join him, as if Therrik might attack her, and he intended to protect her as well as himself.

Ridge didn't think the colonel's propeller was that off kilter, but he took a few steps toward the man, anyway, lifting a placating hand.

"That's what I came to do," Ridge told Tolemek. "Why don't you let me handle the, ah, interrogation, Colonel? Your captains are already at the hangar. There was some debate over the packing list. They could probably use your advice."

Therrik glowered at Ridge, that long knife still clenched in his hand. "Sure, I'll let you and him conspire, then come along on my mission to Cofahre together. That's not insanity, not at all."

Ridge didn't know whether to fight Therrik's sarcasm with sarcasm of his own or to try to get to the bottom of it. What was the curmudgeon so worried about? It wasn't as if Tolemek had been working for the Cofahre a month before. He had been estranged from his homeland for years. Besides, he would be surrounded by military officers out there.

Therrik pointed at Ridge's face. "You may have the king where you want him, but some of us know the truth and aren't going to let you roam free much longer, not with some witch controlling you."

Uh, how had they jumped to Sardelle again? What exactly had Therrik been telling the king before and after Ridge had listened in on that conversation? And what did it have to do with

Tolemek and the mission anyway?

"You can't be trusted any longer, Zirkander. It's not your fault that you were so weak-willed as to fall for some witch's wiles, but it won't be a problem much longer."

"What does that mean?" Ridge whispered, eyes locked with Therrik's. "You didn't have something to do with the break-in this morning, did you?" He doubted it, but there were a lot of people gunning for Sardelle all of the sudden. Was it possible they were all part of the same organization? "Or the explosion?"

Therrik managed to look confused and angry at the same time. "You'll find out."

Ridge clenched his fists. A threat toward him, he could handle—it wouldn't be the first. But threatening Sardelle? Oh, he knew she could handle trouble, too, but if some group of people—Therrik's intelligence buddies?—knew what she was, they might be prepared and come up with ways to hurt her. After all, as powerful as her people had been three hundred years ago, they had been destroyed by soldiers with bombs.

Therrik's gaze lowered to Ridge's fists, and a tight smile formed on his mouth. That challenge had returned to his eyes. Ridge knew it would be stupid to get into a fight with the man, but he was sorely tempted when Therrik stalked in his direction. He unclenched his fists and kept his hands at his sides. Therrik might be an ass, but Ridge doubted he would pummel a fellow officer without provocation. Just retired pirates.

As suspected, Therrik didn't lift a hand as he said, "See you in the morning, Zirkander." He jostled Ridge's shoulder as he angled toward the door. Even the simple brush was enough for Ridge to feel the mass of muscle beneath the colonel's sleeve, and he had to take a step to the side to brace himself. "I trust I won't see that *thing*—" Therrik jerked a thumb over his shoulder, "—standing next to your flier when I get there."

The guard in the hallway—who had doubtlessly been witness to this encounter—scurried out of Therrik's way as the colonel strode out. The door slammed shut.

"Actually he'll be standing next to Lieutenant Ahn's flier," Ridge said. He supposed it was cowardly to wait until after the door was shut to respond, but he didn't want to show his cards before he was ready to play them.

Tolemek gave Ahn a hug and walked out into the open. He had lost most of his pirate clothing, including the shark tooth necklace, spiked bracers, and sleeveless vest he had been wearing when Ridge first met him, but he hadn't cut his goatee or the thick ropes of black hair that hung about his shoulders. Still, he was presentable in the white lab coat and black and grey civilian clothing beneath. Mostly presentable. At the moment, a split lip leaked blood onto the white coat, and he was squinting out of his left eye. He had definitely taken a couple of punches. What was Therrik thinking? Was the man truly that unbalanced? It was hard to explain an officer with twenty years in the military acting so erratically.

Ahn walked over to a sink and wetted a rag. "Healing salve?" she asked.

"There are a bunch of finished vials in that cabinet." Tolemek pointed.

Ridge leaned his hip against a lab station. He would leave the ministrations to Ahn. "So, Tolemek. Are you interested in taking a trip to Cofahre?"

"To get my sister?"

"To analyze a secret Cofah lab that our spies found. They supposedly have dragon blood and are using it to make weapons."

"Yes, I got the gist of the dragon blood problem." Tolemek scowled toward the closed door. "Who was that, anyway? He neglected to give me his name before he started hurling me against walls and lab stations."

Ahn returned to his side with the rag and a vial of greenish-gray gunk that looked about as appealing as thirty-year-old ration bars. She twitched a finger, and Tolemek lowered his face.

"*That*, should you choose to join us on this mission, is our commanding officer," Ridge said.

Tolemek's lips twisted into a displeased grimace. "Maybe I'll stay here."

"Ahn's going."

"Maybe I'll go."

Ridge smirked. "I'd make a joke about the tractability of those newly in love, but..."

"You're too busy being tractable for Sardelle?" Ahn asked, then tacked on a belated, "Sir." She was dabbing the green stuff on Tolemek's wounds with far more gentleness than anything other than her gun usually received from her.

"Oh, I'm way past being tractable and on the verge of doing something really stupid to make sure she's safe." Ridge was worried about Therrik's words and worried about what had happened to Sardelle this morning. She was being targeted by people who seemed to know who and what she was. Leaving her here while he went away on an extended mission... he couldn't do it. Nor did he want to simply send her to his cabin. For one thing, she might not go—he certainly couldn't pretend to have any ownership of her or a right to give her orders. For another, these people already knew she was connected to him. His cabin wasn't a secret, nor was it a long distance out of the city. They would figure out to look there. On the other hand, she *was* interested in going to Cofahre...

"That woman can take care of herself," Tolemek said. "If you think she needs you to engage in stupidity on her behalf, you're delusional." Something about the way his eyebrows rose suggested he thought Ridge was delusional anyway. Enh, he wouldn't be the first to think so.

"Possibly so," Ridge said, "but I'm also thinking of the success of our mission. I'm a little concerned by the unpredictability of Fists as our team leader." He tapped his fingers on the cool granite surface of the lab station. "Tolemek, do you have any potions that could cause a man to lose consciousness for a time?"

"Potions? I'm not some witch stirring up a concoction over a cauldron, you know."

"Is that a yes or a no?"

"He's an expert at knocking people out." Ahn gave him a fond smile.

Ridge tried not to shudder at the double implications of the word. He knew Ahn wasn't referencing Tanglewood, or anyone Tolemek might have killed with his potions, because she wouldn't beam up at a man who could take pride in such things; she didn't even approve of her father's career, and he usually killed criminals and thugs who deserved it.

"If you could give me something in pill form, that should work... extremely well." Ridge smiled as a plan solidified in his mind.

"A pill? Does this look like a pharmacy?"

"Definitely a pill," Ridge said, ignoring the sarcasm. "Maybe you could even give it an appealing flavor."

Tolemek made an exasperated noise.

Ahn was squinting suspiciously at Ridge. "What exactly are you planning, sir?"

"You two will both find out, providing you're at the hangar before dawn." Ridge smiled and headed for the door.

"My sister?" Tolemek asked.

Ridge stopped, his hand on the knob, and looked over his shoulder. Tolemek might come along simply because Ahn asked him, but he would be a truer ally if there was something more concrete in it for him. "How far is she from Brandenstone?" he asked, naming the closest city to the coordinates he had been given.

"A hundred and fifty miles."

Ridge hated to make promises he couldn't keep, but if his plan with the pill worked, keeping it shouldn't be that much of a problem. Keeping his career once he returned to Iskandia, that was more of a question.

"We'll get her," he said and walked out the door.

CHAPTER 4

AFTER SHOWING HER TEMPORARY VISITOR'S pass, Sardelle hurried through the gates of the army fort and toward the darkening residential streets that housed Ridge's little cottage. She clutched a heavy book to her hip, a historical tome that held information on secret orders of the past. In truth, she had no idea if the women who had been spying on her belonged to something as ominous or sophisticated as a "secret order," but the similar dress they all wore made her suspicious of organizational underpinnings. She wished she had seen one with her eyes, and not just her senses, so she could have spotted any pins or markings that might be used to identify them.

You think someone in a secret order would be so obvious? It wouldn't be very secret if they ran around advertising their existence with tattoos or glowing brooches.

Jaxi, have I mentioned how endearing your logic is?

Never, but you're young and irrational; you haven't yet learned to appreciate my unerring pragmatism.

Uh huh. Is Ridge home? Sardelle's library time had been interesting, and she intended to give this book a thorough reading, but she wanted to spend time with him before he left. She hadn't figured out yet whether she was going to stay here or head over to Cofahre herself, but either way, she wouldn't see him again for a while. That sense of loneliness that always lingered at the edge of her thoughts threatened to encroach. An image of a tousle-haired Ridge in bed with the sheets tangled around his bare chest *did* encroach.

He's there. I don't think he has amorous indulgences on his mind.

Why not? Whenever Sardelle had such matters in mind, she had yet to find Ridge in the mood to object to making them a reality.

Yes, yes, he's as horny as you are. But right now he's standing in the back yard, loading saddlebags onto a horse.

Er. Sardelle turned onto his street, jogged past the fountain, and cut into the side yard between Ridge's house and the one next door. The soggy snow clinging to the grass licked at her boots and the hem of her dress, but she ignored it. She rounded the corner to find the situation Jaxi had described, with Ridge near the back door, tightening the packs on a sturdy mare. Horses weren't an uncommon sight in the city, but there were stables at the back of the fort. The horses weren't usually brought over to the residential streets.

"Does this mean you're kicking me out because my sword and I went to do research instead of cleaning your house?" Sardelle asked, angling across the yard toward Ridge. She glanced through the kitchen window. Most of the mess had already been cleaned up. How long had he been home? She should have left the library sooner.

"If I were kicking you out, I wouldn't supply you with a horse." Ridge patted the mare on the neck, then stepped away from the creature to greet her. He smiled that roguishly charming smile of his, the one that made her insides melt like the snow beneath the sun. Then he took her free hand, pulled her to him, and lowered his head for a kiss.

After Jaxi's warning, Sardelle hadn't expected amorous indulgences, and she almost dropped her book. But she leaned against him, happy to return the kiss. His lips were warm next to the chill of the night, and it wasn't long before she had forgotten the horse and was thinking of nothing more than ushering him inside.

When Ridge drew back, he didn't push open the door for them. He merely slid his hands down her back and gazed into her eyes, his face scant inches from hers. "Yup," he finally said, as if he were reaching some decision. "I want you with me in Cofahre." No matter what his orders from the king had been.

He didn't say that last sentence aloud, but this close, with his thoughts burning in his eyes, Sardelle felt the words ring in her head.

"Ridge," she whispered, "I'm delighted that kissing me makes you want to take me on adventures with you, but I've already upset the equilibrium of your life." She lifted a hand to the side of his face, running her thumb along his jaw. "I wouldn't forgive myself if you jeopardized your career. I..." She thought of her earlier musings, the knowledge that she could make life simpler for him by leaving, but all she wished to do was tug him into the bedroom. She didn't want to leave, that was certain. She wanted exactly what he was planning—whatever it was. She wanted to go with him.

"The kissing is nice," Ridge said, "but it's also the fact that you're jabbing me in the gut with a book and a sword hilt that gets me excited about taking you places." He grinned, unaware of or undaunted by her concerns. "That's not a combination I've gotten from many girls." As he spoke, he gazed into her eyes with a fondness that made her heart ache.

"I... oh."

Well, it's not your smooth, gilded tongue that has him excited.

Ssh.

Ridge cleared his throat and stepped back, though he only released her with one arm. The other seemed reluctant to leave her waist. The warmth of his hand seeped through her dress as he massaged her. "I've packed a horse for you, and if you're willing to trust me, I need you to ride most of the night to the north, along the Pin-Kanth Highway. It'll be dark, but it's a smooth road. The horse won't have any trouble following it. It's about twenty miles to Monomy Bay, where you can wait for me to pick you up. You can sleep during our flight tomorrow. In fact, some people find sleeping makes flying with me more bearable."

It took a moment for Sardelle to wrap her mind around this proposed adventure. Possibly because she was distracted by what his hand was doing. "And the reason I need to meet you there is because your superiors would be upset if they saw you loading me into your flier?"

"Among other things." He gave her a lopsided smile. "You'll go? I want you to come. I know you'll be amazing, and I promised Tolemek we would get his sister—I may need some help making that happen. We won't have enough room to bring her back on the fliers."

Sardelle wasn't sure if he had magic in mind or was simply thinking of her as an escort who could bring the girl back on a civilian freighter, but she didn't care, either way. He wanted her to come... and she wanted to go. Hoping she wouldn't regret the choice later, she stepped closer to him again for another kiss.

"I'll go," she whispered after a moment. "Thank you."

"Good," he murmured, his lips against hers, and most of his body against hers too.

"It'll only take a few hours to get to that bay."

"About six, I'd guess, given the darkness."

Lighting the way so the horse could travel at a faster pace than a walk would be an easy matter for her. "When are you leaving?"

"Early," he said, then caught on to what she was asking and grinned. "Eight hours. Time for—"

She cut him off with another kiss. "Good."

* * *

An icy wind was blowing in off the sea, and it was almost three hours before dawn when Ridge walked off the tram at the top of the butte, but the dim, cold conditions couldn't dampen his smile, a smile he was still wearing when he strolled into the hangar and proclaimed, "Good morning, troops," to the four officers who had arrived before him. Captains Nowon and Kaika were there, sitting with their backs against the wall and playing cards, as well as Ahn and Duck, who were loading their gear into the two-seaters that had been driven to the front of the hangar. Everyone turned or stood to give him a salute, but he waved them back to work.

"He's been cheerier than a cock in the mornings of late, hasn't he, Raptor?" Duck asked, not bothering to lower his voice.

"His archaeologist makes him perky," Ahn said, no sly winks or special emphasis on the word archaeologist. She rarely joined in with the squadron's banter, but when she did, her deliveries

LINDSAY BUROKER

tended to be deadpan. She finished strapping her sniper rifle into the cockpit and climbed down.

"Where's *your* perky-maker?" Ridge had assumed Tolemek would spend the night with Ahn and that they would arrive together this morning.

"I left him last night trying to make a grape-flavored pill." Ahn was always on the grumpy side if she had to report to work before dawn, but she gave him a particularly irritated glare.

Which he deserved. "Ah. Well, you two will get to spend the entire day together at least."

"Sure. With me flying and him in the seat behind me. That'll be fun. Maybe he can braid my hair." Ahn tugged at one of the short wispy strands framing her face. "Food and water is loaded in all of the planes, sir. Since we had extra gear to load—" she waved at the two elite troops, "—we were careful with our weight. We only took on enough to get across the sea with a little to spare. We'll have to find more water in Cofahre."

"I've heard they have it there." Ridge started to walk away, but paused, wondering if there might be another reason for Ahn's grumpiness. "Did your father stop by last evening, by chance?"

Her eyebrows drew together. "No. Was he supposed to?"

"I might have suggested it. He knows you're heading off on a potentially dangerous mission." Ridge decided not to mention that Ahnsung knew about Tolemek too.

"So that means he came to see *you*." Ahn managed to look wistfully toward the ceiling and like she wanted to punch something at the same time. "I'm sorry, sir. I don't know why he can't either come talk to me or just go away completely."

"It's all right. He hardly even threatened me this time."

Ridge had meant it as a joke, but Ahn only glowered, making him wish he hadn't brought up the topic at all. He gave her a pat on the shoulder, then headed toward the lead flier, intending to secure his own duffel and double-check the guns and ammunition. The mundane routine would be good for his nerves. He might have left the bedroom in a good mood that morning, but his stomach was a tangle of knots, thanks to the deviation from the mission he had planned. Sardelle had left only a couple of hours ago, but had promised she would reach the rendezvous point in time without letting the horse hurt itself on the dark road. He had a feeling he could have named a meeting point a thousand miles into Cofah territory, and she would have found a way to get there first too.

As Ridge walked past the two captains, he caught a snippet of the conversation Kaika and Nowon were engaged in, mostly Kaika. Nowon didn't seem to talk much unless he was delivering information in a briefing.

"...totally passionless. Here I am, heading off on a dangerous mission into enemy territory, and it was like he was thinking of someone else." Kaika played a card. "I know I was. You seen that blond fellow who works at the tea and massage parlor across from the base? The one whose shirt is always unbuttoned? You think all those muscles are from massaging people?"

Ridge managed to keep from gawking, not so much because of the material of the conversation, but because it was hard to imagine Nowon as a confidant for tales of one's sexual adventures. Indeed, Nowon merely played his card without responding. That didn't keep Kaika from giving Ridge a friendly wave, then continuing with the game—and her speculation.

After he loaded his duffel, Ridge trotted over to his usual flier, climbed up, and unhooked his wooden dragon from its spot in the cockpit. He would need every scrap of luck he could scrounge up this week. Sardelle had been amused—or maybe bemused— by the large prosperity dragon now placed prominently on a shelf above the wood stove, but she hadn't teased him about it. Later, he had caught a random smile on her face when she looked at it, but that was it.

The side door of the hangar opened, and Colonel Therrik strode in, a few snowflakes on his shoulders. His gaze darted around the hangar, lingering on Ahn for a second—was he looking for Tolemek?—before he turned to his own team. The captains abandoned their card game and scrambled to their feet, saluting him sharply. Therrik looked like he expected it. He returned the salute with snappy precision, two fingers touching the brim of his hat. Then he gave Ridge a challenging stare, as if he expected a salute from him too.

"Yeah, we're the same rank, donkey ass," Ridge muttered, turning his back to the man and climbing into the two-seater to hang his dragon. He did it quickly, not wanting some teasing remark from the colonel, though it was probably inevitable since they were riding in the same flier.

"Your people don't salute, Zirkander?" Therrik demanded.

Oh, so that was his problem. Ahn was carrying boxes of ration bars, and Duck was dangling head-down into his engine compartment so he probably hadn't noticed Therrik walking in.

"Not when they're busy," Ridge said.

"What an interesting style of leadership you practice."

"Yes. Want to bring your gear over here so we can get you loaded up?" Not that he would actually need it... Ridge smiled amiably and climbed down the ladder pushed up to the cockpit.

Therrik dropped his duffel at the foot of the ladder, apparently expecting Ridge to load it for him. Before Ridge could decide if he wanted to comment, the side door opened with a gust of wind. Lieutenant Apex walked in, his face frostier than the winter air. The reason became apparent when Tolemek walked in behind him. Apex strode straight to his flier, snapping quick salutes to the senior officers and Colonel Therrik, but not making eye contact with anyone. Until he reached Ridge, at which point he gave an anguished you-betrayed-me-sir look along with his salute.

Ridge opened his mouth, an explanation on his lips, but he found himself rammed up against the side of his flier with his heels off the ground and fists tangled in his jacket. Therrik glared, his hard eyes no more than two inches away.

"What is *he* doing here, Zirkander?"

"Apex? He's a solid pilot and knows a thing or two about dragons."

"You *know* who I mean." Therrik thrust him against the hull again.

Ridge was tall enough and solid enough that he didn't usually get picked up and thrown around, but his attempt to loosen Therrik's grip and escape was easily thwarted. They were about the same height, but the colonel had doubtlessly spent his whole life hurling people around. His smirk and dismissive snort said it would take a lot more than a wrist twist to elude him. He would probably be ready for groin attacks and eye gouges too. Aware of all the other officers watching, Ridge didn't try again. He didn't want to end up with his face smashed into the cement floor and Therrik on his back.

"The king wanted him," Ridge said. "You were at that meeting. You know that. You have a problem with his personnel choices, you go talk to him."

"*I'm* in command of this mission."

"I didn't say otherwise." Ridge might have *thought* it, but he hadn't said it.

"Sir," Captain Kaika said, walking up. "We've loaded all of our gear. Do you have anything except your duffel that needs to go in?"

Captain Nowon joined her, though he spoke to Ridge rather than his commander. "Sir, the Ramisen Arm Lever would be an appropriate way to extricate yourself in this situation. If you wish, I can demonstrate it for you when we are on our mission."

"Thanks," Ridge said dryly. And how was that supposed to help him now?

But Therrik grunted and released him. "Just the duffel, Kaika."

Therrik stalked away, leaving it on the floor. Tolemek was standing back, a couple of small bags of his own in his hands, and he watched the colonel warily. He had left his white coat at his lab and was back in the hide vest he had been wearing when Ridge first met him, albeit he wore a brown long-sleeve shirt beneath it this time. His trousers were different, too, a dark, sturdy material with numerous pockets. A hand drifted toward one of those pockets now, but the colonel walked out the door without moving toward him.

"I suppose there's no point in hoping he's decided he doesn't want to come," Ridge said.

Kaika picked up the colonel's duffel. "Which flier, sir?"

"Mine." Ridge jerked a thumb toward the rear seat.

"That's either noble of you, or you have a masochistic streak."

She climbed the ladder to secure the bag.

"Both," Nowon suggested.

Maybe it was simply a reflection of what he desired, but Ridge thought their tones and presence here meant they might not be Colonel Therrik fanatics.

"Would you miss him if he didn't come?" he asked. Ridge wasn't one to try and get officers to badmouth other officers, but it would be useful to know how much trouble he would have with these two if Therrik... disappeared. He also wanted to know how mission-critical the colonel was. In going through with his plan, would Ridge be jeopardizing everything? He had a hard time believing Sardelle couldn't more than make up for whatever Therrik could offer the team, but still...

"Not me," Kaika said, her legs sticking out of the second seat as she strapped down the pack. "We have a troubled past."

Nowon looked up at her wriggling backside, then lifted his eyes toward the ceiling. "Kaika has a troubled past with *many* men. As for the colonel, he is largely superfluous, assigned to go with us because the king believed we needed an officer with more rank and experience." Nowon wrinkled his nose. "I've spent time in Cofahre, and I know their culture, their history. I can slip unnoticed into any city and disappear, gathering information along the way. Hemelt, the man who was fatally wounded getting the location and details on the dragon blood laboratory, was my brother. He died in my arms. We trained together, came up through the ranks together. This should be *my* mission, my command." For a moment, his expressionless face hardened, and his eyes burned with the intensity of an inferno.

Kaika dropped down beside him, and he found his forgettable blandness.

Given this new information, Ridge could see why the king might not have wanted to put Nowon in charge. At best, it would be difficult for him to be dispassionate about the mission. At worst, he might risk the team for a chance to avenge his brother.

"What's your role on the team?" Ridge asked Kaika.

Kaika rested an elbow on her comrade's shoulder. "Nowon's lover." She waited for Ridge to arch his eyebrows before grinning and going on. "His wife, his mistress, his sister, his arms dealer, his bodyguard, his slave—I'm trying to forget about that one—and, oh, once we were circus performers together. That was fun. I've worked with other people, too, and on my own on occasion, but I like group projects."

"She gets distracted when she's on her own."

"Gathering intelligence from the locals is *not* a distraction."

"Even when it's done from their bedrooms?" Nowon asked.

"Especially then."

"Colonel Zirkander, Captain Kaika is also familiar with the Cofah culture and mannerisms. She can handle herself in a fight, but her true specialty is installing and disarming explosives."

Lieutenant Ahn had been helping Tolemek load his bags into the flier behind Ridge's, but she glanced over at this statement. Maybe she and Kaika could become good friends and chat about all the ways they knew how to kill people.

"And Therrik?" Ridge asked, lowering his voice, because the colonel had opened the door. He flicked a cigarette butt onto the ground outside before walking back inside. "What's his specialty?" Aside from being a gibbon's ass.

"Making people dead," Kaika said.

"Interrogation and combat," Nowon said. "What he lacks in mental acuity he makes up for with physical vigor."

Kaika smirked at the word vigor. Ridge decided he didn't want to imagine the situation where those two had been in bed together.

"Ready to go, sir," Apex said from the flier at the end of the line. He was pointedly not looking in Ridge's direction, since he would have had to look in Tolemek's direction for that too. Oh, this was going to be a happy team of people he had put together.

Since Kaika was a couple of inches taller than Nowon, Ridge doubted there was much of a weight difference between them. He arbitrarily waved for her to join Duck and for Nowon to join Apex, imagining the two men could have interesting conversations, or at least throw big words back and forth to each other. Duck's eyes brightened at Kaika's approach, perhaps an unforeseen perk for him.

Ridge walked over to Ahn and Tolemek. "I'm hoping you have something for me."

"Besides glares for making Tolemek stay up all night?" Ahn asked.

"You've already given me those."

"Here." Tolemek pressed something into his hand, using his body to hide the exchange.

He was no dummy—he must know exactly what Ridge had planned.

"Safe flight," he murmured to them, then returned to his own flier. Ridge waved readiness to his seat mate, and Therrik stalked in his direction. There would be no unforeseen perks for him.

"Let's find some clouds," he announced, then climbed into the cockpit and started the engine. The nerves in his stomach had returned with a vengeance. No one else here needed to start worrying until they neared Cofah space, but he didn't have that luxury. He had twenty miles to subdue someone known for "making people dead," and if he failed... Therrik wasn't going to be happy about the attempt. If he didn't fail, Therrik wouldn't be happy about it, either. Nor would the king.

Chapter 5

Ridge couldn't actually feel Therrik breathing down his neck. It just seemed like it.

He guided the flier off the butte and into the dark sky above the harbor. A cold wind tugged at the wings, but it was nothing like the gales he had faced that night they fought off the pirates. He tugged his scarf up higher and adjusted his goggles, so the draft didn't swirl in to irritate his eyes. As he rose toward the clouds, he thumbed on the communication crystal mounted to the side of the stick. The people who had questioned Sardelle's invention—which he had lied about, claiming the crystals had been archaeological finds, similar to the energy sources that powered the fliers—had stopped doing so as soon as they had seen the usefulness of intra-squadron communications.

"Check in," Ridge said. "Any problems?"

Three "no, sir" replies came back to him.

"Good. Let's fly up the coast for a ways, check the caves and the other pirate spots before turning west."

Nobody questioned his command. It wasn't that odd of a decision—for all they knew, he had been ordered to make this check before heading out. Still, the deviation from the normal route increased the jangling of his nerves. If Sardelle hadn't been up there along the coast waiting for him, he might have backed out on his plan. Bending the rules was nothing new for him, but he only did it when he was certain he was right and that he was saving lives. He wasn't all that sure in this case. At a minimum, he was going against the king's wishes, and he would hear about that later.

As they flew north along the coast, Ridge dipped and weaved a little, flexing his wings. This wouldn't surprise anyone—he was known to do such things "for practice," which most of the squadron knew was his way of saying it was fun, and it didn't hurt anything.

"What are you doing, Zirkander?" Therrik growled.

He didn't sound like he was having fun. Good. Ridge had worried the colonel might have delighted in flying; he *hoped* the man had avoided a naval career because he got horribly seasick. And airsick.

"Just getting a feel for the two-seater," Ridge said in his most professional tone and definitely not his I'm-doing-this-to-annoy-you tone. "They're not quite as maneuverable as the smaller fliers, and I haven't flown one for a while."

Ridge expected a sarcastic response, but Therrik didn't answer. Silence was akin to agreement, wasn't it?

Ridge smiled into his scarf, knowing Therrik couldn't see his face. He touched the crystal. "I thought I saw some smoke. I'm going to swing through Crazy Canyon to make sure there aren't any ships tucked into the little coves on the river. Maintain course. I'll catch up with you."

"Yes, sir," Apex and Duck said.

Ahn, who was flying off his port wing, looked over at him and made a circle with her thumb and index finger, the approval and all-is-well sign. It was always hard to read people's faces when they had their goggles on, but Ridge had a feeling she knew what he was doing. They probably all did. Oh, not the part where he hoped to replace Therrik with Sardelle, but the part where he wanted to make the colonel vomit all over himself.

Ridge pulled back on the stick to do a loop, turning himself and his passenger upside down before corkscrewing down to the canyon. He came out of the spin right before the river mouth, then banked hard to the right, taking them in. He weaved in and out, following the rugged walls, rising over trees, and dipping beneath natural arches that stretched from one side to the other over the river. It was darker than pitch, and he could scarcely *see* the river, but he had flown through this canyon so many times, he could have done it blindfolded. It was a popular training run.

"Zirkander." Therrik sounded sicker than a plague victim.

"Yes?" Ridge asked brightly.

"I'm going to—" Therrik broke off with a gasp and a gurgle

that sounded very much like a man trying not to throw up. "I'm going to beat your ass into sawdust when we're back on the ground."

"That's not a very nice thing to say to the pilot who has your life in his hands." A cliff rose up out the darkness. Ridge pulled up hard, the wheels practically skimming the rock wall. One of the more impressive arches in the canyon loomed above them, leaving a small gap between it and the cliff. Ridge aimed for it, tilting the wings just so. They cruised through with inches to spare. Even without looking he knew Therrik was ducking, because everyone did.

"Gods kill you, Zirkander! I'm going to—" Therrik's threat ended in an abrupt gagging sound.

Ridge flew upside down again, taking them over the arch, then twisting back into the canyon, heading toward the mouth again.

"I guess I was wrong," Ridge announced. "All quiet in here. No smoke." A pile of vomit perhaps, but no smoke. And Ridge would happily clean that out himself and consider the morning a victory.

"Good to know, sir," Ahn said dryly.

"I'm going to kill you," Therrik said weakly as they flew out of the canyon.

"Really? So early in the mission? People usually need to fly with me longer before they feel that way." Ridge pushed the engine to maximum so they could catch the others.

Therrik groaned.

"Listen, Colonel. I'll make a deal with you. You stop threatening me, and I'll give you something to settle your gut."

"Like what?" Therrik sounded suspicious. Not good. Had Ridge been too eager?

"Not everyone up here is a natural. We have tablets for airsickness." Ridge resisted the urge to weave back and forth more times to further sell Tolemek's pill. By now, Therrik was probably miserable just flying straight.

"Fine," the man growled.

Ridge looked down and pretended to fumble around in the

metal first-aid kit snapped in beside his seat. Then he extended his arm over his shoulder, holding out the tablet. Thank Tolemek's crafty side, he had even wrapped it in foil packaging that made it look like something that had come out of a general mercantile rather than a lab.

Therrik took it. Ridge kept himself from craning his neck to look back and see if the man put it in his mouth. He did weave a little excessively as he returned to the formation, taking his position at point. Less than five miles to the meeting spot with Sardelle. Ridge doubted Tolemek's pill would work that quickly, but he could make some excuse and turn back, then catch up with the team again.

A couple of minutes passed with nothing more than the thrum of the propeller for company. Ridge tapped his thumb on the top of the stick, wanting to look back, but afraid Therrik would be back there, glaring at him, and would get suspicious at being checked on.

He caught Ahn looking in his direction and groped for a way to ask her if anything strange was going on with his passenger. She either figured out what he wanted, or made the observation of her own accord.

"I guess Crazy Canyon didn't live up to its name, sir. Colonel Therrik looks bored. Actually, he looks like he's taking a nap."

Ridge twisted in his seat to check. Ah, yes, it had worked. The glow of the energy source in the rear showed Therrik slumped down in his seat, his head against the side of the flier. Ugh, he *had* vomited all over himself. Most people tried to stick their heads over the side at least...

"He's actually sick," Ridge said, wishing the communication devices allowed him to single Ahn out for his message. Unfortunately everyone would hear it, including Therrik's two captains, so he had to make this sound plausible. "I don't think he has the stomach for an ocean crossing. I'm going to take him back. Continue on course, everyone. I'll catch up." He touched the crystal again to dull its glow—and turn it off. He didn't want to field questions from Kaika or Nowon until it was far too late for them to do anything about the situation.

Ridge dropped out of the formation and turned for land again. He imagined Duck, Ahn, and Apex sharing our-commander-has-gone-crazy looks. He wondered if he had. If Sardelle were not in his life, offering herself as an intriguing alternative ally for this mission, he would have simply dealt with command under Therrik. Probably. Maybe. Enh, he might have arranged to accidentally leave the colonel behind anyway. Working with someone so volatile would be dangerous to everyone.

"Sure, Ridge, keep telling yourself that." Sighing, he steered for the dark shoreline, the whites of the waves breaking in Monomy Bay.

Dawn was still a ways off, but he had running lights. He could make the landing on the highway, however dark and empty it was.

An orange glow flared below, and he flinched, alarmed to find someone on his chosen runway. Someone who might catch him at this duplicitous exchange. Then the logical part of his mind caught up with his wild thoughts. If Sardelle could take on an enemy shaman and win, she could surely light up the highway for him.

Ridge aimed for the flat road, the stones black and wet from intermittent precipitation. His usual flier required room for landing and taking off, but the two-seaters, designed for flying important people around the continent, had thrusters and could perch on rooftops, cliffs, and even vessels at sea. He activated those thrusters to come down lightly in front of the light source, what turned out to be a ball of swirling orange flame. It lit the surrounding landscape—fields of high grass with cliffs in one direction and the sand and sea in the other—with its soft glow. To some distant observer, it might appear as a torch, a particularly effective torch.

Ridge lifted his goggles and spotted a familiar horse in the grass with Sardelle standing next to it, holding its reins and keeping it from shying away from the flier. He cut off the engine, unstrapped his harness, and checked his passenger. He didn't know how long Tolemek's pill would last, but Therrik was still snoozing. Good. Ridge didn't want a confrontation, especially one he couldn't win. Sardelle could probably wave her hand and save him, but needing to have one's balls extricated from the dragon's maw was no way to impress one's lady. As it was, levering Therrik's two-hundred-odd-pounds out of the seat and to the ground wouldn't be easy.

"Good morning, Sardelle." Ridge removed his cap, pressed it to his chest, and gave her a little bow, then clambered out of the cockpit to unstrap the colonel. He left his gloves on, since vomit was splattered onto the harness. Speaking of things that wouldn't impress a lady...

"Good morning, Ridge. It's been so long since I've seen you."

"Terribly long. Have you been pining with loneliness?"

"Most assuredly."

With the propeller noise fading, a noshing sound reached his ears. The horse was munching an apple out of Sardelle's hand. The mare wasn't hot and lathered after its swift trip up the coast.

"Lift with your legs, not your back," Ridge muttered and hauled Therrik out of the seat. He rolled him over the edge of the flier, keeping a hold of his belt, so he wouldn't crash down, head first. Back straining, he lowered the bulky man by the belt. It turned out even his butt was solid muscle. Maybe that was what had once drawn Captain Kaika. Ridge didn't let go until the colonel was within three feet of the ground. That was as far as he could reach. At that point, he dropped Therrik, doing his best to keep the man's head from hitting the stone, even if a few cracks to the skull might improve his personality. Ridge hopped down and rolled the colonel to the side of the highway, so he wouldn't risk hitting him during the takeoff—and so any early morning donkey carts wouldn't run over him. Therrik was going to be irked enough without waking up with hoofmarks on his face.

"Do you need help with anything?" Sardelle asked.

"No, thank you. Actually, can you bring the mare over here? Maybe we can find something to tie her reins to. The colonel might be slightly less murderous if there's a horse waiting to take him home."

"She'll wait."

"Without being tied?" It was an army horse, and Ridge hadn't worked with it enough to know what it had been trained to do. He was certain Sardelle had never seen it before that night.

"Yes."

"Discussed it, did you?" Ridge was done with the colonel and stepped back onto the road, wiping moisture and grass off his hands. "I didn't think you were one of those sorceresses who specialized in working with animals." Until he had met Sardelle, he hadn't even known there *were* sorceresses who specialized in animals, speaking with them telepathically and such.

"I'm not, but she's an amenable soul." Sardelle led the mare over to the colonel, stroked its neck a few times, and gazed into its big dark eyes for a moment.

Ridge decided to find the situation precious and definitely not creepy.

Sardelle released the reins and stepped out onto the highway beside him, bringing with her the saddlebags he had packed. Instead of one of her usual dresses, she wore dark leathers that would be appropriate for skulking around in forests or cities at night. They were form-fitting and drew attention to her attractive figure, even in the poor light. She also wore boots, her sword, and a fur-lined cloak appropriate for the chill weather. She carried a small bag, destroying all the tales proclaiming a woman's inability to pack light. Maybe she could magic more things into existence if she needed them.

"Seems a shame to leave her here with such a non-amenable soul," Ridge said.

"I trust you'll explain that on the way across the ocean."

"Explaining his soul might be difficult." Ridge waved her over to the flier, then crouched and linked his fingers to offer her a boost up.

"His presence alongside the road is what I'm more curious about." She stepped into his hands and let him boost her into the flier. She was a lot lighter than Therrik. And her backside was a lot more pleasant to look at. He hadn't made a mistake. He hadn't. And if he had... he would find a way to make it right. "Ridge... is this vomitus on the seat?"

"Er, possibly." He winced. Why hadn't he thought to wipe the seat and toss that gunk over the side?

"I knew flying with you would be an adventure."

"I'll try to make the ride smoother for you." Ridge jumped, caught the edge of the cockpit, and pulled himself up.

"Now, now, don't make promises you can't keep." Sardelle sat in the seat, but not before Ridge saw that it was cleaner than it had been before Therrik climbed in back at the hangar, with even the harness free of detritus.

"Yes, ma'am." Ridge flipped a couple of switches, and they were soon off.

* * *

"Nice of you to rejoin us, sir," came Lieutenant Ahn's voice over the communication crystal.

Sardelle, settled in the seat behind Ridge, smiled, pleased the pilots were using the devices she had made. At least *some*body appreciated her presence in the city, or what she could make anyway.

Except they don't think you made them, remember?

I know, but perhaps someday the truth can be revealed.

Before they succeed in hanging, drowning, or otherwise slaying you, let's hope.

That's the plan, Jaxi.

There's a plan? I had no idea.

It's in its formative stages.

"We can't help but notice Colonel Therrik got prettier while you were gone, sir," a male pilot with a country drawl said. That must be Lieutenant Duck. Ridge had told her who he had selected for the mission—and that the other pilot, Apex, was an academic who would be too busy being frosty about Tolemek's presence to chat much.

At first, Ridge didn't respond to this ribbing, and Sardelle wondered if he would. As the commander, he shouldn't have to explain himself, but then again, if his people believed he was defying orders and doing something that would jeopardize the mission, they might have the right to question him. She wasn't sure what the modern regulations stated. The Iskandian Guard had required absolute obedience to one's superior officers, no matter what, but she had heard Ridge mention more than once a soldier's duty to question unlawful orders. Of course, he might have simply been justifying his own habit of questioning everything.

Ridge finally said, "Due to his extreme illness, Colonel Therrik has been replaced with a civilian expert." He didn't mention *what* she was an expert in.

"Funny how ill people get when they're taken through Crazy Canyon at top speed," Duck said. His words were followed by a muffled chortle, doubtlessly covered with his scarf. At least one of the pilots didn't seem that concerned with the switch.

Sardelle stretched her senses toward the three other fliers, trying to get a feel for how everyone else felt. Since she already knew Ahn and Tolemek, they were easy to identify and read: apparently Tolemek had known this was coming for he was neither surprised, nor alarmed. Ahn was concerned that Ridge had done something that could end his career, but she wouldn't say anything, not when he had once stepped in to protect *her* and risked his career doing so. Sardelle picked up on the bubbly personality of Lieutenant Duck in the next flier over, and even if it wasn't respectful, immediately thought of him as a cheerful young dog, happy to have been taken along on an adventure and not overly worried about where they were going or what was happening along the way. A woman sat behind him—this had to be one of the elite troops Ridge had mentioned—wearing numerous weapons with a duffel full of more weapons, tools, and incendiary devices strapped down at her feet. She had a book clenched in her lap, the wind whipping at the pages, but she was gazing into the sky, which had grown a few shades lighter. She seemed to be considering the situation before coming to a judgment. The last flier held Lieutenant Apex and another man, the other elite soldier presumably. He was guarded, his personality difficult to decipher without digging deeper, and she wouldn't intrude by attempting to do so. The lieutenant was another matter. When Sardelle brushed against his aura, she drew back at the hatred roiling off him. That couldn't be for Ridge, could it? His pilots all seemed to love him.

Look closer, Jaxi suggested. *His family is from Tanglewood.*

Ah. Yes, Apex wasn't glaring at Ridge but looking toward the back of Ahn's flier now and then, toward Tolemek. He was keeping his face neutral, but murderous thoughts of revenge seeped from his aura.

He wants to find a way to ensure Tolemek doesn't return from this mission.

Yes, I see that now. Sardelle plucked away a strand of hair that the wind had whipped into her eyes, glad she had guessed right and pulled most of it into a tight braid. *Ridge doesn't know, does he?*

He knows. Apex is a dragon expert.

Sardelle slumped back into her seat. All the trouble Ridge was choosing for himself for this mission. And would the king even appreciate his efforts? Or had he condemned himself by getting rid of that colonel? And by choosing to bring her?

"Are you now placing yourself in command of the ground incursion, Colonel?" the woman asked, her voice distant and raised to be heard over the wind since the only communications crystals were in front of the pilots' seats.

"No, Kaika," Ridge said. "It's your and Nowon's mission. If you need more manpower, someone to replace Therrik in a combat situation, I've chosen people whose talents may be useful and who are, pardon my bias, probably more versatile than your colonel. And Tolemek could be invaluable to you if there's anything tricky in that lab."

A moment passed before anyone responded, but the two elite officers gave each other long looks from the back seats of their respective fliers.

"I believe Kaika and I would prefer to pursue this mission on our own," the male passenger—that must be Nowon—said, his voice equally distorted by the wind. "We've worked together often, and incorporating another person could create more complications than solutions. We will discuss it further when we arrive at our destination."

"Understood," Ridge said. "When we land, we can let you

know everyone's specialties in case you change your mind. I'm probably the only one here who's only good at flying and shooting things."

"Thank you, Colonel."

Now it was Tolemek's turn to give Ridge a long look, though Ridge wasn't looking back in his direction. Tolemek doubtlessly wanted to go look for his sister, and if the special unit didn't want him, it might be the perfect opportunity for him to slip away.

It sounded like the unit didn't want *her*, either, not that they knew about her abilities. Sardelle wondered whether Ridge had been including her in that line about sharing everyone's specialties. She wouldn't be averse to helping the Iskandian military, as she once had, but it would mean revealing what she could do. It might not matter at this point, given that quite a few people had somehow figured it out—including those women spying on her and attempting to bury her in caved-in basements. Still, she wanted to discuss it with Ridge before revealing her talents and being sent off with two strangers. Fulfilling her promise to Tolemek was her priority here.

Perhaps you could have discussed it last night if you hadn't been bouncing around in bed like rutting bonobos in the treetops.

Sardelle had thought she was past the point of being embarrassed by any of Jaxi's commentary, but she found herself blushing and sinking lower in the seat. Probably because she was right.

Of course I'm right. I'm always right. I've been in this sword for a long time. It's made me venerable and wise.

You sound like a dragon. Or someone who thinks she's a dragon.

I always wanted to meet a dragon. They were long gone even when I was alive.

Maybe not all of them. If the Cofah truly have dragon blood, it came from somewhere. Sardelle smiled, remembering the time Jaxi had admitted she had read oodles and oodles of romance stories involving humans falling in love with dragons, and vice versa, as a girl. That would have been before the printing press was invented, but the Referatu had used magic to make copies, and fiction as well as non-fiction had always been well-represented in the libraries in Galmok Mountain. Perhaps that infatuation was part of the reason she hadn't found a human boy to have a relationship with before it was too late.

No... I was pimple-faced, pig-tailed, and precocious. The human boys wanted nothing to do with me. Also, I could fry their balls off with a thought. I think that intimidated some of them.

Perhaps it was more the fact that you made that known... frequently. Sardelle hadn't been there, but she knew Jaxi well enough to believe her guess accurate. The haughty sniff she got by way of a response confirmed it.

Ridge looked back at her, a challenge since she was positioned directly behind him. "Are you doing all right back there?" he called.

Only a couple of feet separated them, but the propeller's constant drone made it difficult to converse, and the wind rushing past would have stolen his words if he had spoken any more softly. The wind was trying to steal his scarf, too, or at least its end—it had a tendency to escape his coat and whip free behind him. She had almost taken a fringe in the eye a couple of times. It wasn't the ideal spot for a heart-to-heart discussion, but she had the feeling the mission would start as soon as they landed, and she had questions that she hadn't, for reasons Jaxi had noted, asked the night before.

"Yes," she said.

Ridge touched his ear, and she leaned forward and repeated herself.

"Do you want a scarf or goggles?" he asked. "I brought extras."

"I'm fine." By slumping in the seat, keeping her cloak wrapped around her body, and using him as a wind block, she found the ever-present gale tolerable. It was amazing how much colder it was up there, partially from the wind they created and partially from the altitude. The breadth of the ocean made it hard to tell how far up they were, but they definitely weren't in danger of being shot at from below if they should pass an enemy warship. She wondered if the Iskandians had considered enclosing their cockpits with glass—perhaps it would be too fragile for the pressures of flying and combat. "How far until we reach Cofahre?"

"Not until after dark."

Considering it would take a sailing ship weeks, that was impressive speed, but she did find herself curious about what happened when the inevitable occurred and she had to use the latrine. An image of herself perched on the side with her rear end hanging over the edge of the flier came to mind. She couldn't imagine that not being messy. "What happens when the need to engage in bodily functions makes itself known?"

Ridge glanced back, touching his ear again.

Sardelle sighed and leaned forward. "Where do you pee?" This was a frustrating way to talk, especially when she had an alternative. Could she convince him to give it a try?

This time he grinned when he glanced back. "There's a tube under the seat. Most of us just don't drink or eat much when we're up here."

A tube? That didn't sound female friendly. Of all the problems she had used magic to solve, she had never thought that would be one.

"Ridge?" Sardelle checked to make sure the communication crystal wasn't transmitting, then laid a hand on his shoulder. "I know talk of magic makes you uneasy, but would you consider…" Hm, how to phrase this? He would understand the term telepathy, she was certain, but might object to it on principle. "You know how I talk to Jaxi? In my mind? Is that something you would be comfortable with? Or could become comfortable with? In situations such as this, it would be convenient. Also when we wish to converse with each other in private and there are other people around." She bit her lip to keep from going on with her list of benefits.

He hadn't looked back at her again, and there was nothing exciting ahead of the flier that would require his attention, so he was either thinking about it, searching for a way to reject it, or hadn't heard her that clearly. No, he would have touched his ear if that had been the case. He must have gotten the gist.

"What would I have to do?" he finally asked over his shoulder.

"Nothing. Just… don't get startled and let your flier drop out of the sky."

He gave her a circle hand sign and said something that sounded like, "I don't even do that when people are shooting at me."

Sardelle waited a few seconds, letting him grow more accustomed to the idea, and left her hand on his shoulder. *Thank you. It's quieter in here.*

Ridge glanced back, like he might be about to answer out loud, but he closed his mouth, giving her a thoughtful look instead. *You haven't been in here long, if you think that.* He raised his eyebrows. *Did you hear that?*

She squeezed his shoulder. *Yes.*

Huh.

I'll have to be monitoring you—know you want to speak—for me to 'hear' you, but all you have to do is think the words to respond to me. I know you're not comfortable with magic or anything associated with sorcerers, so we can reserve this for emergencies, or flying, if you like.

It's all right. Not exactly a ringing endorsement. But then he added, *I want to be comfortable with you—what you can do. I just have to get used to things. Sometimes that takes a while. I'm not as young as I act, you know.*

Perhaps not, but I've noticed your commanding officers are all the ones with the gray hair.

Someday, I'll have to command someone as obnoxious as I am, and my hair will turn white overnight.

You'll still be handsome.

Ugh, Jaxi thought. *This is so cloyingly sweet, I may gag.*

At first, Sardelle assumed the interjection was for her mind alone, but Ridge's shoulders stiffened. *Jaxi!* She groaned.

What?

If you start talking to him about bonobos, I'm going to drop you into the ocean.

Highly doubtful.

That's… the sword, right? You, ah, didn't mention that it would be speaking to me too. Fortunately, Ridge only sounded mildly alarmed. Or maybe mildly affronted.

I didn't invite her to do so, but she's rude.

Jaxi made a rude noise in her mind. *If you don't correct him on calling me an* it, *I'm going to make bonobo noises in his mind all night long the next time you two are rutting.*

Sardelle stared at the back of Ridge's head, afraid Jaxi had shared that bit of disrespect with him as well, but he didn't turn around and gape at her in disbelief.

I'm not that tactless. Not on first contact anyway. Although technically I spoke to him before, to warn him people were trying to blow you up.

For future reference, Ridge, Jaxi is a she, and has threatened to show you her truly tactless side if you call her an it. Also, I apologize for the interruption. I'm used to her waltzing about in my head, but I know it can be startling to others. You can compare notes with Tolemek if you wish.

A couple of moments passed without a response from Ridge. Sardelle flexed her fingers in her gloves, hoping this wasn't too much for him. She would have preferred to wait to bring in Jaxi. Or perhaps never to have brought in Jaxi.

Oh, sure, keep him for yourself. Do you have any idea how few people I dare communicate with? It's a lonely existence these days.

You can talk to some of our Cofah enemies when we arrive, ideally while they're thinking about shooting at us.

I guess if Tolemek can handle a talking sword, I can too, Ridge thought. *But it's a little... daunting to realize she's like a real person and that she knows what I'm thinking and saying to you when I've never really met her.*

Thinking and saying? Tell him it doesn't stop there. I even know about that thing he does with his tongue that you like.

Sardelle dropped her chin to her chest with a groan. To think, when she had been staying up all night with Ridge, then riding out on the horse, she had thought she could nap during this flight. *I'm not telling him that, and you better not, either.*

Fine. You can tell him that I appreciate him already elevating me to "like a real person." That's quick progress considering I was an "it" thirty seconds ago.

I'd actually like to finish this conversation with him in private, if you don't mind. And not discuss you with him at this time. Someday, when you find your dragon lover, I'll stay out of your relationship.

A hollow promise, given the odds of finding a dragon.

Well, maybe you'll find another soulblade who adores your scintillating personality. There must be some of those still around. Sardelle had no idea how they might actually have a relationship that had anything to do with tongues, but with two powerful souls, who knew what was possible? Dragons had been known for shape-shifting, and she remembered a few legends about early soulblades having the power to do the same, though she had never seen that happen in her own lifetime. Maybe legend was all it was.

I'd have to do some research. It's not anything I studied or read much about as a kid. Jaxi sounded vaguely intrigued.

Good, she had something to think about while Sardelle finished her original conversation.

Ridge looked over his shoulder. "Did you hear that last one?"

Yes, sorry, I was trying to arrange for a more private conversation for us. Sardelle groped for a politic way to say that Jaxi came with her and that was just how it was. But she hadn't told him that up front, and it seemed unfair to foist it on him now. Besides, she didn't want to risk it being too much for him to handle. With time, he ought to be able to get used to the idea, but maybe this had been a mistake. Maybe this would all be too weird for him.

You're not giving him enough credit, Jaxi suggested.

I can understand your discomfort, Sardelle told Ridge. *Even having known about soulblades for my whole life, it took me a long time to get used to having someone practically living in my head when Jaxi and I first bonded. She comments on everything from my sex life to my dietary choices to my latrine experiences.*

Yeah? What's she think of the tube?

Though she was truly worried about what Ridge would think of this new experience, she couldn't help but laugh at his question. She hoped the appearance of his humor meant he wasn't *too* disturbed by any of this. *Oddly, she didn't comment on that one. She's probably holding back until I make a mess attempting to use it.*

Yes, Jaxi thought.

Maybe the experience will inspire you to invent some more ancient archaeological devices for my squadron. Your people used to ride dragons in the old days, didn't they? Maybe they had something more sophisticated than a tube.

I believe their flights were short. Sardelle lifted her hand from Ridge's shoulder to a tentative touch of his cheek. She was wearing gloves, so it probably wasn't that endearing of a gesture, but she wanted to let him know... she didn't know what, really. That she cared. That she understood this was strange for him. *Does this latrine banter mean you've gotten past the oddness of telepathy and sentient swords, or that you're focusing on a lighter subject to avoid dealing with it?*

He chewed on her question before answering it. *Can it be some of both?*

Yes.

He clasped her hand in his and held it for a moment before letting go.

Sardelle leaned back in her seat. *The reason I wanted to talk like this is I was wondering if you were planning to use me on your mission here.*

He glanced back at her, and she sensed his confusion.

When you explain to those two captains what your people can do and ask them if they want to take any of us along with them on the infiltration, are you thinking they should know about me and what I can do?

No. Of course not. I'm not telling anyone your secrets, not when it could get you killed.

I thought you might have decided that since I'm being targeted already... the secret was already out.

If it is, it's not widely out. But no, none of that. You wanted to fulfill your promise to Tolemek, right? Find his sister? That's why I'm bringing you. And him too. Oh, sure, I'm hoping your memories and knowledge might be useful if our elite troops bring back something kooky and inexplicable—or something that would be too dangerous to fly home with—but as soon as we land, I was planning to send you two off to find that sanitarium. You should have time while Nowon and Kaika are infiltrating that lab.

Now it was Sardelle's turn to take some time digesting his words. *You mean you're risking your career by dumping that colonel all so we can get Tolemek's sister?* She could have done that on her own without his sacrifice. Granted, she wouldn't have an easy time navigating Cofahre alone, but she would never have asked him for this.

I'd be lying if I didn't say I also had the thought that it'd be nice to have you—and your snarky glowing sword—there if a flock of birds flies into the propeller during this mission. I have a hunch this is going to be more challenging than the king or Nowon thinks, and I had a bad feeling about Therrik too. Not just because he was fantasizing about shoving my face into a meat grinder. Not only *because of that, anyway. He seemed... I don't know. It was strange that he showed up at Tolemek's lab and started threatening him. It was strange, too, that he knew about you. We're not in the same unit, and we'd never talked before meeting with the king. I'll admit I'm well known in the military and in the capital, but I haven't known you long enough for anyone except close friends and colleagues to associate you with me.*

Should you have voiced those concerns to the king or your General Ort before taking the initiative of drugging the man and dumping him out of your flier?

Of course not. Didn't Referatu children have the same rule as regular Iskandian children have?

Sardelle squinted at the back of his head. *Which rule is that?*

It's easier to receive forgiveness later if you didn't first ask for permission and get denied.

Ah. That sounds vaguely familiar. The logic of ten-year-olds.

And pilots. Now, sit back and enjoy the flight. If you want to sleep, I'll let you know when we're close to Cofahre.

She leaned her head against the back of the seat, resolving to follow his suggestion, though she found herself wondering if she might do more on the continent than help locate Tolemek's sister. Maybe she could find a way to prove herself on this mission. She didn't think she needed to prove herself to Ridge, but if the Iskandian king, who apparently already knew about her, found out she could be an asset... maybe she could, one action at a time, clear the image of the Referatu and cut a trail for any other gifted people in the country. It would be much easier to find and train new students if she and they didn't have to spend their lives camouflaging their talents.

"One step at a time," she whispered.

CHAPTER 6

RIDGE YAWNED AND WISHED HE had some coffee. The sun had dipped below the horizon, and darkness was returning. The squadron had turned to the northwest, following the Cofahre shoreline at a distance, a long distance. They were up high, skimming through the clouds, and when land came into sight, it was a faint smudge on the horizon. The encroaching darkness would camouflage them as much as the clouds, but the last thing they wanted was for an overly assiduous lighthouse worker or a sailor in a crow's nest to spot them.

He turned in his seat and called, "Sardelle?"

She had taken his advice and slept most of the morning, then read in the afternoon, and was dozing again now, the book she had borrowed from the library in her lap. She, at least, would be fresh when they arrived. He and his pilots would need to find a spot to rest after the early morning and the long flight. They had detoured twice to avoid freighters and pirate airships in the distance. He didn't think they had been seen, but it had definitely kept them alert to their surroundings.

Ridge couldn't reach farther than her knee without unbuckling his harness, but it was enough. Her blue eyes opened, focusing on him immediately.

"We're almost there." He wondered if she would respond in his mind. He hadn't found their mental conversation as disturbing as he might have expected—probably because it was her and not some stranger—but having the sword pop into his thoughts... *That* had been bizarre. Even though Sardelle had alluded to having some kind of relationship with it, it had never occurred to him that *it* might be a *she* and have the personality, intelligence, and sarcasm of a human being.

Sardelle peered through the clouds to the west. *We're cutting inland over the Alteron Steppes?*

For some reason, Ridge hadn't expected her to be familiar with the area. He didn't know why. She had probably been here when she had been working with the Iskandian army of old. Maybe because she talked so little of her old life that he didn't know what to expect from her past.

"Yes, it's—" He switched to thinking his words, figuring she might expect that now. *It's the logical place, since the mountains are to the north and the desert to the south. It's not a populous area.*

No, it never was. Horrible dust storms in addition to poor soil. And you can talk to me in whatever way is comfortable to you. She rubbed her face and wiped her mouth—afraid she had been drooling in her sleep? He hadn't caught her at it yet, but even if she had been… it would be a mild offense compared to what Therrik had done in that seat.

Good. We're going to cut for land soon. I wanted to warn you in case—

Sardelle jerked her hand up and frowned toward the shoreline. The clouds had thickened, so she wouldn't be able to see anything. Not with her eyes anyway. He looked that way anyway. Clouds scudded across the horizon, and the first stars had come out above. He shivered through his jacket. Their route had taken them farther from the equator, and the air felt much cooler than it had off the Iskandian shore, reminding him of the mountaintop mine where he had met Sardelle.

There are eight airships waiting out there, over the coast. She met his eyes. *They're strung in a line, each just within sight of the next, so they can cover a lot of territory.*

You're sure?

Positive.

Ridge jabbed at the communication crystal. "Everyone awake? Good. Cover your power crystals and hide any hint of light in your cockpits. We're getting close. We're going to change our original route to avoid being predictable and to fly in over the mountains."

"The very white mountains with the storm clouds over them, sir?" Duck asked.

"Yes." Ridge wondered if Duck had better eyes than he did or if he had been paying more attention. "Stay close and fly safe."

"Yes, sir."

Apex and Ahn echoed the words. They both sounded as tired as he felt, and he was picking a tougher route, but if there were unfriendly eyes watching, it made sense to take a few risks to avoid detection. The question was how had those unfriendly eyes known Wolf Squadron was coming? An assumption based on the fact that some spies had escaped? Or had someone warned them that Ridge and his team were coming through tonight? He couldn't imagine that the king had told many people about this mission, but that old castle doubtlessly had a lot of servants wandering about in it, not to mention old crevices and nooks that might support eavesdropping ears.

Ridge was tempted to fly closer to land, to make sure he turned west at the right moment to take them into the shrouded mountains, but he didn't want to be spotted—or heard—by an airship by veering inland too early, either. He couldn't see much through the clouds.

A little farther. There's one directly to our west, then one at the southern foothills of the mountains about four miles past it. That's the last one.

Thank you. Ridge looked at the clock on the control panel, checked the air speed indicator on his wing, and used the time to count off the miles. He waited until the sixth mile, then dipped the flier's nose and wiggled his tail to signal a turn. He could have used the communication crystal, but the old signals were ingrained in him.

You're clear. The Cofah shouldn't be able to see you.

He trusted Sardelle, but his shoulders were tense nonetheless as they flew west, the rough air within the clouds battering at his wings. He could correct the flier easily enough and hurried to do so. He still felt the need to impress Sardelle, and this was his milieu—and her first time in it. He wanted to give her as smooth a ride as possible.

The clouds parted for a moment, opening up the view to the south and west. Ridge spotted the steppes and the mountains looming ahead before the fliers were swallowed by the haze again. He thought he glimpsed that northernmost airship, too, but it had also cut out its lights, so he couldn't be sure.

"That's uncanny, sir," Duck breathed. "How did you know?"

"Know what?" Apex asked.

"About the airship," Ahn said.

Great, two out of three of his pilots had better eyes than he did. He was getting old.

"Just a hunch," Ridge said. He hated to take credit for Sardelle's clairvoyance, but he wasn't going to announce her sorceress skills to his people in this manner, either. Or in any other manner. It wasn't his secret to announce.

You can take credit. I don't mind. I think it's nice the way they look up to you. Obviously, you've achieved that without my help, but I'm happy to contribute to the extraordinariness of the legend.

Ridge snorted. *I'm about as extraordinary as a sock. I thank you for your help, though. You've already kept us out of trouble, and we haven't even crossed over Cofah soil yet.* He had no idea how the telepathy worked, but he tried to impart a sense of appreciation along with his thoughts. There weren't words to articulate how relieved and glad he was to have her back there instead of Colonel Thugly. It was hard to articulate, too, how much it meant to him when someone helped keep his people from getting hurt.

Sardelle gripped his shoulder, then touched his cheek again before settling back to let him fly. She understood. Good.

They soon flew over the shoreline, passing into snow-dusted foothills, then snow-buried peaks. The storm clouds Duck had noted grew darker and denser, and flecks of snow stuck to Ridge's goggles. He wiped at them with his scarf. *Can you sense any other trouble ahead?*

Not at this time. There's nothing else in the air in our immediate vicinity. There are some villages near the streams down there, so I wouldn't fly too low. Your propellers are noisy.

Yeah. That is one thing airships can do that we can't: coast.

"Heading out to the steppes," Ridge said when the coastline had disappeared behind them. "We're going to fly north of Brandenstone, then west another fifty miles to our coordinates.

We'll find a landing spot and then send our worker bees off on their mission."

"While we nap like turtles in a sunbeam, sir?" Duck asked, his words garbled by a yawn.

"While we take turns camouflaging our fliers, then maintaining a vigilant and professional watch over them and our surroundings, alertly awaiting the return of our allies."

"I can nap while doing those things."

"I did see him sleeping on the gun range once," Apex said. It was one of the first things he had said all day that wasn't a response to a direct question. Ridge planned to split him and Tolemek up as soon as the squadron arrived. "The cacophonous explosions going off all around him did not disturb his slumber."

"I wasn't sleeping. I was practicing feigning death, the way hog-nosed snakes do, so if I'm overrun in a big battle someday, the enemy will ignore me and go on to someone else. Someone with a big mouth full of big words maybe."

"If you're referring to thanatosis, the process by which some animals deter predators, then I believe it's done without snoring."

Ridge smiled, glad to have Apex speaking again. He hoped Apex would speak to *him* at some point, too, and that he wouldn't be lumped into the enemy camp for having brought Tolemek along.

"Village lights below," Ahn said. "And something bigger and brighter on that tower."

Ridge saw it. There was a conical beam coming out of the top of the four- or five-story stone tower. They were too far inland for a lighthouse. Could the Cofah have some kind of searchlights for watching for intruders by night? He had flown all over the sea between Iskandia and Cofahre, but the king rarely ordered missions that actually breached enemy borders.

"Anyone know what that is?" Ridge asked.

It wasn't here the last time I was in Cofahre, but that doesn't mean much, Sardelle thought dryly. *It looks like a mill converted into a watchtower. There's a single person in a room at the top.*

"Nowon says the Cofah have watchtowers in all of their villages within fifty miles of the ocean," Apex said. "Their status as an aggressive and conquering nation has earned them enemies from all over the world, but they're particularly concerned about Iskandian fliers, so these lights can be trained toward the skies." After a pause, he added, "He's also heard that some of the towers are equipped with defenses."

"Like what?" Ridge asked. They were thousands of feet off the ground, so he couldn't imagine anything ground-based bothering them.

"Nowon could only speculate. He's always come to Cofahre by sea and traveled into this area by land. As far as he knows, we're the first team performing an aerial incursion."

"So we get to be the experimental mice in... some scientist's lab, eh?" He had almost said Tolemek's lab, and didn't know if he had caught himself too late. Any mention of labs might remind Apex of his unwelcome ally.

"Apparently, sir." Yes, Apex's tone had chilled several degrees there.

Getting them to work together and get to know each other might be preferable to keeping them separated, Sardelle suggested. *Despite his reputation and past mistakes—and, no, I do not mean to make light of what he was responsible for—he's not a heartless, megalomaniacal tyrant when you talk to him. He's actually pleasant and personable. That surprised me. Perhaps Apex will be able to, if not forgive him, forget about his past most of the time and learn to regard him as a coworker.*

Pleasant and personable? That wasn't quite how Ridge would have described the pirate.

Your Lieutenant Ahn finds him so.

Are you sure she didn't use the words handsome and loyal to her to explain his appeal?

These are my observations, not hers. Though I'll be happy to let him know you find him attractive.

Ridge grunted.

You learned to tolerate him during our shared weekends together, Sardelle added more seriously.

Mostly by avoiding him... *I wouldn't recommend he start a snowball fight with Apex. He's not the playful spirit I am.*

You know Ahn started that fight, right?

I suspected. I know my pilots well.

"That light is definitely probing the sky," Ahn said. "It's powerful for a gas lamp. What? Oh."

Ridge was on the verge of asking her what she meant, then realized Tolemek must be saying something. The conical beam coming from the tower had lifted toward the sky and was sweeping across the clouds. Ridge didn't like the way it was turning in their direction.

"Tolemek says the towers use oil burners, the same as their lighthouses, and an optical lens system to focus the intensity of the light. They're on moveable somethings that can be tilted and turned." Tolemek said something Ridge couldn't hear—a correction probably, because Ahn added, "Close enough."

"Well, that light is moving in our direction," Duck said.

"Veer away," Ridge said. "We'll fly over the mountains until we're past the city." *I don't suppose you have any way of quieting our propellers, Sardelle?*

I could, but your own people would notice. Do you want me to do it anyway?

He grimaced, not wanting to reveal her powers. If it had just been his squadron, maybe, but he didn't know Nowon and Kaika that well. Therrik had certainly been full of threats when he had found out about Sardelle. Whenever and however that had happened.

No, never mind.

Ridge led the way toward the mountains again, though he didn't like the heavy clouds wreathing them, obscuring the crags and ridges. Snow was falling, even out on the steppes, and something more akin to a blizzard lay ahead of them. He trusted his pilots to handle their fliers in winds and poor visibility, but at the same time, they were a long way from home without any spare parts or mechanics if they needed to do repairs. Only a few weeks had passed since that pirate battle over the harbor, where Tiger Squadron had lost two fliers and one pilot. Sardelle might be able to heal human beings, but cobbling a flier together and making it airworthy for a thousand-mile flight? He couldn't count on that.

Something's coming.

Ridge wiped his goggles and scanned the trees, rocks, and snow on the mountain slopes ahead. *What? Where?*

From behind and below. Two somethings. I don't know what they are. They're mechanical.

He loosened his harness and peered over the sides of his flier. Snow fell diagonally, thick flakes that hid the terrain. He could still make out the light being cast into the sky by that watchtower and thought he glimpsed something flying through it, perhaps halfway between that village and their current location. But as soon as it flew out of the beam of light, he lost it. The distance and snow made it hard to tell how large it had been. But smaller than an airship, he was certain of it. Another aircraft like a flier? The Cofah were reputed to be working on such technology, but nothing of that ilk had been spotted in Iskandian space yet.

"You see something, sir?" Duck asked.

"Maybe. I'm going to swing back and take a look. Everyone else, stay on course. If we get separated, meet at the first set of coordinates."

"You want help, sir?" Ahn asked, and he imagined her patting the sniper rifle mounted in the cockpit next to her.

"Let me see what we're dealing with first. You three have passengers that need to make it to the landing spot. If there's trouble, and I can delay it... that's acceptable."

The mumbles and murmurs he got in reply didn't seem to agree. Oh, well.

Ridge pushed forward on the stick, dipping below the rest of the fliers and turning back toward the watchtower.

Definitely not airships, Sardelle thought. *But nothing natural. Almost like small versions of your fliers, but without pilots.*

How is that possible? Ridge's mind raced even as his eyes darted back and forth, searching the snowy night sky. *Some kind of magic?* Even with the Iskandian power sources, his people couldn't put fliers in the sky without pilots.

I don't sense anything like your energy sources, but there is... something.

That something buzzed out of the sky, not from below but from above, angling straight toward the cockpit. A black flying contraption with three sets of parallel wings stacked atop each other and a cylindrical body dove for him. Though startled, Ridge kept his calm, veering away smoothly. That calm, however, was threatened when the sound of machine gun fire rattled the heavens.

It wasn't coming from the first contraption but from the second, which also came in from above, diving straight toward him on his new course. There hadn't been a person, or even a cockpit—he couldn't have missed that. Who in all the hells was firing at him?

"Hang on," he yelled for Sardelle's sake, then swooped upward, much as he had in Crazy Canyon. He looped, turning upside down so he could come back down, this time with the pair of contraptions in his sights.

Sardelle popped into his thoughts, "speaking" rapidly, probably not wanting to break his concentration. *I could keep their bullets from hitting us, but you wouldn't be able to fire through the shield I erected.*

No shield. Ridge didn't say more, because he had the first contraption in view now. It hadn't changed course. His path brought him toward it from the side, and he thumbed the firing trigger. His own bullets streaked out, every fifth one an incendiary. One of those struck, and a burst of orange lit the sky for a moment. Ridge weaved and dipped, in case the second contraption was targeting him. But he caught sight of it over his left shoulder. It was on the same course as the first. They were flying in tandem, Ridge realized, now that he could see the puzzle from outside of it rather than from within. Interesting. If they stayed together, that would make them easy to take out, but he didn't assume that they would. He didn't know *what* these things were or what to expect.

The first was damaged, but still flying, coming around toward him, the same as its buddy. This time, Ridge dove instead of pulling upward to make a loop. He twisted as he dove, then leveled out, wanting a better look at them as he passed under them.

Their guns fired again, but he thought he was safe, since their front ends were facing where he had been rather than where he was or where he was going. But in the poor lighting, he realized almost too late that they could fire in more directions than straight. More because of instinct than anything he saw, he pulled up again. Just in time. Bullets pounded the air where he had been.

A light flared behind him, but he ignored it, concentrating on these strange new foes. He did another loop, adjusting his fall so he came down behind them this time. He showed no mercy on the trigger, hammering the back end of the closest one. They had propellers in the front, like his flier, but he couldn't know for sure where the engine was. In the rear? Or buried under some armor farther toward the front? If there had been a pilot, he could have aimed at the person...

Hoping for luck, he continued to pound ammunition into the craft. It banked and swerved, trying to avoid him, but he hung on like a tick on a dog's tail. Finally, one of his bullets struck something vital. Black smoke poured from the back of the contraption, and it lost all of its momentum. It dipped, spiraling toward the mountainside below. Without taking time to admire his handiwork, Ridge accelerated after the second one. They were as fast as his craft, and more maneuverable thanks to their smaller size—and lack of passengers—but whoever or *whatever* was controlling them was used to horizontal movement and didn't think about the three dimensions offered by the sky. The remaining contraption tried to turn for home, but Ridge cut it off, slamming rounds into it again. This time, it exploded spectacularly, lighting up the night sky so much that he had to raise his arm to shield his eyes.

That wasn't my incendiary bullet, he thought dryly.

Jaxi wanted to help. She got excited, thinking we might deflect some bullets, or burn them out of the air, but you were too adept at swooping around and avoiding getting hit.

Ah, so that explained the glow. Sardelle had her sword out, the way she had the night she had battled that shaman and his

Cofah bodyguards, the magical blade melting bullets out of the sky before they could reach her. *Sorry, I'll try to be less efficient next time.*

No need for that. But in future battles, please let me know if there's anything I can do to help.

Ridge smiled, pleased by her calm demeanor. Her first flight, and she hadn't thought anything of the upside down loops or being shot at. Colonel Thugly probably would have been digging his nails into his shoulder. For a brief moment, Ridge entertained himself with the idea of recruiting Sardelle for his squadron, but a lot of rules and beliefs would have to change before that could be a possibility. In the meantime, they had other worries.

You can help me by figuring out exactly what those things were.

Hard from here. Can we go down and take a look at one?

"Sir? Everything all right?" Ahn asked.

Ridge didn't know how far the communication crystals worked, and he glanced up at first, expecting to see her flier nearby. But he and Sardelle were alone in the snowy sky.

"Two unmanned mechanical aircraft tried to shoot us out of the night," Ridge said.

"*Unmanned?*"

"The Cofah don't have that kind of technology," Apex said. "We don't, either, and we've been flying longer than they have."

"We downed them and are going to take a look," Ridge said. "Unless Nowon already knows all about them and wants to share that information."

"I have no knowledge of them," Nowon called, doubtlessly leaning up to Apex's shoulder to be heard. "They must be extremely new. I would appreciate it if you would retrieve a sample for me."

There was something off about a captain asking a colonel to go sample collecting for him, but Ridge merely said, "I'll see what we can do. Just finding the crash sites in the snow will be a challenge."

"Understood."

I can direct you to one.

Oh? Ridge thought of the avalanche she had dug a number of soldiers out of, including himself. *Because you saw where they went down and have a mathematical formula?*

Not exactly.

Ridge headed in the direction the first one had crashed, figuring there would be more remaining of that one, since it hadn't been obliterated in a fiery ball.

Jaxi is now feeling sheepish, Sardelle announced.

Oh? From our brief conversations and from what you've told me, I didn't think that was an emotion she could feel.

It's an extremely infrequent visitor for her. That's why I thought it might be worth sharing.

Ridge slowed down as they drew closer to the ground. The snow brightened the landscape somewhat, but he still couldn't see much. The last thing he wanted was to successfully fight off the enemy attack only to bury himself in a snow bank because he wasn't paying attention.

About two hundred feet lower on the mountainside and ten degrees to port. As Ridge nudged the flier in the indicated direction, Sardelle added, *Do pilots use nautical directions?*

The hands on the clock usually. He leaned forward in his seat, his harness digging at his shoulders. Was that something black lying in the snow down there? Something besides a log?

A soft orange glow appeared in the direction he was looking. If he hadn't seen the same effect on the highway north of Pinoth, it would have alarmed him, but he merely said, "Thank you." It lit up the ground, but it shouldn't be visible from far away. Which was good, because they weren't *that* far from the village. For all he knew, a squad of soldiers was on its way out to investigate the crashed contraptions.

No soldiers yet, but I'll let you know if that changes.

How far out can you sense? With the light, Ridge could tell the dark blob on the snow was the wreck rather than a log, and he took them close, circling and trying to find a landing spot on the sloped and treed hillside.

A few miles usually. But Jaxi is closer to fifty, and she can communicate with me from an even greater distance.

Really? Is she more powerful than you? Up until the morning's conversation, Ridge had been thinking of the sword as a tool, rather than an entity, and he had certainly never considered that its powers might be so great.

That question resulted in her losing all of her sheepishness and growing very smug.

Oh, sorry.

Ridge found a flat area about a half mile from the wreck, the snow largely swept free of the rock by prevailing winds. He wished he could get closer, but mountains weren't known for offering many landing spots. Sardelle's light was still guiding him, so he took them down. Even though the two-seater had been unwieldy during the skirmish, he was glad for the thrusters at the moment. He never could have landed his regular flier anywhere except a road or maybe a field out on the steppes.

Jaxi was born more than three hundred years before I was. She's that many generations closer to those original humans who were daring enough to mate with dragons and whose offspring received some of their powers. As the dragon blood was diluted over the centuries, sorcerers grew less and less powerful. A weak one from Jaxi's generation would have been considered a moderately or even very powerful magic user in my generation. I believe the shaman I faced outside of Galmok Mountain was an example of a very powerful magic user in this generation. I defeated him, but I wasn't considered powerful by my generation's standards. As for Jaxi, she can't do all that she could do as a mortal, but she's still quite capable.

Ridge settled on the stone outcropping, the thrusters and heat of the engine melting the snow in the crevices of the rock. He unfastened his harness, climbed down, and turned, intending to give Sardelle a hand, but she hopped down and landed beside him.

"Let's go see what you brought down," she said with a smile.

"Yes, ma'am." It was almost strange speaking out loud after all of their silent conversations, but with the propeller stopped and the wind a mere breeze, softened by the snowfall, there was no need. Ridge gazed out toward the steppes for a moment, making sure there wasn't any obvious sign of pursuit, then headed up the slope.

"I think that village is exactly what it looked like," Sardelle said. "Something simple and rural that just happened to have someone stationed in a watchtower. There are probably only one or two soldiers for the post."

"One or two soldiers can rouse a village of people with bows and pitchforks." Ridge grimaced as his boots sank into the snow up to his knees. This was going to be quite the slog, maybe taking longer than he had realized. So much for the night's sleep—or standing watch professionally—that he had been waiting for.

Sardelle didn't debate his statement. They clambered up the slope in silence, though they were soon breathing hard from their exertions. Ridge wasn't out of shape, but this was hard work. He kept looking up the hillside, hoping to spot the thing, but it had to be close to a half hour before the black wreckage came into sight. The three sets of wings had been torn off in the crash, and littered the mountainside. The rest of the battered body was half sunken into the snow.

Wiping sweat from his brow, he pushed his way toward it. "Nowon better appreciate his sample. Even if all I feel like lugging back is a screw."

Sardelle increased the intensity of the light that had been guiding their way, but stood back to leave the investigating to him. "My engineering knowledge is rudimentary."

"And here I thought it was a secret passion when you were summarizing *Denhoft's Theories on Aerodynamic and Aerostatic Flight* to me."

Her light was just bright enough that he could make out the redness of her cheeks. That wasn't all from exertion, he didn't think.

Ridge stepped toward the wreck, wanting to touch the remains of the hull to see if the black was paint or some strange metal he wasn't familiar with, but paused, his hand hovering above the fuselage. "It doesn't have any magical alarms or traps that will go off if I touch it, does it?"

"None that I can sense."

"You didn't think it was magic before. Are you still of that opinion?"

"I'm... not sure. I do sense something not entirely mundane, but it's not like the tools and baubles that sorcerers can make." She groped in the air with her gloved hands, as if she could find the proper term to explain her feeling there.

Ridge prodded the hull with a finger. Nothing happened. Emboldened, he patted around the cylindrical hull, searching for an access panel. There wasn't a cockpit, nor would the contraption have been able to support the weight of a man. It was only a third of the size of a one-man flier. Even the guns were scaled down, though he didn't doubt that they could have damaged his craft if their bullets had struck. The hull did seem to be painted, so his thoughts of strange new metals were unfounded.

"Got something," he said, his gloves sliding over a crack in the side. He pulled out his utility knife and levered the panel open. He expected some burst of light to shine out, something similar to what his flier's power crystal emitted, but there was nothing of the sort. There were wheels and levers inside with wires all going to a little box. It had been dented in the crash, but he managed to pull it out, not worrying about the wires snapping. He pried it open, then leaned closer to Sardelle's light.

A thumbnail-sized glass dome was mounted on something that reminded him of the punch cards used in machines back home. He couldn't believe the technology he was familiar with could have directed these two aircraft. Not a chance.

He tilted the little dome toward the light and was surprised when a bubble of air moved around inside. "Huh."

"A liquid?" Sardelle asked.

"A *crimson* liquid." Ridge held it toward her. "Is that the source of your not-entirely-mundane feeling?"

Sardelle nodded without taking the board. Her eyes had grown wide.

"Dragon blood?" Ridge asked.

"I... think we should test it before making that assumption. Your king's report, he didn't mention anything like *this*, did he?" She spread her fingers toward the wreck.

"No." Ridge pocketed the small board. Nowon was going to

get a very interesting sample. "Let's hope Tolemek has something in his bag for examining it. I can tell you one thing, right now."

"What's that?"

"I've looked this craft over from nose to tail, and there's nothing else on here that could be a fuel source, not that my brain can fathom anyway."

"I'm not aware that dragon blood was ever used for fuel. The mind boggles at the notion of a dragon *allowing* its blood to be used thusly. Or used at all, for that matter. All the legends tell us they were the most formidable creatures in the world. And arrogant and prickly by nature. That said... I don't know of anyone who was trying to power machines a thousand years ago. Your archaeologist pilot may have more insight, but you were pretty sophisticated if you were using whale oil lamps instead of candles back then."

If the king's spies had learned of this, Ridge understood the reasoning—the urgency—behind this mission.

His body had chilled, so he waved for them to head back to the flier. The weather wouldn't be pleasant tonight wherever the squadron landed, but he hoped it would be a few degrees warmer on the flats beneath the mountains. He gave the wreck several long looks over his shoulder as he and Sardelle picked their way back along the trail they had broken.

"Something else bothering you?" she asked.

"Just thinking that whatever we're dealing with, it's far more advanced than anything the Cofah have brought to Iskandia before. If there are more machines like this, we could be in trouble."

CHAPTER 7

S ARDELLE RUBBED HER ARMS, SHIVERING in the cold air and watching Ridge try to stifle yawn after yawn. She wanted to drag him off to bed, or to a bedroll, as the case was. Instead, as the midnight snow fell, he was crouching over a map with Nowon and Kaika, pointing and discussing an extraction plan with them, while the other pilots checked the fliers for damage or maintenance needs. A couple of bullets had clipped the wings of Ridge's craft during the skirmish with the Cofah constructs.

Since landing, Sardelle had gotten her first good look at the elite troops captains, but they hadn't done more than give her curious and slightly suspicious looks. The pilots, too, were giving her the squint eye. Duck had been sent off on some mission as soon as they arrived, but Apex kept frowning in Sardelle's direction. Everyone had to be wondering what Ridge had been thinking in bringing her, especially considering the unorthodox manner in which she had been added to the team. She had been thinking of how she might prove herself to the king, but perhaps she needed to start with them.

Without revealing *yourself?*

I don't know, Jaxi.

While Ridge and the others worked, Sardelle loitered near Tolemek, wanting to hear his assessment of the liquid trapped in the bubble. Strange that he was the person here she was most comfortable with now, aside from Ridge. A few weeks ago, she never would have thought she would have any sort of relationship with him, but as the only other non-military person here, she felt a kinship with him. Maybe it was because he was getting even darker glares than she from Apex and from the captains too. Ahn was the only one who saw him as anything other than Deathmaker.

At the moment, Tolemek was kneeling on a bare patch of ground, a lantern burning beside him as he poked into one of his bags. He was assembling something.

"A microscope?" Sardelle guessed as the pieces came together.

"Yes, a very small and weak one. My equipment selection was severely limited due to the weight restrictions someone imposed upon me." He leveled a stare, not at Ridge but at Ahn.

"It's not my fault your muscles weigh so much," Ahn said. "You should be happy we didn't overheat the engine and fall out of the sky over Hariti."

"Yes... my massive brawn is an ever-present burden. It's amazing I can fit through doorways without having to turn sideways."

"He's just cranky because he doesn't have all of his beakers, test tubes, crucibles, and snakes with him," Ahn told Sardelle.

"Snakes?"

"And spiders. Haven't you seen his terrariums?"

"I haven't been up to the lab, no."

"The lab assistant has assured me the creatures will be tended," Tolemek said, pulling a slide out of a case. "It's largely the Micon Burner I'm missing right now. It's useful for sterilization, combustion, and heating my hands when they're cold." He grimaced and flexed his fingers—he had removed his gloves to set up. "Zirkander, can I break this bubble?" He held up the board from the wreck.

"Did Nowon get to look at the intact sample?" Ridge asked.

The captain trotted over before Tolemek could answer and knelt beside the microscope. Tolemek handed him the board with its captured liquid and fiddled with the microscope settings while Nowon studied the machine innards by the light.

"Interesting. If this is what they're doing with the dragon blood, it's not at all what my brother thought. He mentioned weapons, yes, but the last I heard, he believed the Cofah were going to inject it into humans to enhance people, possibly giving them the power of the sorcerers of old."

"Maybe they tried and that didn't work." Tolemek took back the board. He jabbed a needle into the back of it, drawing out some of the liquid inside the bubble without breaking the glass.

"Perhaps," Sardelle said, "they still bear the prejudices toward sorcerers that their ancestors did. In my studies, I've learned that the Cofah had a… purging similar to the one on Iskandia." She swallowed down emotion that welled up into her throat, reminding herself that this was distant history to these people and that they wouldn't understand how recent it all had been for her. Except Ridge. She caught him gazing across the camp at her, his eyes gentle with understanding. "Supposing it's actually possible to give a human being powers by injecting dragon blood into their veins—and I don't know if that's feasible or if such blood would be rejected or destroyed by the immune system— the Cofah may fear that in creating sorcerers, they would be bringing about their own destruction… or creating their own masters."

Nowon was watching her intently. "What is your specialty?" he asked. The and-why-are-you-here hung unspoken in the air.

"I am a student of healing and history," Sardelle said, then glanced at Lieutenant Apex. He'd only known her as an archaeologist, as per Ridge's cover story. Would he be suspicious if she now claimed a doctor's talents?

But he was frowning at the microscope. "Aren't we prematurely believing we have dragon blood? I fail to see how it could be acquired unless the Cofah have found dragons, and that's highly unlikely."

Sardelle imagined some sealed amphora that could have been unearthed by archaeologists. Or miners. But even if someone a dozen centuries ago had found a dead dragon and exsanguinated it for some reason, the blood couldn't still be *alive* today.

"I'm taking a look now," Tolemek said, "though I confess I don't know if dragon blood looks different from human blood at the microscopic level or not. I've never seen any before nor seen it described in textbooks. Dragons predate modern science. They predate most primitive science too."

Sardelle found herself leaning over his shoulder as he peered into the microscope. Nowon did too. Even Ridge came over, apparently more intrigued by the results than by his map.

"The cells are still alive," Tolemek said. "Interesting. There's no nuclei in them, so it's not human blood. Nor is it mammal blood. The cells are large, but that doesn't necessarily mean much. Frogs have larger cells than humans."

"There's nothing that reeks of magic, eh?" Ahn asked.

"There are anomalies. You'll have to let me know what qualifies as reeking of magic."

"Weird concoctions that have a creepy blue glow even after all the lights are turned off at night."

Tolemek frowned over at her. "I assure you there's nothing magical about Illumination Goo Number Four. Bioluminescent plankton are the source of that glow. I captured the dinoflagellates from your own harbor."

Nowon and Ridge shifted uneasily, and Apex openly scowled over at Tolemek. It might have been the talk of magic or the reminder of Tolemek's scientific nature—and what he had done with it in the past.

Ahn noticed the reactions and looked like she wished she hadn't spoken in the first place.

"Like a jar full of fireflies," Sardelle suggested, though she suspected Tolemek might have applied some magic without even realizing it—she had seen the evidence of that in a number of his concoctions—if only to keep the plankton alive indefinitely. Like her, he would have to tread carefully in the modern world.

"Oh," Ridge said. "That would make a useful light, I guess."

Tolemek fished in his bag. "I'll test the blood for an electrical current or some kind of charge that might suggest... *enhanced* properties."

"We saw it power an aircraft and shoot at us," Ridge said. "You don't think that's proof of enhanced properties?"

"It's possible someone was using magic to control the craft from afar." Tolemek withdrew a device similar in look and size to a thick compass, but with bolts for attaching wires.

Ridge met Sardelle's eyes. She shook her head once. She would have felt something like that.

Tolemek attached probes on wires to the testing contraption.

Galvanometer, Jaxi supplied.

How do you know that? Are you poking around in his thoughts?

Of course not. I'm simply a student of the sciences.

And tools that hadn't been invented yet when last we walked the world?

We've been free for weeks now. It's not my fault you haven't applied yourself to catching up and acquiring a modern education.

Why don't I believe you, Jaxi?

I have no idea, but that is dragon blood as sure as I'm a powerful sorceress residing in a sword. You people could just ask me if there's any uncertainty with these things. Also, you might want to keep him from poking around in there.

What? Why?

Before Jaxi could answer, one of Tolemek's needles brushed the damp blood on his slide. A sizzle sounded, charging the air, and he was hurled away from the microscope. He flew several feet, knocking Ridge over, before landing on his back. His already unruly hair stuck out in more directions than usual, as if he had been struck by lightning. His eyes were frozen open, stunned.

Stunned... or dead.

Afraid his heart had stopped, Sardelle rushed to his side, laying a hand on his chest. It hadn't stopped, but the beats were jumpy and erratic. Healing electrocution victims was not something she had much experience with, but she did her best to sooth the muscle and return it to its usual beat pattern. Fortunately, Tolemek's body seemed able to recover with minimal intervention. He gasped in a breath and blinked a few times.

"Are you all right, sir?" Apex asked.

He and Captain Kaika had come to either side of Ridge, each offering a hand to help him up. Ahn rushed to Tolemek's side, frowning with concern and clasping his hand at the same time.

"Yes, fine. Thanks." Ridge waved his soldiers back and sat up, propping an elbow on one knee. He waited until Tolemek lifted his head and was clearly alive, then asked, "Should I feel jealous that you rushed over to check on him before me?"

Sardelle couldn't imagine he'd had many occasions in his life to be jealous, at least not of women choosing other men over him. "From what you've told me and from what I've garnered from your superior officers, if I fell to the ground beside you every time someone knocked you on your lower cheeks, all the skin on my knees would be scraped off."

"Probably true," Ridge said.

"Lower cheeks?" Captain Kaika's lip wrinkled up in disbelief. "Who says that?"

"She's very proper," Nowon observed.

"It's called being civilized," Ridge said, rolling to his feet, "And well-mannered. Unlike most soldiers I know."

Sardelle raised an eyebrow. She was accustomed to soldiers and knew that they would often choose different words to describe the anatomy, but it was a novelty to have them teasing her. She tried to decide if that signaled a modicum of acceptance or if it simply meant she was an aberration for more reasons than one.

"My manners are perfectly adequate," Nowon said.

"Mine aren't," Kaika said.

"That is a truth."

"Are you all right?" Ahn murmured to Tolemek. She didn't seem the type to fling herself onto a man to demonstrate love and relief, at least when others were around, but she had a firm grip on his hand.

"I think so." He rubbed his head. A charred scent lingered in the air around him.

"So, what did that teach us?" Ridge brushed snow off his hands and his... lower cheeks. "Besides that it's a bad idea to stick a little metal prong into a strange blood specimen."

"That whatever this is, it has tremendous energy potential," Tolemek said.

Huh. He wasn't willing to call it dragon blood yet. A hallmark of a scientist, Sardelle supposed. It always took them a few metric tons of proof before they were willing to upgrade something from a hypothesis to a theory, and even then, they used chalk rather than ink.

Because they don't have smart swords that could simply tell them the truth.

And how can you be so positive that it's dragon blood and not some strange new liquid that was made with technology or sorcery?

I can sense it, the same way I can sense whether a person has a hint of dragon blood in them. And you could sense it, too, if you opened your mind and paid attention.

Sardelle had sensed *something*, but, like Tolemek, she wasn't quick to glom onto the possibility that the Cofah had somehow acquired a substance that hadn't existed in the world for a thousand years.

That we know of. I have one more tidbit of information for you, one you're welcome to share with your new friends. That dragon blood isn't cut with human blood.

So it's not from the offspring of a human and dragon union?

It's not.

The thud of hooves sounded in the darkness beyond their encampment.

"Duck," Ridge said, even before Sardelle stretched out her senses in that direction. He jogged to the edge of the camp and waved into the darkness.

The dark forms of five horses came into view, picking their way around the dead clumps of grass thrusting up through the snowy steppes. All of the creatures had saddles, but only one had a rider.

Lieutenant Duck slid off and saluted his commander. He had reins, but the rest of the horses had simply followed him. "Got your order here, sir."

"Are these stolen horses?" Sardelle couldn't imagine the lieutenant, goofy big ears and big grin, sauntering into a market to *buy* the horses—he looked no more Cofah than she did—nor was this the hour for horse markets.

"These are *borrowed* horses, ma'am," Duck said earnestly. "I went a-visiting to a farm over yonder with a couple of apples in my pocket, made friends with this big fellow here—" he patted the dark stallion's neck, "—and I guess that made him inclined to follow me when I opened the gate in his paddock. Some of his friends followed too. They must have heard about the apples."

"And they saddled themselves up for you as well," Sardelle said. "Impressive."

"Horses like to dress up and look good when they go out, ma'am."

"You needn't be so suspicious of your gift, Sardelle," Ridge said.

"Gift?"

"Those three are for you, Tolemek, and the person he aims to bring back."

"We're going tonight?" Tolemek asked.

"It's a ways to ride, and I expect you'll need to sneak aboard a train at some point," Ridge said, "but this is as close as we dare bring the fliers. The region gets a lot more populated closer to the river." He waved toward his map, still sprawled in the snow. "You'll need to find a way to ship your sister home, because we don't have any more seats in the fliers. If you want to go with her, that's fine, but I need Lieutenant Ahn back here to fly her craft home. We're not leaving any of these in the Cofah's back yard."

Tolemek massaged the back of his head. He had a dumbfounded expression on his face, and Sardelle wondered if the jolt had affected more than his heart.

"Sir," Apex said, "you're going to let him *leave*? And trust him to come back home when he feels like it? He could report to some Cofah military outpost and tell them everything he knows."

"If he tried, he'd be thrown back in a dungeon," Ahn said.

"If we don't send him away, he'll be here in camp, experimenting with that blood," Ridge said. "He'll probably blow us all up."

Tolemek's dumbfounded look faded, but he still seemed as surprised as Apex that he was being allowed to go. As if Sardelle wouldn't keep an eye on him. She didn't believe he meant to flee back to his people—he cared for Ahn and was being allowed to pursue the work he was passionate about in Iskandia—but she could stop him from wandering off if she had to.

I can if you can't, Jaxi put in brightly.

"I will gather what I need," Tolemek said.

"Sir, I would like to go with them," Ahn said, her fingers twitching toward one of the horses, as if she wanted to run over and hop on at any second.

"I know you would, Lieutenant, but we're moving the fliers as soon as everybody leaves. There are too many paths leading back to us." He waved toward the horses, but he must be thinking of those crashed unmanned fliers too. "I need you here."

"But after that, we'll most likely just be waiting in camp until everyone gets back from their missions, right? I could help move the camp, then catch up with them."

"Given that the Cofah have some new technology—" Ridge waved toward the spot where Tolemek had been examining the blood, "—I'm not feeling that secure in the notion that we'll be able to stay in one spot undetected for days. We may have to move every night."

Ahn clenched her jaw, but she didn't continue to argue. She watched Tolemek pack, then ran over to her flier and pulled out her own bag. For a moment, Sardelle thought she meant to disobey, to throw the bag on one of the horses and ride off, but Ahn only pulled something out, then jumped down from the flier. She strode over to Tolemek, who pushed his hair behind his shoulders, and gazed down at her.

"Here." She held out a pistol in a holster. "It's a Maverick Eight-Eighty. Most accurate pistol in the world, as fine as all but the best sniper rifles and good for close quarters."

"You think I'll need to shoot my way into my sister's..." Tolemek glanced around, saw a couple of others listening, and finished with, "hospital?"

"You might find all sorts of trouble on the way there. Especially with that hair. You don't exactly look like a Cofah soldier anymore."

"Maybe I should cut it off. You've made that suggestion a few times."

"I suggested cutting it, not cutting it off. If you come back to me bald, I'll pour that illumination goop on your head. Now here." She thrust out the pistol again, and this time he took it.

"Ridge? May I speak with you?" Sardelle tilted her head

toward a dark, private spot behind the fliers.

He nodded, but had a few more orders to deliver before joining her. "Nowon and Kaika, there are horses for you too. You're sure you don't want to take any of my people with you?"

"You're not offering yourself, sir? You did remove *our* colonel from the mission, after all." Kaika didn't sound serious, but Sardelle watched Ridge, not liking the idea of him heading off into a secret and doubtlessly well-guarded Cofah installation, not when he was sending her off in another direction.

Nowon rolled his eyes.

"I don't have the special skills the others have," Ridge said. "I just fly and shoot things."

"We have no need of extra assistance," Nowon said, and Kaika didn't argue.

"It's your mission," Ridge said, though he gazed thoughtfully over at Sardelle.

Do you want me *to go with them? Tolemek can probably retrieve his sister by himself.*

His eyes widened slightly at her telepathic question, but he recovered quickly. *I wish I could send you with them, but it doesn't sound like they want help. They might not be comfortable with your kind of help, either. After all, it took me a while to grow cozy with the idea, and I'm delightfully open-minded.*

Sure, you are. You nearly fell over when I teased you about the possibility that you might be telepathic.

Falling over wasn't what was on my mind that night. He gave her a quick wink. *But back to this. I know Ahn trusts Tolemek, but I'm not ready to let him wander off alone. You're the one person he won't think to cross if for some reason he's tempted.*

You're thinking of Jaxi. She's already threatened to kill him a couple of times. He's quite polite with her.

He won't cross you, either. He looks at you with respect. And wariness.

While Sardelle was debating whether she agreed with this assessment, Ridge faced the captains again. "We'll be waiting at the coordinates I pointed out on the map for your return in three nights, unless that spot is compromised, in which case our contingency pick-up location will be the Miarga River Fork on the other side of the mountains. If we have to move again... put up a flare from the river. We'll be watching and come get you."

"Understood, sir," Kaika and Nowon said at the same time, then ran off to grab their bags.

Nowon headed out of the camp, a dark quiet form without a parting word for anyone. Kaika, on the other hand, thumped Ahn and Duck on the arms as she passed, saying, "Don't get too much napping in while you're back here in the rear, kids."

"Kids? Napping?" Duck stood up painfully straight. "I've been rummaging all up and down the countryside, hunting like a coonhound to find you all horses. And I flew you all the way over here, while you were snoring in the back."

Kaika had been on the move as she had spoken, and she waved over her shoulder at his protest. She did pause in front of Apex, who was standing in the shadows, glowering out at the night and sneaking glances at Tolemek.

"You always this grumpy, L.T.? You've been wearing my granddad's face since I met you. He's got colitis. What's your excuse?"

Apex opened and closed his mouth a couple of times. Flustered? Sardelle hadn't seen the two talking much. Duck seemed a little moon-eyed toward Kaika, but Apex either hadn't noticed she was a woman with some curves under her uniform, or he didn't care.

"I am not grumpy," he said. "I'm... perturbed."

"Well, relax some, will you?" Kaika gave him a kiss on the cheek, then sauntered out to the horses.

Now it was Duck's turn to open and close his mouth a number of times, before stammering, "What just happened?"

"Captain Kaika is more into grumps than horses," Ridge said, then walked over to Sardelle. He turned his back on the two lieutenants, Duck looking like he wanted to strangle Apex and Apex looking confused. In a lower voice, Ridge asked, "Did you still want to talk to me, or, ah, did we already do it?" He pointed two fingers at his eyes, then at hers.

Sardelle took his hand—there were enough shadows that

nobody should notice, not that he ever worried that much about displaying affection in front of his people. "If Tolemek chooses to find alternative transportation back with his sister, do you want me to stay with them or come back to you?"

Ridge looked out toward the horses, where Tolemek was finishing packing. The two captains were already riding away. "I wish there was a way to communicate with you from afar. The... mind thing, that's only for close range, right? I think I remember you saying that."

"For me, it is. Jaxi can communicate with me over a couple hundred miles, at least."

"Could she relay messages to me?"

Not unless he jabs some of that dragon blood into his veins and learns to improve his mental reception to slightly greater than that of a rock.

"Jaxi says it's doubtful."

Jaxi made an obnoxious noise in Sardelle's head, something between a snort and a bout of flatulence.

Bout of flatulence? That captain is right. You're overly socialized.

She didn't say that.

She was thinking it.

"I could leave Jaxi with you," Sardelle said, the idea not all that repellent at the moment.

What? You're tromping into enemy territory with a pirate. You may need me.

Ridge's face screwed up, as doubtful as Jaxi's thoughts.

I'm sure I can muster my meager skills enough to defend myself. On the other hand, if Ridge and his team are discovered, they have nothing except mundane weapons for defense. "That way we could communicate through Jaxi, and you could let me know what you think—and if any trouble finds you back here." Sardelle would find a way to hurry back here if that happened. "Those aircraft at the watchtower may be nothing more than a hint as to what they're doing with that blood."

"I guess it wouldn't matter to me," Ridge said. "I hate to deny you your companion."

Sardelle unbuckled her sword belt and handed it to him,

almost laughing because she had found it amusing that Ahn had given Tolemek her favorite gun. How was this different?

I could cut her favorite gun in half with a thought, that's how. Now Jaxi sounded grumpy. Too bad Kaika wasn't here to kiss her.

Ugh, I'll hold out for the dragon.

Ridge accepted the belt gingerly. "Any special instructions?"

"Don't leave her under a bed."

"Should I wear the belt, or would she be offended by that? I can put her in the cockpit of my flier if that's best."

"Wear the belt if you go anywhere, please. As you've seen, Jaxi can protect herself—with hurled kitchen pots and pictures if nothing else."

Pardon you, but I was only responsible for two pots. And no pictures. The burglars made the rest of that mess. You better take that book along and figure out who those people were before heading back to Iskandia.

I'm not sure I'll be going back, or at least not staying long if I do. Sardelle smiled to Ridge, trying not to let the sad thought show on her face. "I would be upset if she were somehow lost."

He clasped her hands. "I know you would."

What do you mean you might not be going back?

I haven't decided yet, but it's what we talked about before. I'm afraid I've complicated his life, and not in a good way.

"I'll keep her safe," Ridge said and lowered his head, kissing her gently, his affection wrapping around her like a favorite cloak on a cold night. It made her heart ache, and tears pricked at her eyes.

Afraid he would notice, Sardelle stepped back, breaking the kiss. "I better not delay him. Traveling at night will be easier." She took a step, but paused, reaching up to run her hand down the side of his face, as if she could memorize the contours with her fingers.

"Safe journey, Sardelle," he said, a hint of concern in his voice, not just for her journey, she sensed, but because he thought she was acting a little oddly.

"You too," she whispered. She would explain later. This wasn't the time.

CHAPTER 8

THE FIRST LIGHT OF DAWN seeped through the gaps between the slats on the freight train. It was the second morning since Sardelle and Tolemek had left Ridge and the others. She leaned against the wall, her eyes closed, her senses open. They had left the countryside and entered Mason Valley, a more populated area where the asylum waited.

Cattle filled the car, and in the hours they had been cooped up, Tolemek had been pinned a couple of times by furry haunches. That was his fault for trying to pace in the crowded area. Sardelle simply stood in one spot, and the animals avoided her, but he kept gnawing on his knuckles and walking back and forth. A testament to his distraction, he had apologized more than once to the big animals when he bumped one. Or maybe he was simply a more polite ex-pirate than she had realized. He hadn't been talking to *her* that much. She was inclined to give him his privacy, but if he had some plan in mind, she would need to know about it soon.

"Will they let us in if we smell like a farm?" she asked over the *clicketyclack* of the train wheels.

"What?" Tolemek lifted his head, his dark ropy tangles of hair shadowing his face.

In the wan lighting, Sardelle couldn't see his expression, but she sensed the nervousness emanating from him and snatches of thought floating on the surface of his mind. Would his sister still be there? He hadn't visited in three years. Would they be able to get in? Would she want to go with him if she was there? If his father had been visiting, he could have been telling her lies about him. Or the truth. Just as bad. Would she even remember him? She had been mad with moments of lucidity the last time he had seen her. What if she had grown worse since then?

"You've stepped in cow dung at least three times during your pacing," Sardelle said, thinking he might appreciate a distraction from his musings. "And we both smell fragrant."

He stared at her, apparently unamused by her attempt at distracting him. She shouldn't be that surprised. She had never been the class jokester during her school days.

"I wasn't planning to walk up to the reception desk and ask for permission to see her," Tolemek said.

"No?"

"There's a kitchen in the back of the building. I thought we'd go through that door, sneak up to the second floor, find her room, and simply..."

"Kidnap her?" Sardelle suggested.

"It would only be kidnapping if she didn't want to come." He lifted his eyes toward the wooden ceiling of the car. "Which is a possibility, I fear."

"I thought you two were close at one point." Sardelle already understood his concerns, but he might feel better if he spoke about them.

"We were. After my brother died..." He sighed. "It doesn't matter right now. I just need to find her first and see how much of her... of *her* remains."

Of her sanity, that had been what he'd almost said.

"If it helps, I haven't heard of many cases where the ability to use magic drives someone crazy," Sardelle said. "It can account for moodiness, and I've heard of suicides, especially in those who weren't trained, but split personalities and other personality disorders are rare, or at least not any more common among the gifted than in the mundane."

"Was that supposed to be comforting?" he snapped.

She drew back, startled at his anger. Then she realized he had latched onto one of her words. Suicides.

"I'm sorry." Tolemek bowed his head in a further apology. "I don't have the right to question you or snarl at you."

Sardelle spread a hand. "Of course you do. I'm just a person."

He gave her a wry shake of his head. "No, you're not. Regardless, I appreciate you coming with me. And Zirkander arranging this. I honestly didn't expect any of that."

"I gave you my word I would help when you saved the city."

"I know, but you were desperate. And keeping your word to an enemy, that's not something most people would bother with, especially someone…" Tolemek extended a hand toward her.

"I'm not supposed to keep my word because I'm a sorceress?"

"It's not as if there would be repercussions that could affect you if you didn't."

"That's when integrity matters most, isn't it?" Sardelle frowned, disturbed that he thought so little of her, or maybe it was of sorcerers in general. Had she done something to give him a poor impression of her? She knew people sometimes mistook her quiet reserve for aloofness or indifference, but she didn't feel that way.

"I'm not fit to judge a person's integrity," he said dryly.

Ah, maybe that was what lay behind his reasoning—his own mistakes in the past. He didn't believe he was worthy of someone's word?

"It *was* the magic affecting her," Tolemek said. "I'm certain of it. I tested her in every manner I knew how, and I couldn't find a mundane explanation for her change."

"The mind is a complicated organ. Science may have advanced a great deal in the last few hundred years, but I think it'll be a few hundred more before the brain is completely understood."

Tolemek shifted to avoid a restless cow with the ability to crush his foot with one misstep.

"When *did* she change?" Sardelle asked. "She was normal growing up?"

"A little quirky, but mostly normal, yes."

She wagered that his family would have described him as a quirky kid too.

"It was after our older brother died, and after I gave up on my dream and entered the military to appease my father. I came back on leave when I was… twenty-one, or so, I guess. We're twelve years apart, so she was nine then. She remembered me, but she also kept talking to herself when nobody was around. Sometimes she seemed to be talking to someone else. She displayed a few powers, being able to knock things over with her mind when she was angry, and my parents grew afraid. My mother was afraid *for* her, but my father was more afraid of what the neighbors would think."

"He sounds like a lovely man." Sardelle wondered if Tolemek and Ahn had shared stories of their fathers with each other. Maybe that had facilitated their unlikely relationship.

A steam whistle screeched. The car shuddered as the engine slowed down.

"We should get out before it comes to a full stop. We'll be less likely to be spotted that way." Tolemek eyed the sliding door on the side of the car. Five or six tightly packed cows stood between him and it. Odd that a scientist who had concocted countless clever potions and devices should seem daunted by animals. Granted, they *were* large and did tend to give a person flat, unfriendly stares.

Sardelle gave them gentle nudges with her mind, and they shifted aside to let her pass. Tolemek followed in her wake.

She slid the door open, revealing warehouses and factories in the bowl of the valley with houses dotting the hillsides. Night lingered, and lanterns burned all over the city, but people were already walking and riding in the streets. There weren't any lights in the cargo car, and she doubted anyone would notice the open door. As soon as the train slowed to a speed where they could jump out without breaking any bones, Tolemek hopped into the gravel lining the tracks. Sardelle jumped after him and, with a flick of her mind, closed the door behind her, so the cattle would stay put. She had no sooner landed than a voice rang out above the chugging of the train.

"Stowaways!"

A deep-voiced dog bayed a cry that must have meant something similar.

"Run," Tolemek urged, sprinting through the gravel and toward a chain-link fence with barbed wire lining the top. These Cofah were serious about keeping their cattle from escaping.

Tolemek, being taller and more athletic than she, sprang to the top of the fence and leaped over, scarcely impeded by the barbed wire. As Sardelle reached the bottom and was about to climb after him, the first shots fired. A bullet skipped off the gravel, inches from her heels.

"The hells with climbing," she muttered and flung out a hand, slicing through the chain with her mind. She raised a barrier about herself in case another bullet came while she was pushing through.

But the next shot came from three feet away: Tolemek firing toward the guard charging down the gravel path toward them. He didn't hit the man—the bullet clanged off the side of the moving train rolling past a couple of feet away. The guard faltered, probably realizing he wasn't dealing with a couple of unarmed kids.

Sardelle had time to squeeze through the fence and sprint into an alley. Tolemek was waiting for her at the mouth, but he took off as soon as she joined him. She pushed herself to match his long legs and keep up with him.

"Was that because he spotted my pale skin, or do all stowaways get shot on sight here?" Sardelle asked.

"Dodging the fare is a crime. He was probably shooting to scare, but I couldn't be sure."

They ran three blocks before Tolemek turned onto a broad residential street lined with gas lamps. No, those were kerosene lamps, Sardelle realized. Maybe gas lighting wasn't as common here yet as it was in the cities of Iskandia.

A donkey-drawn wagon rolled past in front of them, and Tolemek slowed to a walk. He slipped his pistol into its holster and covered it with his coat.

"Lieutenant Ahn will be disappointed in you," Sardelle said, catching her breath.

"Because I shot at someone with her gun? I think that's why she gave it to me."

"Because you *missed*."

"Oh. That was intentional. I would prefer not to leave piles of bodies behind on this quest. My sister was always a gentle soul, despite the moments of craziness where she occasionally hurt people. She wouldn't approve of me using violence to get her out."

"Good." Even if Sardelle had always considered the Cofah enemies, it was their military and government she had a problem with, not the average subject. "I do appreciate you watching out for me." She kept her voice low, since there were people out in the street, and they would doubtlessly find it odd to hear an Iskandian accent in their town. She had pulled up the hood of her cloak, as well, and wore gloves to hide her pale hands.

Tolemek gave her a sidelong look. "I suspect you would have been fine without my help. I... sensed you doing something." His voice had taken on an odd note.

She had given him a few lessons on developing his power at Ridge's cabin in the woods, but Tolemek had yet to grow accustomed to using his talents or truly comfortable with the idea that he might *have* talents. Non-mundane ones, anyway.

"Cutting through the fence and erecting an invisible barrier around myself to protect against projectiles," she said. "And pokey fence pieces."

Tolemek snorted and raised his own hand. It was too dark to make out details, but there was a dark smudge on his palm? Blood? Maybe he hadn't cleared that barbed wire as easily as it had seemed.

"The sanitarium is on the hill up there." He pointed toward the end of the residential area and to a gray stone building perched on the ridge. Two dark towers rose like gargoyles, scowling down into the valley.

"That looks more like a prison than a hospital."

"Now you know why I hated the idea of my sister being sent there." Thoughts of his father arose in his head again, of a violent fight that had involved blows.

Sardelle turned her focus elsewhere, toward the people they passed. She needed to know if any of them found these two strangers odd. It wasn't a small town, but Mason Valley lacked the anonymity of a metropolis. Most were worried about getting to work rather than watching for strangers.

They climbed a dirt road that ran up the slope in switchbacks. In the town, the snow had been cleared from the streets, but out here, the only bare spots were muddy ruts cut by wagons.

Sardelle eyed the towers. She didn't sense anyone in them, but asked the question that came to mind, nonetheless.

"Will anybody be on guard and watching our approach?"

"I doubt it. It used to be a castle, and there are spots for guards, but I've never seen anyone up there. There *are* guards who walk the halls inside however. There's more danger of the patients trying to escape than anyone breaking in."

Instead of continuing to the front gate, Tolemek veered off the road and into the snow. He walked along the thick gray building toward the first corner. A few windows dotted the walls, but they were more like arrow slits than anything designed to allow in light and air. Sardelle couldn't imagine the rooms—cells?—inside were comfortable, and a quiet rage began to grow in her breast for this girl who had been imprisoned here because her father had been worried about what the neighbors might think of her unexplained outbursts.

Not as bad as being chained up with rocks and hurled into a lake to drown. Jaxi's voice sounded more faintly in her head than usual—the train had taken them over a hundred and fifty miles, on top of the ten they had ridden before arriving in a town with a station.

I'm not so sure about that. Sardelle eyed the drab building as Tolemek led her around another corner. *How is Ridge?*

Pining in your absence.

Sardelle snorted. *I meant how is the camp? No trouble since they moved the fliers?*

Your virile lover has woken his troops to perform physical exercises. When you return, his chest will be as hard and muscular as ever. You would be a fool not to come back to him.

So in summary, your answer is, no, there's no trouble at camp.

Correct. In my spare time, I have been reading your pilfered library book.

That book was borrowed. Sardelle followed Tolemek around yet another tower, and he pointed at what must be the kitchen door he had mentioned. She had better end this conversation so she could concentrate.

Yes, much like Lieutenant Duck's horses. Strange how the definitions of words have changed over the centuries. I believe I've selected three possible organizations that might be troubling you.

Oh?

The Alabaster Motherhood has been watching out for soldiers for several hundred years. Perhaps some wizened mother or grandmother is irritated by your influence on Ridge.

Sardelle thought of the officer next door and his nosy grandmother. It was hard to imagine that woman as more than an innocent gossip. *And the other two?*

Tolemek stopped in front of the door and slipped a vial out of his bag, unfastening an eye-dropper lid.

The Heartwood Sisterhood was founded over a millennium ago to protect innocent young men from the nefarious advances of female dragons.

Oh, please. As if that was ever a big problem.

Tolemek dabbed something into the door lock. Smoke wafted out. Sardelle could have simply opened the lock, but Jaxi had her distracted. Always better to empower men than make them feel unneeded anyway, right?

Apparently a lot of men went on quests, hoping to find dragon lovers and leaving suitable young women back in their villages. A lot of those men found dragons who liked to toast humans like skewers of meat on the fire. This left a lot of eligible women who couldn't find men to marry. It also left a shortage of men to plant and harvest the crops. Those dragons, such rabble-rousers.

Jaxi, are you teasing me about this group?

Not at all. They're the seventh entry in the book. I'm just summarizing what's there.

You mean the part about toasting humans like skewers of meat isn't actually in the text?

That's part of my summary.

Tolemek turned the knob and eased the door open. He listened, then stepped inside, holding it for Sardelle. Clanks and thuds came from the front of the kitchen, but nothing except counters, oversized stew pots, and iceboxes was visible. He and Sardelle weaved past crates of potatoes, apples, and onions, as Tolemek headed away from the noise and voices up front. He found another door and escaped into the hallway without being noticed—until he turned and smacked into someone who had been about to enter the kitchen.

"Who—" the man got out before Tolemek rammed his palm into his nose.

The person flew backward, his shoulder slamming into the wall. Tolemek followed him, producing a rag from somewhere and pressing it to the man's nose. He flailed, trying to punch Tolemek, but the blows soon grew weak and ineffective. A few seconds later, the man's eyes rolled back into his head, and he slumped down like a rag doll. Tolemek caught him and removed a key ring Sardelle hadn't noticed from the man's waist—there were also a pistol and handcuffs there. Tolemek dragged the inert man down the hall, past three doors, then opened a fourth. A broom closet.

"I get the feeling you've broken into a lot of places in your life," Sardelle whispered.

"A few. I've also broken in *here* before."

Tolemek handcuffed the guard's wrist and looked around the closet for something secure to attach him to. Unfortunately, there weren't any pipes or rods or the like. He settled for chaining the poor fellow to the mop bucket. He waved to acknowledge the uselessness of the choice and said, "He sucked in enough of my inhalant that he should be unconscious for the next half hour."

Sardelle jammed the locking mechanism after they shut the door and walked away. It might buy them a little more time. Just in case collecting the sister wasn't a matter of a simple in-and-out. "You haven't told me your sister's name," she realized as they climbed stairs to the second level.

"Tylie." He stopped on the landing to listen and look in both directions. The slender windows on either end did not let in much light. A few oil lamps guttered on the walls, soot staining the old stone above each one. Only every third was lit. The rooms were close together up here, with unadorned solid oak doors every few feet. Each had a number hanging on it, but nothing else to identify the occupants.

By now, people ought to be up and about, doing morning ablutions and lining up for breakfast. Aside from the guard, they hadn't seen anyone in the halls. Maybe they served breakfast in bed here. Or breakfast locked behind one's cell door, anyway.

Tolemek trod softly down the hall, his lock-melting vial of goo in hand. A long-suffering moan came from behind one door, and Sardelle paused and touched her fingers to the wood. With her senses, she could tell the person was a confused forlorn man sitting in a corner, his legs pulled to his chest as he rocked back and forth. His mind seemed disturbed by more than his condition, and she thought some drug or another might account for the hazy thoughts.

A notion of setting all of these people free strode through her mind. But what good would that do? They wouldn't be able to escape or fend for themselves, not in this state, and she could scarcely set up a healer's tent at the base of the hill.

You can't help everyone.

I know. Still, Sardelle wondered if she might do some good in the half hour they had until that guard woke up.

You better help pirate boy, first. And you haven't asked me about the third organization that might have been responsible for blowing up the archives basement. It's even better than the last.

Does "better" mean more ridiculous sounding?

You know me well.

Tolemek stopped at the last door on the right and bent over the lock. Jaxi continued on as Sardelle walked toward him.

The Davaran Trinity, founded by three witches, swore to keep magic a secret through the centuries, knowing outsiders would fear them. They might be targeting you because you're openly striding around the city on a soldier's arm instead of hunkering in a thatched hut in the woods and tossing frog eyes and leeches into cauldrons.

The Davaran Trinity? Sardelle joined Tolemek in front of the door, where smoke was wafting from the lock. *That name sounds familiar.*

Yes, because none of the so-called witches in it had an iota of dragon blood in their veins. They thought they did and made all sorts of potions to inflict evils on people. Crazies like them are part of the reason there are so many unflattering images of sorcerers in people's minds.

Are you sure these were the most likely organizations in the book and not the least likely?

They were the only organizations started and made up of women. Only the Davaran Trinity is still rumored to be in existence today, or at least when that book was published. Fifty years ago, according to the creation date.

Just because we've only seen women doesn't mean they're not part of an organization that recruits both sexes, Sardelle pointed out.

Most of the other entities mentioned were brotherhoods or otherwise male-only orders. It seems men and women can't create secret organizations for clandestine purposes in unison.

We'll figure it out later.

Sardelle touched the door in front of them. "Are you sure this is the right room?"

"No," Tolemek said. "This is where she was last time, but it's been years since my visit—they forbade me to return after the last time, when I broke her out and stole her away to cure her... only to realize that wasn't within my powers." He scowled at the door, his fingers curling into a fist.

"I don't sense anyone inside."

Tolemek nodded, as if he had expected as much. "We'll have to sneak into the file room and look up her room number."

Sardelle wasn't aware that she made a strange face, but she must have, because he asked, "What?"

"I have a recent and awkward history with file rooms." She had been thinking about her attempt to convince Ridge, then Fort Commander Zirkander, that she was a legitimate prisoner in that awful mine, but Tolemek gave her a grave nod.

"I heard about the explosion in the archives building. If you need research done at a further point, you can ask me, and I'll do it for you." His expression grew wry. "My reputation may fade with time, but for now, it's quite effective at convincing people to leave me alone."

The offer surprised Sardelle, but she managed a, "Thank you," before he pushed open the door.

It revealed a dark room that smelled of paint, fresh paint. Odd. Had they moved the occupant, then painted the walls for some reason?

"You're right. There's nobody here." Tolemek sighed. The tiny arrow-slit window faced north, and it was too dim inside the room to see much.

A clatter sounded back in the direction of the stairs. "Careful, Moshi, you'll spill eggs all over me."

"Because you were in my way. Mind your own platter, you big oaf."

"Inside," Tolemek whispered, stepping through the doorway.

Sardelle entered after him. Something clanked, tipping onto the floor, and Tolemek grunted. Sardelle rushed to close the door, afraid the sound would have traveled down the hallway. She hoped the guards would think it had come from one of the other rooms.

"What are these?" Tolemek grumbled. "Paint cans?"

Sardelle created a soft orange ball of light that shouldn't shine too brightly to be seen from the hallway. She gasped in surprise at what it revealed. When she had been imagining a freshly painted room, she had assumed it would be of the same boring milky gray that adorned the stone walls in the hallway. But this...

Mouth agape, she turned slow circles, taking in the colorful fields, skies, lakes, mountains, and dragons painted all over the walls, ceiling, and even the floor. There must have been twenty dragons flying, striding, or swimming in the various scenes, all silver, all similar in features: the long tail, powerful torso, four legs with clawed reptilian feet, and wings familiar from cave paintings and illustrations of old, the figures magnificent even in the two dimensional form.

As beautiful as they were, something about seeing them here, now when Ridge had this mission to search for dragon blood, made an uneasy chill run up Sardelle's spine. The two quests were unrelated—the king shouldn't even know about Tolemek's sister—so they couldn't have anything in common, but it struck her as strange, nonetheless.

People have been painting dragons for centuries.

I know.

At least we can be sure the girl isn't a member of the Heartwood

Sisterhood. All the dragons would have spears through their hearts.

Thank you, Jaxi. You're very helpful. Sardelle touched one of the paintings, where the great dragon seemed to be gazing out of the landscape and into her soul. "This is incredible. I wouldn't have expected her—anyone in this privy hole—to have access to paints." She looked at Tolemek, wondering if he had known this artwork was here or not.

He was scowling down at the paint cans. "My father isn't a complete bear. He sent her paints and books. She always liked art."

"Was she always this—" the word that came to mind was obsessed, but Sardelle changed it mid-sentence, "interested in dragons?"

"Not as a little girl, but in her teenage years, yes. She had painted a couple of these the last time I was here."

Sardelle tore her gaze from that of the dragon. Tolemek was still staring at the paint cans. She sniffed, wondering if they were the source of the fresh paint she had smelled, but they didn't appear to have been opened yet.

"She's gone," Tolemek said numbly.

"Yes, but we can check the file room, and find out where they moved her. As you said."

He was shaking his head before she finished speaking. "She didn't get moved to another room. She was taken away. Why else would they be up here, preparing to paint over the murals? They probably *just* took her."

"You can't know for sure that they didn't move her to another room for some... administrative purpose." That sounded pathetic even as she said it. Obviously, his sister had been in the same room, one chosen with their father's approval, for years, for long enough to paint all of this. Why, indeed, would she be switched to another room after years in this one? "You believe they knew you were coming somehow?"

"Why else would she have been moved? Hidden?"

"I don't know, but maybe we should check that file room before making assumptions."

Tolemek stared at her for a moment, then nodded. "Yes."

He stepped over the paint cans and strode for the door, but stopped before his hand reached the knob. As with the rest of the room, the oak was covered in vibrant color. Tolemek was staring at... an image of himself. In the picture, he was clad in the sleeveless hide vest, shark tooth necklace, and spiky bracers he'd worn the first time Sardelle saw him, and the black ropes of hair hung about his face as they did now. A landscape unique to the door lay behind him, a dense tangle of jungle foliage such as one might find in Southern Cofahre or on the islands around the equator, perhaps even on Daguboor, the big continent in the Southern Hemisphere.

"Your wardrobe hasn't changed much over the years," Sardelle noted.

She was teasing and didn't expect the wide-eyed expression he turned over his shoulder. His bronze face had gone a few shades paler. "But it has," he whispered. "My hair was shorter the last time she saw me, and I wasn't wearing..." He looked thoughtfully toward the ceiling for a moment before deciding, "I had the shark tooth, but nothing else."

"Ah. There are seers among those with the gift, people who can sense what's happening, especially with close friends and loved ones, across hundreds or even thousands of miles."

"What about this?" Tolemek stepped back, revealing a portion of the door his body had been blocking, and pointed.

At the bottom of the picture, red paint spelled out, "Help me. They are taking me here."

* * *

Wan morning sunlight filtered through the camouflage netting the pilots had stretched over the fliers and onto the snow-dusted earth. Ridge watched the pattern of shadows and light on his gloved hand as he maintained a rigid single-armed push-up position.

"Seven," he said and lowered himself until his chest was an inch above the ground, then rose again.

"Seven?" Duck complained. "That was at *least* seventeen."

Duck, Ahn, and Apex were spread out in a circle, their bodies also in rigid push-up positions.

"We're not counting the ones we did on the other side," Ridge said. "Eight." He hated one-armed push-ups as much as the next person, but they made the regular ones seem easier than swigging beer, and the squadron had its athletics tests coming up next month. He would be remiss in letting training slide when they had time for it. And they had too much time, in his opinion. He hated sitting on his hands and *waiting*. They had moved the camp the day before, set up camouflage to hide the fliers, and were now back to waiting. "Nine. Ten. Eleven."

"Eleven?" Duck moaned. "Didn't you say we were only doing ten?"

"I don't remember announcing a number ahead of time. Twelve... you keeping up?" Ridge's own arm was starting to quiver, but what was new? He always ended up doing more than his body considered wise in these group exercise sessions. A squadron leader couldn't let himself look bad in front of the young pups.

"He's too busy complaining to keep up, sir," Apex said. "And it's rather pathetic considering *Ahn* isn't complaining."

Lieutenant Ahn's eyebrows were in danger of twitching, but she didn't respond.

"Ahn weighs eighty pounds," Duck said. "What's she have to complain about? Try putting a couple of machine guns on her back and see if that little arm can still do a push-up."

"*Little?*" This time her eyebrows *did* twitch.

"It's slender. I've seen you with your sleeves rolled up."

"It's proportioned. And I weigh more than eighty pounds."

Apex flexed his back. He might not complain, but his arm was quivering too. "Duck, did it ever occur to you to wonder why you have such a puny nickname, compared to Raptor?" He tilted his head toward Ahn.

"I assumed it was because of my swimming ability. I'm like a fish out there."

"Something we never would have known if you hadn't crashed your first flier into the harbor twice. And then *complained* about how poorly it handled."

"How about we all stop talking so we can finish this set and don't have to stay like this all day?" Ahn suggested.

Ridge smiled. Ever the practical one. "Thirteen," he announced and led the team in a few more to bring it to twenty.

Duck collapsed.

Ridge felt like collapsing, too, but he pushed himself to his feet and walked out of their little camp, intending to check the steppe and the foothills behind them. He halted before he had taken more than a step out from under the camouflage. An airship floated in the air to the south, its dark wooden body and gray balloon standing out against the pale blue sky. He backed up a few steps and watched it from a hole in their netting rather than from outside of it.

"Problem, sir?" Ahn came up to stand beside him and answered her own question with an, "Oh."

"They're more than two miles away and shouldn't be able to distinguish our camouflage hump from the surrounding foothills."

"But?" she asked, correctly assuming he would say more.

"But we'll pack everything up and ready the fliers. According to our latest intelligence, this isn't one of their flight paths, commercial or military."

"Think they're looking for us?"

Remembering the aircraft he had shot down—and the one Sardelle's sword had utterly destroyed—Ridge nodded. "They may not know who's here exactly, but they know an enemy has been flying through their skies."

"Will we move the camp again tonight?"

"We'll see."

The more they moved around, the more chance they would be spotted in the skies, if not by official military watchers then by shepherds wandering around with goat herds. Everyone was a potential spy here.

The airship turned, heading toward the mountains. They weren't coming straight toward the fliers, but on their new trajectory, they would pass within a half mile of the camp. The white-and-tan camouflage netting worked great at a distance, but the closer one came, the less natural it looked.

Ridge faced Ahn and the others—Apex and Duck had both come to peer out across the steppes too. "Prepare to fly. We'll hope they don't discover us, but if they do, we have to be ready."

"Ready to run, sir?" Ahn asked. "Or ready to fight?"

Ridge stuck his hand into his pocket and rubbed the back of his dragon statuette. None of his people appeared daunted by the idea of battling an airship, even with only four fliers, but it was the mission as a whole that he had to consider. Right now, the Cofah might *suspect* an Iskandian incursion, but they couldn't know for sure yet. The empire had many enemies, and most of them had flight technology. But if they left an airship riddled with machine gun fire, and if witnesses identified him and his team, their chances of escaping the continent would go down. Even if they did escape, Iskandia risked retribution.

"If they spot us, we'll run first, try to lead them up into the mountains—" Ridge waved toward the craggy peaks north of the steppes, "—and if they follow, we'll fight them there. If we can force them down on a high mountainside or in a deep canyon, it'll take them a while to hike back to an outpost to warn the rest of their people."

"Would it be better if... everyone died in the crash, sir?" Ahn asked.

She wasn't lobbying for that, he knew, but she was pointing out the most logical scenario. If there was no one to report back, the Cofah would have no way of knowing what had happened out here, and it might be days or weeks before they even found their downed aircraft.

"It would be better if we weren't discovered at all." Ridge gazed toward the approaching airship. "As to the rest, we'll figure it out if they follow us and we manage to take them down. That's not a given, especially if their airship has some of those unmanned craft to throw at us."

"Would it be considered evil if a person would rather shoot at Cofah airships than go back to doing push-ups?" Duck asked Apex as they walked away.

"It would be considered egotistical, perverse and possibly psychopathic."

"But not evil?"

Apex frowned at him before climbing into his flier. "You're lucky you received as noble a nickname as Duck."

Ridge gazed out at the airship and took his cap and goggles out of his jacket pocket.

He had a feeling they would be flying within the hour.

CHAPTER 9

H ELP ME. THEY ARE TAKING *me here.* The red paint strokes had been made hastily, with the last two words barely legible, a definite contrast to the precision of the murals.

"Wherever *here* is, it isn't anywhere around this part of the empire." Sardelle looked out the narrow window, toward the valley beyond, a valley cloaked in snow.

Tolemek was still staring at the painting, his fingers tracing the mural, his eyes searching. For more clues? "This could be anywhere. Well, not anywhere, but at least two continents and countless islands and smaller land masses." He pushed his hair away from his face; he looked like he wanted to tear it out.

"Not anywhere." Sardelle pointed at a rich purple cascade of bell-shaped flowers falling around a central stem. "This is a…"

Marsoothimum, Jaxi?

Yes. As a soulblade, Jaxi had traveled the world countless times with her previous handlers, and she had a memory that Sardelle never failed to envy.

"Marsoothimum," Sardelle said. "It's native to Daguboor and some of the islands around the northern horn. Some of this other foliage seems familiar too." *Know any of these other flowers, Jaxi?*

Just because I traveled the world, doesn't mean I ever had a handler interested in botany. Hektor used to eat flowers, but that's not the same thing.

"We can look them up," Sardelle said.

Tolemek stepped back. "I'll try to be optimistic and not think that all we've managed is to narrow things down to a continent. Or a lush greenhouse at any random point in the world."

"That's unlikely. We might be able to refine our guesses further later." Sardelle touched the three other flowers that were represented in enough detail to suggest they were real rather than random background creations. She tried to memorize them. If the marsoothimum was real, these other flowers should be too.

"I want to check the file room anyway," Tolemek said. "There might be a record of where they took her."

A clank sounded in the hallway, reminding Sardelle they weren't alone—and that there was an unconscious man in a downstairs closet who could wake up at any time. The two guards were the ones responsible for the noise, making their way closer as they delivered breakfast to the patients—or inmates, as she kept wanting to call them. A man in a nearby cell started singly loudly. The utterances piercing the walls were nonsense except that the word breakfast came out in every line. Judging by the indifferent attitudes of the guards, this was a common occurrence. Sardelle thought of trying to dig Tylie's location from their thoughts, but unless they were thinking about her, it would be hard to glean that information from their minds. They probably wouldn't have been told anyway.

Tolemek had his ear pressed to the door.

"They've both gone into a room if you want to try to sneak past," Sardelle said. It would be safer to wait until they were done serving breakfast, but that guard downstairs might wake up before then.

"Let's go." Tolemek slipped a leather ball out of his pocket and opened the door.

Sardelle walked into the hall after him. He slowed next to the open door—the obnoxious singing was coming from that cell— and glanced back at her before passing it.

"Can't he just eat without it being a dragons-cursed event every day?" one of the guards growled.

They were standing in front of the patient, feeding him by hand. A restraint jacket kept the man's arms secured around his torso. Sardelle nodded at Tolemek, and they slipped past the door.

They hadn't gone more than three steps when one of the guards said, "Who was that?"

Erg, he must have seen them out of the corner of his eye.

Sardelle flicked a hand, unfastening the patient's restraint jacket. The man lashed out, knocking the breakfast tray from one guard's hands and leaping onto the back of the other. She raised a gust of wind and blew the door shut, then disabled the lock as she had done below.

"Go, go," Sardelle urged, shooing Tolemek toward the stairs.

His face was grim. He knew it wasn't likely they would have a chance to spend much time in the files room now.

"If you don't care if they figure out who was breaking in, head for the files room," she said as they ran down the stairs. "I'll keep them off your back while you search."

Tolemek turned left at the bottom of the stairs, running toward the front of the building instead of back toward the kitchen. Sardelle shook out her arms, loosening her muscles as if she were about to jump into a physical battle, and readied her mind for what might become a large-scale confrontation.

The main hallway was still empty, but four people were working at desks in the front room that Tolemek charged into. He tossed his leather ball into the middle of them, then backed out. Sardelle almost crashed into him, but she had seen the ball work before and realized what he planned. She scrambled back into the hallway, knowing the smoky air that wafted out would affect them if they were too close.

"Who are those people?" someone shouted.

"Get them!"

Despite the order and the ensuing footfalls, nobody made it to the hallway. A thump sounded as someone bumped into a desk, staggered, and collapsed to the floor. The other three people slumped unconscious before making it two steps from their seats.

Sardelle took the moment to destroy the locks in other doors off the hallway. There were more offices, furnace rooms, and storage areas down here, so there weren't as many doors to deal with as on the floor above. Still, it took a few minutes, and Tolemek had already charged inside by the time she finished. He must have a way to extinguish his device once it had done its job, because the smoke had already cleared.

Someone in the room across the hall had heard the shouts from the admins and had already discovered he was locked inside. He banged at the locked door. There were more people in that room. It wouldn't take long for someone to grab an axe or other heavy tool to force his way out.

Sardelle joined Tolemek inside a storage area full of shelves and boxes adjacent to the main room. He had already found a lantern and was skimming the labels. There wasn't another exit, so they risked being trapped inside.

"Here." He grabbed a box that wasn't as dusty as the others and tore off the lid. He flipped through the files and yanked one out. Two seconds of reading was all it took before he started shaking his head. "Transferred by order of the emperor. Two days ago."

"The *emperor*?" Sardelle wouldn't have thought the emperor knew of Tolemek or his family's existence. His dominion was a hundred times more populated than that of her homeland, and in all the stories and histories, he had always been a far more distant figure than the kings of Iskandia.

"It doesn't mean he personally gave the order." Tolemek stuffed the file back into the box. "It could have been one of the thousand-odd peons authorized to carry out the law in his name. There's nothing about where she was sent." He looked like he wanted to kick over one of the stacks of boxes, but he settled for slamming the side of his fist against a wall and striding for the door.

The bang of a pistol echoed from the hallway, followed by the slam of wood against a stone wall.

"Someone found a way past my disabled door locks," Sardelle observed. It hadn't even taken an axe.

Tolemek poked his head into the hallway. They weren't far from the front door.

"Maybe there's still time to run for the exit," Sardelle whispered.

Tolemek jerked back inside at the same time as a gun fired again. A bullet smashed into the wooden doorjamb where his head had been.

"Maybe not," she amended.

"Guard the door," Tolemek said, slamming it shut. He locked it and shoved a heavy desk in front of it, then ran for the file room again, his hand dipping into his bag.

Concerned about what he was planning—so far he had proven he preferred non-fatal methods of dealing with people, but he was irritated now—Sardelle brushed across his thoughts. An image of an explosion flashed across the front of his mind.

"Uhm." She noted the four unconscious people in the main room with her, people whose only crimes were working in an inhospitable asylum. "You're not planning on bringing down the building, are you?"

"Just a part of it."

Footsteps thundered up the hall, stopping in front of their door. There were four people out there, and they were shouting for more to help them. The knob rattled.

Tolemek ran out of the file room, slamming the door behind him. "Can you make it so nobody can go out the front or through the kitchen for the next ten minutes or so?"

"I can try... so long as you're not blowing up the building in a way that people might be trapped and crushed inside."

His head tilted. "I'm not blowing up anything, simply removing a portion of the exterior wall."

That... wasn't what she had seen in his mind. "You were only *thinking* of blowing up the building?"

"That bit of fantasy might have crossed my mind, but, no, I'm not causing an explosion. Your sword is far better at that than I. Should I be offended that you were reading my thoughts?" His face grew a little sad, as if he knew she didn't trust him.

A dozen excuses popped into Sardelle's mind—it was one thing to snoop in another's thoughts and another to get caught doing it—but she admitted that she wasn't in the right here. "Yes, you should be. And I should be ashamed for doing so."

Guns fired in the hallway, and she dropped to a crouch, expecting bullets to plow through the wood. The oak was thicker than that though, and she made it to Tolemek's side without injury.

"Are you?" he asked.

"Am I what?" She was focused on the men in the hallway. One had an axe now.

"Ashamed."

"Yes. There are—*were*—a lot of rules about respecting people's privacy and not rifling through their thoughts. There are, admittedly, a lot of surface thoughts you receive simply by opening yourself up to those around you, but most sorcerers learn early on to block them out. It's amazing how tempted you are to break rules when there's nobody around to enforce them." An acrid stench reached Sardelle's nose. "Is that your work?"

"Yes. The doors?"

She lifted a hand and pushed her thoughts past the men knocking the hinges and doorknob off with their axe and to the front entrance. She broke the latch assembly so it would be stuck in the extended position. Such finesse was a little harder across a larger distance, and a twinge of pain started behind her eyes, but she managed to break the kitchen backdoor lock too. She would have a headache all day, but had doubtlessly needed the practice with fine-touch kinesis, anyway.

"Done," she said. "It's a good thing the windows are all too small to climb through." The idea of trying to break a hundred more locks made her brain hurt even more.

Tolemek led her into the file room, where a cold draft and a surprising amount of light greeted them. A large circular hole in the back wall now provided a window onto the snowy ridge beyond the building. The wall was more than six inches thick. Smoke wafted from the edges of the hole.

"You did that with a vial and an eye dropper?" she whispered, following him to the new exit.

"A flask and a specially treated wire brush, actually." Tolemek made sure nobody was waiting outside, then hopped through, landing in the snow. "I suggest we run."

Sardelle clambered through awkwardly, not wanting to touch the smoking edges with her hands, but took off at top speed as soon as she landed. They slogged through the snow, this time heading straight down the steep slope instead of bothering with the road.

"We'll have to steal horses," Tolemek said over his shoulder, checking on her and the looming towers of the asylum as well. "No trains in the station, and the guards down there are probably on their toes right now anyway, watching for vagabonds." He waved at the empty tracks running through the middle of the town.

"Not surprising." Sardelle sucked in large breaths of cold air. Plowing through the snow wasn't easy, and she stumbled more than once. "We might have to steal skis instead of horses. Or a dogsled."

"The main road into town has been cleared," Tolemek said dryly. "The tracks too."

"And where are we going with our stolen horses?" Sardelle was ready to return to Ridge, but she didn't know if Tolemek would want to beeline for the nearest library to look up those flowers.

He hesitated before answering her. "Wherever she is, we'll probably need airships or sailing ships—or fliers—to reach her."

The fliers may not be available.

What?

The camp has visitors.

* * *

Ridge sat backward in the cockpit of his flyer, a spyglass to his eye as he tracked the airship through the holes in the camo netting. The craft was still sailing along on the same course, heading toward the mountains, but there was a lot of activity on deck. The soft *thwump-thwump-thwump* of its propellers drifted down from a thousand feet in the air. Its massive balloon blotted out the sun and much of the sky.

"I think they've figured out we're in here," Ahn whispered.

All of the fliers were packed and ready, everything except the camouflage stowed for takeoff. They would have to abandon the poles and netting and take it as a loss. Their propellers weren't running yet—the noise would be a giveaway—but they could start them at a touch. The fliers' glowing energy crystals were covered, so the light wouldn't seep out. It shouldn't be noticeable from afar in the daylight, anyway, but they couldn't risk that something would glint or gleam. Even a spyglass reflecting the sun could be visible from a long distance away, and that would instantly tell those watching that something fishy was going on inside the mound tucked into the base of the foothills.

"Maybe not," Duck whispered. "They haven't stopped. They're still floating toward the mountains."

They hadn't stopped, but they weren't moving at anything near their full speed. And all those people running around on deck made Ridge nervous. He slid into the cockpit, fastened his harness, and rested his fingers on the propeller ignition button. He ought to give the order to fly right now. Only his knowledge that the greater mission was at risk of failing if the fliers were discovered stayed his hand. More than that, Nowon and Kaika would be at risk if the soldiers guarding the installation were alerted.

Still, he had a hunch they were in trouble if they didn't move.

"It's time," Ridge said. "We're taking them on."

"Are you sure, sir?" Apex asked.

He was going to have to be. Ridge mashed on the ignition switch, and his propeller ripped to life. "Follow me," he said, then remembered to tap the communication crystal to activate it. Otherwise his people wouldn't be able to hear him over the noise of their own propellers roaring to life.

He rolled toward the break in the camo net at the back, a gap large enough for the fliers to escape through. He almost knocked over a pole, but squeezed past without dropping the netting. The last thing he needed was to get his propeller tangled in his own camo.

"They're launching something," Ahn shouted.

"Aircraft?" Ridge asked, thinking of the unmanned fliers. He cleared the netting and jabbed the thruster switch. A steep slope rose right ahead of him, so there was no time for a runway-style takeoff.

Explosive, came a warning in his mind. *Get out of there.*

"Move," Ridge barked, not questioning the sword. "It's a bomb! Out, now!"

He was already in the air, angling up and away from the Cofah craft—he had wanted to pick up speed and come in from above rather than risking its guns from below, but he craned his neck, trying to spot the bomb.

"I hit the gods damned pole," Duck said.

"Don't worry about the netting," Ahn said. "Go straight up."

Cold wind scraped across Ridge's cheeks and whipped his scarf about, but he spotted his target. The bomb. He swooped toward the falling cylinder, firing and hoping. If the airship hadn't been so far above them, there never would have been time, but if he could catch it as it dropped through his sights...

He wasn't sure he hit it until it exploded with an ear-splitting boom. A fiery sun filled the sky above the camo mound, shrapnel flying in every direction. Ridge ducked as he flew through the explosion zone. Shards slammed into his windshield, and glass cracked. The camo netting itself had been close enough to the blast that it caught fire, and flames leaped up from what had appeared to be a mound of earth a moment before.

He wondered if he had been responsible for hitting the bomb or if the sword had helped him.

That was you, hero. Our flier got out, so I was worried more about what's going on up there now.

Our flier. Ridge supposed it was good that Jaxi, secured beneath the back seat, considered herself in the same predicament as he even if she might survive an explosion.

Might?

Knowing he would be a target to the airship above him, Ridge didn't take the time to respond. He banked and picked a weaving route through the air. He also checked on his people as he swooped about.

"Did everyone get out?" he asked, searching the sky. There was Ahn and Apex... "Duck?"

"Over here, sir." Duck sounded miserable, but he sounded alive too.

Ridge finally spotted him. He wasn't in the air—his flyer was bumbling and rolling across the snowy steppe, a portion of the netting tangled in his propeller. "Figure that out and get into the air, Duck."

"Yes, sir." So that was what mortified sounded like.

Ridge streaked into the air, knowing he would have to distract the airship for a while before his team could form up and fly north, as he had planned. His lack of preparedness embarrassed him. He should have known all along that the Cofah would spot them. What a mess.

A cannonball screamed over his wing, reminding Ridge to focus on the fight and worry about being embarrassed at their showing later.

Jaxi—what did you mean earlier? What is going on up there now?

He didn't get an answer. He would have to see for himself.

With his unpredictable zigging, he dodged three more cannonballs on his way up. He finally climbed above the airship, firing rounds at the big gray envelope as he rose. He had a look at the deck on his way up and tried to guess what might have been worrying Jaxi. He caught a glimpse of something in the back near the cabin—several large metallic somethings, but the balloon blocked his view before he could identify them.

Duck's flier had shaken free from the netting and found the air, more than a mile out over the steppes. It would be a couple of minutes before he circled around and got into the fight, but Ahn and Apex were rising behind Ridge, also evading the cannons firing in their direction.

"Keep the men on deck busy for now," Ridge said. "Remember, we don't want to bring it down until we reach the mountains. Finish your coffee and join us, Duck."

"Very funny, sir."

"It's my wit that keeps me in the general's good graces." Ridge left a few holes in the airship's balloon, then dove down to follow his own instructions. He aimed at the gunners manning the cannons, but even more, he wanted a look at those metal machines. Were they some kind of new weapon?

A circular disk spun out from an unusual launcher on the aft deck. Ridge avoided it easily, but it surprised him by exploding

in the sky. Even from twenty meters away, the force rocked his
flier. He kept control, but a cable moaned ominously.

"Watch the disks," he said. "They're bombs."

Ridge looped upward, then flipped and came down again,
this time gunning for the man hurling those disks. His bullets
strafed the deck, and his target ducked down behind the big
artillery weapon. Ridge shot at it, hoping he might cause one of
the disks to explode.

"The Cofah have been busy upgrading their weapons this
past year," Apex observed.

"They could have had the technology for a while," Ridge said,
not taking his eyes from the launcher he was targeting. "They're
probably trying things out at home before revealing them to us."

"Or maybe they just think we're so unimportant that
they don't bring their best equipment when they attack our
homeland," Ahn said.

"I don't have a problem with that," Duck said. "I have trouble
enough with our own equipment."

"So we see."

One of Ridge's incendiary bullets found the ammunition pile.
The explosion demolished the launcher and blew away a chunk
of the deck and railing.

Before he could congratulate himself, a grim-sounding Ahn
spoke. "Those are fliers. Manned ones this time."

"Four of them," Apex added.

Ridge banked, turning away from the smoke and fire he had
created, and coasted along the length of the airship, closer than
he should have dared—he wanted to see what his pilots had seen.
Yes, the metallic contraptions he had glimpsed earlier had wings,
bodies, and propellers. These must be the new Cofah fliers he
had heard about. They were in motion, too, rolling along the
deck, toward an opening in the railing. They were picking up
speed to take off, using the airship as a launching pad.

A number of Cofah warriors with rifles were racing toward
Ridge's side of the deck. He turned his belly toward them and
flew down and away. They weren't going to catch him gawking.
A few bullets streaked in his direction, but they missed as he

bobbed and dipped.

"Now's the time," Ridge said. "Head north. Let them think we're afraid of them."

"Afraid?" Duck said. "I can't wait to see what they can do."

"This from the man who got his propeller tangled in his own camo netting," Apex said.

"Well, I wasn't planning on challenging them personally. I thought I'd fly around, distracting them so Raptor can tear into them with her guns."

"What are you going to do to be that distracting?" Ahn asked, rare amusement in her voice.

"Haven't you seen me in the annual Harvest Show? I juggled pumpkins last year while flying with my foot."

"Yes, that was the *third* time you ended up in the harbor." Ridge took point, and the three other fliers fell into position beside and behind him. "We didn't put that one on his official record, since he was flying in some retired festival plane for a private businessman, one who will be carrying more insurance for future festivals, I understand."

"The flier was still perfectly serviceable after the event," Duck said. "And it wasn't as if I crashed. Water landings are a legitimate option. The passenger fliers that take the doctors around in the country do them all the time."

"Those fliers have floats instead of wheels." Ridge twisted to look behind him. The four Cofah craft were in the air and had formed a modified arrowhead formation, not dissimilar to that of Ridge's own squadron. He wondered if the empire had studied Iskandian techniques. Either way, the enemy fliers were coming after them, and it looked like the airship was giving chase too.

"A minor detail," Duck said.

"They're not as fast as us," Apex said. "They're falling behind."

"Ease back a bit. Let them think they can catch us. In fact..." Ridge fished in the emergency supply kit fastened to the side of his seat. He pulled out a flare, lit it, and tossed it into the foot well of the seat behind him. It would fall out as soon as he flew upside down, but in the meantime, a stream of gray-blue smoke poured from the end.

He wobbled his wings and started dipping, then pulling back up, as if he were having trouble controlling the flier.

"That's an act, right, sir?" Duck asked.

"Yup, pretending to be a little injured." By now, the snow-covered steppes had turned into snow-covered mountain slopes, with thick stands of evergreens blanketing the hillsides below. They flew over a craggy ridge, and more peaks rose up, along with numerous rocky cliffs and crevices. "I believe I'm going to have so much trouble that I nearly crash in that canyon."

"You want us to go in with you, sir?" Ahn asked.

"Keep flying and see how many of them take the bait. If they all swoop down after me, you're welcome to help." Ridge wanted a close look at one of those fliers. The intel he had heard placed some kind of fossil fuel as the source of their power, and he wanted to know if that was true, or if this dragon blood might be responsible for the manned Cofah aircraft too. This might not be the intelligence the king had sent Ridge's team to retrieve, but it was the kind *he* cared about. General Ort would care too.

"But if only three swoop down after you, you'll be fine?" Ahn asked dryly.

"Use your discretion, Lieutenant." Ridge was approaching the canyon, so there wasn't time for greater discussion. "Just don't lose track of the airship. Gunfire is irritating, but one cannonball could knock us out of the sky."

"Understood, sir," Ahn said, and the others responded with, "Yes, sir" as well.

"Time to make this look good," Ridge muttered.

Ridge jerked on the stick a couple of times, ducking and rising, like a man struggling to stay horizontal. In the end, he lost the battle and dipped toward the canyon, tailspinning as smoke streamed up behind him. Between rotations, he glimpsed the other fliers against the blue sky. One veered away from its formation to follow him.

He felt a little indignant at the lone stalker. Even injured, shouldn't the Cofah consider him, the infamous Colonel Ridgewalker Zirkander, dangerous? Maybe they didn't know he was the pilot. He wasn't in his usual craft, after all.

Does Sardelle find that arrogance appealing?

Even though the sword had been in his head earlier, Ridge flinched at the intrusion, nearly scraping his wings off on a cliff wall.

Sorry.

"It's fine," Ridge said, regaining his concentration and moving farther from the rocks.

"Sir?" Ahn asked.

"Nothing."

As he abandoned the tailspin and leveled off, he reminded himself that he could talk *silently* to the sword. He headed back the way he had come, hoping the Cofah flier would enter farther up the canyon. He sailed toward a shadowy ledge blown bare of snow; it might be dark enough to hide the bronze of his flier from someone sweeping in from the top, especially if that someone was looking up canyon. He slowed down and activated the thrusters, so he hovered over the ledge.

I keep the arrogance inside my head where it doesn't bother most *people,* Ridge informed the sword as he watched the blue slice of sky above the canyon. It made him a little nervous that he couldn't see the rest of his pilots, but he wanted to spring this trap, and he trusted the others to take care of themselves for a couple of moments.

Now that you have more people poking around in your head, you should watch your thoughts.

Thanks for the advice.

Here's some more: I'm not an expert on engineering, but their engines look to be near replicas of yours.

Bastards. Ridge barely kept the curse from spilling from his lips.

And they're powered by little vials of dragon blood.

Hells, are you sure? Where are the Cofah getting all of this blood?

I could only speculate, but I'm imagining a dragon working with them. Or imprisoned by them, though it's hard to imagine how humans could hold a dragon against its wishes. Their power, magically and physically is—

Ssh, Ridge thought. The Cofah flier had come into view. Ah, and there was a second. They weren't streaking recklessly into the canyon but following cautiously. They were wary of him after all. Good. That would make this more interesting.

Interesting will be when you realize the repercussions for shushing a soulblade, Jaxi grumped.

Focused on the fliers, Ridge barely registered the comment. The Cofah craft dipped into the canyon, flying in the direction he had been heading when he had disappeared from their view. They would look behind them, but it was hard to keep track of enemies on one's rear, especially enemies located lower than one's own flier.

When the two Cofah craft were committed to the search, flying side by side in the narrow canyon, Ridge switched from thruster to propeller power and took off after them. He stayed below them, putting himself in their blind spot, believing their inexperience would allow him to sneak up on them. Of course, he was gambling on inexperience due to the newness of the Cofah fliers. He couldn't let himself get too cocky or make too many assumptions.

His nerves jittered as he crept closer. Coming in for the kill, as his old flight instructor would have called it. Except this wasn't some slow-moving airship; these craft were much more maneuverable, something demonstrated by the way they glided up and around the contours of the snowy canyon, rock formations, bends, and sometimes dipping low to follow the frozen river meandering below, its banks just visible beneath the layers of white. Watching them was surreal; if the craft had been painted bronze instead of black, Ridge might have believed them to be from his own hangar.

His thumb massaged the trigger of the guns. Almost time.

The drumming of the propellers echoed off the canyon walls, his own melding with theirs. One of the pilots glanced back. Ridge didn't think the man saw him, but he must suspect a tagalong.

Ridge angled his nose up, toward what should be the engine area of one of the fliers, and fired. He pounded several rounds into the rear of the craft before both pilots reacted. His target pulled up, doubtlessly intending to fly upside down, make a loop, and come down behind Ridge. Having performed that maneuver countless times, Ridge knew it well and he followed, but let himself pummel the second flier with rounds on his way by.

The Cofah pilot's face was obscured by goggles and some kind of head wrap, but Ridge knew what the angry shaking of a fist meant. The man was yanking a pistol out as Ridge zoomed upward beside him. He better focus on his flying, or he would end up smashing into that rock formation coming up. Not Ridge's problem. He corkscrewed upward, flying parallel to the canyon walls for a moment, then angled away in time to fire at the first craft. Bullets ripped into the hull near the cockpit, and the pilot ducked, his head disappearing from view. A ribbon of smoke flowed into the air behind his craft. It should already be done for, but Ridge circled to come in again to make sure—and to make sure the other pilot hadn't figured out an effective attack, either.

He needn't have worried about that flier—its distracted pilot had flown it into the rock formation. Or maybe the damage Ridge had done on the way by had stolen its ability to steer. Either way, he only had one flier to finish off, and he cut in mercilessly, targeting the engine again. The smoke streaming behind the craft doubled. The pilot was trying to land, but there was nowhere safe in the rugged canyon. His wing clipped a cliff wall, and the craft spun out of control, then bashed against the cliff again and tumbled to the snowy floor.

"Sir, the airship is veering away, but we're having trouble with our—" Ahn grunted, cursed, and resumed, her voice tense. "If you have any suggestions on how to deal with the rockets, we'd appreciate it, sir. Duck is—" the screech of some projectile whistling near her cockpit drowned out the rest of the words, and she didn't speak again.

"Ahn?"

Ridge zoomed for the top of the canyon, needing to see what was going on up there. Rockets? What rockets?

"Ahn, give me your status when you're able. Or Duck or

Apex." He kept his voice calm, but their silence filled him with anxiety.

He twisted in his seat to look in all directions as he neared the top of the canyon. If he had dealt with two fliers, and the others were having trouble with one, that left one unaccounted for.

As soon as he crested the lip of the canyon, he spotted it. It was flying along the rim and zipped by so close, it almost gave him a haircut. The other pilot jerked in his seat, as surprised to see Ridge as Ridge was to see him. They were heading in opposite directions, and Ridge banked to turn back toward the other flier without hesitation. He expected the Cofah pilot to do the same, to want a fight with him, especially if he hadn't seen what happened to his comrades in the canyon, but the man kept flying in the direction he was already going. Ahead of him, the three Iskandian fliers were playing cat-and-mouse with the other Cofah craft, weaving in and out around a pair of craggy mountain peaks. Ridge couldn't understand how one lone enemy flier could be giving his people so much trouble, but he gunned his flier to gain ground on the craft that was now ahead of him. His people were in the sky still; that was enough for now. He would get the news later.

The pilot ahead of him jerked his arm and fired something large, much larger than a bullet or even a cannonball. The sleek oblong projectile leaped into the sky with such power, that a recoil coursed through the craft, making it shudder and buck. For a moment, the pilot struggled to bring his flier under control again. Ridge couldn't understand what he had been firing at— the four craft darting around the peaks were too far ahead to hit—but he arrowed in, hoping to take advantage of the pilot's brief struggle. A few more seconds, and the Cofah flier would be in range...

But the large projectile did the impossible. It curved off its trajectory, banking in the sky like an aircraft. By now, Ridge ought to expect the unexpected from these dragon-blood powered contraptions, but he found himself gaping in stunned disbelief anyway. Until the projectile—the *rocket*—arced a full hundred and eighty degrees and spun through the sky toward him.

"Anyone want to enlighten me on these new Cofah weapons?" Ridge asked, nudging the nose of his craft to alter his course.

"If you haven't seen one yet, be glad," Duck said, his voice quick, almost breathless.

"I'm seeing one now. It's heading right for me and—" The rocket was adjusting course to keep him in its sights—if projectiles even *had* sights—and it had already closed half the distance. "Talk later," he said, knowing he'd need his full concentration.

"Yeah," came Duck's response, grim and full of understanding.

Ridge made a more abrupt correction to his course this time, pitching downward. The canyon was still running along the craggy hills beside him, but he didn't know the terrain and didn't want to get himself stuck with a rocket on his butt. He headed straight for the ground, as if he meant to crash. He kept one eye on the terrain and one on the rocket, which was tilting toward the ground, too, toward him.

He brought his nose up before he hit the trees, though he came close enough that the air from his passing knocked snow off the boughs. The rocket arrowed toward him, its nose aimed straight at the front of his craft. The trees ended, and he dropped even lower, skimming along rock and snow. The rocket filled his vision, its black snub-nose as appealing as a viper's fangs.

Ridge waited until the last second, timing it... timing it... and jerked the stick to the side.

The rocket tried to adjust at the last second, too, but it wasn't quite fast enough. It darted past Ridge's wing, so close he could have read the model number engraved in the side if it hadn't been moving so fast. He expected it to hit the ground—that had been the whole idea—but he didn't expect the cacophonous boom that filled the air, pounding at his eardrums even as the shockwave pounded his craft.

His flier spun out of control, the tail flipping over the nose twice, a wing cracking against the ground. Ridge was jerked around in the cockpit like a puppet on strings. His head slammed against the side, his leather cap offering poor protection. If not for the harness, he would have been thrown free. He almost wished he had been. He tried to regain his senses, to recover somehow and get the flier into the air again—or at least bring it to a stop before it destroyed itself, but the lip of the canyon loomed before him. He'd been flying so close, and he had turned in that direction... He was going in if he couldn't bring the craft to a stop. And it was a long fall to the bottom.

Suddenly, his flier slowed and stopped striking the ground. It righted itself and rose into the air as if someone had snatched it from its mad tumble. Ridge knew that wasn't *his* doing, but he was so disoriented that he couldn't guess what was happening. He wasn't even positive he was alive.

The flier came to a halt and floated over the lip of the canyon, the ground on one side and a fall of two hundred feet on the other. He hovered there. He hadn't activated the thrusters, had he?

My apologies. I thought your maneuver would be sufficient. I didn't realize the projectile would explode.

Jaxi? Ridge touched his head, wincing at a lump already swelling beneath his cap. There was blood dripping down the side of his face too.

Are there other swords that speak into your mind?

I don't think so. But I can barely remember my name right now, so I'm an unreliable source. He twisted to look behind him, looking for the spot where the rocket landed. It wasn't hard to find. A huge crater scarred the ground, with trees uprooted and thrown free all around the circular depression. He was lucky to be alive.

Remembering that he hadn't shot down that flier before it launched its weapon, he jerked his gaze to the sky. *Where's the other pilot? The Cofah?*

His flier fell into the canyon.

Ridge, his mind still a knot of jarred confusion, could only ask, *What?*

I should say his engine exploded, and then his flier fell into the canyon as a result of that. I wasn't sure I could do that—dragon blood isn't flammable, as I found out, but that oily stuff you put in the engines—what do you call it?—that is flammable. Very flammable. If swords could cackle, Jaxi did.

We call it oil. Ridge slumped. His head and body ached and he owed his life to a sorcerous sword. Not his skill or cleverness or… anything.

Remembering the rest of his people, who were also facing rockets, Ridge sat up straight. Self-flagellation would have to wait for later. *Can you help the others?*

A second explosion shook the mountains before Jaxi responded. An orange blaze lit the sky like a small sun. Two bronze Iskandian fliers flew out of the explosion, heading in his direction. His fist clenched. Good. But the third? Where was the third? He didn't see the Cofah craft, either. A small comfort if he had lost a squad member.

"Nice shot, Raptor," Apex said.

"Thank you," Ahn said. They both sounded exhausted. Harried.

"Duck?" Ridge asked.

"I'm here, sir," Duck said. "Just escorting that Cofah flier into a nice mountainside back here. That black paint makes the hull look real good all smashed into the snow. Not sure that goat appreciated us a-visiting, though."

"Visiting," Apex said. "There is no grammatical reason to add extra letters or syllables to the word."

"After what we just went through, you're lecturing me on my word-making?" Duck's craft finally came into view, flying out from behind the mountain.

"The goat asked me to."

Jaxi, can you lower me to the ground? I need to see if this craft can be made airworthy again. I'm assuming I'd drop right out of the sky and into that canyon without your assistance. His sudden ability to hover without thrusters would be difficult to explain to the others as well.

Correct.

Thank you for your help, he added as his mangled flier floated to a flat stretch of ground and settled onto its wheels. Lopsidedly.

Sardelle would have been weepy and inconsolable if you'd died. I probably should have helped earlier, but these mechanical contraptions are beyond my experience. It's also possible your comrades would have found it suspicious if the enemy craft spontaneously combusted before their eyes.

Possible, yes.

"Your flier isn't looking good, sir," Duck said. "My wing was clipped, too, and I'm a little wobbly. Should we land or try to catch the airship?"

"Is it still in sight up there?" From the ground, Ridge couldn't see over the trees. "I was too busy crashing to see what it was doing."

"Last I saw it, it was flying behind that peak over there. It probably kept going. So much for crashing it in here."

Ridge sighed. So much for this whole mission. He should have taken his people's role more seriously from the beginning. But how could he have anticipated these new aircraft and weapons?

"Sorry, sir," Ahn said. "We should have split off and someone should have come to help you when we saw we only had one on our butts, but that one fired that crazy rocket..."

"Each of their fliers was loaded with two rockets," Apex said. "Ahn discovered that her sniper rifle was ineffective for destroying them, but that the machine gun works. For the record, Duck and I tried to discover that, too, but our aim was imprecise."

"My aim was perfectly precise," Duck grumbled. "It's not my fault the rocket kept moving out of the spot I was aiming at."

"Find places to land," Ridge said. "We'll run checks and see who's damaged and how much. I'm afraid this flier might not be airworthy again, not without an engineer and a box of spare parts." Neither of which they had out here. He cursed softly. How was he going to get all of his people out if they were down a flier?

"Yes, sir."

Ridge unfastened his harness and climbed down. His legs were shaking after the crash, so he was glad he had a moment to compose himself before the others joined him. He removed his cap and goggles and slumped against the side of the craft. An icy wind blowing off the mountaintops batted at his scarf. He shivered, his body slicked with cold sweat, as if he had run a marathon instead of simply sitting in a chair up there.

After the others landed, the buzz of propellers faded from the mountains. He considered the sun, hoping it would drop quickly up here and that his people would have the darkness of night to hide them while they did repairs. That airship, and possibly many of its friends, would be back before long.

The airship hasn't left completely.

Ridge straightened immediately. *What? Where is it? Is it coming this way?* He opened his mouth, ready to order his people back into the air and already feeling a surge of anguish that he might not be able to follow them.

It's heading west, but it's leaving a message.

A message? Ridge thought of the rockets. Could the airship be equipped with launchers too? Just because it hadn't used them on their first pass didn't mean it didn't have them.

It's a literal message. Interesting how a sword could make its telepathic words as dry as someone could with a voice. *Might want to climb a tree.*

Ridge didn't feel like climbing anything, except maybe into a bed, but he didn't want to miss whatever lovely message the Cofah had for him. He found an aspen tree with most of its trunk bare and only the snow-covered branches at the top obstructing the sky, creating a latticework he could see through. He unfastened his belt, encircled the trunk with it, and looped the ends around his hands and gripped them. With his boots braced against the trunk, he slid the belt up a couple of feet at a time, his legs following. As he advanced toward the treetop, his movements shook the thin branches overhead, and clumps of snow pelted his shoulders and head.

You could have just told me what the message said, Ridge thought, though he didn't know if the sword would be listening.

Yes, I could have floated you fifty feet into the air, too, but would you have an answer when your people asked how you got up there to read it?

They're not here yet. He wasn't sure where they had landed, but there were limited spots among the trees.

Yes, they are.

"Whatcha doing, sir?" Duck called up.

But by now, Ridge had climbed high enough to see the sky to the west. The airship was a mere speck on the horizon, and the message it had left in smoke was already being blown apart by the wind. He could still read it, though, and it made him drop his head to his chin, a great weariness filling him.

Your spies are dead. Leave or you're next.

CHAPTER 10

SARDELLE AND TOLEMEK SLOGGED ACROSS the snow, cloaks pulled tightly around their bodies and hoods tugged low over their heads. Night hugged the mountains, and after traveling all day, they both needed sleep. After Jaxi's warning, Sardelle had wanted to fly back to Ridge's camp with all speed possible, but they'd had little choice but to return the way they had come: first on train, then on horseback, and finally on stolen snowshoes when the drifts grew too deep for the horses. Jaxi was directing them to the new camp, where the pilots were doing repairs as quickly as possible so they could move before the Cofah returned. Sardelle worried she and Tolemek—who had scarcely said three words since leaving the asylum—would arrive only to find out the others had moved on.

They're still there. I'm helping Mr. Cranky fix his flier.

Mr. Cranky? That couldn't be Ridge.

He's not cranky with his troops, but he's cranky with me. I'm not sure he appreciates my comments in his head, even though I did save him from falling into a canyon yesterday.

Is it the fact that you're commenting that he doesn't appreciate or the fact that your comments are sarcastic and frequently exasperating? Sardelle was starting to regret initiating telepathic communication with Ridge. She hadn't realized Jaxi would take it as an invitation to chat with him at every opportunity.

Please, I'm only infrequently exasperating. You can't believe the restraint I exercise. I could comment on everything you people do. As to the rest, if you didn't want me to chat with him, you shouldn't have left me in his flying contraption.

"Are you sure we're going the right way?" Tolemek stopped on the snow-socked hillside, gazing up at the mountains fencing them. They had been on a trail at one point, but Jaxi had assured Sardelle this was a shortcut.

"We're close to their camp," she said.

"That didn't quite answer my question, did it?"

"Jaxi is certain we're going the right way."

Tolemek grunted and continued up the slope. Sardelle caught the scent of woodsmoke on the breeze. She hoped that meant they were close, but wondered if Ridge would allow fires when enemy airships might be about.

They're using the flames to melt pine pitch to use in their repairs. It's extremely primitive. Ridge did not find it helpful when I informed him thusly. Perhaps the pirate scientist can help them come up with a superior glue.

Sardelle was beginning to see why Ridge might be cranky with Jaxi. She and Tolemek crested a ridge, and she expected a campfire to come into view, but she saw nothing but trees, a canyon in the distance, and a strange crater. Ah, wait. There was a hint of magic in the air.

I'm camouflaging them from anyone who might happen by.

Does Ridge know?

It's the reason he's risking the fire. I'm being very helpful. I told him I could have camouflaged his camp before if he had only asked. That netting they were using was troublesome when they had to leave. A far inferior product to what a sorceress can craft with her mind.

Ridge doesn't know what your abilities are, Sardelle reminded Jaxi. *And he's being careful with our secret.*

There are only the two pilots that don't know about you. Perhaps it would be useful to bring them into the fold, so we can use our power openly to help them.

Perhaps so. I'll discuss it with him. Sardelle thought Ridge trusted all of his pilots, but she didn't know Duck or Apex well yet, and was reluctant to simply walk up and inform them she was a sorceress.

Tolemek stopped. "I… sense something out there." He gave her a curious look.

"It's the camp. That's good that you detected Jaxi's handiwork."

Not that good. It makes me doubt my touch. Am I growing old?

Ancient. But you shouldn't be surprised. You said yourself he has a lot of innate talent. It's a shame we didn't find the sister. I'm curious about her.

Aren't you going to keep looking for her?

Yes, but it sounds like we need to help Ridge and his team first.

Jaxi had summarized the aerial battle, as well as the message the airship had left in the sky. The fact that the Cofah had all of this dragon blood and were using it to build weapons that would inevitably be used on the Iskandians… It was disturbing. This wasn't just about helping Ridge. Her whole continent was in danger.

Between one step and the next, the view changed. What had appeared to be nothing more than trees turned into a cleared area with two fliers in it. Two others hunkered behind a copse of aspens farther back. They appeared fine, but the closer two fliers had black tarry spots over their bronze bodies and patches on the wings. Dozens of dents and scratches marred the hull, and the number of broken branches and pine needles carpeting the surface suggested the propeller had recently doubled as a wood chipper.

In the shadows, Lieutenant Ahn leaned against a stump with a rifle cradled in her arms. Sardelle hadn't noticed her at first, but had a feeling Ahn had noticed *her* hundreds of meters away. The two other lieutenants were standing by a large fire, one adding branches and one stirring the contents of a makeshift pot—was that a tin Cofah helmet? Ridge was straddling the most damaged flier, and he waved a pitch-covered stick at her when she looked at him.

"Tolemek," he called. "Do you have any interesting goos that could help with repairs?"

"Possibly," Tolemek said. "I'll take a look in a moment." He drifted over to Ahn first, giving her a hug and sharing a few quiet words with her.

Apex was on his way to gather another load of firewood. He glared at them, but didn't say a word.

Sardelle knew she shouldn't distract Ridge with secret conversations, but, remembering the way he had teased her about helping Tolemek first when they'd both been knocked down, she touched his mind with a question. *Should I be jealous that you're more excited to see him than you are to see me?*

No, because that's not the case. It's just that I can't leap from my flier and smother you with kisses while everyone is watching. Also, I might get pitch in your hair if I tried. His humor sounded tired and forced. He was weary, but there was more bothering him. The loss of the two captains must weigh heavily on him. Maybe he felt responsible in some way.

"You didn't find what you sought?" Apex asked, walking back into camp with a couple of big branches. He addressed Sardelle instead of Tolemek.

"What we sought had been moved," Sardelle said.

Ridge finished working on the flier, at least for the moment, and climbed down. "Apex, that's enough wood. Everyone, let's have a quick meeting around the fire."

Sardelle wouldn't have minded sitting down after the long trek through the mountains, but the camp lacked seating unless one wanted to climb up into one of the cockpits. Tolemek and the pilots gathered around the flames. Sardelle resisted the urge to lean against Ridge's arm, instead standing a couple of feet behind him.

"If the Cofah can be believed, Captains Nowon and Kaika are dead," Ridge said.

"If they can be believed?" Ahn asked. "You think they were lying, sir?"

"They were precise with their message—two spies—so I think they found our men, but… it's possible they're holding them for questioning and that they're not dead yet."

Ahn nodded grimly.

"If there's a possibility that they're alive, I don't want to leave them in there." Ridge looked at Sardelle for a moment. Did he think she could answer as to this possibility? Her senses couldn't extend more than a few miles. Even Jaxi probably wouldn't be able to see all the way to the city or outpost where they were being held. "There's also the original mission," Ridge went on. "If we leave now, having lost the cargo we were supposed to deliver *and* take home again…" He didn't mention the colonel he had left on a road by the sea, but that had to be in his mind as well. "If we leave now, then this entire mission was for nothing."

"But we've learned some good intelligence, sir," Duck said. "All about this dragon blood and what it can do."

Ridge grunted, clearly not impressed by this tiny snippet of information.

"If we continue with the mission, we may end up facing a dragon," Sardelle said. "All of this blood must be coming from somewhere."

"Maybe Tolemek has some nice dragon-slaying potion in his kit," Ridge said.

Tolemek snorted. "Lizard-slaying, maybe."

"What I want to know," Apex said slowly, his eyes toward Tolemek, "is why he wasn't surprised by the revelation of Nowon and Kaika's death—or capture. Whatever it turns out to be."

Because Jaxi had told Sardelle about it the day before and she had told Tolemek. But she couldn't explain that in a logical, believable way to the pilots who didn't know about her or Jaxi.

Tolemek raised his eyebrows. "After three days of traveling, I am too weary to react to much of anything."

Ahn, standing arm against arm with Tolemek, narrowed her eyes at Apex.

Jaxi told us, Sardelle told Ridge. She wouldn't have shown a visible reaction, either, but Apex hadn't been watching her, only Tolemek.

I gathered. Ridge spread a placating hand. "It doesn't matter. What matters is what we do next."

"Wait, sir." Apex raised his own hand, palm spread. "It *does* matter. We haven't talked about it, but don't you find it suspicious that those Cofah airships were waiting for us when we first flew onto the continent? And then that watchtower knew to search the skies for us."

Duck snapped his fingers. "That's right. They've been all over us like ants on fried chitlins since we got here. How did they know we were coming?"

"It has occurred to me that someone may have leaked information about our mission," Ridge said, "but I don't see how it could be Tolemek, since he didn't know anything about it until the afternoon before we left. The news couldn't have traveled here any faster than we carried it, so it would have had to have been sent ahead of time by someone else who had knowledge of the king's plans."

"Unless the news traveled by sorcerous means," Apex said.

Several people shifted uneasily and frowned at him. The statement made Sardelle uneasy, too, and she waited to see if Apex would look at her. Had he figured out what she was? He was supposed to be an academic. Was he observant? Someone who had deduced that she wasn't the archaeologist Ridge had described her to be?

Apex *did* give her a long look, but when he pointed, his finger extended toward Tolemek. "I've been reading up on some of the alchemical formulas he's made, and while he doesn't publish the ingredients or his methods—" he scowled as he said this, as if it were some crime, and maybe it was some academic faux pas these days, "—I am extremely skeptical that some of his potions could be viable without some sort of otherworldly influence."

Ahn's fingers curled, as if she was thinking of plowing a fist into Apex's nose, but she didn't say anything. Maybe because she knew Apex was right. Sardelle had suspected Tolemek had some dragon blood at their first meeting, and Jaxi had confirmed that suspicion early on. Oddly, Tolemek himself had never suspected until Jaxi had informed him.

"I thought your specialty was archaeology, Apex," Ridge said quietly, "not alchemy."

"It doesn't take an expert to sniff out fishy science."

"Wait," Duck said, "are you saying Deathmaker is a witch?"

"Witches are women, aren't they?" Tolemek murmured to Ahn. He sounded more amused by the accusation than worried about it. He probably thought he could handle Apex, no matter what came up.

"You're asking me?" Ahn muttered. "I don't know the details."

Sardelle could have explained the correct terminology, but she didn't want to call attention to herself, not when this was the topic.

"We'll keep an eye on everything," Ridge said. Nothing about an eye on *Tolemek*. He must truly believe his pirate scientist wasn't to blame. His reasoning had been logical, but maybe he had someone else in mind. "In the meantime, I want your opinions on the mission. I feel I have to carry on with it, but if two of our elite troops were captured, there's a possibility we might fall to the same fate. I'll ask for volunteers. Anyone who's not comfortable going can wait out here. Or fly back with the information we have. Duck's right; what we've learned does need to make it back to the general."

"I'll go," Duck said. "I thought you were picking us for this possibility all along."

"I was," Ridge said.

"Then what're you asking for volunteers for? We're with you, sir." He waved at Ahn and Apex.

Ahn nodded once. Apex was still glaring at Tolemek.

"Is *he* going?" Apex asked.

"He and Sardelle have unique talents that will be extremely useful if we're sneaking into a highly guarded facility, especially if that facility is on the alert because of the failure of our first team. They know we're out here. They'll be ready for us."

Sardelle was glad he hadn't asked for the details of the incursion into the asylum. They might have gotten in and out, but she couldn't imagine anyone calling that smooth. An image of that guard coming to and running down the hallway with the mop bucket chained to his wrist came to mind.

"Unique talents, sir? Like what?" Apex asked.

Ridge looked into Sardelle's eyes, a question there, though he didn't form any thoughts in his mind.

Guessing what the question was, she did it for him. *You want to tell them?*

Do you object?

I think it's going to come out anyway, if we're sneaking in together. I'll be hobbled if I have to worry about not letting them know.

"Magic," Ridge said.

Apex's expression was somewhere between vindication and betrayal. "You *knew*, sir?" He flung his hand toward Tolemek.

"That Tolemek's potions are witchy?" Ridge asked. "No, I just figured that was science and engineering. I was actually referring to Sardelle. I didn't bring her along because she's a good history student."

All of the stares leveled in Sardelle's direction made her uneasy, but she kept her chin up and tried to look wise, helpful, and not particularly witchy, since they all considered that something vile.

"I thought she was here because she'd be better at keeping your bump stick warm at night than Colonel Therrik." Duck rubbed his head. "Are you saying she's... a witch?"

"A sorceress actually," Sardelle said. "Witches tend to be poorly trained, often self-taught, and sometimes completely bogus insofar as having an actual aptitude for magic. I was formally trained." She decided not to volunteer the how and where, since that would take some time to explain.

"You *knew*, sir?" Duck whispered. "And you're still..." He groped in the air, and Sardelle waited to see if the term "bump stick" would come up again. She hadn't heard that one before. Amazing how much the slang for such things changed in three hundred years. "Or is that all an act? Are you two pretending to be a couple, and you're really—" His fingers flexed in the air again. The poor kid was having trouble finding a piece that would fit into his puzzle. "Does the *king* know? Are you *spies*?"

"If Colonel Zirkander is a spy, then I'm a spotted tiger shark," Apex said.

"Your confidence in my ability to suss out information on the sly is disappointing, Apex," Ridge said.

"It's not the sussing I'm questioning, sir; it's the not talking and joking about what had been sussed." Apex wrinkled his brow. "That didn't make sense. I'm as befuddled as Duck usually is, right now." He looked at Tolemek and Ahn. "But I see I'm the only one. Once again Deathmaker seems to already have this information. And, Raptor, you don't look surprised, either."

"I was extremely surprised on a night a few weeks ago," Ahn said.

Apex shook his head and stumbled away from the fire, mumbling something about firewood.

"I'll help," Duck said and jogged after him.

Sardelle touched the back of Ridge's hand. *Is it wise to let the two of them go off together?*

"They'll figure out what they think and if they want to go with us. Each of them may be useful, but I wasn't lying earlier. Someone *should* get this information back to Iskandia. On the chance..."

"We fail utterly?" Tolemek asked.

Ridge shrugged.

"I'm not failing before I find my sister. I don't know why they've moved her, but if the message she left me is true, I know they didn't simply send her back to my father's home. She's in danger because of me, and I'm not going to die in some forsaken wilderness when she's waiting for me to help her."

"Does that mean you don't want to come on this mission?" Ridge asked. "You and your tools would be useful, but it's not your quest. I understand that."

Tolemek looked down at Ahn. She wasn't whispering in his ear or making any facial expressions that suggested she would be disappointed if he didn't come, but he may have seen something there that Sardelle didn't. "I'll go," Tolemek said.

"Good. Ahn?"

"Yes, sir. I'm in."

Ridge gave Sardelle his tired smile. "I hope you're still in too."

"Yes, but can we talk for a moment?" She clasped his hand—and found some of the sticky pitch he had mentioned earlier.

His smile flattened with I-told-you-so wryness.

Tolemek and Ahn had already moved away from the fire, and the two lieutenants were talking—their voices occasionally rising in anger or exasperation—off in another direction. Sardelle didn't have to lead Ridge far to find a private spot.

She dusted snow off a log, sat down facing the fire, and unfastened the snowshoes. Icy air whispered off the mountaintops, licking at her skin, and she pulled her cloak tight. She had a trick for heating blankets, usually reserved for sick patients, that she might have to employ the next time they had a sleep break. Whenever that was. Dawn was only an hour off, and

Ridge would want to be gone before the sky brightened. There was a Cofah airship that knew where they were, and it would have had time to reach a base and gather reinforcements by now.

Ridge sat on the log and put an arm around her. For a moment, Sardelle allowed herself to feel amused that Duck had thought their romance had been an act. Everything else was an act. This was the one true thing. Or was it? Would she truly be considering leaving him if she cared for him? She recaptured his free hand and clasped it in hers. Yes, it was *because* she cared that she was considering it.

Really? I thought it was because you were being cowardly and didn't want to face that secret organization.

I have no problem facing organizations. I just don't want to ruin his career. His life.

Yeah, yeah, why don't you ask him what he thinks about your career-ruining presence and let him decide for himself?

That's... actually somewhat logical, Jaxi.

You needn't sound so surprised. I've been witness to thousands of matings.

Thousands? Either your former handlers were extremely randy, or you have a voyeuristic streak.

If swords could smile, Jaxi did.

Ridge's gaze had drifted toward his flier—he probably needed to get back to the repairs. "Is there something you were wanting to talk about? Or has your time away with a boring and introspective pirate left you aching for someone fun to cuddle with?"

Sardelle thought about defending Tolemek, but he hadn't been a very talkative companion. She might believe Ahn didn't find him boring—she wasn't that talkative, either, so maybe they enjoyed spending time together in silence—but Sardelle preferred Ridge's playful teasing.

"Can we trust them?" Sardelle tilted her chin toward the arguing lieutenants. "Or can *I* trust them, I should ask. I know they won't plot against *you*."

"No, their military indoctrination should keep them from plotting hijinks against a superior officer."

"Hijinks aren't what I'm worried about."

"I don't think they'll risk my ire out here. Once we get back... Enh, that'll probably be the least of my problems when I get back. If I don't get court-martialed for kicking out Therrik, I'll probably get demoted for tarring up the mission."

"How are you responsible for what's gone wrong?" Sardelle asked. "Was that colonel likely to make the captains more effective?"

"Not from what I gathered, but he'll be back there, slobbering all over the king's ear while I'm out here, underestimating Cofah pilots and nearly crashing into canyons." He lowered his voice. "Your sword saved my life."

"I know. She's quite pleased with herself."

"I feel like an idiot. I was overly confident. I wasn't even thinking about the potential of special dragon-blood weapons when I saw those Cofah fliers. And after what we've already seen, I should have been. But I assumed the pilots would be green compared to my people—compared to *me*." His hand flexed and he made a disgusted noise. "Apex is right in that the Cofah seem to have an uncanny amount of data on our whereabouts. I don't know if there's a snitch somewhere or if it's something else they can do with that blood, but I have no reason for overconfidence out here." He scuffed at the snow with his boot. "Sorry, we were supposed to be talking about your concerns, not my... The dragon usually gets this."

Sardelle blinked. "The what?"

"You know, my little figurine."

"You, ah, talk to it?"

"Not *to* it," Ridge said, "but I pace in circles and talk to myself."

"While you're holding it."

"Yes." He squinted at Sardelle. "I've told you before, this isn't that odd. Not any odder than what other pilots do. The job makes us a little crazy. All of us."

"Of course. I understand. And I'm not mocking you." She squeezed his hand, but couldn't help adding, "Do they have asylums in Iskandia these days? Or is that only in Cofahre?"

"I think so, but it wouldn't be within your rights to admit me, unless you were my wife. Even then, I think I'd have to do more than get caught talking to myself."

Unless she was his wife... He was joking, but the words made her pause and dwell on the possibility. Did he want that? Did she? She shook her head. She had better bring up the first discussion first, though commenting on his jokes was easier. "Even if you're rubbing your dragon while you're talking to yourself?"

"Yes. Er." His brow crinkled. "We're still talking about the statuette, right?"

"*I* was."

"Good. Yes. Me too."

She snorted softly.

Ridge leaned closer and kissed her on the cheek, his lips warm against her chilled skin. "Thank you. I don't know if it was your intent, but you've taken my mind off glum thoughts."

"I'm glad, but..." Now it was Sardelle who poked at the snow with her boot. "Some of this court-martial concern of yours... You've made some choices others might question, and you've been put in some compromising situations lately as a result of me—of knowing me and having me in your life."

Ridge gave her a suspicious squint. "Did someone tell you about the vine at the castle?"

"The what?"

That's an entertaining story. Definitely get that from him.

"Nothing," Ridge said. "Go on."

Hm. "I like your company very much—"

His eyes widened with surprise—ugh, did this sound like the beginning of a we-need-to-go-separate-ways speech?

"—and could easily see living with you for many years... or all of them. But I'm afraid I'm getting you in trouble. That you're making choices you wouldn't usually make if you weren't trying to protect me. I was wondering..." She wasn't sure what expression was in his eyes now. She was having a hard time looking at them. "Maybe I should leave for a while, until I've dealt with the people spying on me and your life returns to normal. You have the respect of your people, your superior officers, your king, your pilots... I don't want you to lose any of that because of me."

"Sardelle."

She risked meeting his eyes. He didn't look mad or stunned or devastated, but he did look like he was trying to figure something out. Or figure *her* out.

Good call, genius.

Hush.

"Is this allowed?" Ridge asked. "Talking about leaving right after you teach me to mind-talk and invite your sword to waltz into my head whenever she feels like it?"

"Uhm." She didn't know what to make of his humor, not this time. A defense mechanism? A sign that he didn't understand the ramifications of what she'd asked? No, he wasn't a dull man, even if he hid behind that I-just-like-to-fly-and-shoot-things persona.

"I assumed that was a sign that a marriage proposal was imminent," Ridge said, "or at least that I was worth sharing your innermost secrets and abilities with."

"Marriage proposal? Are the women supposed to do that now? It was always the men in my time." She stopped talking, lest it turn into battling. The topic flustered her. He wasn't seriously suggesting he'd *want* a proposal, was he? No, it was a joke...

"It can come from either sex."

"I assumed I'd wait for you to ask. You instigated our first evening together, after all, even though I'd scarcely known you for three days at that point."

"*I* instigated?" Ridge asked. "You were the one fondling my chest. If that's not an instigation, I don't know what is."

"I was bandaging your wounds."

"There were wounds? Huh, I'd forgotten. Odd which details about a night different people remember, isn't it?"

Sardelle shoved her shoulder against him but smiled anyway. Maybe this was the only answer to her concerns she would get tonight.

But Ridge sobered and dropped his voice again—the others had looked in their direction at the mention of sex, even if they had been using the gender sense of the word. "Listen, Sardelle.

My life has never been normal, and I make dubious choices all the time. I was doing that long before I met you. Ask anyone. No, ask General Ort. He would be happy to give you a list. Or show you my file. All three inches of it. I'm just impulsive and not very disciplined. There aren't many branches of the army where I could have made it more than five years without being bounced out on my a— my lower cheeks, as you call them. I knew that from the beginning. The only reason I joined was because I wanted to fly. That's all I've ever wanted to do. I've put up with the rest of the discipline and chain-of-command cra—wait, do you have a polite civilized word for, ah, fecal droppings?"

"I think you just found one."

"Enh, it doesn't have a very forceful ring. Anyway, what I'm saying is that I've put up with the army because the army keeps me in the air. The only reason the army puts up with *me*, is because I'm good up there. Usually." He grimaced. "The king's good graces mean less to me than they probably should. I see him as a man, nothing more, nothing less. I see everyone that way. I don't like failing—that claws at me—and if I'm dreading a court-martial, it's because I know that in this case it will be deserved, but it's the having failed that will bother me, not the opinions of others."

Ridge slumped down on the log, leaning his elbows against his knees. Sardelle thought about putting her arm around him, but rested her shoulder against him instead. He stared thoughtfully down at his hands. "As long as I can fly, that's what makes it worth the early mornings, the horrible chow, the physical and mental exams, the long work weeks, the days off only when it's convenient for the army to let you go, which is next to never. It's the flying that makes everything else workable. But if there was another way… I've been thinking off and on, ever since you mentioned that you might be able to *make* a power crystal."

He glanced at her, and she gave a nod. She hadn't tried yet but thought she could.

"Maybe I wouldn't *need* the military to have a flier," Ridge said. "I have engineer friends; we might be able to build one from scratch. Even if you couldn't make a power source, or it was too dangerous to, now there's this dragon blood... Just seems like all of a sudden there are options. And I've wondered what it would be like to go off after my dad on one of his crazy world-exploring missions while he's still alive. I've wondered what it would be like to fly all over the world, really. See it all from the sky. Maybe skipping the empire, since my head is apparently adorning bounty posters here. But if we weren't at war with the Cofah, and there were another way to keep flying, I might have retired already. That crossed my mind while I was being flown out to those prison mines, let me tell you. But I figure it would be cowardly to leave as long as the Cofah are a threat and I'm able to keep fighting. But I suppose if the army kicked me out... I wouldn't feel all that bad about it. And if something happened where I had to leave to help protect this particularly fine lady, I wouldn't feel all that bad about that, either." Ridge wiggled his eyebrows at her. "I know you don't need my protecting, but I'd at least like to be able to take my cloak off and lay it across a mud puddle for you, so I can feel useful. I'd do that, by the way, if we ever get somewhere without snow and you're wearing sandals instead of boots."

"I'll keep that in mind." Sardelle should have said something more meaningful to his sharing of dreams, but she sensed that he wasn't being completely straightforward with her. Aspects of the military might irritate him, but he loved his job and the officers who worked under him. He wasn't ready to retire, not unless they made him choose between that or a desk job. And he didn't want to fail or to lose the admiration of those he cared about. That mattered to him. He *liked* being a war hero, even if he waved away the attention and pretended it didn't matter. He even believed it didn't matter to him. Perhaps this was a case of Sardelle being able to sense things in him that he wasn't being honest to himself about. He would be devastated if his career was taken from him and if he was ostracized. On some level, he knew that; he had to. That he wanted her enough to bury those thoughts... she appreciated it, but she feared he would come to resent her one day if she was the one who, however unintentionally, ruined his life.

She stared bleakly at the ground.

"Anyway," Ridge said, flexing his clasped hands and returning his gaze to them. "I can't read you the way you can read me, so I don't know how you truly feel, but I want you to know that if you're looking for an excuse to leave, you don't have to give me a story. Just say that's how it is, and I'll understand. I'll drink myself into a stupor and pine horribly for days, but I'll understand. You're like an eagle, and I'm a crow, and it was probably strange in the beginning that we got all lustful in that cave—I'm still sure that was because of you fondling my chest—but I've been enjoying flying with you, so if you're really just worried that you're affecting my reputation or my career somehow, please don't be. I won't go so far as to say I don't care at all about those things, but at this point in my life, I'm ready to care about someone else... more."

That was a truth, a whole truth.

Sardelle wiped at the corner of her eye. A lump had grown in her throat while he was speaking, else she might have protested his notion that she was an eagle or any sort of magnificent bird or animal. She didn't trust her voice though, and when he gazed over at her, she put her hands on either side of his face and kissed him.

It did seem unfair that she could read him when he could only guess at her true thoughts. She didn't know if it would alarm him, but with the touch of her lips, she tried to share her feelings and emotions with him as well, things that were too hard to prove with words, that she didn't want to leave him but she would never forgive herself for wrecking his life. She also admitted that she was afraid sometimes that she had attached herself to him too soon and with too much zeal because he had been the first nice person to walk into this new life of hers, a life she was still struggling to accept fully. He had been like a life preserver on a rough sea, and she had clung on with more fervor than she usually would have when meeting a man. But at the same time, she knew if they had met three hundred years ago, she would have wanted to explore a relationship with him then too.

She shifted so she could slip her fingers beneath his jacket, running her hand up his waist and around to his back, enjoying the contours of his hard muscles, wanting to slide over into his lap and feel more of him. Yes, falling for him would have been easy in any time period. He was handsome, charming, playful—

And he does that thing with his tongue.

Jaxi!

I'm only interrupting because some people have noticed you're using this log for more than a bench, and it's almost dawn.

Is there a Cofah airship on the way?

Nothing close enough for me to sense. Yet.

Good. Now, go away.

Sardelle would have gone on kissing Ridge for a few more minutes—or hours—and who cared who was watching, but for all his words about being indifferent to what happened to his career, he had a more developed sense of duty than she. He broke the kiss first, though his eyes didn't leave hers. The intensity—the heat—in them made her wonder if he might suggest running off into the woods instead of attending to any sort of duties, but he eventually sighed and leaned back farther. "That is… compelling," he breathed, his voice husky.

"Do you mean, ah, did you sense… me?" Very eloquent, yes. But she didn't want to say she had been trying to foist her emotions onto him if it hadn't worked. Just because he understood her words when she spoke with her mind didn't mean the rest would come through.

"Some fears, concerns, something about a life preserver, but I was mostly talking about the end where you were thinking lustful thoughts about my… back."

She blushed—those hadn't been the feelings she had been trying to share.

He caught her hand when she pulled it out from beneath his jacket, giving it a kiss before releasing her, his eyes holding a promise of later. He eyed the sky, which was no longer as dark as it had been, and the camp—contrary to Jaxi's warning, the others were doing a polite job of *not* looking in this direction. "Looks like it's time to go. Are you ready to storm a secret Cofah compound?"

CHAPTER 11

R IDGE TUCKED HIS SPYGLASS INTO a pocket and picked his way down the spruce that he had been using as a viewing platform. He grimaced as sharp needles scraped his cheeks and branches thwacked him in the back of the skull. He still had a knot back there from the crash. He probably should have given the tree-climbing job to someone else, but after moving the fliers, the squadron had hiked all afternoon and was approaching the coordinates for the secret Cofah facility, and Ridge had wanted to see for himself what awaited.

From the ground, it had almost looked like a forest fire was burning beyond the snowy ridge ahead, because plumes of white-gray smoke rose from numerous spots, drifting up into the clear evening sky. Thanks to his elevated perch and the spyglass, he had found the real reason for the plumes.

When he dropped to the ground, all eyes turned to him. The group was taking a break, resting and waiting for night to fall.

"Fire?" Apex was sitting on a log, with his pistol and weapons cleaning kit out.

"Not fire," Duck said, his boot up on the end of the log. They had been having the same discussion when Ridge had gone up the tree. "Smell the air," Duck added. "It's got sulfur in it."

"So does the air above your bunk at night, but that doesn't preclude a fire in the stove."

Duck didn't look like he grasped the joke. No matter. Ridge wanted to share what he'd seen, not break up a fight.

"It's steam, not smoke," he said. "Looks like a lot of hot springs and geysers. One of the little ponds started shooting steamy water twenty, thirty meters into the air while I was up there watching. There were a lot of spots like that. There's a big mound, almost a mountain, in the middle that might be manmade. At the least, it's been excavated by man—there are some metal doors set into one side, big enough to be hangar doors. I'm not sure how easy it is to get to them. I didn't see a road, and there are a lot of those steaming pools."

Tolemek, who was leaning against a tree near Sardelle and Ahn, nodded. "I thought that might be the source of the smell and the steam. We've gone west far enough to reach the Taiga of Boiling Death."

"Boiling *Death?*" Duck asked.

"I haven't been here myself, but they say swimming isn't recommended. The geysers and pools will scorch your skin off. Even some of the streams run so hot that nothing can live in the water. Just traveling through the nearby forest can be dangerous, because in some spots, there's nothing more than a thin crust over scalding water. If you break through it and fall in, you can get burned to death."

"Burned to death?" Ahn asked. "You don't have a goo to fix that?"

"I did bring some of my healing salve along, but it's not *that* powerful."

"Boiling Death, huh?" Ridge asked. "Sounds like a cozy place for a secret base."

"There are people in the mountain," Sardelle said, "Fifty or sixty. Jaxi isn't positive, but thinks some are guards and some are workers. Researchers or engineers. She says there's a *lot* of dragon blood in there. She can sense it."

"Thank you." Ridge appreciated the intelligence, but he took note of the concerned looks Duck and Apex shared. Maybe he should have sent them back in one of the fliers with an intelligence report for the general, but that would have left them a pilot short, and they had both volunteered to stay with the mission anyway. He was still battling with the decision, though, knowing that someone had to survive and that this intelligence *had* to make it back.

We'll survive, came Sardelle's determined whisper in his mind. He had grown used to that more quickly than he would have imagined. Maybe because it was her, and she was the one person he didn't mind having secret conversations with. The sword was another story.

"Uh, who's Jaxi?" Duck asked, apparently dwelling on Sardelle's report.

"My sword." Sardelle drew the weapon from its scabbard.

"It… talks to you?" He licked his lips, eyes big as he stared at it, then glanced around, like he might flee into the woods at any moment.

"She talks to just about anyone who's willing to listen," Sardelle said.

"And some who aren't," Ridge muttered. "Duck, you want to go scout for me? See if there's a way out to those doors? If anyone can scamper around in a forest and avoid pools of boiling death, it ought to be you."

Duck wore a doubtful expression, but he said, "Yes, sir."

"Want me to go with him, sir?" Ahn asked. "Watch his back? Or pull his butt out of the boiling river when he falls in?"

Duck sniffed. "I don't need anyone to pull me out. I'll be better on my own. You city people are so noisy when you walk in the woods."

"Noisy will be you when you fall into a geyser and start screaming," Ahn muttered.

Duck waved dismissively, grabbed his rifle, and headed off through the trees. Scouting, Ridge assured himself, not fleeing from Sardelle. Duck's speed and the way his shoulders were hunched up to his ears made it seem like the latter, though.

"What constitutes a *lot* of dragon blood?" Tolemek asked. "Is it possible there's a whole dragon inside their base?"

"Jaxi doesn't believe so," Sardelle said. "I think even *I* would sense a dragon at this distance."

"Hm." Something about the set of Tolemek's mouth suggested disappointment.

Ridge would prefer *not* to battle a dragon, so he couldn't share that feeling. "Everyone else, get some rest. We've all been up too long. A couple hours of sleep before attempting an infiltration would be a good idea." Or a couple days of sleep, but they couldn't take that long. The Cofah would be looking for them. He was worried about the fliers too. With Jaxi's help, they had found a large cave to hide them in, so the craft wouldn't be visible to patrols roaming the skies, but leaving them behind without a guard made him nervous. "We'll wait until after midnight to attempt to sneak in. With luck, most of those guards will be snoozing in their racks by then."

Ridge sat on the same log as Apex and flexed his ankles. He wondered if he would be *able* to rest. It was hard to relax while thinking about getting past pools of "Boiling Death" and wondering how and where Kaika and Nowon had been captured. He had watched for tracks in the snow as they drew closer to the coordinates, but he hadn't seen anything except signs of animal activity.

The others had already tossed down their packs, and it didn't take long for their bodies to follow. They had come down out of the mountains, so there was less snow here, but the journey had still been a taxing one. Ridge didn't know if they would have made it without Sardelle along, melting passages through canyons and pointing out less treacherous routes. It had seemed a good way to introduce Duck and Apex to her magic, having it be used in a simple way that assisted the team. Apex hadn't seemed that surprised at what she could do and what she was—maybe he had figured it out a while ago—but Duck kept staring with goggle-eyes and making reflexive hill-folk signs for warding off evil witches.

"Ahn," Ridge said, "since you're in the volunteering mood, why don't you take watch while Duck is off exploring?"

"Yes, sir." She took her sniper rifle and disappeared into the trees. She wasn't the wilderness expert that Duck was, but she could sneak around in any terrain without being spotted.

Soon, everyone else found their rest positions and the little clearing fell silent, save for the soft rasp of a bore brush being pulled through a pistol barrel. Every now and then, Apex glanced in Tolemek's direction as he cleaned his weapon. Tolemek had tossed his pack against a tree, its skirt sheltering the base from the snow, and was lying against it, his repose hardly threatening.

If he was aware of Apex's dark glowers, he was ignoring them.

Time to address this, Ridge supposed, though he doubted he could do anything to change the lieutenant's feelings.

"Are we going to have a problem before this mission is over?" he asked softly.

Apex flinched, perhaps surprised to have been caught glowering so obviously. "Before it's over? No, sir."

"*After* it's over, then?"

Apex scowled down at his disassembled pistol. "No."

"Would you tell me if you were thinking of doing something as foolish as the things I sometimes do?"

Apex hesitated before answering. "No."

"I'm not in love with the man, either," Ridge said, "but seeing what we've seen so far here makes me believe the king did the right thing in hiring him. Instead of shooting him. Whether it's fliers, weapons, or scientific advancements, we dare not fall behind the Cofah. They already have the advantage of population and resources. He can help us."

"We already have good scientists, sir. Men who've never *murdered* innocent people." Apex shook his head. "It's not even murder when it's a whole village. It's, it's *genocide*. It's a crime that can't be forgiven." Apex wasn't keeping his voice that low, and Sardelle glanced over. Tolemek turned his back on the conversation. Ridge doubted that meant he wasn't listening. He must be aware that Apex had a weapon in his hands and was glaring at him.

"Who was it you lost?" Ridge asked, though he'd read Apex's record and knew.

"My brothers and sisters and I had all moved away, but both of my parents were still living there. And I knew..." Apex jammed the brush into the barrel again, even though there couldn't be a speck of carbon left inside. "It was a small town. I knew everyone. The Kraytons had just had a new baby. The Pargrats' little girl... They were good people. All of them."

"I'm not going to be his advocate—you'd have to talk to Ahn for that—but my understanding is that he made the weapon but wouldn't have used it, not like that. Someone betrayed him and unleashed it on Tanglewood and on a Cofah town as well."

"So that makes it less of a crime? Even if that's true, he still made it. He chose to make it. There's no reason to make something that horrible, not unless you're a, a *monster*." Apex threw his brush down and snapped the pistol back together.

Ridge had a hard time disagreeing, but said, "Maybe it wasn't a wise choice, but we're giving him an opportunity to do some good with his potions now. He can help us, and maybe in doing so save lives that would otherwise be lost."

Apex stared at the weapon in his hands. "That doesn't bring back my parents or anyone else in my village, sir."

"I know."

"You know that old fable, about the forlorn tiger, sir?"

Ridge held back a groan, knowing he would get a story. Apex had received his nickname when he had been flying a general up the coast to a meeting, and they had been attacked by pirates along the way. In the midst of an aerial battle at five thousand feet, he had started illustrating a point by quoting historical figures and sharing an obscure myth. The word had gotten around, and other former passengers had mentioned similar experiences— even if pirates hadn't always been involved. This had earned him the sobriquet Story at the Apex. Since the communications crystals had been installed, the entire squadron had been treated to some of these mid-flight tales. "No, go ahead."

"The tiger knew there were poachers in the forest, men that were dangerous because of their rifles. They shot the elephants, but the tiger didn't do anything, because elephants lumber around and rarely bother speaking with tigers. And then the poachers shot the wolves. Maybe the tiger could have done something, but he really didn't care about wolves. They were competition on the hunt. When the poachers returned, they shot the buffalo. Again, the tiger did nothing, because it was a beautiful sunny day, and he didn't want to leave his warm ledge on the rocks. Then one day, the tiger returned home to find that his mate had been shot by the poachers. He was infuriated and tried to round up the forest creatures to help him rid the world of the poachers, but by now, there was nobody except him left to fight. He knew he couldn't take the poachers by himself, so he slunk away, never to be heard from again."

Sometimes the points Apex tried to make with his stories were clear. Sometimes, they left Ridge scratching his head. "So Tolemek is the poacher and you're the tiger?"

The pistol drooped in Apex's hand. "I'm not anything, sir. I'm just afraid that if I do nothing because it's inconvenient or I'm worried about the consequences, and if nobody else does anything, either... then evil is allowed to roam the earth."

Ridge sighed. He had already tried to convince Apex that Tolemek wasn't pure evil, and he didn't know what else he could say.

"He's not a subject, is he?" Apex asked after a moment of silence. "Just an expatriate living on our soil? He might even still be down as a war criminal. Would it still be..." Apex glanced at Tolemek's back and lowered his voice to a whisper. "If I shot him, would it be punishable by death or imprisonment? Would my career be over? I've studied a number of legal systems from historical societies, but haven't paid that much attention to ours. Is that odd?"

Ridge had guessed Apex might be thinking about revenge, but it disturbed him to know the lieutenant had been seriously mulling over the ramifications. It made sense, Ridge supposed. A younger, brasher man might act without considering the consequences, but Apex was old enough to know better. Still, there was something chilling about one of his men so logically debating whether or not to murder someone. He opted to lighten the conversation. "No, the modern ones are complicated and the law books are exceedingly boring to read. Military justice books are especially dry. I'll spare you the story about why I had the task to read several chapters once—and write essays on them."

Apex didn't smile. So much for lightening the conversation.

"He's not a subject, nor has the king granted him provisional citizenship, but he does have a protected status. I don't want to lose you, Anders," Ridge said, using the lieutenant's first name for once, "so I hope you're not seriously considering murder."

Apex flinched again. Maybe he couldn't believe he was

considering murder, either, but saw it as the only acceptable path for revenge. Or justice. Yes, that might be more what rankled him than anything. The fact that Tolemek had been responsible for so many deaths and was allowed to walk freely in the very country where he had killed hundreds. And nobody was *doing* anything about it. Maybe he felt he had to be the one.

"If you can't find another solution for your heart, maybe you can challenge him to a duel," Ridge said.

"Dueling is illegal, sir," Apex said glumly.

"Among soldiers and officers, yes, but not among civilians." Granted it had fallen out of fashion over the last couple of decades, with the Iskandians busy fighting off invaders and frowning upon anything that caused young men, men who could be defending their country, to be killed foolishly.

Apex lifted his chin and gazed into the forest. "Perhaps, hm."

When he didn't say anything else, Ridge patted him on the shoulder and walked away. He didn't know if he had solved anything, or merely postponed the inevitable, but he hoped Apex would at least avoid shooting Tolemek in the back in the middle of Ridge's mission.

Ridge's mission. He snorted as he headed over to check on Sardelle. His self-appointed mission, maybe. Wasn't he just supposed to be the flying rickshaw driver? How had he ended up taking responsibility for this?

I believe it started when you drugged that officer and punted him out of your flier.

Jaxi. Ridge frowned at the intrusion—and at the fact that someone besides Sardelle was privy to his private thoughts. *Everyone is resting. Don't you need naps too?*

Not at all. Sardelle is sleeping, though, so I thought I'd inform you directly.

Inform me of what?

The man floating above the mountain base in a balloon.

Ridge halted, his foot halfway between one step and the next. *What?*

A man is sitting in a basket under a balloon and looking out at the land around the mountain with a large spyglass.

Ridge sighed. He'd been thinking of lying down and cuddling with Sardelle—and maybe doing some of that very interesting kissing where he could tell what she was thinking, especially the part about her imagining him naked—not heading back up a tree, but he grabbed his rifle and left camp.

"Problem, sir?" Ahn called softly from behind some snow-covered ferns. In the darkness, he hadn't seen her.

"Maybe. Want to come take a look with me?"

She slipped out of the brush and joined him. He opted for walking toward the crest of the hill that lay between them and the start of the steaming pools instead of climbing a tree. Someone up in a balloon might spot some strangely moving branches. Especially if that someone was on the alert and expecting spies. Just because the Cofah airship had warned him to leave didn't mean they believed he would.

It took Ridge and Ahn fifteen minutes of climbing to reach the top of the hill—there was probably no need to worry about passing that physical exam next month. It was covered with the charred remains of trunks still standing after some past forest fire, and he had no trouble seeing the sky and out to the dark silhouette of the mountain, an almost perfect conical shape rising a hundred feet above the surrounding grounds.

"That looks man-made," Ahn said.

"It might be. Here, stay back against this brush, so we won't stand out. Do you see anything in the sky?" Clouds had rolled in, otherwise the stars would be visible by now. He searched for Jaxi's balloon and spotted it a heartbeat before Ahn spoke and pointed.

"There. Observation balloon."

"Good eye. Hm, it's drifting north, but I wouldn't be surprised if it loops toward our camp." Ridge licked a finger and tested the wind. Those balloons had some directional abilities, but weren't as navigable as an airship with engines and propellers. Without the fliers, they ought to be able to hide from the observer, especially at night, although… "Maybe we'd *like* it to visit our camp."

"So we can shoot the observer?" Ahn asked.

"It's not the *observer* I want. Come on, I need to talk to Sardelle." Ridge hustled back down the hill.

* * *

Sardelle woke when Lieutenant Duck returned to camp. He padded in quietly, but started talking to Apex right away. "Where's the colonel?"

"Off to check on something with Raptor."

Sardelle pushed herself up. She didn't think she had been asleep that long, but full darkness had fallen. The cold earth didn't make a comfortable bed, but she had been so tired from the day of marching through snow—and using magic to clear it—that she had been asleep before her head touched the pack. She hadn't heard Ridge leave and swept out with her senses. Ah, there he was. Jogging back toward the group.

"Well, I couldn't find a way out to that mountain," Duck said. "There are pools all over the place, and they're hotter than lava to the touch. I tried to find a place where you could walk between them, but Deathmaker was right. The limestone or calcium or whatever that whitish gunk is makes up a thin layer, and there's water beneath it if you break through. I didn't see a landing pad around that mountain, but I'm figuring you have to fly out there somehow."

"You do," came Ridge's voice from the trees. "Sardelle, I'm in need of your assistance again. Could you convince that balloon to come visit us?"

"Balloon?" She yawned and crawled out from beneath her tree. She couldn't see anyone in the darkness, but sensed people's positions. Tolemek and Apex hadn't moved, or killed each other yet. That was good.

Up and to the northwest, Jaxi supplied.

Thank you. "All right. I see it."

"I'd like for it to have a hot air problem and be forced to the ground nearby, if that's doable." Ridge found her and wrapped an arm around her. "Sorry, it's probably not polite to wake you early and ask for favors without a hug." He gave her a kiss on the cheek too.

Sardelle leaned into him, happy for the warmth, then rested her cheek against his chest while she examined the hot air balloon more closely.

"How come we don't get hugs when he wants favors from us?" Duck asked.

"I think there's a rule against officers hugging other officers," Ahn said.

"There's a rule against physical relationships and displays of affection," Apex said, "but I don't believe friendly hugs are mentioned in the regulations."

"That's more than a friendly hug. I'm fairly certain he's touching her butt."

Sardelle was concentrating on the balloon and trying to ignore them, but caught herself flushing anyway.

"I am not," Ridge protested. "That's her hip. I think. It's dark out here tonight."

"Actually, it's neither," Sardelle said, deciding to go along with the teasing rather than try to protest it.

Ridge found something softer to squeeze than her hip, and she sensed his grin even if she couldn't see it. "So, I see."

"Am I correct that you don't want the balloon damaged?" she asked.

"Yes, we can patch it if need be, but that's going to be our ride out to the mountain."

"What about the pilot?" Sardelle started nudging the large balloon in their direction, forming channels of air, similar to what she had done to divert that giant owl familiar back on Galmok Mountain.

"He's not invited," Ridge said.

"What I mean is that I wouldn't care to bring him down into our midst to see him shot in front of my eyes."

"We can gag him and tie him to a tree. That ought to hold him for a few hours. That should be all we need."

"All right. I should have his craft down in a few minutes if you want to hide to ambush him." Once he got closer, Sardelle might be able to convince him to fall asleep so a violent ambush could be avoided. Then again, he had already realized his balloon was fighting him more than it should. He would be alert when she funneled out some of his hot air, forcing him to land.

"I'll take care of that," Tolemek said from his tree. He rolled to his feet, something in his hand. One of those little leather balls.

The hot air balloon came into sight over the treetops. Sardelle blew out the fire in its burner, eliciting a startled protest from the handler. She funneled air out of the balloon, too, and it descended rapidly. The wind came up, fighting her, and she struggled to keep it from getting caught in the trees. Unfortunately, the unwieldy craft defied her, and the balloon snagged on the skeletal branches of a birch. Several snaps sounded, and she thought the balloon might fall to the ground, but enough large branches caught to support the weight of the pilot and basket.

"Sorry," Sardelle whispered, embarrassed by her lack of accuracy.

Tolemek handed his ball to Ahn. "I have a feeling you'll be better at hitting that target than I. Push that indention before you throw it."

"Got it." Ahn jogged a couple of steps and chucked the ball.

It arced up toward the tree and landed in the basket.

The pilot, alternating between trying to relight his burner and push the branches out of his basket, didn't notice it land at his feet. A minute later, all of his activity stopped.

"Nice work," Ridge said. "Now, who's going to climb up there, extract the pilot, and get the balloon down without ripping it into a thousand pieces?"

No one rushed to volunteer. The balloon was a good twenty feet up in that tree.

"It depends, sir," Duck said. "Are hugs involved?"

"If a hug from me is what it takes to motivate you, Lieutenant, I suppose in this situation, I'd consider that a fair trade-off."

"Maybe he wants a hug from Sardelle," Tolemek said.

"Er." Duck shifted his weight, the snow crunching beneath his feet.

Sardelle had a feeling that might have been an acceptable reward at one time, but now he was uncomfortable at the idea of her coming close. Ridge had been once, too, she reminded herself.

I'll do it for a nice oiling of my blade.

From whom?

Anyone with a gentle hand. That Apex is handsome when he's not being surly about pirate boy.

"Jaxi and I will handle it," Sardelle said.

You forgot to mention my oiling.

I'm not sure this group is ready to hear about your quirky needs.

They're not quirky. You like being oiled now and then too. I've seen it.

Sardelle resisted the impulse to explain the difference between massages and having one's blade protected from moisture. She was busy lifting the unconscious pilot from his basket and lowering him to the ground. Ahn stood at her shoulder, her rifle ready in case he woke up. But Tolemek's smoke had worked again, and the man remained inert.

Jaxi handled the branches and the balloon, repairing rips as she went. Sardelle relit the coal in the burner, and by the time the basket touched down, it was almost ready to take off again. Her head ached by the time she finished all of these tasks. The thirty minutes of sleep she had gotten hadn't been as refreshing as she had hoped.

"Apex, Duck, tie the prisoner, please." Ridge walked to the basket and inspected it as much with his hands as with his eyes in the dark. "This isn't very big. We'll all be hugging and touching butts. At least it's not a long journey." He removed a rope and tied the basket to a tree. With the burner running again, the balloon was threatening to rise.

"Are we going to wait to go in?" Sardelle asked, hoping for a few hours of sleep before breaking into an ultra modern and secure Cofah laboratory.

"Yeah." Duck yawned. "I could get more excited about butt touching after a nap."

"An appealing notion," Ridge said—whether he referred to naps or butt touches wasn't entirely clear. "But this fellow might be missed. We better go in now. Maybe we'll finish our mission in thirty minutes and celebrate by finding an only mildly heated hot spring to lounge in after that."

Nobody did anything more optimistic than snorting. If things were going to be easy, the two elite troops wouldn't have been captured. Or killed.

"Grab your gear," Ridge said, his voice more sober. "It's time to go."

CHAPTER 12

THE RAILING OF THE BASKET was digging into Ridge's ribcage. He wasn't sure whose elbow was in his back, but it wasn't Sardelle's. She was plastered into the corner beside him. The entire team had fit into the basket, but not comfortably, and the balloon hadn't budged, merely hovering above them with placid indifference when they removed the rope anchoring it to a tree.

"Guess we shouldn't have done all those push-ups," Duck had said. "It made our muscles grow too heavy."

"More likely all that beer you swill made your belly grow too heavy," Apex muttered.

Fortunately Sardelle, or maybe Jaxi, had done something, causing the balloon to swell until it appeared ready to burst, and the basket had floated into the air. Now they were drifting slowly toward the mountain, across the steaming pools and through air that stank of sulfur and decomposing things. The moon was poking through the clouds, a development Ridge wasn't enthused by, since anyone watching from the mountain would be able to notice the balloon—and the abnormal number of people stuffed into the basket.

Hot eddies rose up from below, creating strange air currents that tugged at the balloon. Pools and mud pots burbled as the craft passed over them, and, after hearing Tolemek's warning, Ridge knew he wouldn't want to crash. The wicker basket would make a poor shield to keep near-boiling water from seeping inside.

Without warning, a geyser erupted in front of them. They were floating more than fifty feet above the ground, but the top of the water jet reached far above them. The breeze blew the steam and water droplets toward the balloon. The basket rocked precariously as people shifted away from the spewing hot water.

"Stay steady," Ridge said, not leaving his rail. "Even out the weight." He raised a gloved hand to protect his face from the spray—it was a fine mist at this distance, but the tiny specks still burned. "Sardelle, take us around that, please." He didn't know how long the geyser would keep erupting, but the balloon was heading straight for it.

"Working on it," she said, her voice tense.

"Thanks." He wondered if he should apologize. Just because she had magic, didn't mean hot air balloons would be a simple thing to navigate. But if she didn't maneuver them away from the jet soon, they would pass through it, and find out just how much power propelled that water. Ridge's knuckles tightened as he imagined his men being knocked from the basket, flung out like dolls, to drop fifty feet and land in those bubbling pools.

"Got any concoctions that will turn that thing off?" Ahn asked.

"No," Tolemek said. "Had someone informed me that this was our destination, I might have brought more useful tools."

"More likely specimen kits for collecting samples of that weird green stuff growing around the pools down there."

"Anyone ever tell you that you have freakishly good eyesight, Ahn?" Ridge asked, though he kept glancing through his gloves to that geyser. More spray was hitting his clothing now, and the hot water bit like acid where it struck flesh. Someone jerked away from what must have been a big splash and cursed.

"Yes, they have," Ahn said. "And I'd like to take this moment to thank you tall, looming people for protecting me from the water."

The breeze gusted harder, and Ridge realized why Sardelle was having trouble directing them away from the geyser. She was moving them against it, trying to curve around the spraying water. If they went the way the wind wanted to carry them, in the same direction that spray was blowing, that would be an unpleasant trip.

The balloon pushed into the wind. Sardelle wiped her brow. Sweating in this cold weather? It was hard to imagine using one's mind could be that taxing, but he appreciated that she was working that hard for them.

They drew even with the geyser and inched past it. Some of the tension ebbed from Ridge's shoulders. So long as Sardelle's concentration didn't give out, so the wind couldn't push them into it, they should be fine. Seconds after the balloon cleared the geyser, the spray died down. Within a few more seconds, it disappeared completely. Only a steaming pool below signaled that a geyser existed at all.

Duck snorted. "*Now* it goes out."

"The timing was… precise," Tolemek noted.

Ridge frowned over Ahn's head at him. "Are you saying your people can control when these things shoot off?" Did that mean someone inside already knew his team was out here and sneaking in on a stolen balloon?

"I have no idea what these scientists can do. I would not think that possible without magic, but this is not my area of expertise." Tolemek sounded stiff, as if he resented being lumped in with these people.

Well, Ridge could soothe his ruffled feathers later. Maybe they could bond over another snowball fight.

"Even with magic, controlling the geysers would be difficult if not impossible," Sardelle said. "That's usually the case when it comes to nature."

Ridge remembered the avalanche she had dug him out of. She had later admitted she had tried and failed to divert the snow slide.

"Neither Jaxi nor I sensed magic being used," she added.

One of the mud pots belched loudly below, the stink in the air intensifying.

"Let's just get to that mountain as quickly as possible," Ridge said, then, realizing that sounded like an order, laid a hand on Sardelle's to let her know he appreciated all she was doing for them. He had to remember that neither she nor Tolemek were his troops, sworn to obey senior officers in the duty of the king. They had volunteered to come along.

Sardelle leaned against his shoulder. He didn't know if that was a sign of understanding or acceptance, or if it meant she was tired. She wasn't talking in his head at the moment.

He left his hand on hers and, as they drifted closer to the mountain, watched for lights or some sign that another person waited outside, prepared to receive signals from the balloon observer—there had been a light and mirror kit in the bottom of the basket, presumably for that purpose. But he didn't see a soul.

"Anyone out here?" he murmured to Sardelle.

"I sense people inside, but not outside."

"Still no dragons, right?" Ridge smiled, meaning it as a joke, but not entirely. If they had nearly been taken out by a geyser, he didn't want to imagine how vulnerable they would be to something that could fly and breathe fire.

"Trust me, I'll let you know if a creature believed extinct for the last thousand years plucks at my senses."

Ridge gazed toward the mountains rising to the north, the same ones they had been flying along and through since leaving the sea. In focusing on this mound among the geysers, he had neglected considering watchtowers or outposts that might overlook the area from those peaks. He thought of the old legends that always had dragons living in caves in mountains. But if Sardelle didn't sense anything, he would trust that there was nothing out there.

"We better go down soon," Duck said, "or we'll overshoot the mound and end up landing on a geyser."

"Can you magic us down there?" Ridge asked Sardelle.

She leaned past Ahn and dumped the coals into the ashbin to put out the flames heating the air.

"Or we could do it that way," Ridge said.

"I'll try to bring us down on that little strip of gravel next to the doors," Sardelle said.

They were above the mountain now, and Ridge could see a ledge about six feet wide that circled the conical base. Or outpost. Or laboratory. He wouldn't know what to call it until he had the tour. He could also make out a couple of vents near the top, each spewing puffs of smoke. Nothing that might be a window or peephole had come into view, though. He wondered if it was too much to hope their approach wouldn't be noticed.

"Not much of a target," Tolemek said.

"It'll have to do." Sardelle had her eyes closed as the balloon dipped down.

Ridge decided not to find that alarming. Sorcerers could see with their minds, right? "If you land us on it without tipping the basket into that pool, we'll make you an honorary Wolf Squadron pilot."

Another geyser erupted, this one farther out and not as boisterous as the first. Maybe they were simply natural occurrences after all. Ridge still didn't see a road or path of any kind leading to the metal double doors, but he couldn't imagine venturing out there on foot even if there had been one.

The corner of the basket scraped against the rocky side of the miniature mountain, jostling everyone against everyone else. Sardelle was erring on the safe side, and Ridge couldn't blame her for that, but he hoped nobody on the other side of that wall would be able to hear the scrapes and bumps.

"When the colonel promised butt touching, he wasn't kidding," Duck said. "Watch out for Raptor. Her guns are poky."

"As the commanding officer, and presumably the most mature person present, I'm going to resist the urge to make a lewd comment," Ridge announced. They scraped the wall again, but they were only eight feet from the ground now. Almost safe. From the balloon flight anyway.

"Who told you that you were mature, Zirkander?" Tolemek asked.

"Perhaps I should have said advanced in years."

"Perhaps."

With another soft scrape, the balloon settled onto the ground. The corner was tilted upward, resting on the slope of the mountain, but Ridge couldn't fault Sardelle's aim, not when a bubbling and gurgling pool lay less than a foot away in the other direction.

He climbed out first, landing on packed gravel. Sardelle had said nobody was out here, but he kept a pistol in hand, nonetheless.

"How does one deflate the balloon without having it smother

the basket and fall into the water?" Tolemek wondered, eyeing the black-and-gray material above them. It hadn't yet lost the swell of its shape, but it probably would before long. "Do we need to leave someone here to make sure we can get away again once we're ready to leave?"

"There must be something inside that can take the workers away from here if need be," Ridge said. "After all, *this* thing came from somewhere in there." He didn't want to separate the team and start leaving people behind anyway.

Tolemek didn't question him further.

While the others hopped out of the basket, Ridge walked along the base of the mountain toward the alcove that held the doors. They were tall enough and wide enough that a two-seat flyer could have navigated through them, though he couldn't imagine landing and taking off without a runway, unless that was built into the mountain itself somehow.

He froze as soon as he poked his head around the corner for a better look. Clearly what Sardelle had meant was that there was nobody *living* out here. He gulped as he stared at two bodies hanging on hooks on either side of the closed doors.

Though Ridge wasn't certain he wanted to see better, he had to know who the people were—who they had been. He dug into his utility pouch for his small tin of matches. He lit one, the flame flaring and reflecting off heavy rivets on the steel door. It also illuminated the bodies.

On both of them, the skin had been flayed—no burned—off, leaving the facial features unrecognizable, but the shredded remains of gray-and-blue Iskandian army uniforms were all too familiar. Much of the hair had been removed—burned or melted away, but from the sizes and shapes, one clearly feminine, Ridge was fairly certain he was looking at the bodies of Captains Nowon and Kaika. He let the match fall to the ground and dropped his chin to his fist, guilt and regret gnawing at him. If he hadn't left that posturing colonel behind, was it possible the mission would have gone more smoothly? That the elite troops team might still be alive?

"Oh hells," Duck whispered, stopping beside Ridge. The

others soon gathered in front of the doors too.

Tolemek shook his head slowly. Sardelle closed her eyes and looked away. It was a disturbing image. Ridge was glad the sulfurous scent all around them overrode the butcher-house smell that had to be lingering around the bodies.

"Should we cut them down, sir?" Ahn asked.

"If we can get them on the way out, we will." Ridge would like to give the officers burials somewhere, but the sooner they finished what they had come for, the sooner they might escape with their own lives intact. He didn't want to see the rest of his team suffer this fate.

Ridge took a breath and walked up to the double doors. There wasn't a handle, latch, or even a keyhole. He looked back at Sardelle.

"Tolemek has a knack for opening doors or making them where they don't exist." She sounded weary, like she would prefer to hand this task off to another.

"Yes, he does," Ahn said.

If there was an alternative, Ridge would gladly save Sardelle's powers for when they truly needed them. "Tolemek?"

"It will take a couple of minutes." Tolemek stepped forward, and the satchel he always carried clanked as he dug into it.

Ridge tried pushing and pulling on the doors while he waited. He didn't expect them to budge—and they didn't—but one had to try. In the darkness, he wasn't positive what Tolemek was doing, but he seemed to be drawing a circle on one of the doors. After a moment, he stepped back.

Ridge shifted his weight from foot to foot, resisting the urge to demand what was supposed to be happening. Eventually, Tolemek planted a boot on the center of the circle and shoved. To Ridge's surprise, the movement dislodged the metal. With a resounding clang that made Ridge wince, the circle fell through, landing on a stone floor on the other side. Light spilled out from within. Ridge dropped to his knee to the side of the hole, pistol in hand, and leaned in, prepared for a firefight if legions of guards were descending on the door.

But the chamber inside, a cavernous space with ceilings so

high he couldn't see them from the doorway, was silent. Black marble tiles stretched out in all directions. There were doors to what might have been a lift at the far end of the space. He glimpsed alcoves and recessed doors in the side walls, too, though they were also a long walk from his observing point. Everything was. This chamber looked to take up most of the ground floor of the mountain base. Maybe it *was* a hangar. Many of the tiles were chipped or cracked, and he spotted a couple of old oil stains.

The only sign of humanity was a guard in a crimson Cofah uniform lying on the floor a couple feet from the big metal circle. Ridge's first thought was that he had been crushed by the massive falling disk, but no part of his body was trapped beneath it.

"Looks clear, sir," Ahn whispered. She had knelt on the other side of the hole from him, her rifle at the ready.

Without taking his eyes from the room, Ridge stepped through the hole. The large chamber was lit from above, dozens of bulb-shaped paper lamps hanging suspended from the ceiling at all different heights. Some were even moving about. Strange. Ah, but no, they weren't hanging at all but floating. The candles or whatever fuel was burning must be heating the air within the lampshade, like the burner had heated the hot air balloon outside.

Interesting, but not the ultra modern technology they had been sent here to learn about. Ridge shifted to the side, so the others could enter, and so he could check the guard. It was one thing seeing dead enemies of the Cofah hung up as a warning in front of their secret laboratory, but one didn't expect the guards to be dead too.

The man's neck had been slit. No need to check the pulse, but Ridge touched his skin anyway, trying to get a gauge for when this had happened—and who might have done it. If his people had both died, did this mean they had some other ally in here? Or maybe the Cofah had some other enemy worried about secret bases and dragon blood. The guard's skin was faintly warm.

"This didn't happen long ago," Ridge said, then chastised himself for stating the obvious. Of course, it had to have happened after the balloon observer left, or the man wouldn't have gone out on his normal rounds. Then again, Ridge couldn't prove the balloon man had left through these doors. He couldn't imagine where else such a craft might be launched, but there weren't any other baskets lined up along the walls.

By now, the rest of the squadron had entered the chamber, and everyone was looking at him. That didn't normally faze him—he was in charge, after all—but he had no idea where they should start searching. He turned three hundred and sixty degrees, seeking inspiration from the chamber. He halted to stare at notable decorations, ones he hadn't registered on his first inspection because they were so big as to seem like part of the architecture.

"Uhm?" Ridge muttered, stepping back and nearly tripping over his heels as he craned his neck to see into the shadows above the lanterns.

What he had mistaken for columns were the legs of enormous blocky statues. With patchwork metal bodies of bronze, steel, and more alloys Ridge couldn't identify, they looked like some child's project composed from junkyard scraps, except on an enormous scale. They were humanoid with rectangular torsos and square heads that sat flush against the broad flat shoulders, with nothing resembling a neck. They had simple faces, rectangular holes for mouths, circular holes for noses, and vertical rectangles for eyes, the latter appearing closed, metal lids drawn down in sleep.

"I believe those represent the Tangula Tarath from Cofah mythology," Apex noted. "The ambulatory statues protected the gods' sky palaces from dragons, back when humans were dwelling in caves and hunting mammoths with stone-tipped spears."

"Whatever they are, I really hope they don't come to life," Duck said.

Ridge almost snorted. Come to life. How could they? But he caught himself before he expelled that breath. If unmanned aircraft could be powered and directed by dragon blood, what if giant statues could be too?

"Let's get moving before they decide to," Ridge said. "Sardelle, any idea of where the stash of blood might be?"

Her eyes stared off into the distance. He was starting to recognize that expression as the one she wore when she was discussing things with her sword. With Jaxi, he amended. Somehow it sounded less odd to his mundane little mind to think of Jaxi as a person rather than a pointy stick.

Good for your mind. I'm less likely to harass people who use my name.

Before Ridge could reply, or decide if he should flush with embarrassment, Sardelle was answering his question.

"The heaviest concentration is up there." She pointed toward the ceiling.

"Let's try that way then." Ridge pointed toward the far wall where sliding metal doors waited—all of the other exits from the chamber were single doors. "It looks like a lift."

Nobody objected to his assessment. Either they thought he had a clue, or they didn't have any better ideas. Inspiring.

He, Ahn, Duck, and Apex walked on either side of the group, their rifles cradled in their arms and pointed toward the perimeter, ready to shoot if any guards trotted out of those doors. Ahn looked alert and unintimidated, her calm gaze roaming about, taking in everything as they advanced. Duck and Apex didn't look quite as professional. Their boots clomped a little loudly, and their shoulders were tense, as were the fingers on the triggers. Ridge tried not to think about how Kaika and Nowon, true professionals when it came to sneaking into places, had been discovered. He had Sardelle and Tolemek. That ought to give Ridge an advantage they hadn't had, no matter how skilled they had been at stealth, attack, and evasion. Still, the lack of columns or any sort of features that could be used for cover in a firefight made him nervous as they traveled across the very large, very open chamber.

The group had walked halfway to the lift when a soft clink-clank-clink-clank sound came from behind them. It reminded Ridge of the drawbridge being raised back in the king's castle. Or of a clockwork machine being wound up. He and his pilots spun in the direction of the noise, their rifles ready. Sardelle and

Tolemek faced in that direction, too, though they didn't reach for weapons, as if they knew that whatever they might face wouldn't be harmed by mere bullets.

Nothing back there was moving, save for the floating lamps that drifted lazily on currents of air, but the mechanical noises continued. Then Ridge spotted something that had changed: the eyes on the statues were open. And they were glowing red.

"You still not sensing any magic, Sardelle?" Ridge pointed to the eyes.

"Not magic, in the traditional sense, but there is dragon blood in those statues."

"You didn't think that was important to mention before?" He regretted the sarcasm immediately, but there was no time for apologies. "Back up, everyone. Keep heading to the lift. Let's see if we can get out of here before we get a demonstration of what those things can do."

"Yes, sir."

He hardly needed to give the order—no one was charging down the room to engage those things. Half of the team turned and ran for the lift doors. Ridge backed away more slowly, watching those statues. What had Apex said? Ambulatory? They looked too top-heavy to move, but he wasn't willing to make a bet against that.

The tone of the clink-clanks shifted, as if smaller gears were moving than had been before, and the left arms on both of the statues began to rise. The next step before the metal contraptions started walking?

"The doors are locked again," Duck said, reaching the lift first.

"Tolemek?" Ridge prompted.

"If it is indeed a lift, burning through the doors may render it inoperable."

"Sardelle?"

The arms of the statues had risen to roughly forty-five degree angles and stopped. Ridge didn't like the way they seemed to be pointing at his team. If something crazy happened, they could still escape through the front doors, but they would have to run a hundred meters to reach them.

"It's a lift system, yes," Sardelle said. "I can sense that there's a vertical shaft behind the doors. There's not a cage or cabin or anything on the other side, though. It might be at the top."

Ridge had been prompting her to open the doors, but that information was valuable too. "Then burning a hole shouldn't make a difference, eh? While Tolemek does that, someone see if there are any levers around to call the lift down to our level. I'm going to be—"

Without warning, a *thik-thunk* came from the other side of the room, and something flew from the tip of one of those arms. Ridge jumped to the side, though it was more luck than skill that kept him from being skewered. Something clacked into the marble floor beside him with enough force to crack the tile and leave a hole. It ricocheted off, landing with a ping somewhere else in the room.

"—dodging for my life," he finished with a grimace.

Ridge looked around, but he had already studied the room with defenses in mind, and he knew there was no place to hide, no cover to be taken. The firing noise came again, and Ridge dodged to the side again, as he might in a firefight in the sky, but he was just guessing that he was a target.

This time, the projectile thudded into something behind him. He glanced back, his heart jumping into his throat. If it had hit Sardelle or one of his men...

But the weapon was stuck in the lift door—it had ripped into the outer metal layer and was sticking out, still quivering. A knife? No, it had several points. A large version of a Cofah throwing star, but it was more like a saw blade at this size.

"Hurry, hurry," Duck whispered.

"I'm going to second that." Ridge raised his rifle to aim at the head of one of the statues, but he was reluctant to shoot and make noise. The statues weren't *that* loud by themselves, but someone was bound to hear gunfire and wake up to check on intruders.

Sardelle stepped up beside Ridge, her sword out now. Out and glowing.

"Jaxi and I will protect the group from fire," she said.

The *thik-thunk* came again. Despite her words, Ridge's instincts were to throw himself to the ground to make a smaller target.

The throwing star hurtled out of the shadows toward them, but burst into fire ten feet away. Ridge swallowed. That had been an accurate throw. It might have cleaved one of them in half.

"How're those doors coming, Tolemek?" Ridge asked, wishing he didn't feel so useless. He fingered the trigger of his rifle. Would a bullet even do anything against a metal statue? Maybe if one shot at the holes from which the stars were being ejected. From this far across the chamber, that would be a job for Ahn.

"I've applied the dissolving goo."

"It's smoking," Duck added helpfully.

"No sign of a lever," Apex added, less helpfully.

Ridge started to ask Sardelle if she could call the lift down from whatever level it was on, but the statues shot again. She was busy. He hated relying on her for everything anyway. He dropped his rucksack and pulled out a coil of rope. Maybe there would be something inside the shaft they could anchor it to so they could climb up to the next level, or at least out of reach of the statues.

A creak and a groan came on the heels of the next round of projectiles. The arms weren't moving this time; it was the legs. A shudder ran through the floor with the statues' first ponderous steps.

"I appreciate you and Jaxi keeping us from being shot," Ridge said. "Are you going to be able to keep us from being crushed by ten tons of metal too?"

The doubtful expression on her face said a lot. Nothing he wanted to hear.

"Ahn and anyone else who's not helping with the doors, come up here," Ridge said, raising his rifle again. "Stealth probably became useless as soon as we knocked open their front door. Time to see if we can find a vulnerable spot on those statues."

"You'll have to stand over there to do so." Sardelle pointed to the side. "I have a barrier up in front of the doors and the group, and your bullets would be bounced back at us."

"Good to know before we start shooting." Ridge and Ahn stepped to the spot where she had indicated, and she gave him a nod.

"I assume we're in danger here too?" Ahn asked.

"I'll keep my eye on you, but you might want to lunge back over here before they shoot each round."

"Understood." Ridge fired his first shot, aiming at one of the red eyes. Those things were eerie.

But the statues were still a hundred meters away, their heads obscured by the shadows above the lamps. His bullet clanged into the nose hole instead. A few clangs sounded—the shell bouncing around inside its head? Well, maybe that would do some damage too.

Ahn must have guessed his original target, for she aimed in the same direction. Her bullet took the statue in the right eye. The red glow blinked a couple of times, but then returned to a steady crimson light.

"Guess the eyes aren't the most vulnerable part of a statue." Ridge thought about firing at the monster's crotch, more out of spite than because he believed that would be a vulnerable spot, but that seemed a touch immature. Besides, he was busy jumping back into Sardelle's sphere of protection, for the statues were firing again. Firing and walking. As slow and ponderous as those steps were, the monsters were drawing ever closer.

A soft metal clang sounded behind him.

"I've made a hole," Tolemek said.

"Duck, take my spot," Ridge said and joined Tolemek at the lift door, bringing his coil of rope. It was probably foolish to think there would be anything up there he could hook it on, but it was worth a look. He had a collapsible grappling hook in his pack too.

"We're on the ground floor," Tolemek said, pulling his head out of the still smoking hole. Amazingly, his shaggy ropes of hair didn't catch fire in the process. "I can't tell how high up the shaft goes. It's dark. There's not a ladder or anything on the wall to climb; I could tell that much."

"I don't think lighting lift shafts is a priority in many places." Ridge ignored the shots firing behind him, even though the blazes that occurred when Sardelle stopped a throwing star were bright and spectacular, and eyeballed some of the nearest floating lanterns. Some of them weren't that high up there. He made a quick lasso with the rope and gave himself room to throw. "Sardelle is busy at the moment, but she floated that Cofah observer out of the balloon. Maybe she can float us up too. Or call down the lift." That would probably be less taxing for her.

"Except that we might not be able to spare her out there." Tolemek nodded his head. "Those statues are going to be here soon. We might have to abandon this and run back to the front door."

Ridge set his jaw. Retreating was better than dying, but if they ran out, they might not get another opportunity to slip in. He was surprised nobody had come down to check on them as it was. Or maybe the Cofah knew they had guests but trusted their statues to handle it.

Ridge caught the lamp he was aiming for, though it took a delicate touch to guide it down to them. The thin paper lanterns were lightweight. He handed it to Tolemek. "Add some more oil and see if you can get it hot enough to float up the shaft. I'll try to get another one."

"Your aim is surprisingly good. Did you rope cattle before becoming a pilot?"

Ridge squinted at him, not sure if that was a compliment or the setup for a joke where he was the butt. "There's a pub in town where you can rope mechanical rabbits that run back and forth on a clockwork track. If you get five in a row, you get a free beer. Naturally, I'm well-practiced."

He tossed his lasso again and brought down another light. The floor was shivering more than ever now as the statues closed the distance. Another twenty steps and they would be upon the group. Sardelle, Duck, and Ahn would have to back up soon. If Ridge thought simply climbing through the hole Tolemek had made would save them, he would order it, but what happened if someone above chose that moment to send the lift down? And what happened if the statues could simply smash through the door with those colossal legs?

Ridge handed the second lantern to Tolemek, then stuck his head through. The first was already inside, lighting the shaft as it rose. The smooth walls didn't offer any hooks, nor were there more doors for more than fifty feet—of course, with the high ceiling of this chamber there wouldn't be. Climbing up there would be impossible, and his rope wouldn't reach anything useful. He *did* see the bottom of what appeared to be a lift cage, though.

"Sardelle, want to see if you can bring this down?" Ridge asked, leaning out and grabbing his rifle again. The statues were so close that they towered over the group now, their heads nearly brushing the ceiling, rice paper lamps bouncing off their chests. "Ahn and I will try to distract the statues."

"We will?" Ahn asked.

"Just like dodging cannonballs in your flier."

Ridge took a step toward her, but a quake ran through the floor. At first, he assumed it was just another reverberation caused by the colossal statues' steps, but the seam in the tiles under his feet parted, then dropped open.

Ridge twisted and tried to grab at the lift doors, but he was too far away. The space that opened up in the tiles was too large. It was a door of some kind, a trap door. And he had been standing in the wrong spot. He fell into darkness and could do nothing except cry out Sardelle's name as he plummeted. He wasn't sure if it was a call for help or a protest that they were being parted, but it was the last thing he got out before the darkness consumed him.

CHAPTER 13

R IDGE!" SARDELLE CRIED, HER CONCENTRATION lapsing. She hadn't been looking toward the lift when the trapdoor opened, and she hadn't seen the men fall, but Ridge, Apex, and Tolemek were gone, swallowed by a black pit.

"Sardelle," Ahn snapped. "Watch the—"

Sardelle was yanked to the side. One of the huge throwing stars screamed past her ear, slamming into the floor and chipping marble.

"Sorry, yes, thanks," she blurted, yanking back her focus, forcing herself to wait until they were out of danger to worry about Ridge. Even if she wanted to scream and jump into that hole after him. Which might not be a bad idea if it meant escaping from these behemoths. *Figure out how to melt whatever's making them move and shoot yet, Jaxi?*

Working on it. Machines aren't my forte, you know. Jaxi sounded tense and defensive, a rarity for her. That did nothing to soothe Sardelle's nerves as she reestablished the barrier that would protect the team from the projectiles. Not "the team." Just her, Ahn, and Duck.

Clang!

The trapdoor had reset itself. The hole was gone. *Ridge* was gone.

Sardelle struggled to keep the bleakness from overwhelming her, stealing her already flagging energy. "Duck, over here. You're not within my sphere of protection."

"We should retreat to the front door," Duck said, running over to join Sardelle and Ahn. "Think about how to destroy them from out there."

"Assuming they don't follow," Ahn said. "Those doors are big. Can the statues bend over? We might be better ducking into the elevator shaft. Sardelle, you floated that Cofah observer out of the tree. Can you float us up to another floor?"

After defending them from the statues, Sardelle didn't feel up to floating a pencil onto a table. "Maybe. But not while I'm protecting us from them. Give me a second. Jaxi is trying to figure out what operates them so we can melt it. She already tried to destroy the dragon blood inside, but it's not easy to burn, vaporize, or otherwise demolish. The metal hull is so thick that we weren't able to melt it, either."

I could eventually, Jaxi put in. *With a sustained burn. But they're not giving us much time.*

Indeed—as Jaxi was speaking, Sardelle had to jump to the side to avoid a giant stomping foot. The metal monstrosities had long since reached the lift and were doing their best to crush her and the others. Her defensive barrier might be able to stop bullets, but she wasn't ready to try standing beneath a ten-ton foot to see if the statue would bounce off. Her people hadn't been able to keep a mountain from crushing them, after all; there was a limit to what sorcery could accomplish. She had already tried without success to knock the statues over.

"Is it my imagination," Duck asked, "or is it trying to herd us toward the lift—toward that trapdoor in the floor?"

"It's herding us," Sardelle said.

"Any chance that wouldn't be a death sentence? Can you tell if the colonel is still alive?" Duck had a desperate look in his eyes. He probably had no idea what a sorceress could do and was simply hoping she had answers.

"I…" Sardelle stretched out with her senses, trying to locate Ridge. "No," she said, a feeling of bewilderment coming over her. Had he fallen so far and so fast that he was already out of her range? *Jaxi? Do you know what happened to Ridge?*

No, and I'm busy with your other assignment, right now.

But can you at least check? Do you sense him out there at all?

Jaxi was silent. Sardelle and the others danced away from more stomping feet. Ahn stepped out from behind the barrier and fired a couple more rounds at the statues. Her aim was accurate, but none of the bullets caused the machine to falter or slow in any way.

"You can't vaporize the blood, right?" Ahn asked. "But couldn't you vaporize the glass?"

"What?" Sardelle asked, barely hearing her, distressed by her inability to feel Ridge out there. *Jaxi? Are you busy, or...?*

I don't sense him, Sardelle. Or the others. I'm sorry.

Because they've fallen out of range? She couldn't see how that could happen. Jaxi could sense twenty or thirty miles, at least.

I don't think so.

The only other explanation was that they were dead. No, Sardelle couldn't accept that.

"If the blood is on some controller board, the way it was in those unmanned fliers, couldn't you just burn the board? Or the glass bubble holding it on there?" Ahn asked.

Oh. Maybe... yes, let me try.

Sardelle, still numb with the implication of Jaxi's previous words, didn't respond. She barely managed to keep her shield up when another throwing star spun down at them. How much ammunition could these stupid machines have, anyway? A surge of rage filled her, and she longed to run over and chop at one of those lumbering legs, as if it were some tree she could hew down.

She paused at the thought. Maybe it *was* something Jaxi could cut through. Sardelle had been too distracted by protecting the group to try—and maybe intimidated by the size too—but a soulblade could cut through things a mundane sword couldn't.

Gripping the weapon in both hands, she was about to lunge forward when the leg she was glowering at stopped moving. Sardelle tilted her head back as far as she could, trying to see the glowing eyes, but the statue towered so near that she couldn't see past its blocky torso. It had definitely stopped moving, though. Not just the leg, but the rest of the body as well. The arms drooped, and nothing new was fired from them.

The second statue, a dozen meters to the side, had stopped as well.

Someone should have suggested that earlier, Jaxi thought, her voice small, barely a presence in Sardelle's mind. *Like when they first started moving. It could have saved... much.*

Sorry. I should have thought of that myself. "Good thinking, Ahn," she made herself say, though it felt like there was a weight sitting on her chest. Talking hurt. So did everything.

I should have too. I don't... Sardelle, this isn't my world anymore. These mechanical things, I don't... I don't understand them. I don't know what to do when they're a threat.

It was the most uncertainty and remorse Sardelle could remember sensing in Jaxi's words in a long time. Maybe ever.

I know. I don't blame you. Sardelle wasn't sure she could say the same thing for herself. Ridge couldn't truly be gone, could he? That quickly? That meaninglessly?

"Are they down there somewhere?" Ahn waved at the trapdoor. "Should we go after them? Sardelle, can you tell? Are they... all right?"

"I can't sense them at all. It's possible the fall—that they... didn't make it."

Ahn's mouth formed a silent, "Oh."

Duck lowered his rifle, apparently realizing the statues were no longer a threat. He stared at the trapdoor for a long moment, then focused on Ahn. "Raptor, you've got two months' seniority on me, on account of your prior service before entering officer training school."

Sardelle looked back and forth between Duck and Ahn for a moment before she realized what was happening. He was ceding command of the mission to her. Something about that made Ridge's death seem real, far more real than Sardelle was yet ready to accept.

Ahn was as practical as anyone Sardelle knew, and she almost expected the young lieutenant to snap right into leadership mode, but she stared at the floor in front of the lift instead, blinking rapidly, her eyes shiny with unshed tears. She had lost Tolemek and her commander, the man who had been a big brother to her for a lot longer than Sardelle had known him. Sardelle didn't know if it would be appreciated, but she walked over and gave Ahn a hug. Maybe she just wanted one herself.

Ahn didn't push away, but she didn't return the hug, either. It was understandable. After a moment, Sardelle stepped back. She probably would have dropped into a weepy pile at any greater sharing of solace anyway. Mourning would have to wait.

"What are your orders?" Duck prompted after a moment of silence. "Go out or try to find a way up?" He pointed at the lift, the hole in the side of the door staring into dark emptiness.

"Up," Ahn whispered, then lifted her chin, her eyes hard. "Up," she repeated more loudly. "We're not crawling out of here with nothing. Not after…" She shook her head and repeated, "Up. Sardelle, can you get us over the trapdoor and up the lift?"

Sardelle tried to keep a calm facade in the face of the young expectant gazes that turned in her direction. It might be a relief that she didn't have to hide her secrets now, but at some point, she would have to explain the limitations of magic, or rather the limitations of the user. The mental strain it put on a person might be minimal after a good night's rest and with no other stresses on one's life, but now… She couldn't keep herself from glancing at that trap door.

I see how it's triggered. I can keep it from falling when you walk on it. Can you help me figure out the workings of the lift? That would be easier than trying to levitate three people up a shaft. And you've got the problem of potentially running into the bottom of the lift. Or having someone order it down while you're in the shaft.

That thought filled Sardelle's mind with a horrifying image.

"Give me a moment, please," Sardelle said. "It's more feasible to bring the lift down." She hoped.

All right, let's try this, Jaxi. It should be relatively simple, simpler than the statue machinery.

So you say. You haven't seen the big steam machine in the room at the top of the shaft.

Sardelle closed her eyes and let her mind's eye travel up the dark vertical passage waiting behind the hole Tolemek had made. There were four levels above this one. The lift cubicle itself was all the way at the top of the shaft, but she got a sense for the cable system that could raise and lower it. It didn't appear to be automated—on levels other than this one, there were levers to pull that presumably called the lift down. There were also levers inside the cubicle itself. The machine room Jaxi had mentioned lay above the shaft, but the cables were fed through holes in the floor. It looked complicated, but they should just need to pull the right lever, right? Whichever one that was. This floor must not be used often. Maybe there was another way to access the mountain, and only intruders with lock picks or corrosive goo were invited through the main doors.

There's a room full of hot air balloons at the very top. I think the peak of the mountain must open up.

That could explain why the outside gravel strip had been so narrow. It had never been meant for landing.

While Sardelle was thoughtfully studying the levers with her mind and trying to trace the various cables up to the machine room, Jaxi started pushing and pulling things randomly.

What are you doing?

The cable system engaged, and the lift started descending.

That. Jaxi sounded smug. Then the lift stopped on a floor well above theirs. *Huh.* Jaxi pulled another lever.

A few clanks drifted out of the shaft from above. The lieutenants watched the doors, waiting expectantly. Sardelle was glad they couldn't *see* the lift going up and down the way she could. There might have been numbers or instructions beside the various levers, but Sardelle couldn't sense things in that great of detail. Jaxi might have been able to—she could allegedly read books in a library while buried under a mountain hundreds of meters below—but she wasn't having much luck with the system.

There aren't any labels; I would have noticed that. You probably get a tour when you're hired. Here, I think it's coming down now.

Sardelle might have laughed at the randomness of their infiltration strategy—and her lack of qualifications for leading a group of people through this technological miasma—but her soul lacked the capacity for humor at the moment. She felt bleakness rather than triumph when the lift finally stopped on their level.

"Is it safe to cross now?" Ahn pointed at the trapdoor, the outline disguised by the cracks between the tiles.

I think I've jammed the mechanism that made the floor drop away, but double-check, please.

Had I realized machines could make you polite, I would have locked you in an engineer's lab centuries ago. Sardelle found the gears and pulley system built into the floor beside the trap door. If she hadn't been busy defending against giant statues, she might have noticed all that down there earlier. Or perhaps not. She wouldn't have known to look for such things. She vowed to check around every doorway, stair landing, and cupboard for the rest of the time they were in the mountain.

"It's safe." Sardelle led the way across the treacherous patch of floor and ducked through the hole Tolemek had made. A lantern burned inside the lift cubicle, which was open on both sides. Nothing but a rock wall was behind them, but she was getting a sense of the installation layout now and knew that some passages opened up in that direction higher up. She supposed they wouldn't find a map lying around anywhere.

There are some people gathering up on the floor we want to go to, Jaxi said as soon as everyone was inside.

Maybe we should go to a different floor then.

The highest concentration of dragon blood is up there. In a small storage room, I think.

Sardelle imagined a dragon slumbering in a broom closet with a lot of syringe holes punctured in its hide.

I'd know if there were a dragon here. It would be sentient and have a soul I could sense. Also it wouldn't fit in a closet.

I know. I was just... never mind. How many people are up there?

About six right now. They're gathering for something, preparing themselves.

For us?

Maybe. Let me see if I can direct the lift to the right floor.

"There are going to be people waiting for us when we step out," Sardelle said.

"Good." Ahn had already reloaded her rifle, but she checked it again.

Duck nodded once, his face grim.

With a clank and a shiver, the lift started rising.

"How many people?" Ahn asked.

"At least six."

"I'll step out and go left. Duck, you go right. Sardelle, can you and your sword glow and attract their attention?"

"Yes." *Keep us alive, Jaxi. We're the bait.*

Getting shot at doesn't bother me.

Maybe I'll just throw you into the room and let you *glow then.*

We're almost there.

Are they expecting us?

They're facing the door, wondering who it is. They were about to come down to make sure the statues had finished us off.

"Be ready," Sardelle murmured as the lift came to a stop.

The doors didn't open. Sardelle sighed. Would they have to wait for the guards to let them in?

Ahn pushed a button on the side of the door. The doors slid open.

People in this century are so smart.

Sardelle was too busy creating a shield to answer. She would have to be careful to cover Ahn and Duck as they stepped out but not block them from firing. If one of their bullets bounced back and struck her in the chest... Jaxi wasn't the healer she was, so that could be a death sentence.

They stepped out, not into an open room or corridor, but into a haze of brown smoke that stung her eyes and throat and limited visibility to a couple of feet. She kept the shield up, and it was a good thing: guns fired and bullets flew out of the smoke.

I guess they figured out who was coming. Jaxi added a silver flare to Sardelle's shield, making the boundaries visible to anyone close enough to see through the smoke. At first, Sardelle didn't know why—it would make her shield visible to their enemies too—but when Duck and Ahn started shooting around the edge while keeping their bodies protected, she understood.

Slowly, she walked forward, in the direction the barrage of bullets was coming from. The six people were split into two groups, kneeling and standing behind columns to shoot. Ahn and Duck wouldn't be able to see them through the smoke, and Sardelle groped for a way to explain where their enemies were exactly. She could have attacked them, but not without dropping the shield. The acrid smoke was already distracting enough that she struggled to maintain her concentration. It bit at the insides of her nostrils and tears streamed down her eyes.

A cry of pain came from ahead. Someone's bullet striking a Cofah, even through the smoke.

Sardelle kept walking and was halfway to the closest column when Ahn dove to the side, rolling across the floor and disappearing into the smoke. Though surprised, Sardelle kept going. She wiped her eyes, and the outline of one of the thick columns came into view.

Four rapid shots came from the wall to her left. Even though Ahn had gone in that direction, Sardelle's first thought was that the Cofah had crept around them and were firing from the side, where her shield wasn't up to protect them. But no, she sensed the Cofah ahead still, and, yes, that was Ahn over there. Shouts and grunts of pain signaled the bullets finding flesh. Two of the Cofah behind the near column crumpled to the floor; the third turned and ran, clutching at his thigh.

Sardelle shifted toward the other column. Bullets were still pinging off her shield, but the Cofah had figured out the intruders had split up, and they were firing at Ahn now too. Since Sardelle couldn't extend her shield to protect her, not without blocking her ability to fire, she rushed the column instead. No need to walk when one could run.

Close your eyes, Jaxi warned.

Sardelle did so, and a flash of light like a sun exploding erupted against her eyelids. The Cofah stumbled back, and the smoke vanished. Taking advantage of their blindness, Sardelle charged in, letting her shield drop and wielding Jaxi like the sword she was. The men knew she was coming and flung out their rifles, swinging them like clubs and trying to keep her at bay, but Jaxi cut through them faster than Tolemek's goo cut through metal doors. She took one man in the chest at the same time as someone's bullet slammed into the second's forehead. Both guards dropped to the floor. Duck leaped into the fray and caught the third one from behind, pressing a knife to his throat. Ahn charged toward a corridor at the back of the room, following a blood trail.

"Be careful," Sardelle called and almost ran after her, fearing traps under every floor tile.

But Duck's prisoner was struggling, despite the blade at his throat. He opened his hand, dropping something, and more of the smoke spewed into the air. It must have surprised Duck, because the man was able to get his arms up and push the dagger away. He spun toward Duck, a blade of his own in his hand. Duck backed away, but clipped his shoulder against the column. The guard lunged. Sardelle lifted a hand, intending to throw a shield between the two men. But Jaxi attacked first, flaring, and blasted the Cofah with a stream of fire.

Duck stumbled away from the heat, but he wasn't injured. Jaxi flared again, burning away the smoke.

I think he wanted to keep that man alive for questioning, Sardelle noted.

You don't think he would have found that difficult if he himself were dead?

Duck stared at Sardelle and the soulblade, his eyes round. Jaxi's glow had faded but not left entirely, and Duck's expression was more one of terror than gratitude.

"We better catch up with Ahn," Sardelle said. "She went—"

A shot fired from the direction in which she had run.

Duck nodded. "Got it."

The clank of machinery came from the direction of the lift. Sardelle stepped out from behind the column to look as a huge metal wall slammed down with a thunderous boom. She gaped. It was more than a door sliding closed. The thick slab had fallen out of a gap in the ceiling to completely cover the lift and the entire length of the wall on either side.

Rifle in hand, Duck jumped over the charred Cofah and ran for the corridor Ahn had gone down. Maybe she hadn't been the one to fire that shot; maybe the Cofah had escaped and activated this new trap.

Duck was about to turn into the corridor when a grim-faced Ahn strode out of it.

He skidded to a stop. "Are you all right? Did you get the Cofah?"

"Yes, but he smacked some lever in a little room before I caught up with him." Ahn flung a disgusted hand toward the metal wall blocking the lift. "I assume that's what he activated."

"We didn't want to leave yet anyway, right?" Duck said.

The way Ahn's lips thinned wasn't a smile. "Let's find that blood."

She led the way down the corridor, with Sardelle and Duck following. Doors lined the route on either side, some open and some closed. Small, dark rooms lay behind them, all with glass walls on the far side. They came to one with lanterns lit inside.

"Wait." Sardelle wanted to see what was behind the glass. She stepped inside of what turned out to be an observation room overlooking a lab on a lower floor. There weren't any people in it, but the workbenches piled with tools and machinery looked like they had been used recently.

She ticked the glass with a nail, wondering if they might break it and escape that way when they were ready to go. It sounded thick.

More than six inches. Given enough time, I might be able to melt through it, but there's something in there.

What?

As if in response to the question, something moved in the shadows of a far corner. Sardelle was about to stretch out her senses to get a feel for it, but it moved first. It *flew.*

A construct similar in size to the unmanned flier floated up to the observation window. Instead of having a propeller on the nose, like the other one, this craft had a propeller circling above it, allowing it to hover in place. Small rockets were mounted beneath its compact frame.

Those look like the ones that stalked Ridge's flier, then exploded, Jaxi observed.

Maybe we'll keep looking for another way out.

Maybe a good idea.

By the time she returned to the corridor, Duck and Ahn had reached the end and were standing in front of another big metal door. It took up the whole back wall and appeared as sturdy as the slab that had fallen to block the lift. Before Sardelle got close, she could feel energy humming from it. No, *through* it.

"That's our spot," she said.

"How can you tell?" Duck asked.

"I just can." Sardelle was surprised they couldn't feel any of the power. It crackled in the air around them like electricity.

"Any ideas on how to get in?" Ahn touched three shallow divots on one side of the door. They were the only markings. "Does a key go here, or…?"

"I'll try to figure it out." Sardelle stepped closer and touched the cool, smooth metal. It was hard not to jerk her hand back. The power swarmed over her skin like fire ants, ants that bit and nipped at her fingers.

Good luck. I've already looked at the locking mechanism. It's a lot more complicated than what operated the trapdoor, and if I melt it, I think we'll just permanently lock ourselves out.

Maybe the sides of the room—vault?—are less secure and we can cut our way in from another direction.

It's all metal. They like metal here. As heavy as this mountain must be, I'm surprised the whole thing doesn't sink into the hot springs out there.

The facility did have a lot of metal. The floors and walls weren't made of it, thankfully, or the iron in the steel would have interfered with Sardelle's ability to sense their surroundings. Her thoughts hiccupped. Was that why she couldn't sense Ridge and the others? Maybe they hadn't fallen to their deaths, after all. Maybe they were simply buried under too much metal for her to sift through.

She looked at Ahn, opening her mouth.

The walls and floors aren't metal, Jaxi pointed out. *You were just acknowledging that.*

Sardelle closed her mouth. She would wait to say anything to Ahn until she had more proof, but maybe if they could find a map, she could see what was down below the entrance chamber. Once they had the blood, they could check on Ridge and the others. She wouldn't leave them unless she knew without a doubt that they were gone.

We haven't even figured out how to get the blood or get off this floor yet.

Then we have a project.

Better hurry it along. There's a lot of activity now in the rest of the compound. It's a foregone conclusion that the rest of the guards know where we are. I doubt they're going to let us sit here and pry our way into their vault unopposed.

Your cheerful optimism is always a pleasure to be around.

"Got something?" Ahn asked.

"Just thinking," Sardelle said. "While I'm working on the door, you two might want to consider how to defend us if guards show up."

"You think that's likely with the lift blocked?" Duck asked.

"If there are other ways in, they'll know about them."

"We'll be ready." Ahn hefted her rifle.

Sardelle faced the vault door and shut out the rest of the world to focus on the locking mechanism. She tried not to find the complex system daunting, but failed. As Jaxi had said, if they melted or broke the lock, they would prevent the door from opening. That might be desirable when an angry and armed guard was on the other side, but not now.

We're going to have to sign up for some engineering courses, Jaxi.

I already read Denhoft's Theories on Aerodynamic and Aerostatic Flight, *and those two extremely dry engineering books in that prison library. They were not illuminating.*

Sardelle found the latch and tried to lift it out of the door, but it couldn't move until the mechanism behind it disengaged. She left that area and probed around the other walls, trying to determine if they were metal too. Unfortunately, they were made from the same thick steel as the door. As was the floor and ceiling. It was interesting that she could sense the dragon blood through the walls, since iron blocked magic, and there was plenty of iron in steel. Maybe there was simply so much power that it bled through.

I should have asked Tolemek for one of his jars of burning goo, Sardelle thought. *Or I should have had him teach me how to make it.*

Maybe I could melt a hole in the door. It's even thicker than that glass, so it would take a while, but I've melted cast iron before.

A hole? Why not melt the whole door?

You don't want much, do you?
It's either that or we have to master the lock.
I'll melt the door.

CHAPTER 14

R IDGE TUMBLED THROUGH THE DARKNESS, his back, then shoulders, then head striking against the sides of some kind of diagonal shaft. Knowing he might break every bone in his body when he landed—*if* he ever landed—he tried to slow himself down by grabbing at the walls. But they were cold and smooth and too far apart for him to brace himself against. And then they disappeared. Ridge fell straight down, plummeting through emptiness, and in the dark, he couldn't prepare himself for a landing.

He fell into a surprisingly soft pile of dust that flew up everywhere, coating his eyes and tongue. The landing was still jarring, but not nearly as much as if he had struck stone or dirt.

Something heavy smacked his chest, and he let out a pained, "Oof."

That hurt more than the landing. Ridge pushed the object away, only to realize it was someone's arm. Had the whole team fallen into that hole? That trap, he amended with a mental kick to his own butt. He'd allowed his people to be herded right toward it. And here he'd thought having a sorceress along would make everything easier, that it would let him succeed where Kaika and Nowon had failed. What a fool.

Judging by the thud and the flinging of more dust in every direction, someone else landed.

"Sardelle?" Ridge hoped she was with them, because if she wasn't... she was stuck up there with those statues.

"No," Tolemek said, removing his arm from Ridge's hand. "She, Cas, and your other lieutenant were farther away."

"Duck?" Ridge asked.

"Yes."

"Apex, are you down here too?"

A groan came from a few feet away.

"I'll take that for a yes," Ridge said. That had definitely been a masculine groan. "I have a first-aid kit somewhere." His rucksack hadn't come off his shoulders during the fall. "Are you injured?"

"Yes," Apex said, a wince in his voice, "but if you're the only option for medical services, I think I'd rather leave my health to fate."

"There's nothing wrong with my medical skills." Ridge groped his way over to Apex.

"Aren't you the one who offered to staple General Paltimer's nostrils shut to heal his sinus infection, last fall?"

"That had nothing to do with clogged sinuses. I was going to staple his nostrils shut so he wouldn't be offended by the stench of Tiger Squadron's failure—his words—on the Dasikar Bay mission. I thought that was quite polite of me." And if it had earned him a demerit, it had been worth it, for the look on that pompous ass's face.

"Ah, I was mistaken." Apex's breathing was labored, his voice weak.

Ridge shrugged off his pack. "Let me find a match, see how you look. See where we are, too, maybe."

"Underground," Tolemek said.

"Yes, that's obvious. But what is this? The garbage dump? The prison where idiot trespassers are deposited?" Ridge wiped his eyes. Whatever that dust was, it was clinging to every part of him. It was humid and hot down here as well, almost as if they had fallen into a furnace room. Maybe they had. This might be ash they had landed in.

"Obvious because we fell, perhaps, but confusing since we shouldn't have," Tolemek said. "How could there possibly be a basement when the ground all around this mountain is full of water under pressure and heat? You'd think any attempt to dig out earth down here would result in it being flooded. The mountain *itself* is odd."

"I'll trust you on that one. I was too busy making paper fliers to pay much attention during my geology class in school." Ridge had two emergency candles in his pack. The first one he found was broken, but he pulled out a second one intact. "The other science classes too. And when I had that extremely tedious math teacher in third year, I spent at least a month perfecting a launching catapult for my flier. Or was it a trebuchet? I get those two mixed up."

"It's reassuring to know the man leading our mission is so well-educated," Tolemek said.

"I know my weaknesses. That's why you're along. Did nobody tell you that you'd be the brains out here?"

Apex grunted. "Please."

"I assumed I would be the cannon fodder, should things go wrong." After a moment where he was probably contemplating the subterranean darkness, Tolemek added, "Wronger."

Ridge lit the candle. "Only if you don't have a bottle of goo in your bag that can get us back to the others."

The weak flame didn't reveal much beyond the grime-smeared faces of the two men sitting on top of a pile of dirt with him. No, it *was* ash. He had been right. If there was a furnace somewhere, he couldn't see it in the shadows beyond the candle's influence. He had the sense of another large room, not as big as that entrance chamber perhaps, but the ceiling—he could just make out the black hole they must have been dumped through—was about twenty feet above them. They were lucky they hadn't all been killed in the fall.

Apex was lying on his back. His cap had fallen off somewhere, and the fine ash had turned his hair gray. His face was pale too. Ridge did a quick survey of him and didn't find any blood, but the way he gripped his ribs and kept his inhalations shallow told him much.

"I'll bandage your ribs," Ridge said. "No staples."

Apex managed a quick smile, but his eyes were haunted. Ridge knew that look, the sense of fear when one's mortality caught up with a man, the awareness that this might be the last mission. If he had internal bleeding, he might have a reason for that fear, but he couldn't know. Best to make him believe he would be fine.

"It's probably just a couple of cracked ribs," Ridge said. "You'll be able to walk, shoot Cofah, and find a way out with us." Ridge wished his candle had hinted at a set of stairs leading up. Tolemek was rooting in his satchel. Maybe he had some more candles and could do a search. "And we'll catch back up with Sardelle. She can heal you."

"She can do that?" A hint of hope brightened Apex's eyes.

"Yup, that's what she was trained to do back when she... oh, that's a long story. And probably more hers to tell than mine."

"Is it the story of how she came to be in our world—in our *time*? Because she doesn't really fit here."

Huh, Ridge wouldn't have guessed Apex had been paying that much attention or could have guessed that. "What clued you in?"

"There are some words she says like they said them a few centuries ago. And the instruction note in the box that held the communication crystals—I looked over it after we dealt with the pirates—there were diaereses over half of the vowels. Those fell by the wayside about two hundred years ago, at least on Iskandia. The Cofah still use them, but nothing else added up to Sardelle being Cofah."

Ridge wasn't sure whether he should encourage Apex to talk when he was hurt, but it seemed to be distracting him from his pain. He had to be the only one in the squadron who could find linguistics talk distracting, instead of painful in its own right.

"How long have you known? And sit up, will you? So I can wrap you." Ridge held up the roll of bandage. "Here, hold this candle, too, eh?" He helped Apex sit up, grimacing at the gasps of pain his pilot made.

"You're a demanding doctor," Apex rasped.

"A demanding doctor who's cranky because his nostrils are caked with ash." And because he didn't have enough hands free to do everything he wanted.

"Perhaps you should have stapled them shut."

"Perhaps."

Tolemek stood up, a small, sphere-shaped lantern in his hand. "I'm going to look around."

"Good. Find us the way out, will you?" Ridge said.

Apex only glowered silently at him. Ah, yes, being trapped in a garbage dump in an enemy fortress with the two people who loathed each other. This would be fun.

Tolemek walked by as he headed off the ash mound, pressing something into Ridge's hand as he passed. Apex, looking the other way, didn't notice the exchange. The small ceramic jar was labeled healing salve. Ah, yes. Ridge had heard about this and that it was very effective. Good.

Maybe thinking that the two men loathed each other had been inaccurate—only Apex seemed to loathe Tolemek. What would Tolemek do, Ridge wondered, if Apex challenged him to that duel one day?

"I've seen your school records, sir," Apex muttered when Tolemek was out of earshot. "You paid attention at least some of the time."

"You've *seen* my school records?" Ridge squinted at the jar—the single candle in Apex's hand didn't shed a lot of light—but didn't see anything resembling directions. He slipped the lid off. "If they're on display somewhere besides my mom's icebox, I'm going to be appalled."

"They're not on display. I snooped. When I received invitations to join both Wolf Squadron and Eagle Squadron, I was trying to decide where I wanted to go. Since Eagle is stationed up north, it would have been closer to my home grounds, not that there's much up there for me anymore." He didn't bother glowering at Tolemek this time, but Apex did watch him walking the perimeter of the chamber, searching for exits with his small lantern.

"Isn't Colonel Kensingbar a math and engineering maestro? I know he taught classes at the academy when he was on the disabled list a couple of years ago." Ridge's grades hadn't been *that* impressive. There had to be another explanation. He dipped a corner of bandage into the salve jar and smeared it on Apex's ribs.

"Kensingbar failed two history classes and barely passed Iskandian Literature. That's unacceptable."

"And here I thought you'd joined my squadron because I bought you a beer."

Apex frowned down at Ridge's ministrations. "What is that?"

"An antiseptic?"

"It's not the army one."

"No." Ridge set it down, so he could start wrapping bandages before Apex started doing something juvenile, like rubbing the salve off.

Apex scowled at the corner of the chamber Tolemek was inspecting, then scowled at Ridge. "You're putting his cursed witch brews on me. I don't want—"

"Too bad," Ridge said. "Now, stay still."

Apex tried to pull away, but the sudden movement made him hiss with pain. "I refuse. That's not army-tested and approved. I don't want his dragons-damned slime on me."

Ridge gripped Apex's shoulder before he could stand up and hurt himself further. "Sit *down*, Lieutenant." He hated pretending to be a disciplinarian—him of all people, who made a habit of lipping off to senior officers—but he wasn't going to let the friction between these two threaten the mission—or a man's health. "I didn't ask for your opinion on the goo, and I don't care about it, quite frankly. You are welcome to file a complaint when we get back. My willingness to use an unapproved healing product will be a minor crime compared to what else goes on the docket for my court-martial, but maybe your grievance will be addressed." He hurried to finish wrapping Apex's ribs, while he was sitting still.

"My grievance isn't with *you*, sir," Apex said, his eyes pained, probably not from his wounds this time.

"I know, and you can challenge him to a duel later, but I don't want any trouble until we're out of here." Ridge didn't want it later, either, but he'd figure out a way to deal with that when the time came.

Apex sighed dramatically but didn't protest.

"These walls are iron," Tolemek said from the far end of the chamber. "I think the ceiling is too. There are some tubes in the floor over here. And in the walls too. I think they might be for taking samples."

"To make sure the magma chamber isn't heating up so much that the mountain will blow?" Ridge asked.

Tolemek looked over. "Sounds like you didn't sleep through your *entire* geology class."

"No, volcanoes are interesting. Any boy will perk up at the prospect of things exploding, erupting, or otherwise making booms. And if there's a way we could blow up this mountain once we have those samples and get our people out of here, I'd be very open to hearing about it."

"Judging by the size of the Taiga of Boiling Death, there wouldn't be a safe place to hide within hundreds of miles if a volcano-like eruption occurred."

Tolemek stopped in front of a couple of machines. *Weapons,* if the huge gun-barrel-like protuberances were an indication. And they were pointing right at the ash pile—and those on top of it. Ridge hoped those were simple artillery weapons and nothing powered by dragon blood, or that possessed glowing red eyes. He looked ceiling-ward, thinking of Sardelle again. He hoped she and the others were all right. She should have been able to help the team run out past those statues if there was no way up the lift. Having them safe would be good, but it also might mean Ridge, Tolemek, and Apex were the only ones who might be able to complete the mission.

"Interesting," Tolemek said. "These machines are attached to pipes that run into the walls, and there's some kind of..." He wandered around a metal box on the ground. "Engine? Generator? I'd have to take off the cover to know for certain. Maybe. Engineering isn't my specialty. But it looks like the scientists here might be experimenting with using the heat supplied by the hot springs to power these weapons."

"And here I was thinking we'd been tossed into the garbage dump," Ridge said.

"This may be a testing facility." Tolemek pointed at the ash pile. "That could be the remains of whatever they've been testing the weapons on."

"Like... the last people who fell down the trap?" Ridge looked at the gray powder smearing the back of his hand. "Comforting."

"I suspect there's too much ash for human beings to have been the sole contributors to the pile," Apex said, tugging down his shirt—Ridge had finished the bandaging job.

"There's ash on the floor back here, too," Tolemek said. "It's everywhere."

"What I'd really like to hear about is a door." Ridge took back his candle and slid down the powdery slope to the floor. He kicked aside some of the layer of ash Tolemek had mentioned. The floor beneath it looked like iron too. "Am I correct in guessing that iron has a higher melting point than the temperature of lava?"

"Yes," Tolemek and Apex said together.

"I can't imagine how they engineered this though," Tolemek added. "I hadn't thought... This whole facility seems far more advanced than what I'd expect from my people. I always thought— it's not general knowledge, of course, but those with an iota of global awareness know we've fallen behind on technological advancements in favor of focusing on military resources."

"Those guns look like military resources to me." Ridge pointed at the pair of monstrosities near the wall, then a door in the shadows nearby drew his attention.

"Yes... this facility must have been built here with the intent of figuring out how to weaponize the geysers or the magma below them. When they found the dragon blood, they must have thought of this place, since it has such an inhospitable location."

"Let's worry about the historical details later." Ridge tried the knob on the door he had found. Locked. Of course. The sturdy metal didn't look like anything one could kick down, either. "The others will be worried about us. Tolemek, can you open this door?"

Tolemek joined him and dug into his satchel for his vial again. The contents had gone down considerably.

"How many more doors will you be able to do?" Ridge asked, watching Tolemek brush the substance on.

"Not many. I'm on my last vial now. I used quite a bit at the asylum." Tolemek lowered his voice to mutter, "For naught."

"I heard you got some clues at least."

Tolemek's grunt wasn't enthused.

"You're not giving up, are you?"

"No."

A deep clank emanated from the wall behind the weapons. Soft clicks came from the metal boxes Tolemek had been looking at earlier. They were attached to the big guns by thick pipes that also attached to the wall. A faint hum started up from the weapons themselves, a deep note that reverberated through the entire chamber.

"Now what?" Apex grumbled, as he slowly made his way over to join them.

"Now we open that door even faster," Ridge said. "Need any help with that, Tee?"

"No." Tolemek eyed him through his ropes of hair. "Tee?"

"Your name's too long, and I haven't come up with a suitable nickname for you yet."

"Yet? I thought that dubious honor was reserved for your pilots."

"Anyone's a fair target." Ridge drummed his fingers on the wall as the circle of goo started to smoke. He eyed the weapons. "They're pointed at the ash pile, not us, so we should be fine, right?"

"Maybe," Apex said. "Maybe not. We fell into a security system. You wouldn't think you could avoid being incinerated by simply moving out of the way."

"There *is* ash everywhere." Tolemek knelt back from the door, apparently having done all he could until the goop finished eating through the metal.

Ridge hoped it wasn't a *thick* door. "It's getting hotter. The weapons. They're radiating heat like furnaces." The hum was growing louder, too, with the pitch becoming less deep.

"I think it's a fancy crematorium." Apex pointed at the layers of ash. "Everything that falls down here gets incinerated, not just what's in the pile. There's just a pile because more things fall over there." He backed up until he bumped into the wall next to the smoking door. "And if we're in here when the weapons go off, we'll be incinerated too."

"A reasonable hypothesis," Tolemek said.

Ridge thought of Nowon's body, the way his skin had been melted off. Had *he* fallen down here? Or into some other trap powered by the heat of the earth?

"How's that door coming along?" Ridge almost gave it a kick

236

LINDSAY BUROKER

to check for himself, but he didn't know if doing that too early might disrupt the goo.

"Soon," Tolemek said.

The hum was growing higher and higher in pitch. "It's definitely building to something." Ridge jerked a thumb at the door. "Will we be safe as soon as we get out?"

"Eventually. I'm not sure *how* far we'll have to be. The heat could pour through my hole, and if it's just a tunnel or staircase on the other side, it could be quite intense out there." Tolemek gave the door a kick.

"Go, go," Ridge urged. He wanted to leap through himself, but ushered Apex through. Thanks to his injury, he would be slowest and needed any head start he could get.

Thankfully, he didn't object. Apex cried out as the sides scraped his ribs, but he hurled himself through the hole without hesitation. Tolemek grabbed his bag and dove through next. With the high-pitched hum so loud and powerful it felt as if it were tunneling through his eardrums, Ridge scrambled after them.

His candle went out, but Tolemek still had his lantern and led the way up a set of cement stairs. An impossibly long set of stairs that disappeared into the darkness above. Ridge sprinted up them and could have passed the others. Instead, he urged them on with pats on the back. They might have been shoves. All he could think about was the expression, "Heat rises."

The hum culminated in a strange wail and flash so intense it flooded through the hole and up the stairs, lighting every shadow with the power of the sun. A wave of heat slammed into Ridge's back, wrapping around him like water. *Hot* water. It seared his skin, and he was terrified that it might be melting his flesh right from his bones. No, that would hurt more. It had to, didn't it? The heat was uncomfortable, but he wasn't in agony. Not yet. He kept running, sprinting up those stairs even though his thigh muscles burned, and the air he breathed seared his lungs and scraped his throat raw.

Something burned his hand, and he cursed, imagining skin melting off. Tolemek's lantern didn't provide enough light for him to see the wound. Maybe that was for the best. He ran on.

After an eternity or two, the heat finally faded. The machines cycling off? Or maybe they had simply run out of reach.

Apex stumbled and went down, grasping his ribs. "A minute. Please. Just need—"

"Take it." Ridge stopped, putting a hand on his shoulder. The door they had escaped through had fallen back into darkness and disappeared from view.

"The top is ahead," Tolemek said. "I see another door."

It felt like they had climbed enough stairs to have run out the top of the mountain and up into the heavens by now. Ridge rested a hand against the wall. There was something lumpy on the side of his palm, deadening his feeling. He gulped, remembering that pain he had felt. He held his hand up toward Tolemek's light, afraid of what he would see.

Then he laughed.

"Glad you find the news so promising," Tolemek said.

"My hand is covered with wax," Ridge said.

Both men stared at him.

"The candle melted," Ridge explained. "I thought—never mind. A door, you say? Any chance this one isn't locked?" He doubted it.

Apex shifted, and Ridge helped him stand up.

"I'm fine, sir."

"Good."

"It *is* unlocked," Tolemek said.

"I hope whatever's on the other side is cool," Ridge said. "My skin feels like... I don't even know. A bad sunburn."

"Be glad that's all we got." Tolemek pressed an ear to the door, listened, then shook his head. "I don't hear anything."

Ridge eased past Apex, drew his pistol, and nodded for Tolemek to open the door. "Ready."

He stepped past Tolemek and into a cement hallway, ready to fire in either direction. A second or two passed before he realized there was a dead guard on the floor. Like the first one they had encountered, his neck had been slit.

"When nothing's going your way, it's comforting to know that things aren't going the enemy's way, either," Ridge murmured.

Ridge?

He jumped, surprised by the voice, even though he recognized it an instant later. *Sardelle?*

You're alive! The relief that came through the link almost brought tears to his eyes. He was relieved to know Sardelle was alive, too, but her emotion was more intense.

You thought I wasn't?

I couldn't sense you. Neither could Jaxi. I thought...

Oh. We were in a, a crematorium, I guess you could call it. The walls were metal. Iron.

Sardelle had admitted once that she couldn't sense things through iron. *Ah.*

Where are you now? Are Ahn and Duck all right too? Did you have to go back out?

We're all here. We deactivated the statues and went up. But we're... in a little trouble now. If you could find us, we could use Tolemek's help.

Just his? Not mine?

Maybe you can hold his bag.

Very funny. I don't know where we are. You haven't found a map, have you?

"Sir?"

"Hm?"

"I asked if you had a preference as to which way."

"Hold on. I'm seeing if we can get directions."

A surprisingly strong grip latched onto his forearm. "Caslin?" Tolemek asked. "Is she all right?"

Ridge nodded. "Yes, they went up."

Jaxi says for you to take the wider hallway, go up two more flights of stairs, and look for the lift on the floor with all the labs. There are some stairs at the other end that should lead to our level, one up from there. We're on the other side of the lift though, so you'll have to figure out a way to burn through a metal wall to get to us. Oh, also, there are people along your route. If they're like the people we've run into, they'll be expecting trouble. Us.

At this point, I'd be delighted to deal with something as normal as "people." Ridge pointed down the wider hallway and started walking. "This way. Stay alert." *Where are you now? You said you needed help?*

We've found the vault, but we've been shut off from the lift. Sardelle sounded sheepish. *We're locked in for the moment.*

The vault? The vault full of dragon blood?

Yes. But if Jaxi can't melt a hole in the door, that's where we'll need Tolemek. She thinks she can handle it, but she does have a high opinion of her abilities.

I'd never have guessed.

By the way, Jaxi has had time to inspect the mountain and says the peak can open and that the hot air balloons are stored up there. That may be our way out once we're done.

Understood. We'll get to you. Don't take any chances until we get the team back together, all right?

They had been "speaking" back and forth rapidly, and Ridge expected a prompt answer. He followed Apex up the first set of stairs Jaxi had mentioned—since he was distracted, he was letting Apex lead—and onto the second set before prompting Sardelle again.

Right?

No answer.

He cursed softly.

"Sir?" Apex.

"I'm afraid the others are... taking chances."

CHAPTER 15

S ARDELLE?" CAME AHN'S SOFT CALL from the front of the corridor.

"What is it?" Sardelle had been about to finish talking with Ridge and join the two lieutenants—Jaxi was heating up, preparing herself for her attempt to melt the door, and it was about to be far too hot for a human to stand close.

She had no more than reached Ahn and Duck when a soft scrape came from the ceiling in the corner of the big lift room. There was a square hole there that she hadn't noticed before. It looked like some kind of vent or duct entrance with the grate removed. Ah, there was the grate lying on the floor. Ahn and Duck were both aiming at the hole.

Ridge was asking something, and Sardelle was about to answer when a tin canister dropped through the hole. Duck fired.

"Wait," Ahn whispered, "we don't know what it is." The warning came too late. The bullet took the canister in the side, and smoke poured out of the hole.

It was a different color than the earlier smoke weapon, a reddish-pink this time, and Sardelle's stomach roiled as soon as the first fumes reached her nose.

"Hold your breath," Duck said. He kept standing there, like he meant to hold his breath and shoot whoever came out of the duct, but Sardelle's senses screamed that this was more dangerous than the other smoke, that it had toxic properties.

"Get back," she whispered. "Both of you."

She could have made a shield, an airtight bubble around herself, but she wouldn't be able to attack through it, so she pushed past them and focused on the smoke billowing from the can. She drew air from the room behind her and pushed it against the air in that corner. Her churning stomach made it hard to concentrate, but she managed to squash the smoke into a small area for a moment.

She was debating on how to destroy the canister and the tainted air completely when the first guard dropped through the hole. Well armed—and wearing a mask—he landed in a crouch.

Sardelle waved her hand and ripped the mask from his face at the same time as a second guard landed, this one aiming straight at her. A shot came before she could raise a shield to protect herself. But the shot came from behind her, not from the man. Ahn had leaned around the corner, risking the smoke. The man in the mask pitched to the floor.

The guard who had dropped into the room first had fallen to his knees and was clutching his neck. Eyes huge, he reached for the mask Sardelle had ripped off, but he collapsed before he touched it. She didn't know whether he was dead or unconscious, but the ramifications horrified her either way.

"Get back," she repeated to Ahn and returned to trying to confine the smoke. Sticking it back into the canister was impossible, but she did what she should have done immediately. Using the surrounding air again, she pushed the smoke up to the ceiling and into the hole—she could sense more people in the ductworks up there, now that she was looking for them. She tried to usher the gas toward them. It was like trying to throw sand through a hole, but if she could at least get most of it out of their space...

Her stomach interrupted her fight. Clutching at her gut, she ran from the room. She could have vomited right there, but she didn't want the people in the duct to hear her and believe they had affected her. Instead she ran back to the first observation room, just managing to pass through the doorway before heaving her dinner all over the floor. She gripped the wall, her sides and chest aching from the effort even as she was unable to stop the spasms. What *was* that gas? She thought of the inhalant Tolemek had created. It couldn't be related to that, could it be? If it was, would she die in seconds?

Don't die. I'm working on the door. Getting through it.

Sardelle finished throwing up, but she couldn't manage the

mental energy to respond. Her body was shaking, and sweat poured down the sides of her face. She wanted to collapse on the floor, but that was a mess now, and her dignity overrode her physical weakness. She staggered toward the hall, hoping to find a clean place to slump against a wall. She also hoped nobody would notice the mess she had made if she closed the door behind her.

But Duck was standing in the corridor outside. His face was flushed red and bathed in sweat, and he looked like he had thrown up somewhere too. He gave her a lopsided smile, though.

"You're human."

Yes, sorcerers could vomit, the same as anyone else. All she said was, "Apparently so."

"That's not." Duck stepped aside to nod toward the back of the corridor.

Jaxi lay on the floor, where Sardelle had left her, but a bright two-inch-thick orange stream of energy shot out of the tip of her blade, flames dancing along the beam. Sardelle didn't think the flames were necessary. Jaxi had probably added them for flair.

"No, that is a special soul." Sardelle turned toward the open end of the corridor. "Ahn?"

"Here," Ahn called softly. "There are more vent grates in that room. I'm watching them, but we should check in those little rooms too." Her face was also flushed, and her hands shook, but she hadn't dropped her gun, and she looked like she would die there in the mouth of the corridor rather than leave her self-assigned post.

"Ridge and Tolemek are alive," Sardelle said.

Ahn glanced back at her.

"Apex too. I thought you should know before you decided to get suicidal defending us."

"Good." Ahn didn't deny the suicidal bit. Hm.

"I'll watch with you," Sardelle said. "I'll know how to react now. Canister goes back up into the hole before it explodes."

"Or some idiot shoots it," Duck muttered from behind them.

"I'm sure it was designed to spit the gas out anyway," Ahn said.

Sardelle's stomach gave another little twinge. She wasn't sure if she had gotten enough of the gas out of the room to keep them from suffering further deleterious effects, but she hoped so. That guard still wasn't moving. The first one had been shot dead, but she felt compelled to check on the second. If he was still alive, she might be able to do something for him. But he must have caught an entire lungful of that gas, or maybe his body tolerated it less well than others. Either way, he was dead.

Remembering that she had been communicating with Ridge when all of this had started, Sardelle reached out to him again. *Ridge?*

Sardelle, you're all right?

She decided not to mention the vomit. Or the fact that her belly was still shivering with the aftereffects of that vile concoction. Tolemek must have a like-minded soul here. She shuddered, imagining going up against that person.

For the moment, we're fine. Still stuck, but fine.

Good. We're trying to get to you. We're—

Busy? Sardelle guessed when a moment passed without a response. She stretched out, trying to find him in the maze of a mountain, but she ran into the Cofah first. There were more guards moving around in the ducts above the front room, and a pair of them were crawling along on elbows and knees, making their way over the laboratories. They must be angling for a vent in one of those observation rooms.

She almost missed Ridge's response of, *Yeah.*

We have more trouble to deal with here, she told him. *Be careful. I'll check on you as soon as I can.*

Wait, Ridge added. *Do you know how those soldiers blew up your mountain three hundred years ago?*

What? I mean, why do you want to know?

I'd like to do the same thing here, if possible. After we leave.

Sardelle shuddered at the idea of collapsing the mountain with people in it, even if they were Cofah soldiers and scientists making deadly weapons to fling at her homeland. She didn't have an answer for him anyway. *I don't know what they used exactly. It was all a blur of running to the meeting point and assuming others would make it too. I didn't see any of the detonations myself and don't even know if it was some form of magic or not—though it seems strange that they would have used magic against the very magic users they feared and wanted to destroy.*

All right. A determination accompanied his words, like he meant to succeed with that plan, one way or another.

She trusted he would warn her in advance, so she would worry about the most pressing problem first.

"Ahn," Sardelle whispered, "two are trying to come in behind us. I'll be right back."

Ahn gave her a quick salute. There wasn't likely any thought behind it, beyond acknowledging her words, but it made Sardelle smile anyway. It was as if she had been accepted as part of the squadron. Who knew vomit would do that?

She walked back toward Jaxi. Heat was rolling off that vault door, and noxious smoke as well—their lungs would all need the attention of a healer after this—but Sardelle couldn't tell if the soulblade had broken through yet. She would ask for an update after she dealt with the two guards.

She slipped into an unlit observation room. Whatever lay beyond the glass in this one, it was too dark to tell. What lay above the ceiling was more concerning. Enough light seeped in from the corridor that she made out a vent in one corner. She closed her eyes and once again located the approaching men. Inspired by Jaxi's heat wave, she applied some energy of her own to the bottom of the duct, close to the vent. Her mind ached, and her eyes felt gritty, like she needed to close them for a few hours—or a few days. She had been expending too much of her power and feared her muscles were trembling from more than the effects of that poison. Still, she managed to heat the thin duct metal nicely and was rewarded with a yelp of pain when the first man reached it, placing his hand on the hot spot.

He shuffled back in a rush, bumping into the guard behind him. They were right above Sardelle, with tools in hand to remove the vent covering. She wasn't going to allow that. In fact... she examined them more closely until she found another of those canisters. She yanked it from the pouch where the second man had it stored. If the vent grate had already been removed, she would have pulled it down into the room with her, so she could stuff it in a cabinet somewhere the Cofah couldn't use it. Instead she hurled it down the duct behind the guards. She sensed other men nearby, all jerking their heads up in alarm at the sound of the tin can clattering toward them. She contemplated puncturing a hole and letting that gas spew forth, but not when someone had died after exposure to it. She couldn't do that, even to her enemies. With luck, simply hearing the canister clanging around would distract the men for a time. They would wonder if it might have been triggered, and they would have trouble finding it in the dark.

Good plan. Jaxi sounded tired, exhausted. Even if a soulblade had no physical body that required food and rest, its stores of power weren't unlimited. Jaxi, too, would need a break to recharge.

When Sardelle returned to the corridor—it was like stepping into a sauna—the increase in energy crackling in the air told her that the vault had been breached before her eyes did. Her own weariness combined with the intensity of the power almost forced her to her knees. She braced her hand on the doorjamb. It wasn't malevolent power or benevolent power. Just power. A lot of power.

I'm done. Jaxi's beam winked out.

The light level fell, but there were enough lanterns lit in nearby rooms that Sardelle could see the end of the hall. And she could see a giant hole in the door, its ragged sides melted like candle wax with drops of molten steel spattered on the tile floor.

"That's impressive," Sardelle murmured.

Thank you.

"What's going on up there, Sardelle?" Ahn asked from the front of the corridor, jerking her chin toward the ceiling. Duck stood next to her, frowning upward too.

"A little confusion. We should have a moment before they try anything else." Sardelle walked to Jaxi, intending to sheath her, but so much heat radiated from the blade that she was afraid the hilt would burn her hand.

Give me a moment to cool down. I'm sizzling. You couldn't handle me.

No surprise there. You need a dragon to handle your heat.

Jaxi snorted. *Alas, he's not here. Just his blood. And considering how much blood has been carted in here, I doubt he's in very good condition wherever he is.*

"Is it safe to go in?" Ahn had crept up beside Sardelle. Duck remained on guard, or maybe he wasn't comfortable walking past a naked soulblade and into a vault filled with magical blood.

"Should be." Sardelle had already searched the area around the door thoroughly and didn't think any traps had eluded her. "Just watch out for the dripping steel."

The drips were already hardening, creating a strange image, almost like the top of a cave with numerous small stalactites dangling down. The Cofah would doubtlessly wonder what had happened to their technologically superior door.

When Ahn didn't rush inside, Sardelle grabbed a lantern and went first. Entering the hole was almost like walking underwater, pushing against the current of power. For her anyway. Ahn breezed inside as if there was nothing abnormal about the place.

There wouldn't have been room for anyone else in the small vault. A wooden crate in the center took up most of the floor space. It was covered with FRAGILE warnings and shipping labels. The back wall held shelves, mostly empty, with one supporting a rack of test tubes filled with blood. Several empty racks occupied other shelves.

"Does that mean they're almost out of their supply?" Ahn pointed at the empty racks.

"I don't think so." Sardelle touched the crate. "Most of the energy is coming from here."

"Energy?"

"Yes, I can feel it. It's very intense."

"Should we open it?"

Sardelle knelt and examined the shipping labels. It had been checked in at Port Krunlow and Bekany Bay, both along the Cofah coast, but the label that would have mentioned its origins had been ripped off.

Ahn lifted one corner. "The crate is heavy, but two of us could carry it. Maybe we should just take the whole thing."

"Carry it where? We haven't figured out how to get off this floor yet."

"The Cofah are getting here through the vents."

Yes, and she would have to tell Ridge about that possibility as an access point. And about the canisters. She shuddered at the idea of him running into that smoke.

"Guess we can't carry this box through a vent though," Ahn said.

"No. Let's open it."

Ahn slung her rifle onto her back and withdrew a big utility knife. Though it looked like a simple shipping crate, Sardelle tried to sense the insides before Ahn broke in. If there was a trap, she couldn't tell. She had a vague sense of numerous tubes of blood, but their power distorted their surroundings. At the moment, Sardelle would have a hard time sensing her own gender.

Fortunately not something that's likely to have changed in the last five minutes.

Let's hope so.

Unless that smoke had some very strange side effects.

I see you're recovering well from your ordeal, Jaxi.

I'm exhausted. I'm going to need you to carry me out of here.

Sardelle snorted.

At the noise, Ahn paused in the middle of sliding her blade into the crack under the lid and looked up.

"Just... soulblade humor. Carry on."

"Uh, all right."

Ahn popped open the crate and pushed aside the top. Inside, packed in wads of dried foliage, lay racks of test tubes. There must have been two hundred and fifty vials, all full of blood.

"Huh. I was sort of expecting them to glow or something," Ahn said.

"Energy doesn't glow. It just is."

Ahn sniffed. "Smells good, though. I assume that's this stuff and not the blood." She picked up a handful of dried leaves and flowers.

Sardelle stared at the foliage. It had clearly been used for nothing more than insulation, to keep the tubes from breaking, but that purple flower... She plucked it out of Ahn's hand.

"Something wrong?" Ahn asked.

"I've seen this recently," Sardelle whispered.

"Where? It looks tropical."

"On the wall of an asylum room two hundred miles from here."

* * *

They found a third dead Cofah at the top of the last set of stairs. The man had been killed in the same manner as the others, with a slit throat. Ridge, Tolemek, and Apex had already fought their way past a group of scientists whose hearts hadn't been in the battle. They had hurled a few flasks of smoking compounds at them, but the men and women had looked like they had been in the middle of packing. Either way, they hadn't been trained warriors and had fled as soon as Ridge's team proved capable of putting up a fight. Not wanting to shoot civilians, Ridge had let them go. He hoped he wouldn't regret that later.

As they stepped over the body, Ridge wondered once more who was inadvertently helping them storm the mountain. All of the kills had been recent.

"I wonder if we'll stumble across our ally soon," Apex said.

"I'd like to stumble across the rest of our squadron first." Ridge led them down a wide corridor with glass-walled labs on both sides. These were similar to the ones on the level below, and though he didn't see anyone scurrying around, there were also boxes and bags out, half stuffed with equipment and notebooks. "Were they packing because of us? Or do they know something we don't know?"

A soft clank came from above. Ridge jerked his rifle upward. There were no floating lanterns on this level, and shadows cloaked the ceiling. A long moment passed, and nothing moved. He lowered his weapon, but vowed to glance upward often. At this point, Ridge wouldn't be surprised by anything they crossed. In addition to the laboratories, they had passed chambers full of half-assembled fliers and unmanned craft, along with rooms full of devices for containing and studying the steam and hot water from the geyser field.

Tolemek walked to a lab table full of beakers and a complicated maze of glass tubes—Ridge couldn't guess what it was for, though some green liquid rested in a spherical ball in the middle of it. A notebook open on the table was what drew Tolemek's eye. He stared at the page, then flipped to the front, then glowered at the glass apparatus.

"Something important?" Ridge wanted to keep going, to find the others and the blood and to figure out a way to escape, preferably while destroying most of the scientists' work on the way.

"I *thought* so," Tolemek growled, sounding more like a riled bear than a man.

"What?" Ridge asked.

"That formula they hit us with downstairs, it seemed familiar. This is my work. Based on it anyway. It looks like someone lifted my notes from a few years ago and mailed them here." Tolemek slammed the book shut. "If it was Goroth, I'll kill him again."

"Their fliers are clearly based on our designs," Apex said. "The Cofah seem to struggle with originality."

Tolemek gave him a flat look, knocked the apparatus on the floor with a great shattering of glass, and strode onward.

"Good idea," Ridge said. "Let's make sure the enemy knows exactly where we are at all steps in our journey."

Tolemek was too busy stalking and glowering to respond. Ridge jogged back into the lead. The lift doors were visible at the end of the lab area. All they had to do now was find a way to reach Sardelle and the others on the other side. A side that was unfortunately blocked. He glanced upward. She had mentioned a top level where the hot air balloons were kept. Maybe there was a way to go up and over.

Ridge?

Yes. We're close.

Men have been attacking us through the vents. You should be able to reach us the same way.

Ridge grimaced, imagining gunfights in a snarl of tight duct passages.

They've quieted down now, Sardelle added. *I think they may be leaving to try something else. If you do run into them, be very careful. They have cans full of a smoke that's killed one person and made the rest of us sick. A big enough inhalation might kill anyone.* Her words came with an image of pale red smoke blowing out of a canister.

Wonderful.

Perhaps better news is that we've gotten into the vault and have the dragon blood.

Ridge lifted his head. That *was* better news. *How much is there?*

A crate full. Carrying it out as is might be problematic, but if we split the burden between all of us, it might be doable.

The king *had* wanted samples. But the true mission was to deny the Cofah of this resource. *No sign of the dragon itself, eh?*

The crate came from, well, we're not sure exactly, but a tropical region. It's traveled quite a ways to get here.

Oh? I'd hate to think the Cofah could simply... order more.

Maybe your next mission will be to find the source. If the king is still talking to you when we get back.

Ridge snorted. A legitimate concern.

There's more. Tell Tolemek... Oh, wait. Jaxi is communicating with him.

Tolemek had stopped walking and his glower had changed to an expression of confusion.

I'll explain further later, Sardelle went on, *but Tolemek's sister may be caught up in all of this somehow. Either to get at him or for... other reasons. It's possible she's been moved to the same location as these vials came from.*

Strange. Do you—

The elevator doors slid open, revealing a cluster of crimson-uniformed guards, all wearing protective vests and all carrying rifles or—

Ridge cursed. Was that a rocket launcher?

He and the others were still twenty meters from the end of

the room. "Take cover," he barked and lunged to the left, toward a lab table piled with books and equipment.

Apex and Tolemek lunged right, finding a thick column to hide behind. The Cofah spotted them right away, and bullets were skipping off the marble floor before Ridge had fully flung himself behind the desk. One struck the pile of books atop it, knocking a tome off onto his head.

"Because my head hasn't taken enough damage this week," he grumbled.

He shot a couple of rounds around the side of the desk, trying to take out a few of the guards before they rushed into the room and also found cover, but another clank came from the ceiling, this one louder than the last. A vent grate dropped to the floor behind Apex and Tolemek. A canister rolled out of the opening in the ceiling, smoke spewing from a hole in the top.

Ridge fired at a shadow moving above the vent. He didn't know if he hit the person, but nobody else came through after the canister.

Tolemek's eyes widened when he spotted the smoke, or maybe when he *smelled* it—his nostrils flared and he grabbed Apex. "We have to move."

Apex shoved him away, refusing to leave the protection of the column. "People are shooting at us!"

A barrage of shots came from the lift area, punctuating his words. Some men had stayed inside, jamming the doors open somehow, and others had lunged behind two columns closet to the lift.

"Get away from that smoke," Ridge yelled. "Sardelle said it's deadly."

A bullet slammed into the back of his desk, and he had to look away before seeing if they complied. The impact hurled one of the drawers onto the ground and made him rethink his hiding spot. More bullets skipped off the floor all around him. He didn't know if he was going to get a chance to run to a new position. He couldn't even lift his head to check on Apex and Tolemek.

Another round slammed into the back of the desk, this one

cutting a hole. If he had been hunkering closer, it might have cut a hole in *him.*

Ridge scooted back, bumping the drawer that had fallen out. Glass clinked. There were several vials and flasks full of colored liquids. He grabbed a few and lofted them over the top of the desk toward the lift. He had no idea what they did, but he doubted the guards did, either. Maybe they would get worried and run back to the lift, or maybe he would get lucky, and the mixture of chemicals breaking onto the floor out there would smoke and hiss terrifyingly.

A whiff of the red stuff that had been thrown through the vent reached him, and his stomach clenched. Sardelle's warning thundered to the front of his mind again. He would *have* to risk changing positions now. The shots coming from the lift had slowed down. Maybe his chemical cocktail was doing something. Or maybe the guards were readying themselves for a more deadly attack. Those two men with rocket launchers filled his mind.

Ridge rushed to reload his rifle, then threw the rest of the drawer's contents and burst out from behind the desk. He fired as he ran, and by luck struck one of the men holding a launcher. The Cofah had just stepped out of the lift with the weapon. The bullet took him in the neck, but it was too late. He had already fired.

A floor-shaking boom erupted from the desk Ridge had been hiding behind. The rocket obliterated the metal frame and all of its contents. Even though he had left the position, Ridge still felt the force of the explosion. It slammed into his back, and he caromed off a column, then stumbled to the floor. He scrambled behind a bookcase before the Cofah figured out where he had gone. Paper confetti flooded the air, floating down everywhere. It was all that remained of the books and papers on that desk.

Taking advantage of the confusion, Ridge rolled into a crouch on the other side of his hiding spot and fired several rounds. He was closer to the lift now and could see the men behind the columns. They were facing the explosion—or maybe Apex and Tolemek were occupying their attention—so Ridge had a good shot at them. He fired twice, taking two men in the legs—those vests they had on were blocking shots to the torso—before the others adjusted their position behind the column and started shooting back at him.

He ducked back behind the bookcase. There were two pieces of furniture back to back; he hoped they would be thick enough to stop bullets. A queasiness had come over him, and he fought against a growing urge to heave the contents of his stomach.

Get back. To the wall. As far as you can. Away from the lift and those men. That was Jaxi's voice, not Sardelle's, but Ridge obeyed it, nonetheless.

Using the bookcases to block his movement, he crawled between two workstations, around a column, and kept going until he reached the wall. At the same time, a second explosion rocked the laboratory. Even though Ridge wasn't as close to this one, it still hammered him into the wall. Furniture toppled down all around him, with glass shattering and breaking as it landed on the floor amid books, drawers, and the gods knew what else.

Ridge scrunched up against the wall, holding his breath, not sure if something toxic might be flowing out of those broken containers—and not sure he should be breathing the smoke in the air, either. Parts of the ceiling had fallen, too, and he spotted cracks in the column nearest him.

It's all right now. I'm communicating with Tolemek too. He's the one who threw that explosive.

"Zirkander," came Tolemek's voice, weary and pained. "You better be alive. I need someone to help me find my dragons-cursed bag before your man dies." A slam sounded, a desk being kicked, and Tolemek cursed and started shoving more things around.

Ridge pushed to his feet, but he didn't make it far before the nauseating feeling that had assailed him before returned fivefold. He clutched his belly and tried to calm his system, but his gut roiled anyway. He dropped his rifle and vomited all over the floor before he managed to stumble away from the wall.

He forced himself to run, passing bodies—and body parts— strewn all over the floor. His beleaguered stomach threatened another round of spasms. On the floor behind a column, there was an inert form that wasn't wearing the crimson Cofah uniform, but the gray and blue of Iskandia. Ridge forced aside his sickness to run to Apex, afraid he was already dead.

Apex's uniform jacket was covered in vomit, his limbs were trembling, his face was drenched with sweat, and saliva beaded at the corners of his mouth. Unfocused eyes stared at the ceiling, and his weak breaths rasped in his throat. Ridge stumbled to his knees beside him and clutched his arm.

"Apex," he said. Uselessly. What more could he say that wouldn't be a lie? Ridge knew a dying man when he saw one.

"I don't know why everyone's vomiting," came Tolemek's voice from a toppled bookcase a few feet away. He heaved the obstacle away and dragged out his bag. "Some Cofah tinkering with the formula."

"Can we discuss that later?" Ridge snapped, annoyed with the science analysis. If Apex had another minute, he'd be shocked. He needed... what, Ridge didn't know. "You know what this gunk is? Can you do anything?"

Apex blinked, his eyes focusing on Ridge. Tears welled in them. "Should... should've listened," he whispered, then took a deep breath, or tried to. He didn't seem to be getting the air he needed.

Tolemek dropped down on the other side of Apex, digging in his bag. He pulled out a jar and a syringe. Ridge held his breath, hoping that was some kind of cure—and that it could be delivered fast enough. And that it would work. What did that mean? A Cofah tinkering with the formula? Was this something of his? That same death toxin that had almost been unleashed in the capital?

With quick, efficient movements, Tolemek filled the syringe from the jar. "I'm not going to try to make a deal with you, Zirkander, but I'd appreciate it if you keep this piranha off me in exchange for this." He pulled out a knife, cut open Apex's trouser leg, and jabbed the needle into his thigh.

Apex didn't react. He didn't even seem aware of them anymore.

"What is it?" Ridge whispered, watching his lieutenant's face, hoping this was some miracle cure.

"Atropine. I make it in my lab from the deadly nightshade plant."

"*Nightshade?*" Ridge lunged across Apex and grabbed Tolemek by the shirtfront. "I thought you had a cure, not a poison." Was all of this just to end Apex's suffering? Seven gods, Ridge could have done *that* with a knife.

"Relax, Zirkander. It's not enough to poison him." Tolemek picked up Apex's wrist, his fingers resting on the pulse. He watched the lieutenant's face and ignored the death grip Ridge had on his shirt. "Even if the Cofah altered the formula, it's still an organophosphate. The symptoms match up, and I can tell from the abbreviated whiff I got."

"I have no idea what you're talking about." But Ridge let go of Tolemek's shirt. Apex's eyes had widened, and his breathing had grown less raspy.

"That's what you get for making paper fliers during your science classes."

"I—"

Movement behind Tolemek drew his eye. A crimson-cloaked figure was dropping down from the ceiling, not ten feet away.

Ridge remembered his rifle—back on the floor where he had left it when he had been vomiting and worrying about Apex. He clawed at the pistol on his belt, but the guard already had a weapon pointed at him. Ridge threw himself to the side and whipped his own gun out at the same time as a shot fired.

He expected a bullet to the chest, but it was the guard who reacted, stumbling forward, then spinning around. Another shot fired. The man tumbled to the floor. Ridge raised his aim to a second guard, who had been in the middle of lowering himself from the vent. He'd paused at the sounds of gunfire, and started to pull himself back up, but Ridge caught him first. His shot struck the man in the side, and the man dropped like a brick. Two more shots—not his—were fired from somewhere behind the Cofah men, both thudding into the figures on the floor. The guards didn't move after that.

Ridge stood, his pistol in his hand, not sure whether he was about to welcome an ally... or something else.

A figure in a torn crimson uniform stepped out from behind a pillar, a Cofah shotgun in one hand and a pistol in the other. Ridge tensed. But the person spoke at the same time as he recognized the bruised, swollen face.

"I wasn't expecting you here, Colonel," Kaika said.

Ridge swallowed. "We weren't expecting you, either."

Kaika looked fierce and scary at the same time as she looked battered almost beyond recognition and wearier than death. "We thought... they said you were dead, and we saw bodies hanging by the door. Wearing your uniforms."

"Yeah." Her eyes closed and she took a shuddering breath. "Nowon is dead. I couldn't figure out how to get into the vault. I questioned a couple of guards and scientists, but they didn't know. They kept saying the woman who knows isn't here. I've been hiding out—I think they thought I was dead, too... after that acid trap thing... whatever it was. But I tricked the scientist who tripped it, pushed her in, then stuck her in my uniform." She was walking toward them as she spoke, her steps slow, her shoulders slumped, as if firing those last shots had taken all of her meager reserves.

Ridge lifted an arm, not knowing if she wanted a hug, but she damned well looked like she needed one. So did Apex, whenever he was strong enough to sit up and receive one.

Kaika slumped against his side, accepting the arm around her shoulders. "I've been skulking around for days, using what I could find—what I could recognize—to make explosives."

"Explosives?" Maybe someone else had his plan in mind.

"I thought if I couldn't get to the dragon blood, I could blow up the mountain so nobody else could, either." She looked at him warily. "The king... I mean, I didn't talk to him directly, but Nowon said he didn't want any of this to survive to be used against us." She waved toward the laboratories. "And I don't think he knew about half of what they've been doing here. Or even a tenth. Are you going to countermand that? Because I was about to light the fuse, but I heard the gunshots and thought—I figured it must be you people. Who else knows this place is here? I didn't want to blow you up."

"Those are the kinds of words I like to hear from my officers. My enemies too. Listen, Sardelle and the others have the dragon blood." Ridge pointed at the lift, in the direction he believed them to be. "So let's not blow this place up yet. If we can get to them, we can bring back some samples for the king and our own scientists." He tilted his chin toward Tolemek, who was helping Apex sit up. Apex still looked like something an alley cat had coughed up, but some of the color had returned to his face. "*Then* we can blow up the mountain."

"Let's make sure we figure out how to get out before considering that route," Tolemek said.

"Welcome back, Captain," Apex said. "You look awful."

Kaika looked at Ridge and jerked a thumb at Apex. "The man knows he's sitting in his own puke, piss, and shit, right? I can't possibly look worse than him."

Apex's face paled a little again as he looked down at himself. Ridge was glad he had only caught the tail end of that smoke—and had ejected most of his own vomit onto the floor. He had notions of a romantic reunion with Sardelle, and that was always easier without puke plastered on one's shirt.

"He does now." Ridge nudged Apex's boot with his own. "Hope you brought a change of clothing, man. Otherwise we might not let you into our hot air balloon."

Apex's expression grew even more mortified. Good. If he could manage to look mortified, he couldn't feel that awful anymore.

Ridge?

Here. We've met some of your ceiling rats. And their smoke bombs.

Did everyone make it?

Thanks to Tolemek, yes.

Good. We've separated the vials into bundles for different people to carry. Should we try to reach you or wait to be rescued?

Ridge snorted softly. *Somehow I doubt the people who figured out how to get into that vault are truly in need of rescuing.*

That depends on whether you want Jaxi randomly melting walls.

She can melt the whole place if she wants. Oh, wait. "Where are the explosives, Kaika?" Ridge asked.

The captain pointed toward the floor. "Lowest level, support columns. I've never done a cone-shaped building before—" she outlined the mountain form with her hands, "—but I found the architectural blueprints, so I think it'll go down smoothly."

Ridge wondered if he and the others had been battling those statues on the ground floor without ever noticing explosives nestled in the shadows of the walls.

"How do you get them to go off all at once?" Tolemek asked. He had repacked his bag, slung it over his shoulder, and appeared ready to march.

"I found some timers I could modify to use. I haven't set them yet. The lift is watched so I haven't been using that. Been climbing all over this place. I haven't slept in... I don't even know what day this is."

Ridge clasped her shoulder. "The day we get out of here and go home. Would you be terribly offended if I sent you back down there to set those timers now?"

Kaika slumped a little, but she said, "No, sir."

"Can you give us... three hours?" Ridge thought they could find the others and the way out Sardelle had mentioned in less than two, but couldn't imagine there was a need to make it close. Other than the fact that the Cofah might find the explosives if they were given more time to do so.

"Most I can do with the clocks I found is an hour," Kaika said.

"Oh." That *would* be close.

Sardelle? he asked, hoping she might be monitoring his mind or whatever it was telepaths did to communicate with non-telepaths, but he didn't receive a response. Guess she wasn't obsessed enough with him to want to stalk his every waking thought. Probably a good thing for his sanity. And hers.

"Sir?" Kaika said. "This is why I was sent. Nowon was supposed to get the blood, and I was supposed to destroy the research facility." She gazed past him, at the wrecked furniture and lab, or maybe at nothing. "I can stay behind to give the rest of you more time to escape."

And get herself killed if she couldn't get out in time, if not in the explosion then in trying to pick a path through those geysers.

"No, we'll all get out of here together," Ridge said. "Set the timers, and meet us at the top floor. There are hot air balloons that we can launch from there to escape." Or so he had been told. He hoped Jaxi's assessment of the mountain proved accurate, or they would all be in trouble.

"Yes, sir."

"I can give you some company if you'd like, Kaika. To watch your back while you work." As soon as he said it, he realized *he* would have to be that company. Tolemek might be needed to burn a way in to free the others, and Apex would be lucky to walk out of here of his own accord.

Or so Ridge thought. Apex pushed himself to his feet, using his rifle for support. "I can help her, sir. I'll, ah, grab one of these Cofah uniforms since mine is in… disrepair. We might be less likely to be shot if we look like them anyway."

Ridge lifted his eyebrows, wondering if Kaika would want someone who had almost been dead ten minutes earlier. He wouldn't have much energy.

From the way her lips screwed up thoughtfully—or was that dubiously?—Kaika was mulling over the same thing. By this point, she might be desperate enough for company to take him anyway. Ridge felt bad about sending her down to the bowels of the mountain again, but she was the demolitions expert. He wouldn't know where to begin to set the charges.

Kaika finally thumped Apex on the shoulder. "Fine. You can hold my rifle while I tie knots. Let's go."

Surprisingly, Apex perked up at this offer. Or maybe it wasn't so surprising. Ridge remembered that Kaika had kissed him the last time they had seen each other. Duck, who had been more openly ogling her, hadn't received similar treatment.

Before heading away, Apex looked back at Tolemek. "Thanks for the help."

It wasn't exactly a peace offering or an apology for all the digs he had taken at Tolemek, but maybe it was a start. Ridge didn't know, but he hoped so. He didn't want to have to reassign

Apex to the other side of the continent to ensure he wouldn't come in contact with his nemesis.

"You're welcome," Tolemek said.

"Well, Tee," Ridge said as the other two walked away, "shall we find our ladies?"

Tolemek looked up at the open duct access point. "Yes. It was foolish of us to misplace them in the first place."

"I agree."

CHAPTER 16

SARDELLE WAITED UNDERNEATH A VENT opening while Duck lugged out the last bag of vials they had packed. They had done their best to insulate them, but glass still clinked when he set it down. Sardelle hated the idea of the containers breaking and spilling their precious contents, but that was better than having the blood used to power weapons that would be employed against Iskandia.

Ahn was up in the duct system already, searching for a route that would get them to the other side of the lift. A couple of shots fired somewhere above and in the distance. Ahn? Taking care of the Cofah? Or someone shooting at her?

"I should have gone up there with her," Duck said.

Sardelle eyed his tall form. "You'll be lucky if you fit. She's the logical one to squirm around in there."

"I know but—"

Soft grunts and bangs drifted down from the ducts. When Ahn had shimmied into the system, she hadn't made a sound. And those were male grunts.

Sardelle backed away, and Duck did, too, raising his rifle toward the hole. Fearing more Cofah with smoke canisters, she reached out mentally to inspect the intruders. The two men jostling their way through the ducts toward them were familiar.

"It's Ridge and Tolemek," she said, placing a hand on Duck's arm so he would lower the weapon.

An upside-down head and a dirt-smudged scarf dangled through the vent hole. The face, when it turned to search the chamber, was equally dirt-smudged.

"Over here." Sardelle walked over and smiled up at Ridge. "Did you cross paths with Ahn?"

"Not yet. We've had to deal with a couple of Cofah scampering around in here, though. We found a way up to the top level too.

Want to hand me those bags? Then we'll pull you up."

"You're not going to come down for a reunion hug? I thought you were dead, you know." Despite her teasing, Sardelle could sense the urgency emanating from him—he had barely returned her smile—and picked up a bag.

"We have less than an hour to get out of here before the mountain blows up." Ridge caught the first bag when she carefully tossed it up to him. He pulled it through, then his head and arms came down for another. "Though if you can jump high, I imagine we can manage a quick upside-down kiss."

"How romantic." Forgoing the jump-kiss, Sardelle tossed him a second bag.

Duck came over and picked up the next one. "Good to see you, sir. I've been keeping your lady safe in your absence."

"Oh?" Ridge shifted out of view to push the bags back behind him. Tolemek grunted and said something too muffled to make out. "Is that why you're so beat up, and she's unscathed?" Ridge added when he returned for the next bag.

"Yes, sir." Duck winked at Sardelle.

She was still amused that sharing a vomiting experience with the man was what had caused him to accept her into the group.

This time, when Ridge disappeared into the duct with a bag, more time passed before his head reappeared.

"Problem, sir?" Duck asked.

A third person had joined them in the duct. Ah, Ahn. Good.

"I just lost my helper to, judging by the noises, some kind of kissing session." Ridge thumped a hand against the side of the duct. "We're on a schedule, you two."

"I see Tolemek is versed in the ways of romantic reunions," Sardelle observed.

A quick exchange of words followed, then Ridge returned to the opening, waving for another bag. "Actually, I think Ahn pounced on *him*." He wriggled his eyebrows at her.

Before she could contemplate a response, a loud, deep gong sounded in the depths of the mountain, the echoes reverberating through the walls. Ridge's suggestive expression turned into a grimace.

"Alarm system?" Sardelle guessed.

"I don't know, but we have even more reason to hurry." Ridge accepted the last bag from Duck, then scooted back so the lieutenant could run, jump, and catch the lip of the duct. Barely. It wasn't a low ceiling.

Ridge pulled him in, but Duck must have lost half the skin off his chest in the process.

Due to the confines of the narrow shaft up there, it took some rearranging before there was room for Sardelle. Bangs and thumps drifted down—the alarm had stopped after three bongs, so she heard them well. It sounded like Duck was trying to push past someone else, so Ridge could return to give her a hand.

Sardelle summoned her reserves to give herself a magical boost to duplicate Duck's athletic feat. She caught the lip of the hole at the same time as Ridge's head reappeared. His eyes widened, but he caught her hand and pulled her in. Thanks to being lighter than Duck, it went more smoothly—she only lost a quarter of the skin on her chest as she was pulled onto her belly in the duct.

She clunked her head and found that she couldn't rise higher than her elbows. How the bigger men were navigating around up here, she couldn't imagine.

"This way," Ridge said, and backed away from her.

It was dark, but Sardelle followed the men's thumps and grunts easily enough. They reached an intersection, and Ridge was able to turn around and face forward. She kept his boots within reach. Nobody had given her a bag to carry, but she could hear the clinking of glass from ahead. She kept herself from nagging at them to be careful—they knew it was a precious load they carried.

"Ridge, Apex isn't with you?" Sardelle asked softly, realizing he was the only one in their group who wasn't in the ducts ahead of her. She hoped they hadn't lost him, but if he had been injured, and there was a possibility that he wasn't dead and that she might help...

"He's with Kaika, down on the first floor."

"Kaika? Wasn't she...?"

264

"Apparently she switched uniforms with someone and tricked the Cofah into believing she was the scorched and disfigured one. That was Nowon we saw, though. Unfortunately." A sense of guilt came with his words, of failure.

Sardelle wanted to comfort him, to remind him that they at least had the blood the king had sent him for, but that would have to wait until they escaped this mountain. He had said there wasn't much time. And if the team was split up, did that mean they needed to retrieve the others before finding those balloons? Wait, he hadn't said *why* they didn't have much time.

"Why aren't they with you?" she asked. "And why do we have less than an hour?"

"They're setting explosives," Ridge said, wariness in his tone.

When he had asked about the Galmok Mountain demolition, Sardelle had been glad she couldn't give him an answer. She wondered how many guards and scientists were left alive in here. The Cofah had been trying to kill them all along, so she shouldn't argue for saving their lives, but this wasn't Iskandia. She and the others had invaded another nation to steal resources and destroy work. Even if it was in the name of protecting her own people, it was hard to justify murder.

"Do they have enough to matter?" Sardelle wondered. "To bring down the mountain?"

"I don't know, but that's what Kaika's specialty is, so if it can be done, she'll know how."

"I see." And was that why the woman had been on the team to start with? Had blowing up this facility always been the plan?

We have a problem, Jaxi announced.

That gonging? It hadn't returned, but it had been loud enough that Sardelle believed it would have been audible all over the mountain.

I think that was just a warning bell to tell the scientists to leave or hide somewhere safe. The problem is the Cofah airships heading in this direction.

What? How many? Sardelle mashed her knuckles against Ridge's boots—he had stopped.

"We're going up here," Ridge said.

From the scuffs and clanks, the others were already heading up some vertical shaft.

"Wait," Sardelle caught his ankle. "The Cofah are coming. Airships."

"You can sense them? How many?"

"They're not in my range yet, but…" *Jaxi?*

They're about ten miles away, at least four of them. Big heavily armed military warships. It won't take them long to cover that distance by air.

"At least four, Jaxi says. Coming fast."

"All right," Ridge said. "Let's get up to the top and we'll assess the situation."

Sardelle let go of his boot, so he could climb. He didn't sound as frantic as this new information made Sardelle feel. Maybe because he didn't know that she didn't have the mental energy to muster much more in the way of magic, and Jaxi was exhausted too. She would have to tell him.

As soon as she tried to climb the vertical duct, she found out her physical energy was depleted as well. Asking for help would have been embarrassing, though, and she didn't see how Ridge could provide it anyway. She jammed her back against the side and pushed herself up with her legs, inch by inch. A clank came from somewhere above, and a hint of light filtered down. She reached up, hoping to find the top. A hand clasped hers and pulled her up, until another hand could grab her belt and hoist her sideways into a new duct, her sword scabbard scraping and banging every inch of the way.

Not dignified, but at least nobody could see her in the darkness. "Guess there was a reason I wore a shirt and trousers instead of a dress," she muttered.

"Handholds are useful." Ridge shifted around, blocking the light for a moment. "We're under the floor of the top level. The exit is just ahead."

His words sounded encouraging. Maybe he had sensed her weariness—or had heard her grunts of distress—and knew she needed encouragement. She crawled after him until she could stick her head through a vent low on a wall in a big room with a high pyramid-shaped ceiling. They had indeed reached the top of the mountain. Four hot air balloon baskets rested in the center of the room, though it wasn't yet apparent how they might escape the confines of the mountain.

Someone had lit lanterns, and Ahn and Duck were already unfolding one of the balloons. It would take time to heat up the air to fly one of the craft, time they might not have.

"I want all four of them readied," Ridge said from the perimeter of the room. He was jogging around, examining the wall and touching things. There weren't any windows, so only the wan flames of the lanterns brightened the space. "Tee, bring your big brain over here, will you? There has to be a way to open up the roof or some kind of big door. Something to let these out."

Sardelle propped her hands on her hips and tried to *see* the contours and cracks of the roof with more than her eyes.

"Why are we getting all of them ready?" Duck asked from inside one of the baskets—he had matches out and was trying to light the burner. "And dare I state that I've never launched a hot air balloon, and have no idea how the balloon is supposed to get from a crumpled mass on the ground to a big bulb above the basket?"

"There's usually some big fan that gets things started." Ridge paused in his hunt to look around.

"Jaxi will get them inflated enough for the burners to take over," Sardelle said.

I will?

I'm tired. I need to save a shred of energy for those Cofah airships. Not that she could imagine what she would do against all of them. Even at full strength, such a battle would be a struggle. If Ridge and his squadron had their fliers, they could attack, too, but what could anyone do from a hot air balloon? Besides be a target?

I'm tired too. I just melted a vault, remember?

Yes, but you have greater strength and stamina than I do.

Flatterer.

Sardelle smiled. *Who, me?*

Blowing up balloons is on the list of things I once deemed too lowly for someone with my skills.

Fortunately, you've changed your mind?

Not really.

Then we'll be stuck here when another mountain blows up, and you might have to wait another three hundred years for someone to pull you out of the rubble.

I'll blow up the balloons.

Good girl.

Amazing how one could feel a sentient sword glowering even when it was tucked away in its scabbard.

"Found something," Ridge said.

Sardelle started to join him, but nobody was working on the fourth balloon yet. She didn't know if Ridge wanted extras in the air to distract the Cofah, or if he intended to split up the team, but he had wanted them all up, and he was busy. A loud thunk sounded as he pushed an arm-sized lever into an up position.

Gears ground behind the wall, and chains rattled and clanked overhead. A whisper of warm sulfuric air wafted in from a new crack—several cracks. Sardelle had been imagining that the peak would flip open on hinges somehow, but the point of the ceiling was splitting in four directions, each quarter leaning back, opening like flower petals. Stars poked through the steam wafting across the dark sky. The geysers did not stop their cycles, even in the middle of the night.

Ridge ran over to the envelope Sardelle had started to unravel—it had been coiled up like a sleeping roll—and they laid it out together, spreading it like a picnic blanket. She smiled at him across the thin material, wishing they were setting up for a picnic someplace quiet and peaceful—and not in danger of exploding.

Hurrying, his face tense, Ridge didn't notice her look. Sardelle fought through her fatigue to pick up her speed too. As soon as the envelope had been unfolded, she willed air in to inflate it part way. Ridge turned the burner up to high, angling it toward the sideways mouth of the partially inflated balloon. Sardelle pushed in more air, until it started to rise, and the burner could continue to heat the air inside on its own.

The airships are six miles away now.

Sardelle stared around the room, noting everyone's progress. Could they possibly escape before the airships were close enough to spot them? If any of the balloons were spotted at all, the Cofah could easily catch them and shoot them down. Possibly right over that field of geysers and scorching pools.

Help Ahn, please, Jaxi. Hers is ready to go. Sardelle turned her own attention to the balloon Tolemek had spread. Duck was still struggling to lay out his.

"Hurry up, Kaika," Ridge muttered. "I'll be right back. Need to find something to anchor this down until we're ready to let it go. Or—" he drummed his fingers on his thigh, "—maybe we should just let it go as soon as it can. Get the Cofah chasing after a dummy." He met Sardelle's eyes. "How close are they now? Are they within sight of the mountain?"

"Soon, but not yet. They're six miles out."

The captain and lieutenant are coming.

Thanks, Jaxi.

"It's occurring to me," Ridge said as he ran over to help Duck with his balloon, "that the lab never was reinforced with extra troops, or not many at any rate. Maybe that airship dropped off a few, but then it must have gone south for reinforcements, and now it's back with friends, friends with orders to utterly destroy us."

"We have all of their dragon blood," Tolemek said. "Can't we use it against them?"

"If you know how to program it to do something special—like blowing up Cofah airships—I'm not going to object to that."

Sardelle gripped a nearby basket for support, then channeled air into Duck's balloon. Her head throbbed, stabbing the backs of her eyes with each beat of her heart. She feared she wouldn't be able to do anything against the Cofah when they finally appeared.

"The blood itself couldn't do that. I'd have to find some of those rockets and figure out how to reprogram them." Tolemek glanced at the vent they had come out of.

"There's no time for going back down and tinkering," Ridge

said. "We'll have to simply hope we can escape before the Cofah show up." He paced over to the next balloon, thumping his fist against his thigh. "And before the mountain blows up. Kaika, Apex, where *are* you two? Sardelle, can you tell if they've run into trouble?"

"Jaxi says they're coming."

"They—"

A clunk-thunk came from the middle of the room, a trapdoor being thrown open.

"...not my fault the lift doesn't come up to this floor," came Kaika's voice before her head appeared.

"I didn't say it was, but you might have informed me we were choosing an alternate route before I ran into those two guards," Apex said.

"You were fine. They were too busy fleeing the building after that gong went off to waste time noticing you."

"One punched me in the eye. I think that fits the definition of noticing."

Kaika searched the room, spotted Ridge, and jogged up to him, giving him a smart salute, a gesture that seemed odd coming from someone dressed in a red Cofah uniform. She looked like she had been punched in the eye a few times too.

"The explosives are set, sir, and were you aware of how whiny some of your pilots are?"

Apex stopped a few paces away and folded his arms over his chest with dramatic flair. He, too, had switched to a Cofah uniform at some point.

"Only some?" Ridge asked and winked at Apex. "You're looking better. Arguing with a woman must agree with you."

Apex sniffed. "Really, sir."

The basket Sardelle was leaning against started bumping across the ground. The balloon had filled and was ready to drift up through the big opening in the ceiling. "Ridge, are we riding out in this one, or letting it go?" The basket tried to lift up, and she had to lean on the rim to push it back down.

Ridge looked at the other balloons, which ranged from a quarter to three quarters inflated. "How long until the explosives go off, Kaika?"

She looked at a pocket watch. "Ten minutes, thirty seven seconds."

Sardelle pushed down on the basket with more of her weight. In a few more seconds it would be dragging her up with it no matter how hard she pushed.

"Are the Cofah within sight yet, Sardelle?" Ridge asked. "Gather your gear, everyone. Kaika, Apex, grab a couple of those bags."

They're... yes. On the horizon.

"They're on the horizon," Sardelle said.

Kaika's brow wrinkled. She hadn't been in the camp when Ridge had decided to share Sardelle's talent with the group. Sardelle wasn't about to try and explain things now.

"Too late to slip out without being spotted then." Ridge gestured for Sardelle to scoot back. "Let that one go. With luck, they'll follow it. We'll take... that roomy one over there."

"Should we consider splitting up, sir?" Ahn asked.

"Sardelle, are you and Jaxi going to be able to give us any magical defenses, and if so would it be easier to protect us if we're all together?"

"I've got our defenses right here, sir." Ahn thumped the side of her rifle, which she had managed to drag all through the ducts with her.

"I'll be counting on that defense, too," Ridge said.

"All together." Sardelle didn't want to promise a lot in the way of "magical defenses." Her main thought was to get them past the geysers so they could drop to the ground, where the trees might hide them from aerial assault. Might. She would hope the Cofah didn't have any of those rockets Ridge had encountered, with the ability to magically find their target. "But in theory, Jaxi can keep an eye on one basket, and I can watch the other." She opened her mouth—this would be the time to tell him that she didn't have much energy left—but he spoke first.

"She doesn't mind you volunteering her for duties?" Ridge waved for everyone to pack their bags into the two larger baskets.

"She minded being volunteered for blowing up balloons. She

gets less perturbed when asked to send streams of flame at the Cofah."

That's the truth.

I know you well.

Tolemek, Ahn, and Duck climbed into one balloon, and Ridge, Sardelle, Kaika, and Apex headed for the other. Sardelle wanted to hop in as smoothly as the men, but her limbs were as weary as her mind. She had to try twice to throw her leg over the rim of the basket, and Ridge ended up catching her in the middle of the second try and pulling her in beside him.

He had given the other half of the team more of the bags of their invaluable cargo. Because they had fewer people, or did he put more stock in Ahn's marksmanship than Sardelle's ability to defend a basket, right now?

Maybe he can tell how tired you are, even without you saying anything.

You're tired too.

I didn't say I wasn't. But Ridge doesn't monitor me as stringently as he does you.

A cannon boomed in the distance.

The first two airships are veering off after that balloon, Jaxi said. *One fired a warning shot.*

They don't think it could be their own people?

No, because they can't see anyone. They think someone might be hiding in it.

Let's hope they're tired of checking by the time we do that.

"How much longer, Kaika?" Ridge was gazing toward the stars, listening to the booms outside of the mountain, but he didn't sound worried.

Sardelle wished she could emulate that sense of calm. As Kaika checked her watch again, the second balloon, with nothing inside the basket to weigh it down, took off. "Six minutes, forty-three seconds."

"Hm," Ridge said.

"We may not want to cut it too close," Sardelle said. "I'm not that certain of my ability to protect the balloon from shrapnel and whatever else comes flying out of this mountain."

Kaika's eyebrows lowered. "It'll be a *controlled* explosion with gravity drawing the mountain down and in on itself. There's no way I could have found enough explosives for flying shrapnel, even if that were the desired result."

"My apologies." Sardelle watched as the second balloon bumped against the sloping ceiling but eventually drifted upward toward the exit. "Explosives aren't my specialty." They hadn't been a common occurrence in her time, unless one counted fireworks at festivals.

"I wouldn't have minded something with shrapnel," Ridge said wistfully, "something that might catch a few of those airships with the force of the explosion, but this will be safer for us."

The basket wobbled beneath Sardelle's feet.

"We're going up first," Apex said. He didn't sound like he was certain that was a good thing.

"Duck down when you get up there," Ridge said. "Everyone. We'll hope that after blowing up two empty baskets, they'll be less certain anything is loaded in these two."

The basket tipped, then rose from the floor. Sardelle sank down before they reached the ceiling hole. Her legs thanked her. Ridge looked down at her, his eyes gentle with concern, then he cut out their lantern, and his face disappeared into shadow.

He crouched down beside her and took her hand. "How are you feeling? You look pale and tired."

"Not sexy and interestingly wan? I seem to remember some fairy tale where a sorceress beleaguered after thirty days and thirty nights of fighting back the Cofah still managed to look interestingly wan, enough so that she attracted the eye of a dragon."

"Your people had strange fairy tales."

Apex and Kaika knelt down so their heads would be below the rim. Someone bumped Sardelle's knee, but she was too tired to adjust her position.

She couldn't see the hole in the ceiling, not with the bulging envelope above them, but knew from the ripples coursing down to the basket that the balloon was already subject to the breeze.

Sardelle gripped Ridge's arm and leaned her head against

his shoulder, even though they probably only had a minute—she could sense the airships out there. The two that had gone after the first balloon had already taken it down, and they were heading toward the mountain. The other pair of airships had fired at the second balloon, demolishing the basket, but hadn't veered off course to follow it down into the geysers. Water spit and erupted somewhere nearby, and the sulfur stink in the air increased.

We might die in the next twenty minutes, Jaxi.

Speak for yourself. I'm living forever.

You don't think you'd melt if you fell into one of those geysers?

Of course not. Jaxi paused thoughtfully. *I might rust, though. That would be unpleasant.*

So, being shot down would be a bad time for all.

The basket cleared the mountain, but Sardelle couldn't see much from the floor of it. A few stars. Steam.

Ridge was crouching rather than sitting, as if he would spring up to defend them somehow.

"You've been through everything I have," Sardelle murmured, patting his thigh. "Yet you seem like you could march another twenty miles while carrying your flier on your back. If there were female dragons around, I'd have to worry about you attracting one."

"Your mind is on dragons tonight."

"I can't imagine why."

They're coming our way. Two ships.

"Jaxi says two ships are coming to check us out." Sardelle didn't move away from Ridge, but she did take a deep breath and pull in her focus. "I'll do my best to shield us. Bullets, I can handle. I'm uncertain about cannonballs right now."

"What about rockets?" Ridge asked.

"I'm even less certain about those."

At first, she tried to wrap her shield around the entire balloon and basket ensemble, but it was like trying to stretch tissue paper. Her efforts ripped and tattered, leaving giant holes.

Focus on the basket. The balloon can take a few holes.

Sardelle nodded at Jaxi's advice. *I'm going to have to.*

I'll shield the other one. Unfortunately, I don't think I can manage any gouts of flame at the same time.

We just need to escape.

"Sir," Kaika said, "what are you and her talking about? Or... do I want to know?"

"Probably not, Captain. But I can explain later."

The wind caught the balloon, and it drifted away from the mountaintop, carrying them north, toward the *real* mountains.

"Time, Captain?" Ridge lifted a hand toward the lip of the basket but caught himself. He doubtlessly wanted to poke his head up to check on the other half of their team, but on the chance the Cofah were thinking of dismissing them, he dared not risk it.

"One minute, thirty-seven seconds."

For the first time, Ridge shifted his weight, a hint of unease escaping his otherwise calm facade. Sardelle was so busy focusing on maintaining her shield, she barely registered it. Gurgles came from below, and a geyser erupted twenty meters to the side of them. Why couldn't one erupt under one of those airships? They were probably too high up for it to matter, though.

A hiss-thud came from the nearest Cofah vessel, and the unexpectedness of the noise broke through Sardelle's concentration. That was a different sound than the cannons made. "Is that—"

Ridge stood up, his rifle in hand. "A rocket."

Sardelle tracked it with her senses. It was heading straight for them.

Jaxi—

Before she could get out her request, a second hiss-thud came from the same ship. This rocket was aiming at Ahn and Tolemek's balloon.

Take care of them, she thought, then threw every shred of energy she had into shoring up the shield on the side closest to the rocket. She tried to increase the area to protect the balloon as well, but she was straining, and the entire ethereal construct threatened to collapse.

The rocket blasted against her barrier and exploded. Yellow

and orange light flared so brightly that it stung her eyes even down in the basket. She expected the force of the explosion to shred the balloon into confetti and hurl them all into the scalding pools below, but the basket scarcely moved.

Thanks, she told Jaxi, knowing she'd had help.

She didn't get a response. Sardelle knelt up to look over the rim and touched Jaxi's hilt at her waist. It was so hot it almost burned her hand. Another flare of light burst into the night sky, almost blinding her. The other balloon. Dread and guilt threatened her equilibrium. Had Jaxi left them undefended in order to save Sardelle?

No, I blew up the second rocket before it reached them. That's better than buffering the explosion. But I don't know how many more I can handle. Those airships are getting ready to throw their whole arsenal at us.

Sardelle could see the Cofah craft now, and they weren't nearly so far away as she wished. The weak wind wasn't moving the hot air balloon anywhere fast. Seven gods, she should have been trying to push the balloons along rather than shielding them. No, she dared not let up on the barrier. She rubbed at her sweaty face and gritty eyes. She wasn't sure if the black spots floating through her vision were aftereffects from seeing that explosion or were a more worrisome side effect of overexertion. The air did seem thin and not nearly substantial enough for her lungs at the moment.

In the other balloon, which had risen to the same height as Sardelle's, Ahn raised her rifle, targeting some Cofah gunner on one of the ships.

"No," Sardelle called, able to sense Jaxi's shield around the other craft. "You're protected." She wasn't sure if her voice carried, but Tolemek put a hand on Ahn's arm, forcing the weapon down, and pointed in front of them.

"More weapons firing," Kaika said, glancing at Ridge and Sardelle.

"A lot more." Ridge clenched his fist. "If I had my flier..."

The first round went toward the other balloon.

Something like a moan echoed in Sardelle's mind as Jaxi

threw everything she had into blowing up the explosives before they reached the team. The next round would be aimed at this balloon, and Sardelle didn't know if she had enough to blow anything up. Or keep the shield alive, either.

Apex eyed the ground below them, as if he knew his sorceress protector was about to fail.

It was too dark to see the geysers and mud pots, the near boiling water bubbling and gurgling in the pools, but Sardelle knew that terrain was still down there. It would take several more minutes to reach the forest and a spot where they might land... or grow tangled in the trees and climb down.

"Here it comes." Ridge gripped the edge of the balloon, his longing to do more washing over Sardelle with its intensity.

A muted boom came from the depths of the mountain. It was a weak sound next to the explosives being launched from the airships, and Sardelle almost missed it. But it made the Cofah stop firing for a moment. Gunners looked back and forth at each other, then over the railing of their ship.

Kaika leaned against the basket next to Ridge, peering down at the mountain. As far as Sardelle could tell, not much was happening.

"Did it work?" Ridge asked.

"Give it a moment." Kaika didn't sound certain. "With the lower supports removed, the levels should collapse in on themselves, under the weight of gravity."

"If we destroy that mountain," Ridge said, "and take the blood... even if it goes down with us in one of those pools, we've won a victory."

"Who's going to live to tell the king about it?" Apex grumbled.

More muted thuds came from the mountain. It was too dark to see what was going on, but the sides didn't seem to be tipping over or crumpling inward.

"Geyser," Ridge warned.

"Under us?" Sardelle leaned forward to look, but the black dots in her eyes turned into black circles, obscuring her vision. A wave of dizziness accompanied the circles. She had definitely pushed herself to the limit.

Ridge caught her arm and pointed toward the ground. "Looks like it's going to be a big one."

Even as he spoke, the funnel of water increased in size, from a few meters to over fifty. Maybe over a hundred. The phenomenon was big enough to see even in the dark. The steam and spray blocked the view of the mountain and two of the ships.

One of the outside ships could still see Sardelle's balloon, though, and orange flashes and booms announced cannonballs firing. Her shield had slipped in her distraction, and she rushed to reassemble it.

A cannonball tore through the balloon twenty feet above them. She couldn't do anything to stop it, could only focus on the basket.

"Down," Kaika barked.

A rocket raced out of the night sky, arrowing straight at their basket.

Can't, Jaxi whispered. *The others—*

I've got it. Sardelle flung a hand in that direction, but she didn't have Jaxi's power, and it wasn't enough. At the last moment, she tried the only other thing she could think of. She turned her energy toward cutting the cables holding the basket to the balloon.

They plummeted. Someone screamed. The rocket soared by overhead, missing them. But, as they fell, she saw it arcing back toward them, angling downward, and remembered the way one had followed Ridge.

She lifted her hand one more time, this time only trying to find and destroy the vial of dragon blood instead of detonating the whole rocket. It worked. The glass burst open, spraying blood all over the inside of the projectile. She could only hope it was enough, because the blackness she had been fighting against finally swept over her. She was aware of the basket slamming into a pool, and water flying everywhere, scalding her skin, and of someone crying out in pain... and then she knew no more.

* * *

The basket rocked so hard it threatened to throw people out. Ridge tried to grab everyone and cover and protect Sardelle all at the same time. Scalding water sloshed in, and Kaika cried out in pain that soon turned to rage, as if she was tired of this entire mission and longed for an enemy to throttle.

"Sardelle?" Ridge whispered as the basket settled—it was floating, for the moment. He prayed to the ancient dragons that it was waterproof.

She didn't respond. He touched her cheek and found it clammy and sweaty. She was breathing. That would have to be enough for now. He had to figure out how to get them to safety and what was happening to the rest of the team.

A plop sounded a few feet away, and he squinted, wondering what had fallen down beside them. He almost laughed, realizing it was the rocket. Whatever Sardelle had done in the end, she must have deactivated it somehow. His humor was short-lived, for he knew there would be more. Possibly aiming at them right now.

He spun, nearly knocking over Apex, who was standing and gaping toward the mountain. What was left of it. The geyser had finished erupting, and the rubble was visible now, the pile only a third of the height it had been before, if that. Unfortunately, the airships remained in the air above it. Most of them. One was flying in their direction.

"Any chance we can paddle this thing to safety?" Ridge asked, turned in the other direction again.

He spotted two things that gave him hope: the trees marking the foothills of the mountains—they weren't that far off—and the silhouette of the other hot air balloon. Since Ridge's basket was now missing its balloon, he hoped the others could get to them, and they could manage to all pile in and fly to safety. The only problem was that the Cofah only had one target now, and Sardelle couldn't defend them if she was unconscious.

Ridge hefted his rifle. They would have to do their best to defend themselves. Too bad nobody had thought to mount cannons or rocket launchers on the hot air balloons.

Waves rocked the basket. His first thought was that Tolemek's balloon had crashed, too, but it was still aloft, still a good twenty meters overhead. They looked like they were having trouble steering.

Three geysers erupted at the same time. The mud pots belched, and the most potent stench yet emanated into the air. Ripples flowed through the pool the basket was sitting in.

"Uh," Kaika said. "The mountain is steaming. What's left of it."

So much smoke was wafting from the giant rubble pile, that Ridge had no trouble seeing it, even by night. It blotted out the stars and obscured the airships, almost as if they had flown into clouds. "That's not your work?"

"Zirkander," Tolemek called down, his voice almost drowned out by the increased noise of popping bubbles and gurgling pools. "We'll be in trouble if we land. Can you catch this rope?"

"Yes," Ridge called back. He didn't see the rope, but he would find a way to catch it anyway. Then he would have to figure out how to climb it with Sardelle slung over his shoulder. Whatever had made her think he still had the energy to march twenty miles?

"There it is." Apex leaned out of the back of the basket, a hand outstretched. "Got it."

"You and Kaika go first." Ridge picked up Sardelle, careful to make sure her sword was still in its scabbard. Jaxi had certainly earned more than to be dumped into a pond and left there.

I should hope so.

Well, at least someone's conscious.

Barely. You people are taxing.

Apex grabbed one of the bags of dragon blood and shimmied up the rope. Kaika did the same and followed before he was more than halfway up. Ridge wasn't certain what was happening exactly, but the water was growing more agitated rather than less. He didn't know if Kaika's explosion could have triggered some twitchy fault down under all these pools and geysers, but if there was about to be an earthquake—or a volcanic eruption— he didn't want to have his nose pressed against the window for it.

"Hurry, Zirkander," Tolemek called down, the urgency in his voice clear even over the noise.

He must know something Ridge only suspected at this point.

"Good luck to us," he whispered to Sardelle, gave her a kiss, then wrapped the rope around his forearm and hand a few times, hoping that would be enough. There was no way he could climb without risking dropping her. "Go," he called up. "I've got a grip."

He thought he might have to explain further, but Tolemek understood. Their balloon had already been trying to drift away. Ridge curled up his legs, letting it pull him from the basket.

But with all the weight, their balloon didn't gain any more lift. It was drifting off in the right direction, toward the trees, but the angry, bubbling water spit and sputtered right beneath Ridge's butt. He was so busy jerking his legs up and sideways—anything to keep from being burned—that he almost missed the first spews of angry orange magma bursting forth from the mound of rubble. Or maybe it was shooting up from behind it, from some new volcano thrusting out of the mire. It was too dark to tell, but whatever was happening was alarming the airships. None of them was shooting or sailing toward the hot air balloon now.

"Ouch," Ridge yelped. His trousers provided *some* protection from the hot water, but not enough. He envisioned one of those geysers blowing right under him.

"A little more altitude would not be unappreciated," Ridge called up.

He smacked into something. Hard.

"What the—" He had wrapped the rope around his arm so many times that he wasn't immediately knocked free, but the blow did send him spinning, and then a second one followed it. Something big and brushy slammed into his face. This time, he *was* knocked free, and he shouted an angry, "No!" as he fell.

He didn't land in scalding water but in cold snow, his limbs tangled with Sardelle's. She moaned but remained unconscious. He grinned, realizing they had made it to the forest. Safety. Well, maybe not. If that new volcano grew serious about erupting, who knew how far it would hurl lava and ash? Maybe the magma would be swallowed by the pools all around the area, but maybe not.

"Sir," Duck called down.

"Here." Ridge gathered up Sardelle again and floundered through the snow, trying to catch up with the balloon. He might have cursed the hapless craft earlier, but they would escape lava flows a lot more easily from the air.

"There he is," Duck called. "We're coming down, sir. Can you meet us in that clearing?"

Ridge had no idea where "that clearing" was, but he followed the balloon, weaving through the trees and fighting snow that went up past his knees. He was stumbling by the end, and only his desire not to drop or hurt Sardelle kept him upright.

"I love you people," he called when he spotted the basket waiting for him, the craft tied down with a rope around a tree. "If I don't get court-martialed, I'll put you all in for awards." His enthusiasm grew even more heartfelt when Duck and Apex grabbed him and Sardelle, hoisting them into the basket. It was a tight fit, but he didn't care, not even when his legs collapsed and he ended up propped up against Tolemek.

"What award can I, as an expatriate civilian, expect?" Tolemek asked.

"I'll fly south to Terra Falls and pick you up the best mango turnover you've ever had."

"A fair reward. Cut that rope, Duck," Tolemek said. "As much as I'd like to observe the eruption of the long theorized but never seen Boiling Pools Volcano, I don't believe this is a safe observation station."

"Definitely not," Ridge mumbled and sank down beside Sardelle, wrapping an arm around her.

Jaxi? Can you hear me? Will she be all right?

I believe so. Humans are much frailer than swords, you know. But they're resilient too.

"I hope so," he murmured and rested his head against hers. If the rest of the team thought it was strange that he was muttering to himself, they didn't said anything.

EPILOGUE

WHEN SHE WOKE UP, A headache pulsing behind her eyes, Sardelle's first thought was to worry about Ridge, her second to worry about herself, and her last to wonder how going to pick up her first student had turned into such an... *event.*

Daylight had come, but it was far darker than it should have been, the sky a hazy dusty gray. It was ash, she realized, not dust. Sardelle could taste it in the cold, thick air. She should have been cold, too, but someone had wrapped her up in parkas before laying her on the frosty ground. The fur lining of Ridge's coat was snugged up protectively over her face—she could smell his masculine scent on it, though it was faint compared to the sulfur and ash in the air. She pulled the warm fur down so she could see her surroundings.

"Where are we?" she croaked, turning her head to look for people.

She was in the shadow of a cliff, surrounded by snow-clad evergreens. The crumpled black-and-gray balloon lay stretched across the snow nearby, but the basket stood empty. There should have been two hot air balloons, except she had destroyed theirs in a vain attempt to avoid that rocket. That rocket that had been arrowing straight toward them. Had she succeeded in disabling it? Had they lost anyone? Her stomach clenched when she didn't see anyone else around. Who had survived? Who hadn't? Why had they left her alone here?

Relax, genius. They're up in the cave, getting the fliers ready. I'm moderately certain Ridge is planning to come back for you. That's a nice coat, after all.

Jaxi. A wave of relief washed over Sardelle. *We made it? Everyone?*

Yes, everyone made it. The Cofah were distracted by the volcano that erupted underneath their airships. That was even better than the storm you were hoping for. We escaped in the other hot air balloon. Jaxi shared an image of Ridge, holding Sardelle while he had one hand latched onto a rope dangling from a basket. *Your soul snozzle gets an award from me for making sure I came along on that ride.*

I think he'd settle for you staying out of his head outside of emergencies.

You want him to miss out on my insightful commentary? That sounds more like a punishment than a reward.

Sardelle pushed herself into a sitting position. *Does anyone have any injuries? I should help instead of sleeping.*

You were unconscious, not sleeping. You pushed yourself too hard.

You did too.

Yes. We should probably recruit and train more sorcerers to send along on your boyfriend's crazy missions.

That was *one of the goals here.* One they had failed at, at least for now. Sardelle hoped they could find Tolemek's sister, wherever she was. At least they hadn't failed at acquiring the dragon blood. She could still feel its power buzzing against her skin. The bags had been moved from the basket up into the cave. Everything had—except for her. Ridge must want to leave as soon as possible.

A good idea. We're not that far from Cofahre's newest volcano. Breathing that ash doesn't affect me, but I'd hate to be buried by a lava flow.

Me too. Sardelle climbed to her feet. The new position did nothing to improve her headache. She felt like a raw student again, foolishly pushing herself too hard to study for exams, then excel at exams, only to wake the morning after with a hangover greater than one would ever receive from alcoholic indulgence.

A rock clattered down from the cliff. Ridge was climbing down. He was filthy—smothered in ash and engine grease—but Sardelle welcomed him with a fierce hug when he reached the ground.

Ridge seemed surprised but quickly wrapped his arms around her. "Does this mean I'm forgiven?"

"Forgiven? For what?"

His expression grew sheepish beneath the grime. "I was up in the cave, realizing how often I snapped orders at you. Magic this. Magic that. Oh, and magic up all of the balloons, will you. I'm used to everyone who's along on my missions being under my command. I didn't mean to, ah… make you pass out."

Sardelle leaned against his chest, touched that he felt guilty, but chagrined too. There was no call for guilt from him. "I made *myself* pass out. And believe it or not, I've taken orders from military commanders before. Granted they were usually grumpy old generals, not cute and charming, if dirty, pilots…" She wiped at a smudge on his face, only to realize her thumb was just as ashy as his cheek. They all needed to find a warm pool somewhere to bathe in, preferably a tepidly warm one, not a scalding and bubbling one that stank of sulfur. "And you take me for granted a lot less than they did. You're quite tactful when you order me to magic this or magic that. You even said please once."

"Oh. Good." He was truly relieved when he hugged her again, adding a kiss this time.

Sardelle decided to find it sweet and romantic even though their lips were coated in a layer of ash. Ridge drew back, the wryness in his eyes suggesting he had noticed the same thing, or maybe she had inadvertently shared the emotion with him. He didn't release the hug, though, and she wondered if he had been worried whether she would wake up or not.

"Is it time to go home?" she asked.

"Home, as in my house in Iskandia?"

"Yes… I dread dealing with those women who were stalking me back in the capital, but I do long for a soak in your bathtub."

"That means you've decided you'll return with me? That you want to?"

"I always wanted to, Ridge. It was just…" Sardelle gazed toward the dusty sky. "I didn't—don't—want to wreck your career."

"I know, but I've told you that that doesn't matter."

"And I, being more empathic than a rock, knew that was a half truth."

He opened his mouth, a protest on his lips, but she raised a single eyebrow, and he stopped. The sheepish expression returned.

"Maybe so, but I want you *and* my career. I don't want to give up on either of you. That's why we all just nearly died to get those vials, and why we're not going home until—"

"Sir," came Apex's call from above, "Captain Kaika and I are ready to go. Do you want us to wait for you to finish canoodling or have you told us everything that you need to?"

"I'm not canoodling," Ridge called up. "I'm... negotiating a consolidation."

"If you're opting for the military definition of that word, to strengthen by rearranging the position of ground combat troops after a successful attack, I don't think your girlfriend counts as a troop unit."

"It's tedious when your young officers have a better vocabulary than you do," Ridge murmured and released Sardelle. He faced the cliff. "We're coming up, but you can take off whenever you're ready. You've got my report for the king, right?"

"The scroll filled with chicken scratches? Yes, I have it."

"You read it?"

"No, but I've seen your reports before. Your maintenance requests and shopping lists too. I trust my assessment is accurate." Apex disappeared back into the cave.

"So glad to see he's feeling better," Ridge muttered, not entirely sarcastically. He picked up the coats and started up the cliff.

Sardelle smiled and headed up the cliff, too, glad it wasn't quite vertical. Her body ached almost as much as her head, but knowing she could rest in the flier made one more climb doable. Ridge waited for her and made sure she wasn't having trouble.

"We're not all going back to the king?" she asked when the ramifications of the men's conversation sank in. Apex and Kaika were leaving first. Meaning everyone else was going somewhere different?

"Not yet."

"Afraid to face him until he has a chance to cool his blood?"

"Not exactly. I'm sending most of the dragon blood back with Apex and Kaika. I think that and the fact that we turned the Cofah secret lab into a volcano should appease him." The way Ridge's mouth twisted suggested he wasn't certain about that, at least not insofar as his indiscretions went. "But in the event that I'm to be punished or relieved of my command again, there's one more thing I want to do before returning home, something that should further appease the king. Eliminate the source of the dragon blood—or otherwise ensure the Cofah can't get any more of it." At some point, Tolemek and Ahn must have explained the painting and the foliage in the crate to him.

"So we're going to the tropics to look for purple flowers?" Sardelle knew from experience that soldiers, even higher-ranking officers, weren't supposed to run off, assigning themselves their own missions, without permission from commanding officers, but she didn't point that out.

"Actually we're going to Mavar Island to look for my dad," Ridge said. "He's supposed to be there this winter. If anyone can identify some tropical location by its flora, it'll be him. He's spent decades exploring all around the equator. Even if he doesn't know, I'm sure he can still point us in the right direction."

"Really, Ridge," she said as she climbed onto the cave ledge. "If you wanted to take me home to meet your parents, all you had to do was say so."

"Does that mean you agree to come? If not—" his expression grew bleak, "—we can drop you off somewhere."

"Of course I'm coming. My potential student is apparently in the same place as the source of that dragon blood."

His face lightened. "Ah."

"And I agree to your offer of consolation, military or otherwise." Knowing they would be separated in the flier, Sardelle took his hands and kissed him once more.

"Come now, sir," Apex said from the cockpit of the closest flier. "That's *definitely* canoodling."

"Jealous, Lieutenant?" Kaika asked from the rear seat. She appeared to be ready to go, several bags of the dragon blood strapped in around her. Sardelle hoped they wouldn't have to dodge any of those unmanned attack fliers on the way out. It would be a shame to lose their samples at this point. With luck, the volcano would be distracting everyone within a couple hundred miles.

"Of course not," Apex said.

"Because if you were, I was going to offer to hold your hand on the way back."

Apex blinked a few times, but seemed too flustered to come up with a response.

Duck strolled up and handed Sardelle a skewered piece of meat on a stick. Rabbit? It was hard to tell under the layer of char.

"Thank you." She decided to add the restaurants in the capital to the list of things she was longing for.

"Knew you needed to fill your empty belly." Duck saluted Ridge. "We're ready to go, too, sir."

Duck climbed into the cockpit of his flier.

Tolemek and Ahn walked out of the depths of the cave, holding hands. There might have been some canoodling going on back there too.

"*If* the flier can get off the ground with all that unauthorized cargo on board." Ahn gave Tolemek a significant look.

"I've never studied volcanology," Tolemek said, "but I don't know when I'll get another chance to acquire fresh samples."

"Including *twenty* vials of ash?"

"Twenty-six. I assure you the combined weight is less than that of a sniper rifle."

The glowers they gave each other weren't particularly fierce.

"Looks like it's time to fly, then," Ridge said.

Apex and Kaika were already rolling toward the cave ledge. She gave a long look over her shoulder at the empty seat in Duck's flier.

"My lady." Ridge offered Sardelle his hand to give her a boost into the flier. "Your conveyance awaits."

She accepted the offer. "And my nap, I hope. Though that doesn't seem fair. You must need one as much as I do, if not more."

"Who says I won't take one?"

"Is that allowed when you're the one *flying* the craft?"

"You'll know if you wake up in the arctic instead of the tropics."

THE END

Made in the USA
Columbia, SC
24 August 2017